THE
WAY
AHEAD

— Book 2 —

THE
WAY
AHEAD

— Book 2 —

Kaleb England
aka NorskDaedalus

Podium

THE
WAY
AHEAD

— Book 2 —

CHAPTER 1

By the Buy

It was nice to be on the road again. Since his crash landing on Joriah, practically the only times that Edwin had actually enjoyed himself had been while traveling. Sure, technically the bulk of his time spent on the System-dominated world had been in a single place, namely Blackstone citadel, and he wouldn't exactly consider "forced into Alchemy-centered slavery" a good time. Then . . . well, yeah. The only other place he'd spent more than one night since then was in the company of *literal serial killers*. That the two locales he'd stayed in had *both* ended with a furious fight for his life was probably a telling sign.

Still, traveling in itself was rather fun. Yes, he'd gone on vacation when he'd lived on Earth, but that had always been a mad rush to see as much as possible in the limited time allotted for each location. Run here, see that view, pause for a picture, then go through a museum, see the sights, and find a restaurant for dinner. Repeat five more times, then fly home. He'd enjoyed it just fine—seeing new things was a bit of a reward unto itself—but he'd always found himself exhausted at the end of it all.

Now that he was walking everywhere, with nothing but his own thoughts to keep himself company, Edwin felt far more rested than he had on any of the family trips supposedly meant to do just that. It helped that he finally wasn't injured (blisters went away easily with a tiny dab of healing salve), wasn't wandering through untamed forests, and had plenty of food (what with the fact he only needed to eat about once a day) and easy enough access to water.

Plus, he was in fantastic shape, though he was *really* getting scruffy. His hair was definitely getting long, and it was nearly blond from how much time he'd been outside. It was probably some three months he'd been on Joriah now, not that he'd been paying *that* much attention to the passing time, but his own two feet had been his primary method of transportation that entire time. Things felt different when it took him an entire day to go as far as he might have in just an hour or two in a car.

It was just all so massive, so grand in scope, and he had far more time to appreciate everything he came across. From magnificent sunsets and sunrises to the flocks of birds that flew overhead, whose feathers seemed to shine like jewels, to the mountains looming in the distance, glittering like sapphires against the azure sky, and even the unusually crystal-clear brooks trickling alongside the road, everything just felt so much more fantastical than what he was used to.

During his breaks and stops for the night (while there was enough light, anyway), Edwin took to reading the *Zosiman Grimoire* Alchemy manual. Of all the things he'd looted from the serial-killing bandits, the *Grimoire* was decidedly the most valuable. Oh sure, the alchemical notes that their leader Niall had left behind were morbidly interesting, but Edwin didn't particularly care to read about the several uses that ground avior bone could be put to.

While the *Grimoire* was tricky to parse in many places and the author seemed to be a bit overfond of their own eloquence, *and* while Edwin couldn't fact-check it very well, it was still a wealth of information that he was delighted to have available to him, particularly in the area of magical plants.

According to the *Grimoire*, water-filtering seagrass grew in places of abundant life and water magic, and its blue-green stalks could actually support fish, which could swim through the grass as though it were water. And, if dried in a particular way, the grass could be spun into exceptionally soft and fine cloth (drying it a different way gave it the water-absorbing properties Edwin had so benefited from in the tower). Mage's lichen changed color and even glowed depending on the sorts of magic it was exposed to. Spiderless webs were a type of fungus with a striking resemblance to cobwebs but were surprisingly nutritious. Royal's cup grew leaves that folded into the shape of a goblet and was nigh impossible to cut, but it had powerful antipoison abilities if you managed to do so and drank from it. Glowleaf was actually an entire family of plants, not a single species (which according to the *Grimoire* was a common misconception), with bioluminescent leaves. Glassleaf trees were actually something Edwin had encountered in the Verdant—the massive, magical forest that he'd first crash landed in—and they allowed green light to pass through them in a single direction only. Atir moss had the strange property of . . .

All the herbology sections came with incredibly lifelike drawings of the substances, which allowed Edwin to recognize a small patch of wild seagrass for what it was, despite its lack of fish. He even took a few blades of the grass for himself, though since he couldn't properly dry it, he just sort of stuffed it into his bag, hoping for the best, and it shriveled up into a state that the *Grimoire* described as useless.

All in all, Edwin was having a blast, and as he ventured back toward Vinstead (or more accurately, the Verdant), he watched as the empty space he traveled through slowly became more and more populated. When he first started out, he might see a person every day or two, particularly shepherds and other herders, tending to animals both familiar and strange on the sea of grasses that dominated the landscape, but now he would regularly encounter a courier, his enhanced senses barely able to catch more than a few glimpses of the (usually human) runners as they dashed past him, kicking up massive plumes of dust, carrying some cargo to places unknown.

He'd also spot flights of avior overhead, the humanoid birdfolk soaring across the lightly clouded skies. It was always slightly cloudy, though on further thought, had it ever rained at all in the time he'd been here? Well, other than that one time two *insanely* powerful mages had summoned a thunderstorm as part of a battle in the skies of course. Edwin . . . didn't think it had. Strange. How was this such a flourishing agricultural area, then? If Vinstead really was the primary breadbasket for all of Liras like he'd been told, then surely it must get water from somewhere, right?

In the distance, the walls of Vinstead loomed, and even from this far away, Edwin could make out clouds of airborne figures surrounding the metropolis, like flies swarming around fallen food. Hmm. He should probably avoid entering the city proper, to help throw any pursuers off his trail by not leaving a paper trail. It was a minor enough point, and assuming he could restock his rations and get a few tools from some store outside the walls, there was no reason for him to enter at all. It wasn't like he had any *particular* incentive to meet Tara or Rizzali, though come to think of it, he wouldn't mind asking the latter a few System-related questions he had . . . no, not yet. He'd stay outside the walls.

A bit of poking around had turned up something of a market, set up alongside the outer walls of Vinstead. Among the colorful fabrics and stalls, Edwin spotted something that seemed perfect. One of the store-fronts, really just a table laden with miscellaneous travel-related goods in front of a bored-looking green-haired kid, maybe twelve years old, had the same sorts of strange, brown, vaguely fruity loaves that Lefi had bought the last time they came through here. Most were already wrapped up in something that seemed reminiscent of parchment paper, and Edwin found himself remembering that just because Joriah had all the trappings of a planet in the mid-1300s, that didn't actually mean that it was. Did they even *have* paper back then?

"How much?" he asked the . . . Keen Assistant, gesturing toward the rations.

The question knocked the boy out of his stupor, and he shook his head, looking at Edwin with really wide eyes. "Sarry, wha?"

He seemed almost stunned to see Edwin. Really, were customers so rare? Ah, whatever.

"The loaves. How much per?"

"E— Uh . . . one ager each." He seemed to switch what he was saying midway through; was he changing his price? Or maybe he just had a bit of a stutter.

Either way, Edwin didn't feel like haggling. He ran through what he remembered Lefi saying about the currency system. A copper coin (ves) was the smallest unit, and one hundred and twenty of them made up one silver coin (ager), which in turn was sixty per gold coin (grai). Standard coin weight was sixty "grains," which to Edwin felt something like forty grams. In any case, it had been really disorienting to Edwin when the Polyglot Skill stopped translating each coin name as just copper/silver/gold and instead started using their actual words. He *tried* to get himself to think about them by their actual names—actually, he ought to try and just learn the language at some point—but he kept slipping.

In any case, one silv—no, *ager*—for each loaf seemed perhaps a little pricey, but then again, Edwin didn't exactly have a very firm grasp on the corresponding currency value. Perhaps it was totally reasonable. In any case, even if he was being *massively* ripped off, he still didn't feel like haggling over it, not here and not with a kid who would probably haggle him into the *ground* if he was a junior shopkeep of some kind. Edwin wanted to preserve some semblance of dignity, so he pulled out a small handful of coins and deftly stacked twelve ager on the table. "Very well."

The boy picked up each of the coins and flipped them between his fingers, studying each with the same sort of intensity Edwin had come to associate with Skill usage. Checking their purity or that they weren't counterfeit, perhaps? If there was a Skill for that sort of thing, did that mean the scale was developed exclusively for alchemical purposes, or something similar? That was an interesting thought, though it did explain why none of the stalls had any sort of measurement tools, if Skills just took care of all that. His thoughts, and associated zoning out, had attracted a curious gaze from the boy, and Edwin shook his head by way of apology. "Sorry, sorry. Just lost in my thoughts for a moment." He quickly scooped up his dozen loaves, packing them away in his belt and backpack, then nodded farewell to the green-haired lad.

Honestly, if the whole green-hair thing weren't so common, Edwin would have likely gotten distracted by *that* as well. He hadn't really noticed it the first time he had come to Vinstead, too distracted by everything else, but probably a good half of the humans wandering around had the unusual color across their head.

The halflings seemed to be unaffected, and the vibrant gnomes seemed to just have green as one of their more common natural hair colors, though did that work the same way? Edwin had yet to see a green beard, though he couldn't recall if that was because green-haired individuals didn't have beards or just because the beards maintained more normal coloration. It probably had something to do with the Verdant's proximity. At least, if he were seeking the origin of people with strangely green aspects of their integumentary system, he'd look at the giant, magical, and untamed forest right next door.

He wished he had some way to analyze the hair, though. From what little he recalled of his anatomy class, sharpened by his Memory Skill, hair color was the result of two different types of melanin—their names escaped him—but that was what allowed for the variety of brown, red, and blond hair colors back on Earth. Was green hair the result of a third type of melanin, then? Or something else entirely? Edwin didn't even know where to begin trying to determine that sort of thing, though, so he let the question fall by the wayside . . . for now. Someday, he'd return to the question and figure out what made Lefi Forolova—the Adventurer who'd been teaching him stuff about the System most recently— have hair that looked like *literal golden fire*. But that day was not today. This day, he shopped.

Edwin continued his foray through the crowds, looking for a few more materials that he'd need if he were to properly try and survive in the wilderness. He wasn't going to blunder around like normal; he was going to prepare and do this *properly*. His search led him to a stall attached to a smithy, where he picked out a short-handled axe, a shovel, a small saw, a really sturdy knife, and a hand drill for twenty ager, and at another stall on his way there, a few good lengths of rope for a half ager———sixty ves and, yes, they did just cut the silver coin in half— before he left the market, purse much lighter. Edwin was content, though. The quality of the tools he'd gotten was easily comparable if not superior to modern-day Earth gear, power tools notwithstanding. Incredibly, despite how much stuff he had in his pack, it still didn't feel all that heavy, no doubt thanks to his Packing Skill. Magic for the win!

Granted, the unfortunate side of magic meant that Edwin had to stay vigilant against essentially invisible thieves, though how he was supposed to do so, he wasn't entirely sure. His coin pouch had been moved to sit on the inside of his belt, behind his temporarily tucked-in shirt, which was probably sufficient, though in a world filled with

Skills, was it really enough? Well, it was still present even once he had escaped the press of people in the city outskirts, so it must have been.

It was only once Edwin had left even the outskirts of Vinstead that he got his first glimpse of the Rhothos River itself, the namesake of apparently this entire region, and his first instinct was that it couldn't *possibly* be that large. The water seemed to stretch for miles, though most of it was on the shallow side. It honestly looked like the river had burst its banks and flooded a massive valley with uncountable gallons of water. But nobody seemed to take any note of it, like this was perfectly normal. In fact, there were even a few buildings in the middle of the lake-river, built atop stilts.

Edwin snapped his fingers. It had to have cyclic flooding of some sort, regular times of the year when the river burst its banks and irrigated the surroundings, inundating it with nutrients, like the Nile. That, combined with whatever "life magic" came from the Verdant, would probably turn this place into truly unmatched farmland.

Actually, did he really know if there *was* something magical about the Verdant? Everyone seemed to think there was, but maybe that was just the result of regular flooding and particularly rich soil? Sure, the sorts of things you could make with talsanenris berries were pretty overtly supernatural, but in a fantasy world that sort of thing might end up happening in all sorts of ways. Still, Edwin *did* have experiences with train-size predators, given the Stonehide Bear he'd encountered way back when he'd first landed on Joriah, though that didn't absolutely require a magical forest.

A road traveled alongside the bank of the Rhothos, which Edwin absentmindedly took as his mind wandered hither and yon, internally debating whether he would ever really be able to figure out if a place was "magical" in the sense that he knew it, or just a place with exceptional, but ultimately mundane, qualities. The people here would have no frame of reference; who knows what all had been chalked up to "just magic" simply because they didn't know any better? Well, that's what he was here for, anyway. He'd just find some cave or promising tree, come up with some clever survival solution, and become a reclusive alchemist-scholar.

Yeah, yeah! Edwin rather liked the idea of having his own private hidden base, a place he could really call his own.

That would be his goal for now, and hopefully he had given any dwarven pursuers coming after him from Clan Blackstone enough of a slip that they would have no clue where to find him. It was in large part because of those pursuers, whoever and wherever they may be, that he didn't set up shop in a city, but solitude had its own benefits beyond the purely emotional. He wouldn't need to deal with keeping people up with explosions or foul smells, he'd be the only one in danger of one of his experiments going wrong, and just in general, there was a reason chemical plants weren't near residential areas.

Shut up, brain. It's a great idea. It's also really cool. Let me have this. Just until I figure out what I'm doing with myself, maybe get a few Skills to a decent level . . . yeah. Just to properly find my feet.

This close to Vinstead, all sorts of individuals were out and about: patrols of generally human guards; workers on barges traversing the shallower sections of flooding, appearing to be planting something even while the water was still rushing beneath them; and laborers hauling sacks of some kind or another. Most of them seemed to be human, which struck Edwin as being rather odd. Vinstead had so many avior that it almost seemed like they were the most populous species in the entire region. And yet, nearly everywhere outside of the city itself (and the caravan) he had found had been human-dominated. Well, not counting the Blackstone citadel or that one halfling village. The thought of the halflings made Edwin cringe at how he had just sort of vanished after all the help they had given him, never saying thanks or providing any acknowledgment beyond a quick nod to the village chief, whatever her name had been. Without Almanac to remind him of people's names, they tended to quickly drain out of his mind. Not that it mattered *that* much when he wasn't with the person in question, he supposed.

Edwin spent the night in one of the shrines Lefi was so fond of, dedicated to the god of travel, Curicna. It didn't have much, but a mattress, no matter how primitive, was far nicer than sleeping on the ground. In some respects, he almost wished he could take one with him, but ignoring the logistical nightmare of trying to do so, stealing from a probably real god didn't strike him as terribly wise.

Well, he could always make one himself. How hard could it be?

Shut up, you'll jinx it.

CHAPTER 2

Into the Unknown

Edwin stood at the frontier, a boundary between the known and the unknown, the civilized and the wild, from the world where your value was determined by your strength and Skills into one where your value was determined by . . . your strength and Skills.

Okay, that's enough melodrama. Get moving.

He wasn't even at the tree line yet, just where the road turned to run parallel to the forest a few hundred feet away. The ground between him and the start of the woods was fairly calm, though Edwin couldn't shake the feeling of a war zone, with stumps littered across the open area and shoots of bushes and new tree growth tenaciously trying to claw back their lost territory.

It wasn't too hazardous to walk through, at least, which Edwin appreciated. He was also quite content with the absence of any witnesses as he literally ventured off the beaten path. It wasn't that he was doing anything *illegal*, at least so far as he knew, but he really didn't want to deal with awkward stares as he traveled into the depths of untamed wilderness, no matter how close it may have been geographically to civilization. Then again, it might well *be* illegal. The Liras Empire had governmentally assigned Skills and Paths here, so anything was possible.

Interestingly, the undergrowth near the edges of the Verdant was actually far thicker than Edwin was used to, when the tree cover started to grow thicker, blocking more prime sunlight . . . and he'd answered his own question before he'd really asked it. Wasn't there something similar that happened in really dense rain forests on Earth or whatever? It did mean he kind of wished that he'd bought a machete or something similar, but his stick worked . . . adequately. Every swing made his tools, tied as they were to the outside of his pack, sway and clatter. It wasn't quite a hindrance, but it was an annoyance. Still, it was ultimately a minor price to pay as he swatted brambles and creeping vines out of his path.

Though his vision was limited, it seemed to Edwin that if flooding occurred in the Verdant itself, it was far more limited than out in the plains. He'd been alongside the riverbank the entire time he'd stayed on the road, but now that he was among the trees, there was no sign of the excess water, not even the sound of a rushing river. Small creeks here and there didn't count, not that he had encountered many of those anyway. Maybe the floodplain just didn't extend into the woods? The river, if not flooding, must have been miles away from him.

Edwin wasn't sure that he could articulate what exactly he was hoping to find, though the ideal situation would be some sort of smallish cave, large enough to live in but not so large as to make him paranoid about possible undiscovered roommates. He also realized he should have tried to buy a pickaxe or something, but he could hopefully make whatever he found work without too much in the way of modification. He wasn't that picky, after all, and between his newly purchased knife—now he had one for Alchemy, for self-defense, and one for everything else—axe, saw, rope, hand drill (or was it an auger? He couldn't remember the difference, or was there even one?), and shovel, he should be all set, so long as he kept them in good repair . . . shoot. He didn't have a whetstone or anything.

Almanac to self, get a sharpening tool next time I'm in town, whenever that might be.

Outsider's Almanac was *great*. Sure, everyone Edwin had told about it thought the ability to make his own tags for his Identify Skill was massively overhyped, but he liked it! He could tag pretty much any-thing, so it had loads of utility, particularly when he didn't want to forget something, as his Memory Skill must have been too low-level to help out there.

It was kind of interesting. Last time he'd been in the Verdant, Edwin hadn't really noticed any animal life, which he had chalked up to being the result of animals having Skills. While he had confirmed via Lefi that pretty much anything Identify worked on by default—not counting the effects of Common Knowledge or other similar Skills—did indeed have Skills, Edwin didn't think any of his own would account for the sudden abundance of birdsong and other small creatures everywhere. At one point, he even caught a glimpse of what looked to be a deer of some sort in the distance, but it vanished before he got any sort of good look at it.

Oh hey, was that a chear tree? It was! No fruits, sadly. He loved the cherry/pear/lemonlike fruits the last time he was in the Verdant; they had kept him alive for . . . well, a few days before he'd found civilization. Cross-referencing the *Grimoire* yielded no results for what the fruits were really called, which probably meant that they didn't have any particularly notable alchemical properties, and that meant Edwin was still calling them chears. Not that he would really switch to calling them anything else at this point.

Camping was far simpler and much more pleasurable when he had the proper tools. Sure, it had been more than a few years since he'd been a Boy Scout, but thanks to Memory, he was able to recall most of his lessons, and with the benefit of hindsight he couldn't help but cringe a little bit at his hopeless stumbling around when he first landed.

These days, survival was basically easy-mode. Thanks to Survival and Nutrition, Edwin only needed a single meal each day to stay fully functional. Athletics, Walking, and Breathing were all high-enough level that, coupled with his increased standard of activity, a full day of hiking across rough terrain barely even winded him. Chopping down a few branches from a dead tree with his new axe got him a crackling fire, and Edwin made an Almanac note to get some canvas or other sturdy fabric next time he went into civilization to make himself a hammock. He wasn't *too* uncomfortable, lying against a pile of leaves and ferns at the base of the tree, covered as he was by his cloak, but it could be way better for comparatively little effort.

Edwin triggered his notifications for the past couple of days, scrolling past a handful of Skill offerings—no, he *didn't* want Axes, Hiking,

Book Smarts (though the name did sound intriguing), but maybe Reading? . . . Nah. Not worth it. Sure, it might have some interesting evolution, but that could hold true for *any* of his Skills, let alone what they might evolve into—and to his levels. He'd had a pretty good haul from the last week or so. He was still figuring out which was more satisfying, seeing it all at once or bit by bit, but this *was* pretty nice.

Level Up!
Skill Points 423→443
Progress to Tier 2: 653/1590
Alchemy Level 51→52
Breathing Level 26→29
Identify Level 40→41
Memory Level 28→31
Nutrition Level 23→24
Outsider's Almanac Level 78→79
Packing Level 20→24
Polyglot Level 34→36
Seeing Level 27→29
Survival Level 19→21
Walking Level 39→40

Hmm. He really should figure out if he wanted any more Skills. If he were offered something really great or broadly applicable, he might take it. Otherwise, he wanted to focus on getting up to Tier 2, evolving all his current Skills one time.

The complication to that idea was Edwin's immense Skill Point debt, born from his ignorance about the System's functions in the early days of his time on Joriah. He'd evolved several of his Skills while they were still low-level and both froze their advancement as well as losing out on dozens to hundreds of easy Skill Points. Combined, it meant that at *some* point he'd need to hold off on evolving his Skills until he could cancel out his debt or risk becoming softlocked in the System, where he wouldn't be able to raise the ever-more-difficult-to-obtain Skill levels to cover the cost of evolving them and resetting the difficulty with a functionally new Skill.

He'd . . . hmm. He'd raise all his Skills to at least . . . 70 or so, then mass-complete a bunch of Paths, then raise the remaining ones up to evolve via his 90-point Paths. Eh, maybe once he passed the universal level 40 mark, he'd complete a 30-point Path as a bit of a reward to himself. He'd miss out a bit on potential Attributes, but it would probably be fine. For now, he'd content himself with finding a good base to call home.

Level Up!
Sleeping Level 27→28

It took a couple of days of not-quite blind (thanks to Almanac letting him know when he'd already passed a given tree or rock) wandering through the woods, but Edwin eventually found something that he felt would suit his purposes. It was an idyllic tiny meadow situated next to a rocky bluff, the ground sloping slightly up to meet the stone; a small rocky outcropping some ten feet up the slope would provide a bit of shelter. The real prize was a stream coming from the top of the bluff, the water cascading over the edge in a small waterfall, collecting in a pristine but unusually deep pool, then winding away. With that, he'd have a convenient way to find his shelter again, a source of water, and if he could find a way to harness the energy of the stream, the option to make some simple machines. Edwin may not have been an engineer, but he wasn't hopeless in the mechanical department, either.

Although his initial target had been a cave, Edwin had abandoned his search for a suitable one after finding several, none of which were anywhere close to being dry enough, large enough, or accessible enough for actual habitation. Fiction, it seemed, had lied to him about the quality of natural homes in woodland caves.

In hindsight, he should probably have been looking for something with better ventilation anyway. So his new plan was to make a log cabin of sorts, by this idyllic woodland pond, and possibly build out from there. He'd need to dry out the wood he would use, yes, but the *Grimoire* actually had some useful advice in that regard! A genuine formula, with steps and everything, was outlined in the "preservation" section of herbology, regarding how to dry out samples taken while preserving desirable properties. It was vague, sure, but he could probably get a workable version without too much trouble. A footnote had mentioned a couple of modifications that could make the process work for food, animal parts, and most crucially, wood.

Even better, Edwin already had a lot of the required ingredients; he did his best to *not* think about *why* Niall would have the reagents needed for preserving alchemical materials. The main thing he was missing for the wood variation was ash from the target tree type, but that was easy enough to obtain. By the ratios listed in the book, he had more than enough for several logs, and he'd even have enough left over to dry out firewood.

. . .

Yeah, no, Edwin was back to thinking about why the serial killer Alchemist would have so many preservatives. That was . . . not a pretty picture. Hey, at least they'd be put to good use now that their original owner hopefully had his head on a pike. Drying out wood would require a fair bit of work, though, so he'd need to get started.

Okay, let's see. Priorities. Shelter, water, and food. Shelter is partially taken care of by the overhang . . . unless there's any wind. Yeah, some temporary shelter is a must-have. Water is taken care of by the stream, though I need to get a firepit dug so I can boil water, cook food . . . can dried beans be grown? I think so, but hmm. Might be worth a try, see if I can't establish a bit of a garden of my own. Will I need to hunt? I mean, I probably will. At least there's actually animal life down here. A passing thought made Edwin chuckle slightly. *I wonder if this is the "low level" area, where the spiders* aren't *superterrifying, and all your standard woodland creatures live. It's only when you venture farther up that the massive bears and invisible prey start showing up? Man, if real life worked that way. . . . Well, I suppose stranger things have happened. I should try and find another spiderweb to see if it's any weaker here.*

Where was I? Oh, right. Shelter. Hmm. It's what, early afternoon? I could probably chop down a smaller tree or two to make a bit of a lean-to against the cliff that should serve me while I make something more permanent.

A tiny part of him whispered that living in the woods wasn't actually a viable strategy long term, but Edwin shut that whisper down. He wanted to enjoy this, darn it!

The first step was to locate an appropriate tree, Edwin knew. He wanted something tall but not too thick, and while there wasn't anything that fully met his specifications around his meadow, the stream had enough young-growth trees that he'd probably find one there. He didn't even have to venture that far, fortunately, before he encountered something that looked like it would work. The tree itself seemed to be somewhere between birch and pine, with white, fibrous bark (could he weave with this stuff, perhaps?), and was probably about six inches in diameter, which he made quick work of with his axe.

Hauling the lumber wasn't all that bad, really. Other than the branches snagging on *anything and everything*—fortunately, Edwin was usually able to unstick by yanking really hard, only having to lop off a single branch to make it all come along—the tree itself wasn't that hard to move, despite being some forty feet tall at least.

Once he actually made it back to camp, Edwin chopped off the branches, piling them on the sandy soil underneath the rocky overhang. He did have a use for them after all, and he left them attached this far just because he didn't want to make multiple trips. Then, he cut the tree, his saw proving its use, into five roughly equal lengths, and with a twist of Visualization, started laying out exactly how his temporary home would work.

His first task was to dig two holes into the rich soil, just shy of eight feet apart and about three feet away from the rocky cliff. Actually, amend that to digging out the area to make it somewhat flat, then a bit more to give the area a bit of a recessed floor, *then* dig out the two holes. Into said holes, Edwin inserted his two logs from the bottom of the trunk, and therefore thickest and sturdiest, leaning them against the stone cliff face. Then, he filled in the holes, compacting the dirt as much as he could, which should theoretically hold his primary supports fairly steady.

After a couple of failed attempts to continue, Edwin repeated the process to give himself a third support in the middle.

That left two more segments of trunk, neither of which was too terribly sturdy. Fortunately, that also meant they weren't terribly heavy, either. He cut some notches into his support and remaining logs, lining them up such that they slotted . . . more or less . . . into one another. Then, he took his rope and bound them in place, providing a nice framework upon which he could lay branches, giving him a fairly cozy roof, though admittedly at the price of keeping three of his four coils of rope occupied (his longer ones, at that). Once he actually had everything assembled, though, he felt it was well worth the trade-off.

The inside was still essentially just fresh dirt, though, so Edwin took the time to get a bunch of longer grass from his meadow and spread it out on the inside. It wasn't *much*, but it was better than nothing.

The final shelter wasn't anything too terribly impressive, but Edwin was still proud of it, especially given he'd done it all in a single afternoon. The interior was a bit earthy-smelling, but it had enough room for Edwin and his stuff. It opened out underneath the overhang, which was also where Edwin had set up his campfire. The other side he had filled in with his extra dirt, to help keep heat in. It may have still not rained (mage fights notwithstanding), but Edwin wasn't going to count on that. He probably should have asked Lefi about the weather patterns, but he hadn't thought of it at the time. Regardless, no rain would put out his fire.

Night was starting to fall, though, so Edwin figured he should start getting ready for bed. Making a fire was trivial at this point, requiring just the snap of his fingers thanks to his Mana Infusion and Firestarting Skills, but it still felt so nice and Edwin fell asleep with a smile on his face.

CHAPTER 3

An Axe to Grind (With)

Edwin awoke to birdsong and stretched, trying to work out a knot in his back from where a branch had been poking him. Yeah, he'd *definitely* need to make some kind of hammock to aid his sleep. Probably easier to make than a mattress, in any case. The stick, for its part, was cast into the fire and destroyed. It was the little things.

Breakfast was nothing much. One of his travel loaves (he was down to eight now) was enough to hold him for the entire day, and even Nutrition seemed content with his decidedly nonbalanced diet. Apparently, with magical assistance it was adequate? He didn't often dwell on the flavor of what he ate, but the rations, somewhere between rye bread and fruitcake, were just barely not bland enough to be tolerable, though not flavorful enough to actually be enjoyable. As he chewed on the tough substance, Edwin couldn't help but wonder if it had been intentionally designed that way. You couldn't hit that balance so perfectly by accident, right?

He stood up as he tossed the last bit of the bread into his mouth, stretching and sincerely wishing he had a chair. Something to work on eventually, he supposed. If only he could accept Woodworking with a clear conscience, this would undoubtedly be a much simpler process, but he couldn't justify to himself such a narrow Skill, not when he was declining ones like Stealth or Reflexes. Maybe if it were broader in application, then he could take it, but for a Skill that would only help him here and now? No. Now, where was that formula for the wood-curing concoction?

The *Zosiman Grimoire*'s instructions were, as always, equal parts frustrating and enlightening. No explanation whatsoever was provided about what each of the different steps was supposed to actually do, just what their final result would supposedly be. Edwin sighed in disbelief. Who would have ever thought that he'd *want* something to be written more like his chem textbooks? At least the instructions were relatively clear, if not terribly precise. He still didn't know how much "a pinch" or "a small handful" was supposed to be, but he also didn't really have anything more precise to measure with, so it more or less balanced out.

Edwin idly wondered if he'd be able to get a grant to pursue research of some sort, but ironically, the closest he'd seen of anything like that here on Joriah was when he was forced into working at Clan Blackstone. Eh, more likely, he'd be able to come up with something he could sell to fund further research, like a good Alchemist, turning scrap to gold. For now, though, he'd live off the land and do experiments on the magical plants that grew in here. That meant he'd need to get to work, though. His musings were enough procrastination for now, though his muscles were already protesting out of sheer anticipation for the amount of work he'd put them through.

Edwin would need about forty, maybe fifty trees for his cabin, if he wanted four walls ten feet tall, each log about a foot in diameter. That meant his first step was to simply find enough appropriate trees. He didn't want to be picky, but at the same time, he did need them all to be tall enough, straight enough, and, annoyingly enough, all the same species. That last requirement was because of the alchemical formula he was following, whose primary ingredient was ash of the target wood.

Well, he could probably make multiple batches with different base woods if he ended up needing to, but he'd rather not complicate things more than needed. It would be tricky enough for him to spread out his ingredients into three small trial runs, budgeting to be on the safe side, allowing for one incorrect batch as his first attempt, an incorrect attempt to fix it, and one correct mixture before his main creation, let alone having to experiment with two different wood ashes, which may or may not affect the rest of the formula.

Edwin had never really been that keen on Identifying trees, which made the fact that he still didn't need to memorize different leaf shapes and types of bark, thanks to shortcutting the entire affair with Almanac, quite enjoyable. He didn't care what Tara and Lefi said, this thing was fantastic as it was. That said, he had two primary contenders he might use to build his house; namely, not-cedar and not-fir. Edwin could Identify plenty of other types of trees as well, a surprisingly diverse amount at that, but they weren't large enough, weren't straight enough, weren't numerous enough, or had any number of other problems. There was one tree with bark that reminded him of a madrona tree, another reminiscent of oak, and plenty with no easy mapping from what Edwin was used to. He'd even come across a couple truly *monstrous* trees, one of which was nearly as big around as the size of the cabin he was trying to build, but after a brief fantasy, he discarded the idea of carving it into something he could live in. That was just asking for trouble.

In any case, neither not-fir or not-cedar were actually too much like the Earth trees beyond general structure (tall and straight) and bark quality (though not-cedar honestly reminded Edwin more of a maple tree), as both were broad-leaved rather than nettled, and even glass-leaves at that, allowing light through selectively. As he studied a leaf, plucked from a nearby low branch, Edwin couldn't help but wonder if he might be able to use the leaves as windows or for light-filtration goggles or *something*. This property was too unique and cool to allow it to sit unused, though nothing in particular sprang to mind quite yet. Maybe the *Grimoire* would have some notes to give him a starting point on how to treat them into something that would last longer than a normal fallen leaf.

Anyway! Not-cedar and not-fir. Nedar and nir, perhaps?
My naming sense is awful.
The nedar had the advantage of not having many branches, and the stringier bark should make it easier to prepare for use. Nir, on the other hand, had way more low-hanging branches, though they would be relatively easy to remove, and the trees themselves were supernumerous,

and though there was far from a scarcity of either, most of the nedar trees were too thick around for his purposes, averaging around two feet in diameter.

Ultimately, Edwin decided to go with the nir. While he would have preferred the nedar, for the simple reason that he liked how it smelled more . . . it was like a rather sweet cedar scent reminiscent of how scented candles portrayed the wood . . . he ultimately had to go with the nir. The overwhelming advantage of having plenty of trees in the proper dimensions was more than enough to tip the balance.

The first tree Edwin picked out was just off the edge of his meadow. Some eighty feet tall—

Oh yeah, I might be able to get multiple logs from a single tree. That would make things much easier!

—and a little over a foot in diameter, so far as he could estimate, it was on the younger side, but that's exactly what he needed, wasn't it?

Edwin was neither an idiot nor a *complete* novice when it came to felling trees (he knew the theory, at least), so he started with his handsaw. Sure, the blade may have only been twice as long as the tree was wide, but he was still able to cut about halfway through the tree without too much hassle. He could have gone farther, yes, but doing so seemed . . . risky. Also, he was sick of it binding in the wood and wanted to take his frustrations out with an axe. As it was, if the tree fell in the direction of the cut, it would fall into the meadow at a bit of a diagonal, so it would lie mostly in the clearing but not obstruct either the stream or crush his shelter.

Once he was done sawing at it, he took his axe to the log, the sharp blade digging into the wood with no trouble, as he wielded it with a surprising amount of ease. Did Survival have a hidden benefit, or was that just Athletics? Maybe Athletics and Flexibility both, to help him strike with such proficiency every time?

It was just a few minutes before Edwin had a sizable divot cut into the log, his axe strokes meeting where he had cut with his saw, and debris surrounding it all. Okay, that should make sure it fell in the right direction, now to actually cut it down. To do that, he took his handsaw once more, this time to the back of the tree, and started cutting.

Once his cut had nearly connected with the giant divot at the front of the tree, the entire nedar began to creak and groan. Not taking any chances, Edwin took that as his cue to vacate the area entirely, fleeing into the woods and sheltering behind a hefty tree. Hopefully, even if the log did fall in his direction, it wouldn't get past his cover.

The tree, so small in comparison to many of its neighbors, yet still titanic by most reasonable measures, swayed slightly as its branches caught in some of its peers. A flock of birds not scared away by Edwin's vigorous chopping of the tree scattered, flying off to places unknown. The base began to splinter slightly, and with the sound of countless branches breaking off far above, the tree began to fall.

As it turned out, Edwin needn't have worried as much as he had. The tree fell in more or less the direction he had been hoping for, though the bottom of the trunk also shot out like a battering ram as it broke from the trunk, utterly demolishing a dead tree behind it. The bulk of the tree fell in the meadow, crashing down with enough force that even Edwin could feel it as it transmitted through the ground. Overall? Other than the pile of splinters that hadn't been there two minutes prior, it was a rousing success! Now, he just needed to deal with the colossal mess of broken and unbroken branches that occupied his meadow.

Edwin took his axe to the nir limbs, lopping them off with usually just a single blow, using his new haul to reinforce the roof of his shelter, though some of the branches were tossed into his fire, where they snapped and popped before being consumed by the flames.

It took a few hours before his tree was adequately trimmed, in large part due to caution and inexperience, which put him securely in the afternoon, but even once he was finished, he was still dealing with an absolutely massive titan of wood and bark, to the point where Edwin was rather intimidated by the whole thing. How was he supposed to render *this* down into logs for his home? It was enormous! Heck, a good twenty feet of the thing's trunk was still in the forest. Well, at the same time, there was nothing to it but getting to work.

Edwin could barely budge the whole thing—it must have weighed a literal ton—but he could move it *just* enough to start making cuts in the log itself. He settled on his logs being about twenty feet long, conveniently the length of his remaining rope, so he'd have plenty of space inside and a bit of grace when actually cutting the notches into the wood for construction. The actual act of cutting was fairly straightforward, and before long he had three full-length logs and one about ten feet long, before the top started to taper, rendering it unusable for an outer wall. Perhaps an inner one, then? Or he could use it as his ash base.

Edwin's stomach rumbled, which caught him off guard. He must have been working hard if his body wanted food already. While loath to do so, he downed another ration loaf and a canteen of water, refilled with water from the waterfall—that was a slippery mess, but doable, and boiled to sanitize it—before his belly could start to overly protest.

Edwin surveyed his day's work, as the sun's light began to slowly vanish, the star itself having descended behind the trees some time previous. One giant tree, felled and cut up to be used in his house, check. Piles of wood cuttings littered the previously pristine grass, but that was a relatively small matter. He could gather some up and toss them into the fire. Should be a good show. Regardless, Edwin hoped future days would go a lot faster. He'd gotten three usable logs, after all, but he'd need fifteen times that for the walls alone, which meant two weeks of just acting as a lumberjack unless he managed to increase his rate to two per day. And if they were all days as hard as this one? Ugh, that meant his ration supply was cut from a week remaining to three days. Perhaps he should try hunting tomorrow? Or boiling up some of his dried foods?

That might be a decent idea, actually. He wasn't hauling some ten pounds of preserved beans, flour, and rice around for fun, after all. It wouldn't be superflavorful, but he could deal with that. He Almanaced himself a note to make a setup that he could boil water with over his fire, gave a satisfied nod at his work so far, and tucked himself in around his fire. It might have been too early to go to bed, but that didn't mean he'd have to push himself any more for the day. Plenty of stuff to do, but there was plenty of time for it.

Edwin scrolled through his notification list for the first time in a while, dismissing his offered Skills. No, neither Woodworking, nor Survivalism, nor Axes was good enough for his final Skill list, though Paths were always nice to get.

Level Up!
Skill Points 444→461
Progress to Tier 2: 670/1590
Athletics Level 33→37
Breathing Level 29→30
Flexibility Level 25→26
Outsider's Almanac Level 79→80
Packing Level 24→27
Survival Level 21→28
Congratulations! For cutting a felled tree into logs, you have
unlocked the Woodsman Path!

CHAPTER 4

Branching Paths

Now that he actually knew what he was doing, the next several trees all went much faster. Edwin found that he was fully capable of cutting down a tree in less than half an hour, though after one started falling well before he was actually ready for it, he slowed down so as to not risk any potential accidents. The more time-consuming aspect of it was actually trimming the limbs, though even that went faster and faster as his levels slowly climbed. Over just the next day, Athletics grew from level 37 to level 41, and he was pushing himself hard enough that even that continued to slowly grow. By the end of the second day, he was at 45, 48 by the third, and when he had finished cutting up his fifteen logs on day three, he had hit level 50 in the Skill, and it wasn't the only one.

Level Up!
Skill Points 461→478
Progress to Tier 2: 687/1590
Athletics Level 37→50
Breathing Level 30→32
Flexibility Level 26→28
Nutrition Level 23→25
Packing Level 27→30

Survival Level 28→32
Visualization Level 42→43

Some combination of Athletics and Packing was really paying off, as well, as Edwin was capable of just *picking up* the twenty-foot logs, some five hundred pounds if his estimations were accurate, like they were less than a fifth of that. Heavy, yes, but *he could do it*. That same strength didn't seem to apply to anything else, unfortunately; just lifting things, which he found out the first time he tried to do push-ups and confirmed by the fact he couldn't splinter some of the larger branches through sheer muscle power. He was slightly stronger, yes, but not by that much. No, clearly something else was going on.

His current hypothesis was that Packing somehow reduced the weight of whatever he tried to pick up, rather than any sort of strength enhancement, and some of his initial testing had seemed to support that hypothesis. When he grabbed a stick by its thin end, it would bend much less than if he just tried propping it up by that same end. Setting it down would make it instantly sag, for example, and if he threw something, it seemed to actually fall slower through the air than if it just fell, though he couldn't measure precisely enough to actually be certain about that. If the effect was there, and not just his imagination, it was really slight. Superman-style superlifting powers were very cool and had all *sorts* of potential for future use. He had one idea in mind that he just couldn't wait to try out once his level got high enough.

Edwin had fortunately managed to get his food problem more or less sorted out. Sure, boiled dried beans weren't exactly tasty, but when combined with his travel loaves, they were still sufficient to keep him going. He had enough for about a week of food just in that stuff, once he finished working so hard, anyway, not counting any he would want to save out for a garden. He'd start trying to hunt and find edible plants tomorrow, he thought. After all, he was finally done chopping trees down!

Off to one side of the clearing, a few piles of logs lay, neatly stacked into position by Edwin testing the limits of his new physical capabilities. His shelter was also seriously buried under piles and piles of branches, giving it loads of insulation, and his floor now consisted of wood chips and sawdust overlayed with the broad leaves, providing a fairly nice, relatively clean surface for him as he slept. He kept finding bugs, though, especially worms, and he was looking forward to getting a proper bed or hammock of some form.

A flex of Visualization helped Edwin plan out his future home. Some fifteen by fifteen feet on the inside, it would primarily be a single room, though he planned to wall off one of the back corners to use as a dedicated laboratory. He walked out the space that it would occupy, and satisfied by what he found, he moved over to his pile, hauling one of the logs off with a heave. He staggered over to where he had moved a few rocks to form a bit of a small stand, to help keep his timber off the ground. With a deep breath, he pulled out his knives, and started to peel the bark away.

It didn't take Edwin too long to figure out there was bound to be a more efficient way to do this. He had quickly abandoned his idea of hand-cutting every little bit of bark from his timber, instead opting to cut a seam of sorts down the top of the log and peeling the bark off like a jacket, but even that still took quite a bit of effort to do and didn't even work all the time. Unfortunately, any of his additional ideas required tools he simply didn't have, so peeling trees like bananas stayed around. At least the bark was generally cooperating.

He could do this. It wasn't that bad.

. . .

He got through two trees before getting frustrated.
You know what? I'm going hunting. That might help.

Edwin wasn't an idiot, no matter how he felt at times—
Or act, or actually am, or am told by other people.
—Ahem.

Edwin wasn't an idiot, at least not a complete one. He knew that any and all hunting would rely on his Throwing Weapons pretty much exclusively, which was nowhere near as effective as a modern rifle would have been, and that there probably wasn't all that much game still in the area, most of it being scared off by his time acting as a lumberjack. Plus, even modern hunters, with all their gear and their tools, frequently would find no prey. He also knew that trying to hunt while angry was a similarly terrible idea. Really, he was mainly just using it as an excuse to go out on a walk, albeit with a handful of decently hefty stones to use as weapons.

As he ventured forward, Edwin dutifully Almanaced every tree he passed, making sure that he'd be able to find his way back. Oh hey, that bird was the same one that had been popping in and out of his clearing. Was it spying on him? Eh, probably not. Most likely, it just lived in the area and he just happened to Identify one he'd already tagged. Hmm. Almanac would be amazing for conservationists or . . . whoever it was that tracked migratory patterns of birds, wouldn't it? A way to uniquely identify a single creature, at range, with no impact to the creature being measured.

A *snap* broke Edwin out of his trance, and he spun around, ready to fight off some bear, rock already in hand and ready to be thrown . . . oh, it was just a deer. Never mi— Hey, wait, a deer!

As it bounded past him at high speeds, Edwin threw his prepared stone as hard as he could at the creature's skull. Incredibly, he managed to hit it right at the back of the head—his Throwing Weapons Skill no doubt helped—and striking with a solid crack. The Mature Blackshoulder Deer didn't drop immediately, but it did seem to disorient the creature, and it seemed to stagger almost drunkenly into a nearby tree, crashing into the unmoving nedar and falling motionlessly onto the ground.

. . .

Well.

Apparently sometimes things did work out in his favor.

It was quite simple to carry the carcass back to his camp. Compared to the logs he'd been getting used to, the deer was practically as light as a feather. While he was somewhat hesitant to try and clean the animal where he lived—who knew what kinds of predators that might attract?—Edwin didn't have too much of a choice. As he hadn't been expecting to actually *succeed* on his hunt, he hadn't thought to bring his sharpest knife, namely his Alchemy knife from the dwarves, instead only keeping with him his woodworking knife, which was adequate for self-defense or cutting branches, but not quite as sharp as he'd generally like. Hence, he needed to return to camp. Well, as a partial precaution, he'd do the field dressing on the far side of the creek. That should hopefully keep any scavengers well away from him as he slept. Heck, maybe he'd even drop it all into the stream. The fish would probably like it.

The walk back seemed to take slightly longer than the walk out, though that may well have just been his imagination, and soon Edwin was closing in on very familiar territory. With a relieved sigh, he tossed his kill onto the ground where he was planning on dealing with it and grabbed his knife.

Sure, he'd never actually gutted and field dressed any animals before, but how hard could it be? He'd never been hunting before, but that turned out just fine.

Hard. It was very hard. Trying to cut his prize open had punctured the stomach or something in the deer's torso, spilling half-digested grass out onto the ground and releasing an absolutely foul stench that had Edwin gagging for a good minute. Even once he had that taken care of, it was absolutely horrid to have to scoop out all the insides when they didn't fall out, strung up as the deer's body was by its front legs, occupying Edwin's last rope. He was *so desperately glad* that he had managed to get gloves from Niall's tower, though he would have to seriously consider throwing them out after this.

He had to borderline punch through some tough membrane (the diaphragm?) to pull out the heart and lungs of the deer and cut out most of the deer's digestive tract, which he was fairly confident he'd done at least mostly correct, but there was also just *so much* blood. It got over everything; he'd have to give it all a solid scrub in the stream and possibly boil it to make sure it didn't stain, and it just kept coming, too. Gah. Edwin just wanted this to be *over*.

Thinking about it slightly more objectively, it wasn't quite the most disgusting thing he'd ever had to do, but it was definitely up there. He'd need to wash his . . . everything, and even then he'd still know what he and his clothes had been through. Still, at least the deed was done. The deer hung from a tree, eyes glassy and blank as what was left of it slowly drained out its blood, its vital organs in a sloppy pile around the corpse.

Edwin eventually got his clothes clean, though it took extensive scrubbing with sand from the bottom of the stream and pond. He was similarly forced to bathe, which reminded him sharply of another thing he had forgotten.

Soap. I need soap next time I head in. Soap, a whetstone, and canvas. Probably some seasonings, too, if I can get them at a decent price.

Once he and his clothes were dry and only a *little* singed, thanks to careful use of Firestarting and his fire, Edwin sighed and decided he really should deal with his waste before it started to smell or get dark. He grabbed his shovel, hopped the stream, and, hauling a giant scoop of innards, dumped the lot in the stream, just below where the pond let out.

The water immediately reacted, the pool erupting into cold boiling, waves and ripples compounding and multiplying, until waves broke the surface and began to coalesce into a shape. Edwin wasted no time in falling into a combat stance, his . . . shovel ready to smack down to the best of his ability whatever water elemental or river spirit he had accidentally disturbed.

He barely even had time to think about what he was really expecting, though one of his half-formed thoughts came true as a distinctly feminine voice called out from where a good amount of the pond was rising into the air, "Ick! Yuck! *No!* For the last time, I *told you*, no more blood sacrifi . . ." The voice trailed off as the water finished solidifying into a humanoid shape, losing its transparency and becoming a distinctly feylike female figure, clothed in leaves, with dark green hair drifting through the air like she was underwater.

Edwin and the nymph (come on, what else would she be?) stared at each other for a few seconds, before she broke the silence, "Now who the Blight are *you*?"

CHAPTER 5

Feyday

"Who am I?" Edwin was taken aback, blurting out the first things that came to mind, "Who are *you*? And where have you been? I've been here for probably a week. Have you just been asleep or something?"

The nymph glared at Edwin suspiciously, eyes narrowing as she presumably Identified him. Well, then, he'd return the favor.

Enchanting Hydromantic Tender-Muse

So she had an actual Class, then. Interesting. Edwin wasn't entirely sure what that meant, but it seemed significant.

"An . . . Alchemist? I didn't . . . huh. Curious . . ." Her voice was soothing and soft, and Edwin had to wrench his brain into order to avoid being lulled into complacency. It didn't even feel like a Skill, or did it? Was he just that bad at paying attention to people when they talked? He hoped not. She went on, "Not a supplicant, then?"

"Uh, no. I suppose not. I was just trying to clean up after a hunt; I didn't know you were in there, my fair lady." Surprise notwithstanding, manners never hurt. "You surprised me is all. I am Edwin."

She shifted her posture in a way that was probably significant but was lost on Edwin. Was she trying to be more formal as well? She was standing straighter now, feet lightly touching the surface of the now-still pond, "Ah, yes. Naturally. As is only natural. My presence is naturally quite surprising to those who may not have been anticipating my presence. Your apology is accepted. What brings you, supplicant Edwin, to my spring in these fine woods?" She looked around at the clearing, assessing the surroundings.

Edwin had to choke back a smile. He may be nearly oblivious to virtually all nonverbal cues, but *nearly* wasn't *completely*, and he knew all too well the signs of someone desperately bluffing their way through a conversation in the vague hope they'd figure out what was going on midway through. His overall fear of the nymph fell a fair bit, and while he still was somewhat wary of her, he couldn't resist the urge to have a bit of fun with her. "Why is it not obvious, my lady? The same reason all of those who came before me have sought your presence. Have you truly forgotten the past so quickly?"

There was a brief, delicious moment of absolute panic on the Muse's face as she attempted to stammer a reply, "N-no. Of course not, I would never . . ." Her eyes narrowed and she glared at Edwin, though without any real malice. "You! You would play such a joke upon one as fine as I?"

Edwin couldn't quite hold it in, and he started chuckling. That got a slight twitch on the corner of the fey's mouth, which only made him start laughing even more. Fortunately, it seemed it was a twitch of amusement rather than annoyance, and she didn't strike him on the spot. He recovered quickly, composing himself before he got too carried away with his laughter. "I'm sorry. I just . . . understand how you feel, all too well." He gave a momentary bow—he nearly extended his hand to shake but that didn't seem like a good idea given the sorts of stories about lake-dwellers drowning careless people—and looked the nymph in the eye. "As I said, my name is Edwin. I came out here, into the Verdant, as a chance to find some freedom in the wilds, escape those who would do me harm, and to hone my capabilities. And you are?"

It was a bit of a risk, treating an in all likelihood very capricious and powerful individual as something approaching a peer, but he was on dry land and there was no *way* he'd be sticking around here if he'd have to deal with someone who demanded excessive levels of respect and supplication. If she did want him to treat her like a local god or something, well . . . Better to get it out of the way early than to put even more time into his work, only to be forced to abandon it. Still, it seemed to pay off, as she didn't immediately blast him with water or anything.

"I'm . . . Inion," she eventually offered. "And you said that this is the Verdant? On Joriah?"

" . . . Yes? Did you expect to be elsewhere?"

She shook her head in partial exasperation. "I merely did not expect such a drastic change from the last time I was awake. Do you happen to know how many years have passed?"

"Lady Inion, I haven't even the faintest clue as to how to even begin to find that out."

"Fair . . . fair." She sat down on the surface of the water and indicated Edwin should do the same. He mentally shrugged and took a seat on a relatively smooth stone next to the water's edge. "What year is it currently?"

Edwin hopelessly shrugged. "I don't know, actually. I'm not local, just passing through."

"I see. Do the Connacht still hold sway? Did the Vossali conquer them?" she inquired and got only a blank stare in response each time. "I see. What kingdom holds the Rhothos, then?" Huh. That was the first time a name had been translated. Well, not counting the coins, at least, though did those really count?

"Uh, no kingdom. The Liras Empire rules the Rhothos, and I think the entire continent other than what's inside the Verdant." He hazarded this information hoping that it wouldn't upset her too much. "Did you . . . enjoy the Connacht's presence?"

Inion raised and lowered her hands in inverse unison, one going up as the other went down. It took a moment before he realized she was imitating scales. "Somewhat. They knew how to treat me properly"— she shot a glance at Edwin—"but they similarly insisted on always holding festivals and rituals in my pond, and *always* insisted on blood sacrifices no matter how much I told them I didn't want it. Leaves a foul taste in my waters. The Liras Empire, though . . ." She thought for a moment. "Oh! Whatsisname Liras! That bird-guy, whatever they're called."

"Avior?" Edwin ventured.

"Ya, them! Back before I fell asleep, all the druids were trying to do some ritual to fight off Conqueror something—Liras, Kares, Arras, Sarris, uhh . . ."

"Do you mean Xares?"

"That's the one! Xares Liras, some pompous featherbeak, wanting to expand the reach of his kingdom onto Korizan"—there was that name-translation again—"but last I heard we were supposedly holding him off or something. I may have some very faint memories about being asked to help with something like that, but . . . no, I don't remember. It's all very fuzzy. How long has he been in charge?"

"Some two thousand years, from what I've heard."

"Two millennia? Really?" For a moment, Edwin thought Inion might freak out, and was preparing to have to fight her, when, "Oh, thank the gods. That means Athirne should have returned by now. Curse that man."

"Returned? Returned where? What did he do?"

"I . . . don't think I can tell you that, but he didn't do anything too bad, we just . . . didn't get along?"

Inion was apparently a terrible liar, but Edwin didn't want to pry into what he presumed was some form of relationship history. "So then . . . You were asleep for two thousand years and I woke you up somehow?"

She shrugged. "Ya, I guess so." Inion flipped upside down, so she was lying on her back while maintaining eye contact with Edwin. Her leaf-woven outfit wasn't perfectly concealing, so Edwin awkwardly looked off to the side slightly. It wasn't lost on Inion, though, and a playful grin crossed her face. "What's the matter? Don't like what you see?"

"Could we . . . talk about something else? Like, anything else?" He'd come out to the middle of nowhere to *escape* awkwardness, darn it. Even excepting that, it seemed like a *really, really* bad idea to get *involved* with a river spirit.

"Aww, but what better way to get to know each other? Back in *my* day, I'll have you know, we—"

"I have at least two more shovels full of guts from my deer, and there's plenty of room in your pond if you feel like continuing that sentence."

Inion shuddered, cutting off whatever she was about to say, and started pouting slightly. "You're no fun."

"Look, could you at least lie on your front or something so I can look at you without feeling awkward?" Edwin returned his gaze to the nymph, who had thankfully obliged with his request. "Thanks. Not that I can't appreciate it, just . . . context. Also, I've heard way too many stories about water nymphs to really trust you yet."

She rolled her eyes at him, pretending to sag with sadness. "I'm insulted! But fine. I'll play along . . . for now." Inion said the last two words suggestively, then switched to a more bouncy tone of voice, one that reminded Edwin more of a burbling book than a serene pond. "But I've apparently been asleep for *ages*. Tell me what's going on in the world! Even the druids never really told me anything."

"Well . . . there's a big empire, conquered like half the planet, and the Rhothos River is flooding,"

"Oh! I love springtime. So much free rein!" She traced a finger along the surface of her pond, then stopped, hesitating. "Weird . . . Something's stopping me from feeling past . . . just a moment, you don't mind?"

Before Edwin could say anything, the nymph turned into water, splashing back into her little pool. He started to get up, but Inion returned before he could fully rise. This time, instead of all the drama from before, she just surfaced as though ascending from a dive, breaking through the water before returning to her lounging position atop its surface. "There's some barrier right at the trees." She grimaced. "Doesn't let me past. That wasn't there before. Also, the trees are *so far back*. It's all so *tiny*." When Edwin didn't provide whatever response she was apparently expecting, Inion dismissed him with a wave of her hand and said, "Humans," to which Edwin could only mutely shrug as he sat back down.

"So what about you? I presume you're some kind of fey or nature spirit, a nymph of some kind?" He didn't know what the proper words would be, but thank heavens for Polyglot, taking care of that sort of thing. He idly wondered what language it was that Inion spoke. Was it some fey language or just really old human speech? Whatever the case, she must have had a Skill similar to Polyglot herself for her speech to come out so decidedly nonaccented.

"You're pretty well informed for a human. Have you met another naiad before?"

"No, just . . . heard stories, essentially. Probably more false than they're true, honestly." Right, *naiad*. Not nymph, those were tree-bound. "And naiad? Is that because you're water-bound?"

Inion did the scale-weighing thing again. "Kinda. Nymphs are bound to living things, but naiads are more like kami; we bind to objects, most commonly—" Her head darted to the side, and she glared at the air. "What do you mean, *warning*? What did I— Oh, right. Well, I didn't need that anyway? It'll be fiiiine."

"Wait, you got a warning? From what? The System?"

"Ya . . . we can't talk about some stuff while we're . . . nope, can't talk about that, either. Just, knowledge that shouldn't be known here. The System is very picky about that. It's a pity, too, because I miss . . . nope, that would be a warning, too. Okay, my turn to say we change topics!"

So there was something that fey weren't able to talk about? It included wherever they "returned" to, and mentioning that naiads bound to objects was off-limits? Could fey just not talk about themselves or their home? Well, time to test that.

"So . . . fey?"

"Ya! Fey!" She sagged. "Not a lot I can tell you there, though, unless . . . you already know it?"

Well, *that* seemed to both be partial confirmation—

No. Bad Edwin. That doesn't tell you anything new, just agrees with what you already observed. No black swan fallacy here.

—but also a great way to put him on the spot. Darn it, he thought he was done with quizzes! *Okay, think.* Fey in mythology and fantasy, regarding naiads—*But those were Greek!*—shut up, brain, and other stuff. "Are you from some place that's like Joriah, but really extreme and full of wild animals and other fey? That humans can sort of visit, but return changed in some way? Then naiads bind to objects, like rivers or rocks or winds?"

"Nah, weather-bound are called sylphs. You do seem to know about Arcadia, though . . ." Inion seemed to be waiting for something with bated breath, only breathing a sigh of relief after more than a few seconds had passed. "Nice. Anyway, ya! Arcadia is where we're from, and we get to Joriah through . . . ways. Do you know what those ways are?" Edwin shook his head. "Ah, no matter. Anyway, place of a buncha life, we sometimes come here, some bind to trees and bushes and other silly stuff, others pick waters and stones, all that good stuff. Okay, my turn! How'd you get to be an Alchemist? First one of those I've seen."

"Really?"

"Ya. Closest they came that I saw was Herbalist, and even those were low-grade stuff."

"Wait, how do you know what an Alchemist is if you've never seen one before?"

". . . S'a secret," she mumbled.

Edwin raised an eyebrow, but he decided not to pursue the matter. It probably wouldn't affect him. "Well, I guess technology has progressed a lot in two thousand years. I just was . . . offered the Path, evolved my Improvisation into Alchemy."

"Riiiight. Forgot about that. Curious that it'd pick Improvisation, though, and just give basic Alchemy."

"Anyway, Physical Alchemist Path, Alchemy Skill, here I am. Hmm . . . You mentioned Herbalist? I don't suppose I might be able to get some help gathering up some herbs for that sort of thing? That's actually why I came to the Verdant instead of some other secluded place, I wanted to benefit from the magical plants. I don't know what I might be able to provide in return, but there's probably something." A mischievous smile crept across Inion's face, and after a second, Edwin realized what she was thinking. "No. Not that."

The naiad stuck her tongue out at him, then seemed to genuinely consider it for a moment. "Ah, sure. It'll be good to stretch my legs a bit, see what's changed, all that stuff."

"Wait, you don't want anything in exchange?"

She shrugged. "Naaahhh. You mortals can be cute to watch scurry around, trying to figure out new stuff. Tossing your little plants in a cauldron and singing at it to cure a fever. It's *adorable*. So long as I get to watch, it's totally worth it. Deal?"

". . . Why do I feel like this is a bad idea?"

"Because Alchemy is an awful idea to begin with! Do you know what the mortality rate is for Alchemists?"

"I'm going to hazard a guess that it's not as high as for people who readily make innocent-sounding deals with fey."

". . . Touché."

CHAPTER 6

Starting Hand

"So, let me get this straight," Edwin finally settled on, "you're offering to help me with my Alchemy, Skills, and homebuilding to the best of your ability, in exchange for just, quote, 'the opportunity to watch you work and get the chance to chat and stuff,' with the added stipulations that you can't do so just to pester me nor when I'm focusing on my work and need to concentrate and you're not allowed to try and make me sleep deprived? Also, that I can't share what I learn from you with other people without your say-so, in exchange for you keeping my secrets as well."

"Ya!" Inion was way too eager. There had to be something hidden in that, but what? "Also, nice quote! Do you have a memory-aid Skill? Ooh! Is it Keen Mind? Or do you have Intelligence?"

"No to both of those, though, yes, I have Memory. I still just . . . don't see what you get out of this, though!"

Inion shrugged, the perfect picture of innocence. "Why do I need to get anything out of it? Can't I just wanna help you?"

"I don't believe that's what's going on for a second."

"Well, I can't help that now, can I?" She teasingly turned her nose up at Edwin. "How am I ever supposed to get the reputation of being generous if you won't accept my gifts? Is this just because I'm a fey? Are you judging me by my heritage? How *dare* you!" Inion looked away, tipping her head in mock outrage.

Edwin could only sigh and rest his head in his hands in response. This combined so much of what he hated about social interactions into one massive package: obscure rules, incomprehensible goals, and people who were clearly just having fun at his expense. Why did he keep doing this to himself? Still, at least Inion was mostly tolerable to be around. She teased him, sure, but it was clearly all in good fun.

"Okay, fine. I'll agree to your terms." Edwin hastily clarified, "On one more condition!" as Inion started to perk up way too fast and too cheerfully. "Honestly and truthfully explain what magical ties, if any, bargains made with you have. Also just what making bargains with other fey does, if it's different. I need to know what I'm getting myself into."

Inion thought about it for a moment, really exaggerating her contemplation as she contorted herself into all manner of poses atop the water's surface, until she said, "Fine. I'll do it."

Edwin waited. After a few seconds, maybe a minute, of silence had passed, only interspersed with the noise of the waterfall in the background, he asked, "Well?"

"Hey! I never said *when* I was gonna do it!"

Edwin sighed. "Well, I suppose I didn't, either." He started to get up. "If you feel like explaining, let me know. I've got work to do."

"Wait, wait! . . . Fine, I guess I'll tell you now," Inion jokingly moped, before perking up once more with a playful shrug. "So basically, like . . . other things I'm *not telling him about*! Okay, sorry about that. Anyway, we're just able to, like, actually take the stuff offered. The other way around also works, if you're stronger and keep your side of the agreement, you could force us to uphold our side, and just . . . take whatever you're owed. It also means you can take more kinds of stuff than normal. I heard Elatha took a guy's ability to see color once with a Bargain, which you normally couldn't, obviously."

Edwin just mentally shrugged. Who knew what you might be able to take with magic?

Inion carried on, unaware of Edwin's musings. "But, like, since you aren't offering anything to me, not really, the Bargain doesn't do much. Some Bargains are really powerful, though, and some of my kin can get really strong through them, or do things they normally can't to fill their end of the Bargain. Also what we can take and give varies based on a whole mess of things, which I can't really elaborate on. Some of the Highcourt can also do this thing where you enter into a Bargain that tweaks the way things work, and how people need to interact with them, just by interacting with them. It's weird and I don't fully get it, but there!" She crossed her arms. "Your turn!"

Edwin sighed. "Okay." He didn't see any problem with the agreement, which just meant that he wasn't thinking broad enough, he was sure. "I agree to the terms laid out, summarized as such: In exchange for instruction, aid, and assistance, I'll talk to you and let you watch as I'm working. In addition, we also agree to keep what we say to each other in confidence."

"And I accept!" The naiad brightened up instantly.

Edwin kept waiting for metaphorical chains to tighten around him, or the wind to change, or glowing lights to spontaneously manifest, but after a minute with nothing, not even a System notification . . . "That's it?"

"Ya! See? Nothing to worry about. Okay! So, first things first . . ." Inion dove beneath the waves and resurfaced a moment later with a . . . strangely glistening pebble strung on what seemed to be a strand of spun water. "Put this on!"

Edwin accepted the rock, but he didn't move to do anything except look at it. He tried Identifying it but got no return. "What is it?"

"It's a Muse Token! I can make one at a time, it'll help your Skills grow faster!"

Well. If that were the case . . .

He checked it with Mana Sense first, just to be sure. It wasn't magical (somehow), so he shrugged it on, letting the rock slip under his shirt. He . . . didn't feel particularly different, though there was something going on that he couldn't quite put his finger on. "Is this a Skill of yours?" he asked, receiving a nod in response. "Wait, how many Skills do you have?"

Inion hesitated in thought as she counted out on her fingers. "Nine."

Edwin furrowed his eyebrows. "Wait, so few?"

The naiad just smiled. "Ya, you humans get so many Skills as kids, don't you? I just get what I actually need. There's lots of ways to gain power.—I don't need that much past just my"—she flicked her hair back, with the strands slowly drifting through the air as they always were, only slightly spoiling the effect—"natural talents."

"I don't suppose you could tell me what you have?"

She shook her head. "I can't tell you all of it, but I have . . . Tender of the Streams, which was originally Aquatic Presence, Bestow Gift from Fey's Presence—with Muse's Token between them—Nature's Warden from Gardening, Seer of the Natural Realm from Identify, Strands of Fate from Status, Appearance of the Natural One from Misty Illusion, Gaze of the Watchful Fey from Seeing, and Maker of the Creek's Bestowal, which started off all so long ago as Basic Hydromancy."

"And the last two?"

"Can't tell you those." She wiggled her fingers and said, "Those are the rules."

Edwin mentally recalibrated the sorts of things he should be expecting from the seemingly airheaded fey, just giving a distracted "'Kay" in response. Inion talking about her Skills got Edwin thinking about his own, and, well, no time like the present?

Level Up!
Skill Points 478→488
Progress to Tier 2: 700/1590
Identify Level 41→42
Nutrition Level 25→26
Packing Level 27→29
First Aid Level 28→30
Memory Level 31→34
Polyglot Level 36→39
Seeing Level 29→31
Survival Level 28→33

Congratulations! For successfully hunting a deer, you have unlocked the Hunter Path!
Congratulations! For field dressing a fresh kill, you have unlocked the Butcher Path!
Congratulations! For performing a basic sacrificial ritual, you have unlocked the Novice Ritualist Path!

> **Congratulations! For successfully awakening an ancient fey, you have unlocked the Feycaller Path!**
> **Congratulations! For peacefully negotiating with an ancient fey, you have unlocked the Fey Friend Path!**
> **Congratulations! For entering into a Bargain with an ancient fey, you have unlocked the Feybound Path!**
> **Congratulations! For gaining a Token from ancient fey, you have unlocked the Feytouched Path!**

Edwin's Paths were the usual fare of 60-point options. Butcher he wasn't interested in, and Hunter, while only 30 points, was also not something he cared too much about. It might be useful, sure, but he couldn't help but feel he was better off trying to focus on what he was good at rather than trying to do everything. The fey Paths were cool, though. He'd take the Feytouched Path this tier, and save the others for later. He'd need to think a bit more about what he was pushing off, though.

He was offered the usual list of new Skills, as always, and readily dismissed most of them. One in particular caught his eye, though. Harvesting seemed . . . like it might be useful. Not only would it help him out with a profoundly unpleasant task, it might help him when he started going after magical creatures for their magical parts. Ultimately, he still decided against it. He would maybe try to get some sort of general-use construction Skill, maybe Assembly or Creation if those were Skills, to help him if he was going to lean further into the Alchemist/Artificer route like he had been. Maybe in the long term he could use it to make golems or something. Other than that . . . maybe another magical Skill? He'd want anything he got to be really special. He had enough moderately cool Skills, he wanted something that would really stand out! Or a Skill to help his thoughts stay focused, that would work too. Bonus points if it also helped him resist the mental manipulation Skills that seemed to be everywhere.

"Sorry, did you say something?"

"No . . ." Inion cocked her head to the side. "You get distracted a lot just on your own, don't you?"

"Ahhh . . . is it really that obvious?" Edwin admitted, "I just think about a bunch of different things at the same time, and what actually gets my attention flips around a lot. It can be really helpful, but some-times it's just annoying. Why do you ask?"

A smile played across her lips. "I see. Well, hopefully my Token will . . . aid you in that endeavor. So, my musee, what may I aid you with?"

Edwin considered his options. "Well, it's getting a bit on the late side tonight, but I'll be processing logs for my home in the morning. Stripping bark, making them more even. Any chance I could get some help with that?"

"Hmm . . . Bring 'em over here, would you?"

Edwin gave Inion a flat look. Packing and Athletics or no, the logs were still something like five hundred pounds. Eventually, he sighed. "Fine. Just give me a few minutes per."

For whatever reason, unless he actually lifted the logs, Packing didn't kick in, which made it ironically easier to pick up and carry the massive tree trunk sections than it was to try and roll them. He was pretty sure it wasn't an actual limitation of the Skill, though, just that there was some trick to it which Edwin hadn't picked up on yet.

When he first got the Skill, it was as much on a whim as anything. It certainly didn't seem to add too much to his arsenal, just the ability to carry more around with him. Admittedly, given his circumstances, that had been really important at the time, and hadn't entirely stopped being so since, but Edwin felt it had so much room for experimenta-tion. Was it like that with all his Skills, or was Packing unique in that regard? If it were the former, then he needed to do a lot of tests to figure out what else his abilities might be able to pull off. If it were the latter, then it only reinforced his decision to ensure every Skill he took could stand entirely on its own merits, instead of him accepting every last one that was offered to him.

As he dropped the first log, letting it thud into the soft ground and trigger a small collapse of the riverbed, Inion gave him a sidelong glance, to which he just shrugged, panting. "What? It was heavy."

He only got a shake of the fey's head in return before she returned her attention to the log. She tapped it with a finger, and quicker than Edwin could track, the bark fell off into thousands of tiny pieces, where they drifted onto the ground and seemed to melt away. Edwin's slightly tired mind instantly snapped to. "What the heck was that?"

"Mm. Nature's Harvest. It was a couple advancements ago from Nature's Warden. Lets me process plants rapidly, so long as they have water in them." She was trying to act nonchalant, but Edwin could tell she was delighted at his sudden reaction. "So, did you want me to do the rest of them?" she added innocently.

Edwin groaned. Well, guess he wasn't done for the night yet after all.

CHAPTER 7

Faeted Introductions

Level Up!
Athletics Level 50→51
Packing Level 29→33

Obvious or not, Inion's Token was definitely impacting Edwin's leveling-up speed. While he might have normally expected a single Packing level, two at most, from carrying his big stack of logs some twenty feet, four and an Athletics level was way more than he would have expected, especially once he stopped outright carrying the logs and just started dragging them after his pile had unexpectedly collapsed.

Edwin was currently lying next to the creek, panting in exhaustion as Inion sat next to his head, chuckling at his sorry state. Still, he'd let her laugh. It was a small price to pay for what would have otherwise been days of work. All his logs lay in a line, completely debarked and ready for curing. It was a satisfying sight, he had to admit. Tomorrow, he'd make his dehydration concoction, but for right now, he could barely even move as he desperately tried to drink wat— No, his *rehydration* potion. Every muscle was beyond sore, and even Breathing wasn't enough for him to catch his breath quite yet.

Level Up!
Breathing Level 51→52

Edwin couldn't help but wonder what, exactly, it was that triggered levels. Survival's effect seemed almost wholly disconnected from what improved it, namely practicing survival Skills, and Packing seemed to level up from both actually packing up bags as well as carrying around heavy loads. That wasn't even getting started on the weirdness that was Firestarting.

It had started off only making fires slightly easier to start, but these days Edwin could use it to summon tiny candle-size flames when he Infused it, though he admittedly felt decently confident that the blue fire was what oxygen looked like when it burned. It didn't explain the blue sparks he summoned, though.

Everything with the System was so confusing, and in the past, Edwin's brief inquiries about where the System had come from had been met with blank stares. Apparently, it was a question that nobody ever wondered about. The System simply existed. There was no mythology about it. Well, at least not in the Liras Empire, anyway; though they seemed fairly nonreligious outside of a few small temples and shrines, there were no stories about its origin or questions about what its purpose might be.

When Edwin had asked about System moderators, he had been very definitively told there were no such individuals, and where had he heard that absurd rumor? As he hadn't been able to tell Lefi about his personal message from one, he didn't have an answer. Now, though . . .

"So, Inion. What can you tell me about Skills and the System?" he inquired, his breath recovered enough to form intelligible words.

Inion's expression went blank. "Skills are the System's gift unto you, that you might grow in strength and capability." Her line was clearly memorized, like she had been given a careful script to follow. Which, Edwin guessed, she probably had. She claimed that the System was very picky about knowledge that should be known here on Joriah, which implied that she knew more about Skills than that line implied. So what could she tell him? Once he had mentioned a fey world, she had been able to confirm that it was called Arcadia. So if he made a few shots at what he thought the System might be, that might allow her to explain further?

"Well . . . okay then. What about the System itself? When was that made? And by whom?"

"The System is as old as the world itself. Neither has ever known existence other than in unison."

"Did the gods make it?"

"The System is as old as the world itself." Inion winced. "I'm sorry, Edwin. But some things I *really* can't even hint at. Some rules are more set in stone than others."

"That's . . . fine, I suppose," Edwin acquiesced. "But you do know a lot about the System, right?"

"Well, ya! You know, I was considered a great sage back in my day." Inion struck a pose, looking dramatically into the distance. "Supplicants would travel from far and wide to get my advice on what Skills would aid them most in their endeavors. Not that many actually took my advice, however," Inion said, pouting. "They always insisted on taking every Skill they could unlock, completely ignoring the fact that they simply didn't *need* that many. Sigh"—wait, did she just *say* "sigh"?—"so many promising individuals, wrecked by their lack of self-control."

The naiad paused for a moment. "How many Skills *do* you have?"

"Twenty-one. I got a bunch before I knew better."

"Eh, that's not too bad. Depends on what they are, though. Are they just random Skills that don't overlap or ones that are just redundant? You don't need both Block Strike and Shield Block, for example, unless you're fighting *really* strong people."

"I do have a fair number of random Skills," Edwin admitted. "I don't have many actual Alchemy-related Skills; honestly, it's more in the direction of a survivalist skill set, which I suppose makes sense given that's how I *got* most of them."

"Oh? Tell me more. How did that happen? Most humans I talk to get nearly that many just while they're young and their parents' warnings fail to sink in. But you got yours through wilderness survival?"

"I'll . . . explain another time," Edwin sheepishly settled on. "Telling people hasn't worked out for me in the past."

"Oooh. A game." Inion wiggled her eyebrows. "I love a good mystery. Let me guess! Were you . . . abandoned in the woods as a child and raised by wolves?"

" . . . No."

"Okaayyyy, well, what about—" Edwin cut off the woman before she could pull them too far off track or he gave away something by accident.

"Can we stay on topic, please?"

"You're no fun. Don't forget your Bargain!"

"Don't you, either. To the best of your ability, remember? And not distracting me?"

Inion started to say something, but she closed her mouth and started thinking, twisting a lock of hair around her finger. "There's . . . room for interpretation there. *But . . .*" She sighed. "Fine. We'll do it your way *this* time. So what did you want to know exactly?"

Edwin shrugged. "A few things. Some of them I'm curious about what you, who is apparently so wise in the ways of the System, say in comparison to others I've talked to. They all—"

"*Now* who's the one getting off track, huh?" Edwin didn't even need to pick up his head from the ground to look at Inion. He could hear the smile in her voice from where he lay.

When no immediate rebuttal came to mind, he switched tactics. "Yeah, yeah. Laugh it up." With a jokingly exasperated sigh, Edwin shook his head and said, "So, a few questions. Is there any limit to how many Skills you can get?"

"Nope! I wouldn't say you should test that, though. Unless you're a Wizard. But you're no Wizard."

"Maximum Skill level?"

That just got a shrug. "If there is, I don't know it. Might vary based on the Skill and the person if it is a thing, but it's stupidly high."

"Can you get rid of Paths you don't want?"

"How do you . . . How do you not know that one, even by accident?" Inion raised an eyebrow and squinted at Edwin. "How many Paths have you completed?"

" . . . Seven? No, eight. I had one unlock Mana."

"And you're how old?" she asked, incredulously.

"Twenty-two, last I checked."

"What the Blight are you doing with only eight completed Paths?" The naiad sighed, then started looking into the distance, thinking about something. "You know what, on second thought, it's to do with your puzzle, isn't it? Hmm. I'll figure it out, I know it."

"Unwanted Paths?"

"Right, right! Well, so Paths sort of represent the kind of things you could do, right? Well, you just need to take a Path that would exclude the other. You can't be both a Patriot and a Traitor at the same time, nor a Slave and an Escapee. Taking one gets rid of the other, though you could still get it again, same as any of the others. It also doesn't get rid of any Skills that advanced from it, it just matters that you don't have the other Path incomplete in your Status."

"So a Path that you got for taking over a location would be removed if you completed a Path referring to destroying that location?"

"And vice versa, ya. What *have* you been up to, hmm?"

"What about other Skills like Status or Identify, which interact with the System? Are there any more of those?"

"Ehhh . . . .. I've *heard* some stories about Notifications, which tell you if you get poisoned or something like that, but I've never actually met someone with it as a base Skill instead of a Status advancement. There's also rumors about Skills that can mimic Skills, but I've never met anyone with them. Plus a few can help speed leveling"—she pointed at her Token where it dangled from Edwin's neck onto the grass beneath him—"but those are all really hard to get and have a really small effect."

"So what does it take to actually unlock a Skill?"

"Oh! That's an easy one." Inion ticked two fingers in the air and counted them off. "Desire and competency. You need to actually be able to accomplish a given task to unlock a Skill, which is obvious enough, but you also need to actually want to improve on the Skill in question. It doesn't matter how good you might be at poking someone with a stick, if you don't want to be better at it, you'll never get the Stick Poke Skill."

Inion paused. "That's probably why it's so hard to unlock Skills that mimic other Skills or help leveling without advancing them."

"So then why are some Skills hard to unlock if you have something similar? Like Walking and Running?"

"That's a new one, actually. Uhhh . . . if I were to *guess*, it's because it's hard to get into the right mindset to try and get something new rather than practicing something old? Walking affects pretty much all foot-based travel, after all. Lets you walk longer, jog longer, sprint longer, all that. Running just makes you able to run *faster*. Increases your limits."

Edwin nodded. That basically matched up with his experiences so far. He could sprint at full speed for some two minutes straight before he needed to start to rest, and with the way Breathing was increasing, he might be able to sprint continuously before too long. He wasn't much faster, though, beyond what tiny improvements that might come from just constant practice, and maybe Athletics.

"Are there worlds other than Arcadia out there?"

"Yeeeesssss . . ."

"Can you tell me about them?"

"Noooo . . ."

So was Inion bound to just not talk about things not on Joriah, then? Edwin asked as much, not expecting much of a response, or maybe even a "I can't tell you that," so he was pleasantly surprised when she actually replied.

"That's the deal, yes. No extraplanar knowledge from me, sorry. The System doesn't like that sort of knowledge being discussed. I can talk about stuff that's here, though!"

Knowledge beyond Joriah? Hmm . . .

"What's the fundamental nature of magic?"

"Ooh, going straight for the throat, eh? Well, sorry to disappoint, but I don't know." She shrugged, now illuminated by a soft blue-green glow emanating from the pool as the light from the sun faded away. "I know a bit of magic, though most of that is by instinct. I'm no scholar, though even they don't know it all. Some think it's inexplicable."

"But you *do* magic, right? How does that work in a non-System way? Is the System magic?"

"The System is magic in a way. I can't go into detail there, though I know *exactly* how it works"—she shifted slightly as though she were uncomfortable—"but it's magic in the same way that a dragon's flight is magical, or a troll's regeneration, or just the undead in general."

So undead really are a thing here. Interesting.

"It's magic in a way that's just part of what the creature is, and no spell can detect it or remove it. It leaves a distinct mark when used that is visible to those who know how to look, though. For my kind, it comes fairly naturally with mere practice, which is how I know you have Breathing, Seeing, a Mana Sense of some variation, at least two body-influencing Skills, Packing and Polyglot."

"You got all that just from looking at me?"

She shrugged. "Well, our Bargain helps me see you a bit better, and Polyglot is trivial to recognize even without the ability to see System enhancements." So she *did* get something from the Bargain. If he were to guess . . . maybe the ability to walk on land and perhaps a general sense of Edwin's whereabouts? Seemed minor enough that he wasn't sure if he had gotten a genuinely good deal or if he were overlooking something awful.

"So anyway, back to magic." He thought for a moment. "What is it?"

"You already asked that." Inion paused with a chuckle, collecting her thoughts before continuing, "Everyone conceptualizes it slightly differently. I think of it like a flowing river that I can divert into doing something else temporarily; others see it as a long, infinite list of instructions they give to reality, some as a star, others as a sort of framework upon which to build. Some even visualize it like it's music, resonating with the multiverse itself. It's something you'll have to figure out yourself in time."

Hmm. That was worth following up on, but Edwin had one more subject he was curious about, "What about the moderators? Who are they, what do they do?"

Inion's confident expression was shattered in an instant, her casual posture wholly replaced with one of complete shock. Even her hair stuttered to a stop. "Wait, you know about the moderators?"

CHAPTER 8

Unusually Helpful

"How do you know about them?" Inion questioned Edwin. While not overtly threatening, Edwin couldn't help but get the distinct impression that she was accusing him of something. "And why couldn't you have led with that?"

"I don't know!" Edwin raised his hands as something of an instinctual shield against the fey. While there was no real impression of danger coming from the naiad, it was still hard not responding in some way. "It . . . slipped my mind, I guess? No, that's not accurate. I just had other questions first? Also, everyone to whom I've mentioned moderators dismisses it as crazy."

"Well, that's good at least. Means things haven't fallen completely apart," she muttered and raised her voice with a sigh, "Tell me what you know about them, as well as what you *think* you know about them."

Edwin hesitated. How could he not? This was treading dangerously close to talking about his status as an Outsider, and talking about *that* didn't have a great track record of actually going well.

He eventually settled upon how he would phrase his response, doing his best to ignore the impatient foot-tapping of Inion in the meantime. "Some time ago, I was involved in an incident that made a bunch of System errors pop up. It required moderator interference to resolve, and I got two Paths about it. One was the Path Less Traveled, the—"

"Wait, Path Less Traveled?"

"You know of it?" Edwin was surprised. Were error messages that common? No, that couldn't be it, so then . . .

"It has something of a . . . reputation, shall we say. It has a particularly noteworthy Path reward. You should complete it as soon as possible."

"It's ninety points, though."

She nodded. "Well worth it."

Edwin sighed. Well, it's not like he had planned to put it off that long, anyway, though the reason would still be nice to know . . . "Can you elaborate?"

"Not *really*. It does give the sort of reward that most people can only dream of, though, which . . . ya . . . I don't think I can say much more than that. How'd you get so wrapped up in error messages that you needed a *moderator* to get involved, though?" Her eyes probed, glaring and assessing him. "You aren't involved with the elves, are you? No— Even Res— Er, never mind. Even they don't get the Path Less Traveled, thankfully. Blight, that would be a nightmare."

She rubbed her forehead as Edwin thought. Res? Res-something, that was sure. Res . . . pawn? Reset? Respec? What would cause an error, though?

"I don't suppose you're going to elaborate on what 'Res' means?"

"Nope!"

Edwin sighed. Figured. Well, he might figure it out eventually.

"You mentioned two Paths, though! What was the other?"

"Well . . . the other was more like a message of sorts. It was a custom Path called more or less 'Character limit, can't talk much, no clue what happened, did my best to help you li—,' and then it cuts off. I presume it cuts off 'live' but I don't actually know for sure."

"Huh. Ya, I see what you mean. It is strange. How many points is it?"

"A hundred and twenty."

"Whoa. That's so many. Whatever you get with that, it's going to be good."

"I can take notes with it."

Ha! The look on Inion's face was *priceless*. "You can what?"

"Take notes with it! It's really cool."

She sighed. "There has to be more to it. What's it called?"

Okay, that one he had to hesitate for. "Hmm. You know what, if you can figure out what my 'secret' is, I'll tell you." Edwin yawned, suddenly realizing how late it was, and amended his statement, "In the morning." A glance around reminded him how this all got started, and he groaned. "I should deal with my deer, shouldn't I? Ugh, I need more light for that. How do you even take care of that sort of thing?"

"Oh, that's fine. I can take care of it for tonight."

"You can?"

"Ya! Just toss it to me. It's mostly finished draining of blood by now, and I can hold it so it's fresh for the morning. I don't know how to actually do the cutty bits, but it's gotta be easier in the daytime, right?"

Well, Edwin couldn't exactly argue with that, though . . . "So what exactly are you going to do with it? It's going to be safe from scavengers and decay, yeah?"

She nodded. "Ya! Fey Circle! It . . . actually, I can't tell you exactly what it does, but it makes time pass way slower for stuff on the inside than on the out. I use it all the time to save stuff best enjoyed fresh, though . . . Huh, I wonder if I fell asleep in there by accident? Usually I just do it to mess with the mortals who like to think they're so much better than me, and I *never* spend more than a few seconds in there if I can help it. Did I get stuck? Would that have been where the time went? Anyway, ya! It'll be in there like a few seconds tops until you pull it out tomorrow or the day after or whenever. Want me to drop it in there?"

". . . Sure? Is there some downside to this?"

"Eh, not really. It's not something I usually offer, but I said I wanna help you!"

"Still don't trust that I didn't screw myself over by doing that," Edwin muttered, which only served to grow Inion's mischievous grin even more. "Okay, fine. Are you also going to hide in there?"

"Eh . . . probably not. There's a lot of places I want to see what's happened to them in the last few thousand years! I'll probably check those out tonight while you sleep or whatever little mortal thing you do. Just don't forget I still have questions for you!"

Edwin sighed, but accepted it for what it was. At least she wasn't being flirty anymore. He paused, to make sure he hadn't jinxed it, then mentally sighed in relief. So Inion couldn't read his mind, at least. Probably. "Sounds fine to me," he eventually settled on and made his way back to his bed, pausing only to drop some fresh wood on his fire.

***

Level Up!
Sleeping Level 28→29

Huh. Edwin hadn't expected Sleeping to level up for at least three more days, given it was roughly a week or two between levels now. That was a pleasant surprise. He also just felt so well-rested it was *fantastic*. All his muscle soreness was completely gone, his head felt nice and clear, and there was no indication of all the frankly ludicrous amount of work he had done the night before.

Even though he didn't strictly need them to help limber up, he did his morning stretches, pulling himself in and out of the lotus position, fitting his feet behind his head, and generally seeing how much he could contort himself. He likely couldn't have done even half as much without the benefits of his Sleeping, and it still managed to yield results of its own.

Level Up!
Flexibility Level 26→27

Edwin reached for his new pendant and pulled it out, studying the strange object that was apparently the origin of these new levels. It was vaguely aquamarine in color, though mostly transparent, and the interior seemed to ripple; the beams of sunlight he exposed it to cast shifting patterns on the ground, light passing through it as though it were a great deal of water instead of a static rock. It wasn't magic, though. He felt no feedback from his Mana Sense when scrutinizing it, which he wasn't sure how to think about. What were the optics of that sort of thing, if it was entirely mundane?

At the top of the teardrop-shaped stone a thin string passed through either the solid rock or a hole so tiny as to be nearly invisible. While he had first thought the string might be solidified water of some sort, it now reminded Edwin more of some strange combination of silk and grass. Was this seagrass treated to be that high-quality thread he had read about?

He could ask Inion about it later, he supposed. Almanac recognized the material as distinct from both living seagrass and the water-absorbing dried stuff. Not that it came as too much of a surprise, as living and drying had also been considered separate from each other. Why Almanac worked like that for some things but not others—he could use Almanac to tell that his axe handle was made from not-oak, after all—he didn't know, but he intended to find out at some point.

When Edwin finally pulled himself out of his lean-to, he found Inion sitting by his fire, tending to a nice if small little blaze. "So you *can* leave the water, then?"

"Obviously. How else would I be able to watch you work? I'm bound to the river and pond, but that doesn't mean I have to always touch it."

Well, served him right for assuming her limitations, he supposed. Though was that just the result of his Bargain? Though wait. Even if it was, then . . . "Then what did you have me drag all those trees over to your river for, if you could have just walked over to them?"

"Because it was fun to watch!" Edwin glared at the all-too-happy naiad. "Also because you wanted me to help you train your Skills to the best of my ability, which I diiid! You wouldn'ta gotten nearly as many levels if I had just walked, now would you, and I'm supposed to help with that," she added innocently, though she couldn't hide the mischievous glimmer in her eyes.

Edwin sighed. It was hard to say she was wrong; he didn't have anything to *really* complain about—he basically knew this was exactly the sort of shenanigans he signed himself up for when dealing with a fey— but *still* . . . "Fine, fine."

He ignored the girl's beaming face to the best of his ability, though it wasn't easy. She was shifting to always be on the opposite side of the fire as him, so his only respite was staring into the glimmering coals. Furthermore, the smoke from the fire never seemed to blow toward *her*, only toward Edwin.

Reaching out with his Skill, Edwin activated Firestarting and watched as the flames slowly turned from orange-red to the clean, blue flame normally associated with Bunsen burners as the wood burned more and more efficiently and cleanly. It cut back on the smoke blowing into Edwin's face, too, until there was nothing beyond distortions in the air from the rising heat while the timber burned with the same steady flame as a gas stove. It had the added consequence of increasing the temperature of the fire by a fair amount, but scooting back just a little bit fixed that problem.

Inion's slightly pouty face told him everything he needed to about her response to his latest trick, which to Edwin seemed indicative that the smoke was indeed her doing, for whatever end. "So, Firestarting, then?"

Edwin nodded. "It's saved my life a few times now."

"Interesting use of the Skill. Normally people can't hold it for more than a single activation. Are you just constantly activating it, or are you somehow maintaining the activation over a prolonged period of time?"

Edwin stopped. He hadn't really thought about that lately, but Firestarting *was* originally just an active Skill of sorts, wasn't it? Casting his Memory back to the Skill description, he recalled it was just "make fire" and that it supposedly got easier with each level. His experiments combining it with Mana Infusion had gotten him used to sustaining it, but these days he could just keep the Skill going. If he kept it active too long, he felt an odd sort of fatigue, like a phantom limb was being overused, but "too long" was in the minutes these days.

"I . . . I don't know. Huh." A thought occurred to him. "Can Skills grow outside their original use?"

"How do you mean?"

"Well, if I combine one of my Skills—Mana Infusion—with other Skills, will the other Skills gradually become more magical on their own?"

"Kinda? It depends a lot on the Skill in question, and how you use magic with it. Skills can grow a bit, though they're usually fairly fixed in form. If you try to expand a Skill well past what it would normally be able to do, that additional effect usually shows up in its advancement. Well, assuming some level of Path compatibility. It's absolutely possible to sort of combine two Skills by just practicing using them at the same time a *ton*, but the System won't help you much there, though you may unlock a Skill that combines the two in some way. If you don't take that, you just gotta do it the hard way."

"Yeah, I've had that happen—been offered a Skill that was just an application of two of my other Skills—a couple times. What about just using magic all on your own, without evolving, or advancing your Skills or whatever? Like if you just tried to get Fireball without combining Skills and had that as one of your only Skills?"

"An aspiring Wizard, are we? Learn magic the hard way? Sure, you could do it, but good luck without any help from the System. Sure, if you pull it off you're budding, but it's arguable if it'd be any faster or easier than just trying to advance some related Skill into the effect you want. Perhaps stronger in the long, *long* run, but can you really manage to spend several decades as you try to unlock the perfect Skills?"

"Can you predict that sort of thing? I was under the impression it was almost impossible."

"Eh?" Inion did the scales-weighing thing again. "Sure, if you want something really specific, good luck predicting that. But generally? It's pretty simple. Just take Paths that correspond with what you want your Class to be like, take Skills that are basically what you want to be able to do, and it'll turn out just fine. The System is good with that sort of thing. After all, it's . . . no, I can't say that, can I?"

"What about predicting what Skill will be evolved by a given Path? So you could complete Paths without risking that it evolves a Skill you still want to level up, but without rejecting the evolution?"

"You could *probably* predict that, but it would be really complicated or it'd involve following someone else's Class exactly. That has problems, obviously, but if you managed it, then yeah, you could just complete the Paths as your Skills got to a high enough level. It'd be great in theory, but who'd be crazy enough to try it?"

Edwin shrugged. "The Empire apparently. Also maybe the High-peak dwarves?"

"Really? How's that work?"

"So far as I've heard, they just record a lot of people's Skills and Paths and see what evolves each time, then they can try to figure out the best set of Skills for a given type of person, whether it's crafting, fighting, or being a merchant."

"Huh, good for them. Seems like it'd be effective. Oh yeah! You still need to answer a question for me."

Edwin raised an eyebrow. What was she talking about?

"We got sidetracked. What do you think the moderators are?"

"Uh, I guess they'd be individuals tasked with ensuring the System runs smoothly? Not quite administrators, so they don't control it, but they presumably have some deeper level of System access and deal with problems that show up. Maybe most things are automatic, and they just deal with more complicated situations?"

Inion seemed more or less satisfied with that answer, nodding to herself. Then, she glanced at the sky, looked around at the clearing and stood up, circling the fire faster than Edwin could escape, kicking his hip lightly. "Anyway! That's enough talking for now. Time for you to get to work. I wanna see you make stuff."

CHAPTER 9

No Place I'd Lather Be

Inion kept to her side of the Bargain quite nicely and didn't bother Edwin as he started following the instructions in the *Grimoire*. It was a nice surprise, that there were no crazy twists that meant he'd screwed himself over . . . well, not yet anyway. But that meant he was able to work without distractions, so it was a win.

First, he needed ash from the tree in question. That was easy enough, he had loads of extra logs that weren't the right size for his cabin that he could burn. They were smaller, too, which meant they were much easier to carry around.

Inion only took a bit of convincing to use her Skill to process these as well, which meant Edwin didn't have to spend the time needed to peel the bark off. He didn't know if leaving the bark on would interfere with the process, but he didn't know that it *wouldn't*, either, and he had enough variables to account for in this formula without adding an additional one. Maybe he'd be able to try it in the future, once he had enough ingredients, though not today.

In any case, Edwin's first attempt at getting ashes failed in a really stupid mistake. He hadn't failed to account for holding the ashes—no, he'd made sure to build the fire inside the metal bowl he was still dragging around from the dwarves—instead, he'd flexed his Firestarting to make the wood burn fast and hot. It worked, even getting a Firestarting level out of it, but it had the unfortunate side effect of burning *so* fast and hot that it didn't leave any ashes.

That had set Inion off laughing for a good ten minutes—what was just *so* funny about that?—and by the time she had recovered, Edwin had his next attempt already well underway. This time, he just let the whole thing slowly burn while he prepared the next ingredient.

Curiously, despite its inclusion in the "preservation of flesh" variant of the recipe, Edwin, fortunately, did not need drying seagrass. After all, he didn't have any left at this point, what with his use of the stuff back when fighting Niall and his minions. Instead, he needed oil. What kind of oil wasn't specified, but given Edwin only had something that looked and smelled vaguely like olive oil, he didn't have very many options and just had to hope it would work.

Stupid vague instructions, not telling anything useful.

According to the book, once he had the ash, he needed to mix it with water to form a paste, then add oil, stirring until the mixture achieved a frothy texture . . .

Hang on, isn't this just how you make soap?

It used oil instead of tallow and didn't involve concentration of lye, but ashes and oil were *the* main ingredients used for soap creation. Was that principle involved somehow? Curious, Edwin reassessed the pages outlining the process.

The mixture was combined with some ground dried firevine leaves, which was a kind of ivy whose leaves looked like tongues of fire. Edwin had a decent supply of them, but he had no clue what they might provide to the creation.

They *were* ever so faintly magical, though. If he focused really hard, he could tell that much. It was also one of the primary constants in all variations of the formula, so whatever it provided, it was clearly important. Maybe it had some kind of fire mana imbued in it that helped burn off the water or canceled out the moisture in some way? The *Grimoire* claimed that it would "leech and burn the lifeblood from the tree, in death as it did in life." He'd . . . need to test it out.

The formula then wanted salt to "replace the removed hydration," which Edwin supposed he *did* have, though he'd forgotten about it when making food—not that he had enough to really use it on his meals. He could deal with the lessened flavor, it had better uses—Now, he was going to use it to make salted logs. Did it even do anything?

Something that Edwin felt even more strongly was probably a vestigial ingredient in the process was fine sand, taken from a riverbed and dried over a fire. It was supposed to be able to flow "as smoothly as water" from his hand. If it were pure white, that was a bonus but not required, as it would be "adequate though left uncleansed of the aquatic essence." Then again, he was dealing with magic, so how could he really know?

Next up was sunstalk, a "common yet endlessly useful grass whose growth traps the essence of the sun." The bundle that Niall had labeled as such just looked like straw to Edwin, though like the firevine, he did feel like it might have the faintest tickle of magic to it; it was so faint, however, it may well have been his imagination at that point.

"To ensure no life is brought forth," he also needed dust. Honestly, Edwin wasn't sure how that was meant to be something to avoid, let alone how the heck that was even supposed to work, let alone how the dust was meant to prevent that. It did mention sawdust was acceptable, but it needed to be fine enough "as to be carried upon the gentlest breezes." Given all the logging he'd been doing, it was easy enough to come by.

Finally, chopped and crushed fresh stalks of rhoreed, "which forms the barrier between the river and the land, separating that which is dry and that which is wet," which so far as Edwin could tell wasn't *exactly* papyrus, but was pretty close. The fact Polyglot didn't translate it as papyrus seemed to indicate that it wasn't exactly the same, but at this point he wasn't sure if any plants or animals were a complete and total match for their Earth equivalents, just pretty close.

Once everything was mixed together, he was to stir it over a fire until it reached a consistency like dried tree sap, which Edwin was skeptical would ever happen considering how many random things were involved in the process. Then, he was to apply it to the logs in question, allow it to sit for a day in the sun, then set it all on fire. Supposedly, the fire wouldn't damage the logs and would just burn off all the moisture inside of them.

Once again, Edwin was skeptical how that was supposed to work, especially with the seemingly minuscule amounts of concoction in comparison to the amount of wood it would supposedly work with, but who was he to argue with the *Grimoire*? That's why he was testing it, anyway.

In any case, rhoreed was perhaps the hardest ingredient for Edwin to properly get ahold of, and while he at first thought he might have to substitute additional dried sunstalk straw, which was apparently a sub-optimal though functional replacement, he thought to ask Inion first.

"Oh, ya! I can totally get you some of that. There's a little bit right before the edge on this one nice little side creek that I found last night that's open enough for the stuff. There's loads there, I can grab you a few armfuls if ya want me to?"

"Uh, sure? Just as much as you can get? I think I can use it for a bunch of stuff, even beyond this."

"Gotcha! I'll be back in a bit!"

Neat. Well, while Inion was taking care of that, Edwin worked to make his totally-not-soap. How might that even work? Thinking about it from a semimagical perspective combined with chemistry . . .

Soap worked because it had a long nonpolar tail and a polar head, which meant it was both hydrophilic and hydrophobic. The nonpolar portions of the molecule were attracted to oils and dirt and anything water couldn't mix with, which enveloped the substance in a bubble of sorts. The outside of the bubble was thus polar and therefore hydrophilic, which meant that it got washed away with water.

Clearly, this couldn't work quite like that. Burning soap (which was more or less not flammable, though at this point Edwin could probably get it to catch on fire with Firestarting) wouldn't carry away whatever it was bound to, it would just leave it all where it once was. Also, the long nonpolar tails would be a hindrance in the process, as there would be way more random debris that bound to the molecule per water molecule that would be able to interact with the polar head.

Edwin's current hypothesis was that some component in the rest of the mixture—he suspected the firevine, though the sunstalk was also a possibility as one of only two seemingly magical ingredients—altered the nonpolar side into something more flammable, possibly only after binding to several water molecules, and could burn it all off without affecting the wood too much.

How all *that* would work, he had no clue, but at the very least he had a working hypothesis. He didn't have the materials needed for a full, rigorous test of everything, but fortunately, he didn't need to. If he truly was making "soap, but backwards" then he could lean into that side of things slightly more than he might otherwise.

By then, Inion had returned with armloads of the rhoreed and Edwin's ashes were finished cooking into a bit of a paste. The oil was easy enough to mix in, though given the tiny quantities he was working with, mixing anything in would be relatively easy.

The firevine addition went essentially as it was supposed to, though nothing in the *Grimoire* made any comments about how the new mixture was supposed to give off heat. His pinch of salt made no discernible impact, though he did his best to scale all proportions correctly. If anything, he might have added a bit too much, though he had his doubts that it would actually have any impact.

Sand may have been in the same category of "does this even do anything," but that didn't stop him from still trying to do everything correctly. This was his more or less control batch, after all. No sense in messing it up just because Edwin wanted to be stingy with the ingredients he had plenty of, after all.

The sunstalk blades were broken and ground as appropriate and tossed in. As Edwin continued, he got the distinct impression that doing so seemed to give the sand already in the mixture a bit of a glimmer. Wait, did the sand actually do something to aid the overall formula? That would be a surprise. There were still some hints of magic throughout the formula, though his sense wasn't even close to being precise enough for Edwin to figure out what parts actually had some magic lurking within it.

In comparison, adding sawdust went exactly as Edwin had anticipated. The thick mixture (he added a bit more water to maintain the pastelike consistency described in the book) took in the small amount of sawdust and began to dry out. To counter that, Edwin added the crushed rhoreed, where the juice from the plant stalks hydrated his creation just enough to make it stirrable.

Perhaps unsurprisingly, his first batch did not turn out well in the slightest. While he only made about a cup, maybe two, of the mixture, nothing happened as it was supposed to once he had everything added together. It never reached any sort of partially liquidlike consistency, just drying out and cracking along the inside of the bowl he was using.

Edwin sighed. Ah, well, that's why he didn't try to do everything at once. It wasn't a complete waste, at least.

Level Up!
Alchemy Level 52→53
Mana Sense Level 32→33

He must have been doing *something* right, even if it wasn't what he wanted.

The second mixture turned out . . . better. He was a bit more generous with adding water this time around, and that resulted in a superior consistency for his final mixture. It was even vaguely syrupy!

Unlike his first attempt, which was an obvious failure, Edwin actually had to test this batch, which meant pulling out a spare log, too small for his log cabin uses but still large enough to work as firewood. Inion wasn't being petty and helped him prepare it for application.

After spreading the unusually liquidlike paste down the length of the entire log and setting it up in the most direct sunlight he could manage, Edwin had nothing to do but wait.

CHAPTER 10

Contractual Obligations

As it turned out, waiting around for something comparable to paint drying wasn't the most exciting thing in the world. As a result, most of Edwin's time was spent talking to Inion. Even when he was working on marginally productive things, they still kept up a faint string of chitchat.

Edwin couldn't entirely follow a lot of the stories she told about her time prenap, and it was of debatable practicality given she only had experience with a civilization some two thousand years gone. It was still quite interesting, though. Especially learning about magic. Magic was *so cool,* even though Inion kept teasing him with no actual details about how it all worked, simply regaling him with tales about noteworthy mages she'd heard of or met during her long, *long* life. Shapechangers, someone who could make mist into solid weapons, a star mage who cast constellations . . .

"Inion." Edwin interrupted the naiad as she made an offhand reference to her current story—about an unstoppable warrior whose blood ran so hot merely her gaze was enough to melt stone—to the dawn of time. "How old is Joriah?"

"Oh, ages and ages old. It's the oldest thing in the world!" she replied, a cocky grin on her face.

"How old are *you?*"

"Don't you know it's rude to ask a lady her age? What if I'm actually old?"

"You're two millennia old at a *minimum*. Once we get into a four- or five-digit age, is it really important?"

"Obviously."

He sighed. "Fine. I'll just assume you're as old as Joriah, so say some six billion years old . . ."

Inion clapped her hands together. "Outsider!"

"What?" Edwin was taken aback. "Ho— Uh . . . what are you talking about? What's an Outsider?"

A triumphant grin spread across her face. "I knew it. So where are you from? The Prime? Kitan? The Void? Wait, no. Six billion. That's *gotta* be a part of the Primes, right? No, that wouldn't fit either. The Void, then? Not even the Prime, unless I missed something and they've been really busy since I last checked . . ."

Edwin stared at her blankly. "I think I follow even less now than I did before. What are the Primes? What's Kitan?"

Inion's face briefly flashed with a moment of panic, but relaxed after a moment of her eyes darting every way, searching and not finding *something*. "No warning . . . huh. So I'm definitely right in some regard. But you're not lying, either. So where *are* you from, then?"

Edwin set aside the rhoreed he was trying to weave into a mat. "I told you. I'm from . . ." He searched his memory for a moment before recalling his cover story. "I'm from Fierisal."

She snorted. "Ha. No you're not."

"And what makes you so confident you know more about my history than I do?"

"Well, for one, you're an awful liar. Particularly by fey standards, but also just anyone with any sort of truth-detecting Skill would see right through you. Two, you're not from Fierisal. You're too *human* for that."

"Wait, then what lives on Fierisal?" Edwin wondered aloud, "I thought nobody knew what was there. How do *you* know what's there?"

"See? That right there. I'm an immortal nature spirit quite literally from beyond the veil. I know a lotta stuff, and what's on the far side of Joriah is one of those things."

"Your information is also *centuries* out of date, isn't it? But fine. Let's say that's the case, what's this Outsider thing that you think I am?"

"See, unless Vis'Daric managed to blow itself up, the Split Peak was fixed, *and* someone cleanly removed the pioneer of Alchemy from history—which I suppose isn't impossible, but is pretty unlikely—*anyone* should know what an Outsider is."

"Well, I don't. I thought the creator of Alchemy was a goddess? Salverria or something?"

"She's said to be a goddess these days? Huh. Moving up in the world a bit, I see. Nah, she was like you, though a lot better at actual Alchemy."

"Hey!"

"Eh, it's true. You know some stuff, and while I'm no expert, you seem to be doing some fairly impressive Alchemy work without much experience. But you just don't know enough basic, basic knowledge about the System—"

"I was confirming what I was told!"

"Half of which you'd know from experience if you hadn't been here for probably a year at most, not to mention only eight Paths completed? Then your moderator interactions, all topped off with throwing out an age for Joriah in the billions? Yeah, you're not from here. So, I ask again, where?"

Edwin opened then closed his mouth. What was he supposed to say? He didn't feel any supernatural obligation to tell the truth to Inion—their Bargain was that he'd talk to her and keep her secrets, not that he couldn't lie or keep some secrets of his own—but then again, he should be able to trust her.

Isn't that what you thought about Rashin?

Wellllll . . . that didn't count. So far as he knew, Tara was keeping his secrets, and Inion had already sworn herself to secrecy. Besides, she'd already figured it out and was operating under the assumption he *was* an Outsider. Him telling her new facts about that wouldn't change what she may or may not tell other people or do herself. Also . . . he'd be lying to himself if he said he wanted to keep his history a secret, and not even the part of him complaining about her being a fey could fully snuff out the desire to just be *honest* with someone.

". . . Fine. So you got me. I'm from a world called Earth."

"Earth?" Inion furrowed her brow, clearly trying to remember something. "I . . . can't say I've ever heard of it. What was it like?"

"Well, I suppose the obvious distinction was that we didn't have magic." Edwin chuckled to himself. "Actually, I suppose that's up for debate. We sort of did have magic, we just explored it and understood it so much we called it science, and electricity. By that logic, that made me something of a *wizard*, learning to harness the power of the universe."

He fell silent, letting the natural sounds of the clearing fill the void as he thought for the first time in a while about his home.

"There were only humans, back there. The next smartest thing we had were ravens, octopi, and monkeys, and there was nothing stronger than an everyday human with a weapon." A rueful smile found its way to Edwin. "Well, at least once you got a big enough weapon. But there was no System, no individual people having the ability to play by different rules of creation than everyone else. Coming here . . . it's eye-opening, and there are just so many countless things that I want to try, to experiment with, to dissect with math and figure out how it all fits together and *works*. I'm a physicist, darn it! The rules of the universe are . . . mine to behold." What began as a triumphant declaration of fact fell into a quiet, contemplative voice as Edwin's conviction trailed off alongside his volume.

Edwin lapsed into silence once more, and Inion moved to place a hand on his shoulder. Unlike what he expected, it felt . . . human. Still, he shrugged it off. He wasn't inclined toward human contact at the moment, to say nothing of the dangers that came with fey. Eventually, he spoke up once more.

"When I was growing up, all I ever wanted to know was the answer to a simple question: Why? Why is the sky blue? Why do things fall when you let go of them? Why is water clear, but rocks aren't? Why does the sun rise and set? Then I started to learn the answers to those questions, but like any good question should, each only offered up more questions in response, and I started looking around and trying to figure out how things worked, what made everything the way it was.

"I lived in the middle of nowhere, no real companions my own age . . . just books. Lots and lots of books. So I took my questions there. I learned loads, and everyone agreed. Took my first chemistry class when

I was eleven, physics when I was twelve, biology when I was thirteen. Everyone kept telling me I was so smart, that I'd be the one to figure out the secrets to life, the universe, and everything.

"Then, I got to college—ah, a higher learning school of sorts—where you could choose what you wanted to become really good at, where you learned the specialized skills to fill a role in society. Well, I liked material sciences, I was good at math, and I liked physics, so my choice was pretty clear. I thought it would be supereasy, and, well . . . it was. I had no real issues with the classes, got good enough grades. I just . . ."

He sighed. "I'm sorry. This is bound to be superboring for you. You didn't want to hear my life story, and I'm sure half of what I'm saying is just nonsense to you anyway."

Inion cocked her head, hair dragged along to match. "No . . . No. Don't worry about that. I'm learning more than you might think about your Earth. Your Polyglot skill is helping, and I think the System itself might be listening."

Well, *that* was intimidating, but also possibly useful. Still, it wasn't like either of them cared about his struggles, more about the sorts of things going on that were different on Earth.

"Ah, well, it doesn't matter that much. Long story short, I never really quite fell into the brilliant role that everyone seemed to expect me to, even with spending almost all my time studying and doing homework. I just kept learning more and more. What else was there to do? Then, one day, I woke up here, surrounded by all kinds of impossible things, and I've been trying to figure out what's been going on ever since.

"I've seen some really crazy things, too. Things that defy all possibility and are both great and terrible. There's wonder in Joriah, and I want to break open the heavens themselves, wrench the stars from the sky and turn them into forges, but I don't know where to even start. I should be dead a dozen times over. And that's why I came out here. I need to be stronger, to know more, to be able to *do* more. If I had a gun, Niall and his minions wouldn't have stood a chance. Heck, if I'd had *gunpowder*, they wouldn't have stood a chance. If I'd . . ." Edwin sighed.

"I just . . . don't know what I'm supposed to do." He chuckled. "We had stories like this back home, someone being thrown into a world they didn't recognize and having to make do with what they had. I always thought I'd be the absolute best at everything, that I'd be able to be the awesome, cool person who could solve every problem, that I could revolutionize the entire world, with just my knowledge.

"Well . . . turns out it's a lot harder than it looks. If I had my lab, things might be slightly different. But here? Where I have to make everything from scratch? I know the precise ratio for thermite but I have no way of *making* the stuff. Aluminum is bound to be insanely rare if it's even a known quantity, and I'd be lucky to find someone who even knows what magnesium *is*, though I probably wouldn't even need it given how good my Firestarting is these days."

Edwin buried his face in his hands, laughing ruefully. "Gah, what does it say about me, that it took me almost a *month* to reinvent cement, but I have the exact formula for thermite memorized?"

Carefully extracting his face, Edwin flopped onto his back, looking up into the cloudless sky. "I'm sorry."

Inion finally broke her silence. "What for?"

"Just . . ." Edwin waved his arm, a hopeless gesture trying to communicate far too much with far too little. "All of this. I know that I'm the least interesting part about me, that I'm obnoxious and annoying and completely unlikable. I bet you're already regretting that contract which said I had to provide conversation, aren't you? I know I would be. . . ."

"No, no. You're the most interesting person I've talked to in *centuries*, Edwin. Lighten up a bit."

"Well, apparently I'm better off being silent than speaking about myself."

"Wait, no, that's not what I'm saying."

Edwin chuckled, having heard that line so many times before. "There's no need to spare my feelings, though I know you will anyway." His gaze peered forward, picking out the incredible detail of all his surroundings, almost cursing his inability to look into nothing these days. Seeing meant that he'd always see something, and be able to interpret it. He almost cursed his inability to keep his mouth shut, frustrated with his own sensitivity as anything.

Then Edwin caught his emotions running rampant. *Go, shoo. Back in your box.*

He diligently corralled his emotions one by one, returning them to their pens. Sadness was the first to go, the easiest to deal with considering he already fought against it whenever he thought about Earth and all the people he left behind. That was followed with remorse, with jealousy, anger, and sadness once more. Those weren't valuable. Happiness could try to stay out, but it always seemed to get lonely, with all its friends locked away.

It would always try to spend time with its *friends*, Edwin liked to think.

That's why it so rarely came out to visit, he felt.

Oh so very rarely.

CHAPTER 11

The Scientific Method

Edwin wasn't really sure how long he sat in silence, staring at the flames as his campfire slowly died down. Inion had tried to say something at one point, trying to get him to continue talking about Earth by trying to persuade him that she really *did* care about his story, and that she did care about him. She seemed almost genuine, too.

Edwin didn't buy it, though. He'd been in this position before. Even if she did legitimately feel bad for him, it wouldn't last. Give it a day, maybe two, and she'd return to however she felt beforehand. She wouldn't ignore him, at least, though in some ways that might be worse.

His emotions began to try and claw their way out of their boxes, wanting him to pay attention to them. But no. He couldn't do that, not yet. If Edwin gave his emotions even an inch, he'd regret it. He'd do something that seemed like a great idea at the time, but just didn't make sense, or made him vulnerable, or something. No, if he was going to open up fully with his emotions, he wanted to find someone who actually cared about him and somewhere to call home first. He was in a completely new world, after all! There was bound to be somewhere just right for him where he could settle down. Heck, that was even partially the point of his cabin-in-progress! If it turned out well, maybe this could be his home. Even if this wasn't it, the world was really big. He could find somewhere to settle down.

The fire swirled into eddies, twisting and dancing as he poked at the burning logs with a spare stick. Edwin tossed the branch into the flames, twisting Firestarting such that it was firmly on fire before it even landed. Well, there was nothing to be gained sitting around feeling sorry for himself. Before he did anything else, though, he stood up, brushing off the dust from sitting, and stretched his cramped legs as he got a few more logs for the fire.

He'd found that Firestarting meant he didn't strictly *need* dried wood, but unless he wanted to keep the Skill constantly active, green wood made a lot more smoke than deadwood. Granted, it would probably help his Skill level if he did so—he dismissed the level 45 notification as it popped up—but the strange fatigue associated with doing so made it firmly not worth it for the time being.

As a result, he only kept Firestarting going long enough for his fresh logs to catch firmly ablaze before releasing it. He then retreated a few feet to escape the smoke, dropping onto the dry ground.

The half-finished rhoreed mat lay next to him, discarded some time before, and Edwin retrieved it, silently picking up where he left off. A few minutes later, Inion returned from wherever she had meandered to, taking up a seat to his left.

"So . . . do you wanna talk about it?"

Over, under. Over, under. Over, under. Okay, that row was done. Grab a new reed, start threading that in . . .

"Look, I'm no expert, but I'm pretty sure you wanna try to deal with that somehow. It's not good for you, keepin' it all locked up like that, y'know?"

Finish the row, then press the stalks together for a tighter weave . . . what Edwin wouldn't give for internet access. He had a vague recollection of Egyptians making boats out of papyrus. How did they get it waterproof? Did they wait until the stalks were dry first, or did they weave it while wet? Rhoreed seemed oddly flexible for something that Edwin's intuition indicated should be stiff, but that was grass for you.

"Come *on*, Edwin. Talk to me. You're obligated to."

" . . . Not when I'm working."

"Not when doing so would *distract* you from working. If you're even half as smart as you like to think you are, you can weave and talk at the same time. You humans have been doing it for *centuries*."

"Guess I'm not that smart, then." Edwin intended his mumble to be almost inaudible, but Inion clearly had better ears than most humans. That, or he was just bad at determining how loud was *too* loud. Probably that one, honestly. He always brought up topics and dialogues that people just did *not* want to hear.

"Come on, now. Don't be like that. You have four mental skills, that's *way* more than most humans ever get." She nudged Edwin for a few minutes until it became more obvious that he wasn't about to budge from his duties. "If you don't wanna talk about yourself, you can talk more about Earth or whatever."

That declaration hardly surprised Edwin. Of course they weren't going to be interested in him, just care about the information he could provide. Not to mention that the only thing of value he could provide was because of the *System*, not anything inherent to him. Just that he had four mental Skills. Well, he'd anticipated as much. Still, he supposed he could oblige, and this time, Edwin made sure to keep his story centered more around what Inion actually cared about.

"So then . . . you were an ongoing student of . . ."

"Physics."

"Right. And that was basically just math. If you wanted to focus more on things, you'd go with . . . chemistry, and biology is life. 'Making things' was engineering."

"Yep. Physics is about taking the most fundamental aspects of reality and turning them into math. Somewhere in my mind is the speed of light, and how objects are put together on the most fundamental levels."

"It's so . . ." Inion eventually settled on "strange . . . that your kind was able to measure something like how fast light itself moves, but without magic to help support you. How big of a population can you really support?"

That earned a few chuckles from Edwin and led that conversation down the path of the scale of Earth, and how a few thousand just wasn't a big town for him, that selecting from hundreds of thousands to millions of individuals was needed to find someone suitable for the most advanced of physics, which even Edwin couldn't manage. Though with his new Skills, he could probably manage it just fine these days.

Over the course of their conversations, Edwin made good progress on his rhoreed mats, finishing off his first one, followed by his second. While the mat was far from luxurious, Edwin welcomed any and all additional layers of comfort between him and the dirt floor of the forest. Still, with nothing else to really do as the sun set and the darkness began creeping in, he bade Inion good night.

The next day proved to be quite eventful. Edwin's batch of wood-drying potion had finished treating his test lumber, and the briefest taps with Firestarting had it burning merrily. Once those flames died down, even a bit of testing showed that the wood had indeed been dehydrated, and the lumber served as excellent fuel for his fire, burning almost as well as the deadwood he'd been utilizing so much of.

The sudden success threw Edwin off-balance. He'd made it work on his second attempt? That wasn't how this was supposed to go, but hey. That just meant he could use his last batch as a bit of an experiment. Time to see if he could improve on the basic concept!

Since his working theory for the mixture was that he was making something of a reverse-soap, Edwin decided to start off by more or less making standard soap, purifying his lye as much as possible, and going from there. His memories, reinforced by Alchemy, involved creating lye by boiling ashes and skimming the solution off the top into a second bowl. Once he'd filled the second bowl, a process which took *hours*, he boiled all *that*, letting the water evaporate until he had nothing but some off-white powder at the bottom of his bowl.

This, if his memories served him properly, was sodium hydroxide. Perhaps not terribly *pure* NaOH, given the slightly yellowish color present, but NaOH nonetheless. He dried off the powder with a bit more heat and ran it through a small sifter, trying to remove any contaminants. With that completed, he placed the final powder in a ceramic beaker off to the side to make room for everything else.

Satisfied with his results, Edwin distilled some water from Inion's pool, collecting the purified springwater in another bowl. From there, it was a simple matter to produce mostly pure lye, slowly mixing his NaOH into a small measure of water, stirring throughout until the powder had completely dissolved. By the time he was finished, the container was actually quite warm, the dissolution having generated a sizable amount of heat.

"So what was the point of all that?" Inion seemed genuinely curious rather than just making conversation, so Edwin didn't ignore her this time. "Was that salt?"

"No, it wasn't salt, though I get the confusion. It's sodium hydroxide, which is *a* salt, but not the kind you're thinking of. Highly corrosive and quite dangerous. Honestly, I should weaponize it . . .

"Anyway, a salt is just a chemical term for something consisting of a cation and anion in a crystalline ionic structure." Inion looked even more confused than when he had started, which . . . fair. "So remember what I said about atoms and molecules? The smallest you can divide a 'thing' until further divisions just result in something different?" She nodded, so Edwin carried on. "There's different ways that they can combine. You guys have lodestones, right? Metallic rocks that can stick to each other or other metals? Good. Basically, cations and anions work like that, just on a really tiny scale. They stick together and make tiny crystals, and that's what a salt is.

"What I made is similar to what you're used to calling salt, but when it's dissolved in water, it makes the water basic. That's . . . the opposite of acidic. This"—he pointed at the beaker where it sat, slowly cooling off—"is as pure as I can make lye, which I suppose finally answers your other question. I went through all that because I have a theory about how the drying-out potion works and need to test it.

"To do that, I need to eliminate as many variables as I possibly can, so I took lye, which I *think* is the active ingredient of the ashes, and purified it as much as possible. That included getting rid of any contaminants in the water—" Edwin stopped as Inion made a vaguely offended choking noise. Then he continued, "I'm not saying your water is dirty, but there's all sorts of things in any water that, well, aren't water. Minerals and the like, which help with flavor, to say nothing of tiny creatures, dust, and more. Distilling the water just means I can be more confident that any water I use, regardless of source, should be essentially the same as any other water. There's a whole bunch of ways to do that, and they should be used together, but I work with what I have, which . . . isn't much, at the moment.

"Now, I *really* wish I could make DI water—ah, deionized water, that is. Like what I was saying about cations and anions, but different—especially given I'm messing around with acids and bases, but I'll take what I can get. There's probably some alchemical methodology I could use to magically purify it, but the *Grimoire* doesn't care about that sort of thing." He muttered, somewhat bitterly, "No, much too practical." What he wouldn't give to get his hands on the notes of Salverria or whoever had supposedly pioneered Alchemy. If she was an Outsider, she might actually have respect for the basics.

"Sorry, I'm getting sidetracked. Anyway, now that I have my lye purified enough, I can use that as my variable for this trial. I'd *like* to try and implement all my desired changes at once, but when it inevitably fails I'll have almost no information about what actually caused the problem. This way, I can just establish my baseline, get a nice, consistent base for future experiments, and hopefully get some high-quality antimoisture potion all at the same time!"

"Seems kinda slow and boring if you ask me."

Edwin shrugged. "Well, that's science. Heck, that's *life*. Hurry up and wait, do lots of boring work for a few moments of success. No job is entirely exciting all the time."

"Well, for you humans anyway! My life is thrilling!"

"Didn't you just sleep for two thousand years?"

"Other than that."

Edwin shook his head and chuckled as he checked the temperature of his lye, lightly tapping the beaker with a bare knuckle before putting his glove back on and picking it up, angling the container to let light shine into it and double-check that there wasn't any undissolved powder still drifting around. There was, so he added a drop of water more, but when it didn't dissolve, he figured it was probably a trace contaminant, dust or something. Ah well.

The rest of the procedure wasn't exciting, just following the steps one at a time until he had his final result. It looked somewhat different, for sure, as it wasn't quite as gray as before thanks to the missing ash, instead primarily green from the added rhoreed, but otherwise had the right consistency and looked like it should work fine.

He applied it to another test log, gave himself a few stretches, and pulled up his notifications. Edwin was expecting a handful, for sure, but was still completely blindsided by just how many he suddenly found himself faced with.

CHAPTER 12

Reconvene and Reassess

Congratulations! For applying knowledge of the physical makeup of the world to an alchemical formula, you have unlocked the Physical Alchemist Path!

Congratulations! For successfully making an alchemical formula with no assistance and minimal gear, you have unlocked the Makeshift Alchemist Path!

Congratulations! For creating a concoction and demonstrating advanced chemical knowledge, you have unlocked the Practical Alchemist Path!

Congratulations! For displaying advanced knowledge regarding physical matter, you have unlocked the Chemist Path!

Congratulations! For displaying advanced knowledge regarding living matter, you have unlocked the Biologist Path!

Congratulations! For displaying advanced knowledge regarding physical laws, you have unlocked the Physicist Path!

Congratulations! For attempting a well-considered variation upon a standardized concoction, you have unlocked the Experimenter Path!

Congratulations! For demonstrating advanced knowledge regarding experimental methodology and physical laws, you have unlocked the Scientific Revolutionary Path!

Congratulations! For experimenting with alchemical formulas utilizing unique insights into creations, you have unlocked the Forerunner Path!
Congratulations! For successfully refining lye, you have unlocked the Purifier Path!
You have unlocked the Purify Skill!
Accept Skill? Y/N
You have unlocked the Lecture Skill!
Accept Skill? Y/N

Level Up!
Skill Points 518→539
Progress to Tier 2: 735/1590
Alchemy Level 53→60
Basic Mana Sense Level 33→36
Firestarting Level 45→46
Identify Level 42→43
Nutrition Level 26→27
Outsider's Almanac Level 80→82
Polyglot Level 30→36
Survival Level 33→34

Almost halfway to Tier 2! Sweet. Edwin was probably due to reassess exactly how close he was at some point, though. He'd gotten a lot of Paths since he had divided everything up, and he sadly couldn't take everything first. At his current rate, though, he should probably wait until he was closer to the time in question.

Purify was . . . tempting. That was exactly the sort of Skill that he'd find useful in Alchemy. But was it really exciting enough for one of his final few Skills? Ehhh . . . maybe. He'd decline it *for the moment*—he'd probably do it by accident if he didn't, anyway—but he knew how to get it now, and he could grab it later.

A passing thought brought up his Status, which always felt satisfying to do.

Name

Edwin Maxlin

Age

22 years

Race

Extraplanar Human

Class

Hedge Alchemist

Attributes

Mana 5

Skills

Magical

Basic Mana Sense: 36, Mana Infusion: 63 (Basic Mana Manipulation: 9)

Physical

Athletics: 52, Breathing: 52, Flexibility: 27, Nutrition: 27, Packing: 29, Seeing: 31, Sleeping: 29, Survival: 34, Walking: 40

Mental

Polyglot: 36 (Language: 36), Mathematics: 39, Memory: 34 (Research: 50), Visualization: 42

Combat

Bomb Throwing: 9 (Throwing Weapons: 48)

Utility

Firestarting: 45, Alchemy: 60 (Improvisation: 14), Outsider's Almanac: 82 (Status: 22), Identify: 43, First Aid: 30

Paths

Skill Points: 539

Progress to Tier 2: 735/1590

Current Plan

Adventurer 0/30, Warrior 0/60, Athlete 0/60, Researcher 0/60, Skilled Arcanist 0/60, Potioneer 0/60, Wanderer 0/60, Stonehide Vanquisher 0/60, Scientist 0/60, Outsider 0/60, Blackstone Conqueror 0/60, Mage 0/60, Novice Pyromancer 0/60, World Traveler 0/60, Physical Arcanist 0/60, Field Medic 0/60, Unkillable 0/90, Path Less Traveled 0/90

Save for Tier 2

Micro-Biomancer 0/90, Realm Traveler 0/120, Alchemical
Warrior 0/90, Pioneer 0/60, Alchemical Medic 0/60, Titan Slayer
0/90, Explorer 0/60, Giant Slayer 0/60, Superior Alchemist 0/60

Maybe

Novice 0/12, Trainee 0/60, Trapper 0/60, System Scholar 0/60,
Survivor 0/60, Daredevil 0/60, Escapee 0/30, Lecturer 0/30,
Steadfast Medic 0/60, Rebel 0/30, Arsonist 0/60

Unsorted

Woodsman 0/30, Hunter 0/30, Novice Ritualist 0/60, Feycaller
0/60, Fey Friend 0/60, Feybound 0/60, Feytouched 0/90, Physical
Alchemist 0/90, Makeshift Alchemist 0/60, Practical Alchemist
0/60, Chemist 0/60, Biologist 0/60, Physicist 0/60, Experimenter
0/60, Scientific Revolutionary 0/90, Forerunner 0/60, Purifier
0/30

Probably Not

Lumberjack 0/60, Way of the Empty Hand 0/60, Pyromaniac
0/30, Exile 0/30, Rebel 0/60, Master of the Ruined Tower 0/60,
Razer of the Ruined Tower 0/60

No

Slave 0/12, Assassin 0/60, Killer 0/30, Traitor 0/60, Burglar 0/60

Completed Paths

CharLimitCanttalkmuchNocluewhathappened
Didmybesttohelpyouli, Mage, Skilled Arcanist, Physical
Alchemist, Bomber, Linguist, Beginner

"Ooh! Are you looking at your Status?" Inion appeared from wherever she had vanished to once he stopped doing interesting things.
"What are your Skills? I wanna help!"

Edwin tucked his head between his hands. "I'm not in the mood for
this right now."

She patted his shoulder reassuringly, which just made him shift
slightly as he recoiled from the touch. "I won't tell you what to do . . .
yet." She poked at him mischievously, her grin falling when she saw that
he wasn't fond of the joke. "Something wrong?"

"No, nothing."

"*Still* an awful liar."

"None of your business, then."

"Nuh-uh! It's absolutely my business. You made a deal that you'd talk to me and that I'd try to help you *to the best of my ability* with your Skills. If you've got some problem that's making you not wanna talk to me about that, it's my duty to *make* you talk. And . . ." She started mimicking some voice or accent Edwin didn't recognize, "We have . . . ways to make you talk."

The naiad waited expectantly for some kind of reaction from Edwin, but when he didn't give one, her face fell, and she said, "I swear, that joke always works," which only prompted a shrug from him.

"Guess your sense of humor is as outdated as the rest of you."

She glared at him. "You're just *asking* for it, aren't you?" As it turned out, even when falling, Inion still drifted as though she were suspended underwater, and as she floated to a seat, she schooled her face into a standard "I absolutely care about you because I'm obligated to" expression. "But seriously, what's wrong?"

Ah, Edwin's favorite form of empathy. Contractually obligated. It was like a youth leader showing concern for him. No kidding, that's what their *job* is. It was the *rest* of the time that . . .

No. No, Edwin. No getting worked up about that anymore. Just answer the question. Inion is practically your therapist at this point, anyway.

"Just . . . everyone has all these expectations of me, now that I'm here. You'd think that being ripped through the fabric of space-time into a wholly separate world would mean I'd finally be able to escape people thinking I need to do this with my life, that I can't go and do *that*, that I need to conform to exactly what they want . . ." He sighed. "Heck, worst of all are the 'you can do whatever you like and we'll be proud of you' sorts of people, because you *know* they have some secret desire for you but refuse to actually share it."

"Can't say I can *relate* exactly, but I do understand. I . . . I . . . yeah. It's not easy, is it? Still, give me a quick rundown on what you have, and we can talk about it some other time, ya? That way I can get a bit of time to think about it."

He sighed. "Fine . . . Fine. Let's start from the top, then? The *first* Skill I got was Basic Mana Sense . . ."

Edwin finished weaving another rhoreed mat by the time they finished, as Inion wanted to know everything about all his Skills and Paths. What they were, what level they were at, what they seemed to do, how he unlocked them, what he thought about them . . . She'd laughed when he outlined his hopes for Packing, but then she'd stopped and considered it and told him it *might* work, she'd just never seen anyone actually *try* it before.

That was good enough for Edwin. It wasn't a high-enough level yet, though. He estimated it would need to be level 50 or so before it was enough to even start, but once he did . . . well, it would be pretty great.

For now, though, he was finally getting around to trying to get meat from his deer. He only needed to eat a little more than once every two days at this point when he wasn't being too physical, which was quite nice. Still, he needed to deal with this carcass sooner or later, and there was still a bit of light, so may as well do so now.

Inion had pulled it out of her pocket dimension or whatever it was exactly. It was as fresh as it had been before, to the point where it was still slightly bloody. Well . . . Edwin could deal with that later. He had the meat hanging from a nearby tree and started trying to cut away the skin. At first, he'd thought he might somehow cut the meat out, rather than the skin away, but had no *clue* how to even start with that, so here he was.

It ended up not being quite as hard as Edwin worried. Still really hard, but it was at least *doable*. A few cuts here and there to get the skin started, ignoring the fur that kept getting on the meat, and then pull the skin off, bit by bit.

Once he was just dealing with a lot of meat, which was honestly pretty blood-free at this point, the last few drops having worked their way out while he'd been working, things . . . well, they weren't more complicated, nor were they less complicated. Things changed in complexity, as now Edwin had some fifty or sixty pounds of meat to deal with, which . . . yeah. He needed to do *something* with all of that.

Cutting off the legs and head left him with six pieces—well, five, really; he didn't want to deal with the deer's crushed head, so he tossed it into the woods—of varying size, which he *really* didn't know what to do with now. It was easier to deal with, at least. He didn't have any convenient way to grill, fry, or bake it, so . . . maybe smoking it or boiling it? The former of those sounded way more convenient, but it could wait for the morning. Edwin passed what he had so far off to Inion, who was sitting at the edge of her pond doing . . . something. Weaving a cord of grass? And he went to bed.

Level Up!
Survival 34→36

The next morning, the drying potion still wasn't done soaking into his test wood, so Edwin decided to deal with his venison instead. After loading up his campfire with as much green wood as he could, making sure he only took branches from a vaguely maple-looking tree—he couldn't remember *why* cedar and fir were bad for smoking, but he'd heard people discussing it at some point—he got the fire started with his Skill and started working with his meat.

He'd never been a big fan of gristle and had use for tallow besides, so his first task was just trimming as much fat as possible from the game. It was all collected inside a jar and set off to the side, partially set into the creek bed to help keep it cool. From there, Edwin started cutting slices from the leg he was working on, about an inch thick and six inches long, and laying them not directly on the coals, but suspended above it on wood-soaked green wood—his makeshift not-a-grill.

With no illusions that his wooden not-a-grill would withstand any level of fire, he kept his campfire going at a slow, but steady rate of coals and embers. It took hours for his meat to look essentially cooked and smoked both on the inside and out, but cutting up the venison was similarly time-consuming, so . . . it more or less balanced out.

It took most of the day for Edwin to get his meat all prepared, and he was pretty certain he'd be utterly *sick* of venison jerky by the time it was all eaten, but it should at least function adequately as food until then.

Level Up!
Survival 36→37
Nutrition 27→28

Edwin declined the Cooking and Harvesting Skills and, his cooking for the night completed, built up his fire again.

His jerky was . . . well, it was technically edible. It was somewhat flavorless and bland, chewy and difficult to eat, but it had the most important aspect: he *could* eat it, and that meant he could at least nominally use it for food. He had enough to last him for *weeks*, assuming he got fresh water (trivial) and some level of veggies and carbohydrates. Hmm. Nutrition might help out there, and he still had his bags of beans. If he could just find some talsanenris berries at some point, he might be able to figure out some kind of speed-growth fertilizer. Plus, Inion had Gardening by her own admission. She would probably help him with it? Eh, he'd deal with all that later, once he'd made more progress on his cabin.

Hmm . . . Now that he thought about it, what exactly were his priorities at the moment? He needed materials and levels, both of which he had some help with from Inion, both of which he lagged massively behind on both Earth and Joriah. He wasn't able to excel as just a physicist, and his Skills were apparently insufficient. A quick call to his Status allowed Edwin's gaze to linger upon one Path in particular, and the corners of his mouth flicked up.

Scientific Revolutionary 0/90

Yeah. He liked the sound of that.

CHAPTER 13

Starting from Scraps

Stone, water, clay, and metal. Those were the four foundational materials for building something substantial. Well, also sand. Arguably wood as well. And maybe—

Okay, so a *lot* of stuff went into pretty much anything, all tangled together in a vast web of interconnected technologies and methodologies, which meant if Edwin wanted to make substantial progress in one area, he'd have to also make progress in other areas. And he'd need to do it all by himself unless he wanted to return to civilization . . .

He cracked his knuckles. Well, nothing to it but to get started then.

Stone was technically easy to find, but it would be hard for him to actually use. Edwin wasn't sure what the cliff face was made of, but it wasn't limestone, unfortunately. In addition, if he wanted anything more than tiny pebbles, he'd need a pickaxe, chisel, and hammer. Doing that would be insanely laborious, though. At the rate his Packing was growing, it might almost be easier for him to get stone from Vinstead or something. Where *they* got their stone from, he had no clue. Maybe they had a quarry in the mountains and shipped it downriver or something? Ah, the details probably didn't matter. If it actually was important, he'd find out eventually.

Water, at least, he had in abundance, but purifying it was starting to get tricky. He only had two proper-size bowls, after all, and even then his second, nondwarven, bowl wasn't anywhere close to being as large as his primary one, and they were both in fairly regular use. Not to mention that he didn't want his drinking water anywhere close to his Alchemy cauldron, no matter how much he scoured it with sand between each use. For the time being, he had just been collecting water in his canteen and suspending that over his fire to boil it all off, but that wasn't really scalable.

Clay took a minute to confirm, but as it turned out he did have a pretty good supply of it in Inion's streambed. Nice and thick, too, though a bit rocky and buried under layers of rock and sand. It would take some work to actually harvest, but he could probably shovel out a fair amount of the stuff. Or, he supposed, he could dig a pit elsewhere in his clearing. The clay wasn't restricted to just the stream, after all; it was just the only place where the topsoil had eroded enough to uncover it.

Metal was the absolute hardest. Even in the unlikely situation he managed to find a vein of iron ore or something, he'd still need to dig it out, incurring all the issues of using stone, before smelting it himself and purifying it by hand. He . . . more or less remembered the Bessemer process (Almanac to self: introduce that at some point), but that didn't help him at the scales he was looking at. Plus, he'd need to work it and twist it . . . no. That was far too much work and hassle for something in which he'd never manage to compete with the professionals in Vinstead. Edwin ran his finger over the maker's mark on his axe, a torch set into a diamond. Nah, if how well it had held up an edge after so much use was any indication, he'd never be able to hold a candle to the skill and Skills of actual metalsmiths.

Sand he had lots of, as the bottom of Inion's pool was filled with the stuff and the riverbed had a fair amount as well. That would be really useful if he wanted to make more cement, let alone if he wanted to try glassmaking. Plus, he still remembered the strange semi-superfluid-like behaviors Infused sand had demonstrated when he'd tested it previously. That in itself was worth investigating once he had a bit of time.

Edwin already had a lot of wood, and he could also pretty easily get more if he needed it. That said, if he wanted to dry any more to turn it into a more easily usable product, he would need to find more firevine and make more oil. Once he had it, though, all kinds of simple machines were makeable. He could use the stream and waterfall as a source of mechanical power fairly trivially, and once he had mechanical muscles doing his work for him, well . . .

No getting ahead of ourselves. First things first.

The experimental drying potion still didn't seem to have soaked all the way into the center of the log, and it hadn't even soaked into the wood past the surface. What was up with that? It didn't seem like it had taken this long last time; did purifying the lye mean it couldn't penetrate the wood anymore? That would be interesting if so, but also really annoying. Well, there was still time left. Maybe last time it had just gone particularly quickly. If it hadn't been absorbed by tomorrow, then he'd look into it more.

Actually, maybe he just couldn't tell if it had been fully absorbed? Previously, he'd seen a slight discoloration everywhere the potion had soaked through, but not this time. Well, perhaps that was because—

Oy. No. Wait until the experiment actually gives a result before making hypotheses about why it failed and what to do next.

Well, in the meantime, he wasn't about to just sit around. The benefits of superhuman athleticism and rest meant he could work himself way harder than normal, day after day. In some ways, Edwin was surprised at how well he was able to stay focused on work, day after day with none off—he certainly couldn't have managed it back on Earth, after all—but then again, he had lots of different projects to jump to whenever he got bored with one of his tasks, and he was making more or less tangible results with every passing day.

He wanted a pottery bowl to boil water with, though, and maybe an entire distillery setup. It would be graceful as a skating stegosaurus, but if he built it right, it might work well.

Getting enough clay was easy in theory, and it wasn't exactly *complicated*, but it still involved Edwin being waist-deep in freezing spring water and trying to dig clay from under the layers of pebbles and sand that had accumulated over decades and centuries. Because he was stuck between not wanting to get hypothermia and not wanting to strip down in front of Inion, he ended up undressing to his underwear and mentally ignoring the naiad's teasing comments as he did so.

His feet were starting to go numb, but as his shovel bit into the thick soil, scooping out and piling up a decent-size pile of clay on the river-bank, Edwin was immensely grateful that he was almost done. Next time, he was going farther downstream to see if there were *any* exposed banks, because he was not doing this again.

None of his Skills were helping—he'd tried. Not that he knew which of his Skills would actually be of any potential use in this, but giving it a go still almost made him feel better.

Then, finally, he was done. As Edwin plopped the final scoop onto his admittedly arbitrarily sized mound of clay, he practically jetted out of the water and rushed to his fire, gratefully relaxing as the radiating heat washed over him like the first rays of summer sunlight after a long winter.

"Y'know," Inion purred as she sidled up next to him teasingly, trailing a finger along his goosebump-covered arm, "you really should clean yourself more often. Aren't you getting dirty from working so much? Yet I think this is the first time I've seen you shirtless, and you aren't that bad of a sight."

Edwin shifted, shivering as he wiped himself down with a spare rag. "Yeah, well, before I woke you up I made sure to clean myself somewhat regularly. Bit of hot water and a rag, a momentary dip in the stream or pond to get dust and sweat off . . . I didn't have soap, but I made do."

"Oh, really?" the naiad drawled. "I guess I missed out."

Edwin shrugged. It was hard to say he *didn't* like attention from a pretty more-or-less girl, but it just felt . . . awkward. None of her teasing really came across as genuine, more just her messing with him. Compounded with his how-to-survive-in-Joriah sense screaming at him to *not* get entangled with a fey in . . . that way . . . he wasn't terribly fond of it. Not that it was enough for him to actually get her to *stop*, but it was enough for him to not reciprocate her teasing in any way. "Guess so."

Dang it, why couldn't anyone have shown this kind of interest in him back on Earth? It would have been so much simpler if they had. Not *easy*, but simpler.

Edwin finished drying off and pulled on his shirt and pants, sighing in appreciation as the warm clothes slid over his still-freezing skin. He looked away from Inion pretending to pout as he pulled on his socks and shoes and wrapped his cloak around him, waiting for his body heat to warm him back up.

. . . screw this, I have magic.

He had to be careful when using Firestarting, to not include any part of himself or his clothing in the effect, but the sudden surge of heat from the flames as they shifted from orange to blue felt *so* nice. Mmmm. He'd tried Infusing Firestarting before, as a replacement for matches or flint and steel, though never once did he already have a blazing fire going. What would happen if he did?

. . .

Level Up!
Skill Points 542→549
Progress to Tier 2: 739/1590
Firestarting 45→46
Mana Infusion Level 63→64
Bomb Throwing Level 9→14

"Yes, you *do* still have your eyebrows, Edwin. You don't need to ask me *again*."

"Are you sure? Because I really don't think . . ."

"It wasn't even that big."

"It literally blew up in my face! I got Skill levels in my explosives Skill!"

"Only a few."

Edwin harrumphed and turned away from the fey, who was badly concealing how much she wanted to laugh. So, as it turned out, when Infused Firestarting was used on something already thoroughly on fire, it seemed to set every part of that object on fire . . . all at once.

The resulting *whumph* had spread burning coals all over the area, setting a *ton* of things on fire. Fortunately, Inion reacted quickly enough to extinguish the embers that landed on Edwin's shelter before the branches that made up his roof could catch fire, and she put out all the flaming chunks of firewood before they could catch the underbrush on fire. It had the unfortunate side effect of drenching a fair amount of the stuff inside, but Edwin would take it over them burning up.

He did lose a few pieces of deer jerky where it was sitting out, and more than a few pieces of firewood ended up in the campfire before he would have otherwise intended, but overall? Not too bad of a mishap. Especially not now that he'd found a new way to get bombs working!

Well, so long as he was able to already get something firmly on fire. And could Infuse Firestarting to target something at a decent range *without* also igniting a lot of other things. Heck, his current range for Firestarting was like twenty feet at most, and Infusion was still barely past touch range.

Overall, a lot of bugs to work out, but also a lot of potential if he could actually get it working. After all, real-life explosives were all about trying to get a bunch of really flammable things burning simultaneously. If he could do that *at will*? With *anything*?

Well, the results would be positively explosive.

"See! You're smiling again! I told you you'd be fine."

Edwin waved off Inion and poked at his fire, making sure the freshly loaded stock of wood was well and truly aflame before he got up to deal with what he'd been trying to work on before accidentally discovering mana-powered grenades.

Clay was easy to sculpt. Well, it was *supposed* to be easy to sculpt, but trying to do so with his newly scooped clay just wasn't working. It was probably too wet, honestly. He'd let it dry some and come back to it later. Hmm. What else could he work on, then? Maybe get some sand out, so that it could start to dry as well for his future use?

Edwin looked at the stream, its icy, frigid water and his shovel discarded next to it. He shuddered.

. . . I'm going back to my fire now, I think.

CHAPTER 14

Fire Rocks!

Level Up!
Sleeping 29→30

Edwin almost wished it would be drizzling when he finally woke up, simply because it would reflect his general mood. Alas, the weather didn't comply, and it retained its normal rain-free behavior. At this point, he was pretty sure that they must be in a rain shadow of some form or another, probably caused by the mountains to the south.

He only half-heartedly pulled himself from his bed and through his morning routine. Sure, most of yesterday had gone so very well, then he had to go and blow up his campfire and sour everything. Well, it could have been worse. He hadn't started a wildfire, hadn't lost much, and he'd had a relatively nice time sitting around the fire later on, watching the flames and generally contemplating life.

Inion wasn't around, but that wasn't too much of a surprise. She would show up at some point, back from doing whatever it was she did at night.

While not especially hungry, Edwin still grabbed a piece of jerky from his food bag and started absently chewing at it, sipping some water in the meantime. Ugh. He'd need to do stuff today, but he just didn't feel up to it. Maybe he could check the results of his experiment?

Nope, it *still* hadn't soaked into the wood. At this point, Edwin was close to declaring it a failed trial, that clearly some part of purifying the lye had meant the formula wouldn't penetrate into the wood. Was the ash really that important?

Hmm. Maybe in a future variation, he could try purifying lye again and adding ash in afterward, to see if that had an impact.

He'd still give it another day. Maybe it was just slow. Mostly, though, he didn't want to have to do fiddly alchemical work when he was feeling so generally dour. He mentally ran through his list of tasks. . . . Yeah, he was feeling up to playing in the mud.

Edwin's experience with pottery more or less boiled down to a single weekend when he was thirteen, and while he might have learned a lot, it was still almost a decade prior and he had no tools this time around. But how hard could it really be? Well, the answer for once seemed to be "not very."

Overnight, his clay pile—Edwin shivered in remembrance of how cold that had been to make—had dried enough to actually be workable, and with a solid block of clay in his hands, Edwin took to making himself a bowl.

Thanks to, well, already *having* one, Edwin was able to pretty easily get the initial shape of his clay to line up with how a bowl ought to be, simply by forming his block to align with the outside of his dwarven-made one. The problems only really began when he was trying to get an even thickness of clay that wasn't too thin but also wasn't too thick.

Once he had *that* mostly taken care of, having dug out a few pebbles that were messing with it, he needed to try and get a mostly even lip. Again, doable but tricky, and Edwin wished he had a pottery wheel. That would probably help him with this, and he wished for it again as he tried to peel away his bowl from its template . . . only to have it fall apart on him again.

Edwin sighed. This was going to be harder than he wanted it to be, wasn't it?

About two hours later, he finally had something that . . . basically looked like a bowl, and a Skill to correspond with it at the same time. He wasn't really interested in Sculpt Clay, though, so passed on it. Ugh. He really needed to reassess exactly what Skills he wanted, which Skills would be made redundant by Attributes, how to get said Attributes, and . . . yeah. When he was feeling better.

Edwin put his bowl next to the fire to help it dry out before he fired it. If he put it in too soon, the water inside would vaporize and crack the sides, breaking the bowl outright at worst or drastically weakening its structure at best. While it was drying, he kept at it. No sense in wasting time after all. Maybe he could make an entire distillery while he was at it?

. . .

As he was working on his next bowl, Edwin was struck by a passing curiosity about what would happen if he Infused clay. There didn't seem to be much of a pattern if he was honest, and he couldn't help but wonder what determined how certain Infused materials would work. Perhaps clay would follow the path stone took, and harden? That would be really useful and would allow him to make a lot of interesting sculpturelike creations. Curious, he gave it a try.

Mana Infusion.

Splat.

The half-shaped bowl in Edwin's hands immediately liquefied, splattering on his legs and the ground.

Dang it! Now he'd have to start over from scratch and . . . *Breathe, Edwin. It's all right.*

Well, he had to admit that he wasn't expecting that to happen. Was this sort of like how sand became almost a superfluid when Infused? Was clay close enough to sand that it just made the clay lose all internal cohesion? Given the way it had spontaneously melted, he guessed it might mimic a ton of water being added all at once.

Edwin tentatively touched a glob of clay and pulled the mana out of it with what little Basic Mana Manipulation he had available to him, letting the mote of magical energy disperse into the atmosphere. The clay didn't solidify exactly, but it did lose a lot of its fluidity and returned more or less to how it was before he had Infused it. Huh.

Well, if it worked how it seemed to, he could absolutely use that. Edwin picked up a dried chunk of clay from where he'd discarded it near the pile. It was too hard and brittle to work normally, but . . .

The barest hint of mana animated from where it was stored in his chest, flowing through unseen channels and to his fingertips, where it exited and seeped into the clay. As it did, the clump of dirt deformed in Edwin's grip ever so slightly, and a smile crept across his face.

Level Up!
Mana Infusion Level 64→65

Edwin had to decline Sculpt Clay twice more, and even a more general Sculpture Skill before he was finally satisfied. By working with already-dry clay, merging clumps together by Infusing them, mixing them, and removing the mana once they were combined to get more material to work with, he was able to make the material much thinner than before. That said, he still needed to keep in mind the fact that this was going to deal with a lot of heat and cold, so he was still a little on the more generous side of thickness, but hey! He didn't need to wait for this one to dry out.

While he didn't have any way to make a proper kiln—yet—Edwin still felt that he could figure out a makeshift one. First, he dug out a hole in the ground a few feet deep, mounding the extra dirt around his normal firepit. Next, he compacted the dirt inside and caked the interior with wet clay. Last, he found a flat-edged rock, easily picking up the wet stone from Inion's pond despite the slippery rock probably weighing a good thirty pounds. It went at the bottom of the pit, which should help ensure that his bowls didn't fuse with their surroundings, and while he almost grabbed a second one to serve as a lid over his kiln, he realized that doing so would probably ensure any fire he lit would just choke itself out. He wasn't dealing with modern appliances, after all. This would be wood-fired.

He only had the one bowl ready for firing at the moment, but that was fine. He could use the meantime to get more ready. He built up a fire inside the kiln and grabbed more clay to keep working.

Edwin's Logbook: Pottery

Test 1: Bowl made via mana-Infused clay inside kiln. Fire built underneath, no cap for the fire.

Result: Failure. Clay partially hardened from the heat but wasn't cured, so mostly melted in water.

Test 2: Bowl made via mundane clay. Fire built underneath, fire capped but with air channels.

Result: Failure. Clay still not cured, though more successful than test 1.

Test 3: Pot made from mundane clay. Fire built all around the pot, fire capped with ventilation.

Result: Failure. Pot was cracked in half. The outside of the pot was maybe slightly cured, but not the inside.

Test 4: Pot made from mana-Infused clay. Fire built around and inside the pot, fire capped with ventilation.

Result: Failure. Pot was cracked in half. Uncertain why. Still not properly cured.

"Having fun?"

Edwin nearly jumped from where he was contemplating his latest failure, spinning to see Inion having finally returned.

"You're back! Where have you been for the last two days?"

"Ah, here and there. Hey, did you know dwarves found their way into the Highpeaks? I didn't even know that . . . doesn't matter!"

Edwin glared at her. "Yeah. I'm aware. Actually"—he frowned—"I think I *did* tell you about them."

"Did you? I don't remember you saying something like that. But I sense a story! Tell me, tell me!"

"I really rather wouldn't . . ."

"Too bad! You're telling me. We have an *agreement*, remember?"

Edwin waited for some kind of tug in his mind, or some form of supernatural compulsion to keep his word, but it never came. Huh. "Well, you've been gone lately. Maybe I don't need to keep up my side of the deal because you haven't been keeping up yours?"

"Nope! Not how it works. Besides, I've been doing my part! I can't help you if I'm not around, but I also can't watchya. It's just on hold while one of us is gone."

Edwin sighed and finally relented, giving a short version of his encounter with the fur-faced . . .

Language, Edwin.

It's my own mind! I can swear if I want to! . . . Not that I will. Habits, right? Sigh.

Still, he gave Inion a bit of an overview of his . . . stay with the Blackstones, and she seemed to be oddly amused at certain parts, particularly when they *enslaved* him.

"So then . . . Oh, come on. Is it really that hilarious?"

The fey stopped laughing long enough to explain, "Just . . . breaking hospitality in that way." She shook her head. "They're going to find themselves in quite a few unfortunate situations in the near future, if they haven't already."

Edwin frowned. "Wait, are you saying that karma is an actual thing here?"

Inion indicated "kind of" with her hands, imitating a scale again. "Not really but also sort of. Normally, you'd need the attention of an . . . yeah, I can say that. The attention of a really powerful Outsider or just really strong ties to Fate, for that to work. Here, though . . . ah, that's too close, sorry."

Something to do with the System, then? Her limitations were essentially regarding speaking about it and about other worlds and their denizens, so Edwin wasn't sure what else it might be. It would be interesting if the System had done something to help him escape, but he wasn't sure how that might work.

"Aaaaanyway, carry on."

" . . . Thank you for your permission."

"Gladly!"

Edwin sighed. Now, where was he? Oh, right, he was preparing the next firing.

Edwin's Logbook: Pottery

Test 5: Built a massive fire over the bowl (made from mana-Infused clay), covering it completely and utterly. I will burn this to a crisp if I need to. No cap, will continue throwing more and more wood on it.

Result: A falling branch crushed the bowl. It was fully cured though!

Test 6: Built tower more carefully this time, completely surrounding and covering the bowl (made via Mana Infusion). Also padded everything with dead leaves. Kept Firestarting going as long as possible. Allowed to cool overnight.

Result: Success! At long, long last. Odd black spots on the clay. Doesn't seem to impact stability or strength.

Test 7: As test 6, though with less Firestarting use and with five bowls and the walls for a distillation setup.

Result: Success! Lost three bowls, which cracked for some unknown reason, but otherwise turned out well.

Edwin looked on with satisfaction at his new water distillation setup. He'd built it such that it could be placed over his kiln, so even after he had expanded it a few more times, it should serve him well for a good while. At the top, he had set one of his metal bowls, filled with freezing water from Inion's spring.

Any water that evaporated would find itself condensing on the metal, then drip down at the center into a collection bowl, which in turn had a channel leading outside of the entire contraption, emptying into a water jug he'd made just for that purpose. At the bottom sat a jug for holding the boiling water, and the entire contraption was enclosed by a ceramic cylinder, to help keep all the water vapor focused.

He'd need to refill it semiregularly, replacing the boiling water at the bottom with the cooling water at the top, but it should work quite well, especially when kept Infused. While he'd yet to figure out what Infusing his cured claywork actually did, if he ran it through Packing, it made the ceramic significantly stronger.

It may have taken him four days in total to get everything working, but Edwin didn't waste his downtime while the kiln ran. In that time, he'd declared his purified drying potion a failure, considered doing another trial with his lye, this time adding ashes—though eventually decided against it—and mixed up his final batch of drying potion.

He'd even applied the potion, making sure it had turned out properly by testing it on a small branch—it had—and was now checking that each of his massive logs had fully absorbed the seemingly too small amount of potion he'd applied to each. Yes, *proportionally* it was the same amount as he'd tried on the branches, but there was still the nervousness that came from actually doing a full-scale run.

The System was magical in so many ways, but letting his recipe turn out properly, more or less first try? Now *that* was utterly amazing.

Edwin took a deep breath, turning to face his pile of wood. Every log showed signs it had fully absorbed all traces of his potion, and that it had soaked all the way through.

It had been about two weeks spent in the wilderness, now, and he was finally ready to start making a more permanent home. It was time. All that was left was to burn off the water, and his construction could begin.

Fire—

"Oh, hey, Edwin!"

"What?" he snapped. "I'm working! What happened to 'no interruptions'?"

Inion replied by sticking her tongue out at him. "I didn't break anything. You can carry on as you were. But do you *really* want to risk burning the logs?"

Edwin nearly responded that this was fine, it had worked perfectly with the smaller scale models . . . but his test log had come out a little singed, and did he really want to risk it?

". . . Fine."

He'd just use a burning stick, then.

Honestly, reality had no sense of drama.

CHAPTER 15

Last-Minute Tuning

Edwin stretched, cracking his neck as he prepared for his next momentous task. He'd settled on a final location for his cabin and now needed to prepare the actual ground for his building. First up, digging out his foundations.

The soft topsoil was broken and hauled out, mounded next to Edwin's kiln as it burned, making a set of smaller bowls that he could use for ingredients. He still had yet to figure out the origin of the black splotches on the generally reddish-brown earthenware, but that didn't matter. What did matter was that the soil was off to the side, but not so far as to be inaccessible in case he figured out a use for it later.

He kept having to dismiss the Digging Skill, annoyingly, but he couldn't figure out how to blacklist a Skill from being offered. There had to be a way, right? Eh, he decided to just turn off notifications for the time being, and check them all once he was done. He wasn't going to accept a Skill at the moment, though maybe soon, and this way he wouldn't be constantly annoyed by the pop-ups.

Edwin kept going through canteens of water, to the point where one bottle had barely cooled by the time he needed to down it all and Inion started to boil the next one. He didn't mind that much, though. It provided a good time to catch his breath. Not . . . that he ever actually needed to do so. He was almost tireless save for hunger and thirst, but the mental break was still appreciated.

Not having to deal with muscle fatigue had its own benefits, though. Even as he—or more accurately, Inion—watched, the ground he'd chosen to work on sank away, and the mound of discarded dirt grew larger and larger.

By the time he stopped, he had dug nearly an entire foot down and cleared off all the loose dirt, leaving far rockier soil. It wasn't a perfect foundation, but it should work.

The first logs he rolled over and set into place with copious amounts of sand and stone. Strangely, Packing seemed to help him carry large amounts of loose objects, which . . . he wasn't expecting but he guessed made sense? If piles of sand had less weight pulling them down, it did seem to fit that it wouldn't collapse as easily.

Once properly set into the ground, Edwin chopped notches into the dry wood, easily chipping into the tree trunk. On the side farther from the stream, he made sure to include an additional notch into the wood, to account for his inner walls.

Then the day was over, and Edwin joined Inion by the fire, gratefully accepting a final canteen of water.

"You know, I have Skills to make my water more drinkable."

Edwin paused his frantic gulping to raise an eyebrow. "And—" He doubled over coughing as he swallowed a bit of water incorrectly. Inion looked at him with some concern, but he waved off her concern. "I'm fine," he croaked. "Just failing at basic human tasks as always."

Much to his annoyance, though not to his surprise, Inion agreed eagerly with that sentiment. He shot a glare at the naiad, who just laughed.

"Anyway. As I was saying, why didn't you mention that earlier?"

"Didn't ask." She shrugged, which just prompted another sigh—and another round of coughing—from Edwin.

With the foundation laid, the rest of the work was fairly routine, and day after day passed in basically the same manner.

In the morning, he'd dig out his cured pottery and start up his kiln for the next batch. While he did still lose most of his would-be earthenware, he was proud of getting up to nearly a 40 percent success rate. The shards he kept off to the side for some unspecified future use.

Most of his day would then consist of carefully measuring and cutting his logs so they would fit together snugly. Two walls with three notches, two with two, and two with one. The hard part came with the natural variation of thickness and the bumps and irregularities in the surface. Those inevitably interrupted the otherwise snug fit between the logs, and whenever he found one, Edwin needed to pull the log off where it was and whittle away the protrusion before returning the tree trunk.

Edwin's evenings were spent fashioning whatever pottery he'd later fire in his kiln. About ten minutes downstream, he'd found a giant bank of dried clay that proved perfect for his purposes, once he'd retrieved enough of it.

By day 4, the walls were mostly assembled.

Day 5, he got the door cutout partially started, cutting just enough of a notch into one of the logs facing most of the meadow, and started on the roof.

Day 6 involved assembling the roof, which proved trickier than he had anticipated. Since Edwin didn't have enough small logs to form a full roof structure, he had to create something of a temporary skeleton with nondry wood. He'd need to replace it eventually, but better the roof than part of the wall.

"I don't suppose you have something you could do to help with the roof?" Edwin asked as he and Inion were relaxing around the campfire that evening. "I didn't adequately account for how much timber I'd need for it, and I'm just curious if you have an easy fix before I spend two days overthinking a solution."

"Is that actual forethought that I sense there?" The naiad ruffled Edwin's hair. "I'm so proud of you!"

"Shaddup." Edwin's rebuttal, much like his efforts to swat Inion's hand away, were half-hearted at most.

"And I do! I have this really cool trick; you want me to do it? I gotta get your say-so to give it a go!"

"Yes, please." Edwin had the sort of bone-deep weariness that only came from endless days of hard work, never mind that he felt just as physically capable as though he had only worked half a day. It was psychological, but he needed to get this in a usable state before he could take a break, just for his own sanity.

"Hmm. But I think that your Skills would benefit from doing it yourself now, wouldn't they?" Inion cheerfully dashed his hopes, too late to prevent them from actually being formed.

Edwin let his head thud against the ground as he groaned. "Well, I'm just training two, maybe three of my Skills doing this. Once I'm done I'll be training my *other* Skills. Arguably"—he rolled his head to face the fey—"finishing this will be more helpful for my Skills than continuing to work on it."

"Hmm." Inion stroked her chin. "Interesting argument. I suppose I can *almost* see your point."

Edwin wasn't interested in games. "What do you want?"

"Hmm. What *do* I want? It's been pretty entertaining watching you scramble around shirtless day after day, stacking sticks for your little home," Inion teased, to which Edwin just rolled his eyes.

"But I *am* interested to see what your next project will be after this. Saaayyyy . . . tell ya what, I'll do it, but you and I are going to sit down and go over your Skill plans tomorrow, ya? Also . . ." She pretended to think for a moment. "You're going to watch, and never share."

Edwin groaned. "Really? After all this time, *now* you want to go over it? Wouldn't it have made more sense to figure that out before my week of work? Also, watch what?"

Inion shook her head. "Nah. Well, maybe. But I didn't feel like doing it then. Now I do!"

He stared blankly at the fey. It could be so easy to forget she wasn't human at times, but when she started yanking him around for whatever reason, it was always a stark reminder. Still, whatever her reasoning, this was meant to be her "best effort," so that meant that . . .

Nope. He didn't feel up to tracking whatever convoluted logic Inion had used, if it even could be traced. Edwin shook his head. "Watch what?" No response. "Okay, sure. Fine, whatever. Just . . . roof, please?"

Inion hopped up with way too much enthusiasm and made a wide circle around the imposing wooden walls of his cabin. Then, she began to sing.

"*Oh, my dreamer . . .*" From the first words, Inion's voice rang through the clearing, seeming to echo her stream, which fell silent—no, it just trickled in time with a cadence that didn't match up to her words, but did to her singing . . . Polyglot was throwing a fit, but Edwin didn't mind. She had a fantastic voice. "*Sing with me, take me home.*"

Wind whistled through the woods as the grass near Inion began to writhe, swaying to her voice.

I see there the woods, I see there the thickets,
I see there the fair and most fertile of meadows;
I see there the deer on the ground in the valleys
Hiding in mantles of mist.

"*Oh, my dreamer . . .*" Inion danced through the clearing, spinning joyously in contrast with the gentler tone of her melody. Edwin's Mana Sense didn't light up in the way he was used to. There was no single source of magic here, yet this was *undeniably* something deep and primal. It felt like the entire forest was waking up and becoming magical. "*Sing with me, take me home.*"

Any other time, Edwin would have dismissed it as merely his imagination, but here and now? No, his new house was beginning to grow together, his carefully cut and fit logs fusing into one large shape. What had he gotten himself into?

Lofty mountains and resplendent ledges,
There dwell my own folk, kind folk of honor.
Light is my step as I leap up to meet them;
'Tis with pleasure I'll stay there awhile.

"*Oh, my dreamer . . .*" A soft, blue-green glow began to suffuse the area, and tiny fireflies—no, not fireflies. These were fairy lights, though he couldn't determine *why* he was so certain about that. It felt like he was intruding on something old, something ancient. Part of him wanted to flee, yet another part felt tied in place, like he was being welcomed in and brought . . . home. "*Sing with me, take me home.*"

Vines began to grow from the ground, around the base of his home, and seemed to almost snake their way up his carefully constructed cabin. Once they reached where the roof should be, they began to weave themselves between his sparse constructions and solidify, forming a leafy top to his home.

Hail to the blue-green grassy hills;
Hail to the grandest skybound mountains;
Hail to the forests, hail to all there,
Content I would live there forever.

"Oh, my dreamer . . ." Inion rose into the air as she spun, feet stepping on the thinnest strands of grass as the fairy lights swirled around her. A warm breeze flowed through the area, coming from everywhere yet nowhere at once. *"Sing with me, take me home."*

Bark grew back upon the logs, undoing weeks of careful work Edwin had put into chopping, cutting, drying, and assembling all that timber. He couldn't really feel mad, though. Instead, he was . . . entranced. The song flowed through him as well, imbuing his very soul with energy and refreshing his body. At the front of the cabin a part of the wall melted away to create an empty doorframe, and the shape of the walls shifted slightly to fit more naturally into its surroundings. The disturbed earth from all across the meadow smoothed out, growing grasses and delicate flowers as the harmonious magic seeped into every inch of his surroundings, a gentle glow suffusing everything in sight.

Let me be among the trees, tall and proud;
Let me dwell amidst the streams, unending and pure;
Let me find myself beneath the endless skies, shining and bright,
For there I'll find myself a home.

The song continued, but Polyglot began to fail Edwin as the words lost individual meaning and instead simply became a melody telling an ancient story, of lost splendor and the beauty of a time long gone.

His cabin . . . well, to call it a cabin was misleading. His handiwork was still present, that much was clear. But it looked to be a living thing, reminiscent of what he had seen in the halflings' village, yet so much more.

Edwin didn't know how long he sat, entranced by the harmony and lost in the fantastical, but before Inion had even finished her song, night had fallen. Silver moonlight flitted through the trees, nary a beam striking the ground outside his clearing. And yet the naiad continued to dance, to a tune older than time itself.

She opened her eyes, her gaze fixed upon Edwin, and she smiled, a smile utterly inhuman in its perfection and allure. Behind Inion's eyes, Edwin saw the calm, serene beauty of a forest glen, the wild majesty of an unstoppable waterfall, and the incomprehensibly massive scale of a mountain. Yet also the gentle call of birdsong in the morning, the soft fur of a rabbit, and the delicate colors of a budding wildflower.

There was a spark, and suddenly Inion felt Edwin's comprehension, his appreciation, and finished her song, the final notes drifting through the air long past her actual voice had faded into memory.

Oh, my dreamer.
Sing with me,
take me home.

CHAPTER 16

Putting Down Roots

Inion stumbled as she touched back down to the ground by the campfire, the spell . . . not exactly broken, but certainly ended. Its effects lingered, the moonlit clearing still luminous with the emerald glow of magic, emanating from every tree and blade of grass but also from the fairy lights, drifting through the air and occasionally extinguishing themselves.

Edwin was caught off guard but still was able to catch the otherworldly fey as she collapsed next to him. "You didn't tell me you could sing."

A tired grin flitted across her face. "Couldn't. Hmm. You're holding me," she tiredly teased Edwin, who rolled his eyes. "And you aren't tossing me away when I say that. Are you finally willing to admit your feelings for me?"

"Let me think. . . . I'll admit you're tired and I know I'd hate to be lying on the ground in your state." She tried to shift to be more in his lap. "Don't push it, though, or I *will* drop you."

Inion stuck her tongue out at him. "You're no fun."

"Singing, though? Was that a Skill?"

"I can't tell you." So yes, then. Why would a Singing Skill need to be a secret? Even if it had some special evolution that needed to be secret, why the *base* Skill?

"Well, it certainly was . . . something. What did you even do?"

"I helped you with your home. Like you asked."

"I . . . don't believe that's all you did."

Inion turned and tried to snuggle further into Edwin's arms, "Mmmm . . . never said it was."

"So then what else did . . . and you're asleep." He sighed. "I didn't even know you *did* sleep."

"Mm . . . don't. Mm . . . mmmmide amakmmmm. . . ."

Edwin gingerly extricated himself from the exhausted naiad and picked up the sleeping figure, easily carrying her to the banks of her pond. His feet sunk into the bank as he deposited her on a bed of newly grown moss.

For the next little while, Edwin sat by the mostly dead campfire, poking its embers idly as he watched the emerald motes of light slowly fade away or drift into the dark tree line, vanishing from view.

As always, his thoughts eventually drifted toward, horror of all horrors, reliving every painful human interaction he'd had . . . pretty much ever, in reverse order. Tonight, he was stuck on his very recent conversation with Inion.

Why couldn't he be normal there? Yeah, yeah. Everyone had those memories of an awkward social situation that kept them up at night. He knew. But just . . . a complete inability to do anything when he literally had an attractive girl who maybe liked him in his arms?

The rational side of his brain berated that line of thinking, though. She wasn't human and he couldn't forget that. She was nice to him, but that didn't mean she really cared about his feelings. She was probably just acting nice because she *was* nice, and just enjoyed messing with him.

Edwin buried his head in his hands. *Why* did people have to be so complicated? Why couldn't anyone actually be nice to him because they actually liked him instead of it just being their default? Everyone else always had such perfect little friend groups where they'd chat and usually let him somewhat join in . . . not that he was ever invited to, or really allowed to, join in the conversation.

Even though he told himself it wasn't possible that *everyone* hated him, it could be so hard to actually feel that way. Not when he'd be laughed at as he was trying to get something off his chest, or when his supposed friends would spend time with him only so long as none of their actual friends were available. Not when people would turn away from him or choose to avoid him when possible.

Even if he was just the second choice for his "friends," being the second choice for *everyone* still just . . . hurt, after a while. Edwin couldn't shake the feeling that was what was happening here. Inion clearly was a fan of people in general, but she was also more or less trapped within the Verdant, or at least claimed to be. Did she only make their Bargain because it was either Edwin or nobody?

He sighed. Probably. At least he could pride himself in being "better than nobody" for a sociable fey, at least for the time being. She'd already shown she could leave whenever, so she'd probably abandon him the moment someone more interesting came along. Just like everyone else.

With another sigh, Edwin got to his feet. There was no point in letting himself sit here in social misery for the entire night. He was alone, just the way he liked it. Who even needed friends? Just a bunch of exhausting individuals who demanded time and attention without offering pretty much anything in exchange.

He tossed a couple of logs on the fire before retiring to his bed, his last night in his little makeshift shelter. Upon seeing the tiny, bioluminescent mushrooms that had sprouted inside, he wasn't sure if he should be disgusted or delighted.

He settled for "asleep."

Morning brought with it daylight and even more birdsong than normal. A bleary-eyed Edwin stumbled out of his lean-to, wishing that he had gotten more sleep, never mind that he was still objectively more rested than if he had spent the entire day lying around and sleeping.

"G'morning, Inion." The naiad was sitting on a rock at the edge of her pond, toe dipped into the water and absently humming an ancient tune.

She turned, broken out of her contemplation. "Ah! Good to see you up." She gave a beaming smile, vivid green eyes sparkling in the early morning illumination. "Big day today."

"Oh?" Edwin dropped himself by the edge of the pond, taking a seat on a decent-size stone. "What's happening?"

"Planning!" she cheered. "We're gonna look over all your Paths and figure out what it is you wanna take first, and figure out what last Skills you wanna take!"

Edwin groaned, at himself as much as at Inion. Yes, that was exactly what he wanted to do today, but why did she have to say it in that manner? Why was it so hard to want to do something cool just because someone else was pressuring you into it? "Can I at least see my new house first?"

She jumped up, landing deftly on the surface of the water and padding over to him. "Of course! I did a lot of work on it, I wanna see your reactions to it." She marched right past him, grabbing his hand and pulling him along. He could have fought against it, but he couldn't marshal the willpower needed to do so.

Edwin did reclaim his hand as they got to the cabin, though, to run his fingers across the walls. They were relatively featureless and fairly uniformly covered in an unfamiliar type of bark. Almanac was no help in determining the type of wood he was dealing with, and its rough surface was distinct from the nir he had used in its construction. It reminded him of something, though, but he couldn't quite put his finger on it (heh).

"Could you have done this from the start?"

"Ehhh . . . *Normally*, I'd say yes. I coulda done something *similar* without your work, for sure, but it wouldn't have been quite the same. When we go over your Paths, I'm sure you'll see what I mean."

"So . . . was all that time I spent working to dry out the wood wasted?"

"No?" Inion cocked her head. "No. Even putting aside your Skill growth, the cabin needed to be properly established and built to last in order to work. Otherwise, awakening it as your home wouldn't have worked the same way."

Edwin's ears perked up at the hint as to what happened and couldn't resist a follow-up probing question. "So, with it being awakened as my home . . . what does that entail? How does that relate to putting a roof on it?"

She stopped and thought for a moment. "It's . . . complicated. Maybe being able to complete it, and fit it into the Wild pattern, made the song especially potent for it, making it truly sheltered *by* the forest, rather than from it? I'm no magi, no scholar, I'm not entirely certain."

"Potent how? Wait, you aren't a mage?"

"I am; I'm simply not a *magi*."

"Those are . . . hang on, say 'mage' then 'magi' in just a moment . . ." He focused on turning his Polyglot off, to see if it was just translation, and signaled for Inion to speak.

"Miseh beag tha, c'hann idann e." Edwin stared at her uncomprehendingly, and she sighed and spoke up again, "Beag, idann."

Edwin turned Polyglot back on. "One last time. The full sentence."

"I'm a mage/beag, not a magi/idann." Inion sighed.

Edwin frowned. Was this the first time the way Polyglot translated words somewhat obscured by their actual meanings? Or just the first time he'd noticed? He should probably try to make an effort to actually learn more languages at some point. He still mostly remembered how to speak Dwarven, and with Polyglot, a higher Research Skill level, and Memory, it should be relatively trivial to pick up more.

"Can you teach me your language at some point? There's definitely something being lost in translation."

Inion beamed at him. No, that wasn't beaming. It seemed too predatory for that. "Why, but of course, Edwin. It will be my *pleasure*."

What had he just gotten himself into?

The inside of Edwin's house was . . . well, magical. There were faint motes of blue and green light floating through the space, illuminating the interior even in the absence of windows. Granted, the illumination was aided by the ceiling—the leafy boughs of some unfamiliar tree allowed golden sunlight to pierce in some places, though when Edwin looked for the corresponding holes in the foliage, he was unsuccessful.

Though the dirt floor was bare, it had been smoothed and compacted, providing a firm base for Edwin to later install actual flooring. The interior walls were much the same as the exterior, made of one mass of living wood.

Edwin's Alchemy corner had been split into two floors, interestingly, with wood in the approximate shape of stairs leading to an upper wooden platform, and the space below it having been slightly dug into the ground, with enough space that Edwin would be able to stand fully upright under the upper floor.

"Nice taste." Inion nodded approvingly as she looked around the space.

"Wait, what do you mean?"

"Well, it's your home. You're the one the song was trying to make comfortable. This is apparently what you wanted?"

"I designed this?"

"Well, sorta."

"Can I . . . grow it, or change it somehow? How can I install a door?"

Inion shrugged. "It's alive, so it should still grow."

"That . . . doesn't answer my question."

"Pity." She ran her hand along the walls, which Edwin realized were . . . huh.

"It's properly sized?"

"Whaddya mean?"

"The inside . . ." Edwin pointed at the walls and ducked his head outside to confirm. "It's not bigger than the outside."

Inion stared at him, uncomprehendingly. "And that's a *surprise*? Didn't you come from somewhere without magic?"

Edwin nodded. "Yeah, but . . . since I've been here, pretty much every building I've seen has been, well, enormous on the inside, regardless of how big they are on the outside."

"That's unusual." She frowned. "*Every* building?"

"Well, so far as I've seen anyway." He dismissed her next question with a shrug. "Not all by the same amount, but yeah."

"Back in my day . . ." Edwin chuckled and Inion shot him a glare. "I'm not *that* old. Back in *my* day there were some shrines like that which I saw, but they were all made by this one guy with a Skill that made whatever he made bigger on the inside. I think he called it Efficient Interior or Efficient Space or something like that. But you said this was common?" Edwin nodded, which made her consider things. "Weird."

Inion tapped her leg in thought. "You said the Liras Empire controls who gets Skills, right?"

Had he mentioned that? "Uh, more or less? They like, have an approved list of what makes a good Class, Skills, and Paths and stuff."

She snapped her fingers. "That's gotta be it. Whoever it is figured out how to reliably get Efficient Space, or whatever, and now it's standard fare for anyone building stuff. That's gotta be *insanely* complicated though. Efficient Space had to have been fourth tier at least, and keeping track of that many possibilities?" She shook her head. "I do not envy whoever is responsible for that. Still, good for them! Reliable reproduction of Skills can be so useful. It's easy to get something going in a general direction, but replicating an exact effect across an entire civilization?"

She eagerly turned on Edwin. "Which brings us to *you*. Time to get to work!"

CHAPTER 17

Skillful Applications

Level Up!
Skill Points 551→610
Progress to Tier 2: 787/1590
Basic Mana Sense Level 36→45
Walking Level 40→42
Athletics Level 52→57
Breathing Level 52→54
Identify Level 43→44
Alchemy Level 60→62
Flexibility Level 27→29
Seeing Level 31→33
Sleeping Level 30→32
Outsider's Almanac Level 82→84
Survival Level 37→39
Visualization Level 42→45
Firestarting Level 45→50
Nutrition Level 28→31
Mathematics Level 39→40
Packing Level 29→37
Mana Infusion Level 65→66

Polyglot Level 36→41
Memory Level 34→36

Wow. Everything except for First Aid and Bomb Throwing had leveled at least once, even Mathematics, which had Edwin confused. He hadn't been using it that much, had he? Or was that just from normal, everyday use, now boosted by Inion's Token?

Heck, why had Alchemy only leveled two times? And Mana Infusion only a single time? With all that pottery? He asked Inion as much.

"Well, you level Skills by mastering them, and it's *really* hard to get them past sixty just using them. Heck, it's hard to get them past *thirty* just through repetition. It takes a *lot* of effort to keep growing afterward."

Edwin frowned. "But my Almanac Skill levels every couple of days, and it just reached eighty-four."

Inion looked at him strangely. "*Really?* Maybe it just levels quickly, then. The only thing that even *might* get it to grow *that* quickly might be absolute constant use and expansion, but it's an active Skill, right? Passive Skills *are* easier to use constantly, but are *also* harder to push, so I'm not sure what you have going on there."

Edwin opened his mouth, then closed it again. "You know what, never mind."

Her gaze redoubled. "How much?"

"Don't worry about it."

"Edwin. How many things in the clearing do you *not* have marked with your Almanac?"

". . . Define 'things.'"

"Anything your Skill works on."

"I'm . . . still working through the leaves on one of the nearby trees."

"How many Almanac entries have you made in the last thirty heartbeats, since we just now started talking?"

" . . . Twel— Thirteen."

Inion shook her head. "I genuinely don't have a response for that. Well. Have fun with that."

Edwin marked off another leaf in the ceiling with Almanac. So what if he recorded every stray thought he ever had with it? Of all his Skills, that seemed to be the one which had no corresponding strain for over-use. It didn't make sense for him to not be using it constantly, with a bare fraction of his 887-character limit used any time.

Anyway, with Skills out of the way . . .

Congratulations! For digging the foundations for a building out on your own, you have unlocked the Physical Laborer Path! Congratulations! For creating your own kiln and successfully making a number of ceramic vessels, you have unlocked the Potter Path! Congratulations! For witnessing and taking part in a Wildsong Ritual, you have unlocked the Primal Ritualist Path! Congratulations! For building a house with the aid of an Elder Fey, you have unlocked the Primal Constructor Path! Congratulations! For finishing construction upon the Hidden Workshop, you have unlocked the Master of the Hidden Workshop Path! Congratulations! For settling in the midst of untamed wilderness, you have unlocked the Recluse Path!

"Aw. It named it for me?"

"Oh, you got a Path that named here? What did it call it?"

"Wait, how did . . ." He shook his head. "The Hidden Workshop. I mean, it's fine, just a bit boring. Can you change it?"

"Ya! Just like you'd do with anything in your Status. Whatcha wanna call it?"

He thought for a moment. "Hmm . . . what's 'laboratory' in your fey speech, whatever it's called?"

"Laboratory." Inion answered quickly enough that she must have *known* she was messing with him, though she managed to— No wait, there was the smile.

"Wait, one moment. Okay, now you can go ahead."

"Obairlann."

"Obairlann. Hmm. I like it." It was pretty simple to make the appropriate change now that he knew what to try for, and the notification blinked in compliance.

**Congratulations! For finishing construction upon Obairlann,
you have unlocked the Master of Obairlann Path!**

Edwin looked through his unlocked Skill offerings. He could say that he wasn't particularly interested in Digging, Carpentry, Clay Sculpting, Axes, or Saws, among others. But there were a bunch that he wasn't sure about. . . . This was getting complicated.

"Inion, what sort of Skills do you think I should get?" Edwin asked as he dropped onto his seat by the fire. Without chairs inside, it didn't make sense to just sit on vaguely stairlike shapes inside Obairlann and be cold when there was a perfectly good fire available. "I want to get something that will be useful and won't take forever to level up. I don't want to take too many more, though, so . . . what should I do?"

"You're an Alchemist, ya?" Edwin nodded. "How many Alchemy-related Skills do you have?"

"Uhhh . . . Depends how you count it, I suppose. I guess Alchemy and Mana Infusion, maybe Firestarting or Nutrition?"

"There's your problem. Sure, you can *do* Alchemy, but your Skills aren't the sort of thing an Alchemist would want. You don't have any Mixing, any Purifying, any Harvesting, Potion-Making, Bottling, Alchemical Potency, Rendering, Herbalism, Ingredient Assessment, Slow Reaction, Caustic Attacks, Catalyze, Separate . . . y'name it. First Aid *sorta* fits a bit, but for the most part, you got *nothin'*. And you might wanna fix that."

"Sure, but what Skills are most important? How many should I take?" A thought crossed his mind. "Hey, didn't you say you'd never met an Alchemist before me? How do you know what Skills they'd want?"

Inion shrugged. "I can fill in the blanks. But ya! *You're* the Alchemist here. What's most important for you? Since you don't want that many more Skills—let's say we bring you up to twenty-four at most, you didn't want to take too many Skills, yeah? I'd say you *probably* should stick with that, because there can be some really, really cool abilities that they give you after a couple advancements, really unique in everything I've seen, which is a *looooot*."

That . . . didn't really help. "Well, what about other Skills? I've been offered Stealth and Reflexes, which have both tempted me."

She shrugged. "Stick with what you'll use, if you ask me—which you are. Sure, Reflexes *might* save your life someday, but you know what else would? Using a Skill you're good at and use regularly creatively. As for Stealth? Well, if you don't wanna fight, you don't have to. Your Flexibility Skill oughta help you there, and if you go for a bunch of Attributes—which you *should*, they're *really* useful for a generalist like yourself with lots of Skills—they'll pick up the slack. Speed'll take care of all your Reactions Skill—"

"Reflexes?"

"Ya, that one. It'll take care of everything you'd get from it and *more*, and might even give more of a benefit than the Skill itself. You improve an Attribute with Paths, after all. Skills you need to practice with. Then again"—she looked off to the side innocently, which immediately put Edwin on guard—"I suppose I *could* help you level up Reflexes if you did pick it up, fairly effectively, too."

What did— Oh. A brief image of Inion throwing rocks at Edwin and forcing him to dodge them with no warning flashed through his mind. Yeah . . . no. She would totally do it, too. He shuddered. "No thanks."

"Awwww. It could be so much *fun*, though!"

"Okay, so just focus on what I'm already doing. Why can't anyone ever offer some kind of *useful* advice? I swear, you guys are worse than a motivational poster. 'Just be yourself!' 'You're on the right track—carry on!' Honestly."

"Hey! Need I remind you that in my day—oh, stop giggling, it doesn't suit you. Knock it off! Back in *my* day, I would have supplicants travel for *days* to receive my advice."

"Uphill in the snow both ways?" Edwin muttered before properly replying, "Yeah? Well, in *my* day it was thirty seconds to find ten times as many empty platitudes as you seem to have."

After a playful glare, Inion shifted such that she was sitting cross-legged. Edwin mirrored her, but pulled himself into a lotus position instead. He'd been decently flexible before Joriah, but having an actual Skill for it brought things to a new level. The fey stuck her tongue out at Edwin's one-upmanship, then allowed her legs to *pass through* each other, momentarily turning to water and re-forming once she was properly contorted.

"Okay then. What do you miss most about your world?"

Edwin thought for a moment. "My lab. The internet. Societal structure. A feeling of safety. Libraries. My mattress—"

"Sorry, sorry," Inion cut him off. "I should have been clearer. What would you want to have *here*, with you now." She thought for a moment, processing Edwin's list. "Did you not have friends that you miss?"

Edwin shrugged, then once he had collected his thoughts spoke up again, "I guess my lab would be most helpful. Also accurate measurements. High-grade chemicals, too. And my chem textbook. I'm sure there are lots of useful reactions that I could turn into alchemical equivalents if I had that."

Inion frowned momentarily at something, then schooled herself. "Well then, okay! You want Skills to make yourself a new lab, and ingredients, right?"

"Uhh . . . sure. But what about measurements and my textbook?"

"Ah, I don't know what basic Skills might help you there. Keep working on Memory, 'kay? That should help with your book. But you want to get high-quality ingredients and lab stuff, right?"

". . . Yes? I feel like I should be concerned."

"Well, the way I see it, you want your final three Skills to be *something* that helps you build non-Alchemy things for your pottery and your lab and all *that* stuff, another that'll assist you when harvesting herbs or bottling griffin blood or whatever, and a last one that'll help you get everything to an"—she puffed out her chest and said in a deep, gravelly voice—"acceptable quality," then broke down laughing at her own joke.

Edwin frowned. "I don't sound like that!" He tried to defend himself, just to be waved off by Inion. "But . . . I guess that makes sense. What about if I'm offered some really impressive Skill, like . . . I don't know . . . Spellcasting? Or Teleport somehow?"

"Then just take it! You don't need to be limited to *just* twenty-four. It'll just be a good marker! If you hit twenty-five or -six, eh. Not *that* big of a deal at that point, though it'd probably be a hassle and a half trying to get it to a decent level, ya?"

"Yeah . . . yeah. I guess that makes sense. Just that everyone seems to think fewer Skills are unilaterally better. Well, except for Lefi, but I don't think following his example is a good idea. It works for him, but . . . Well, maybe one day?"

Inion shrugged. "It's your life. I really just don't care. I am helping you to the best of my capabilities, that's the Bargain, but even if you do something subpar, I *still* can hold up my side. But honestly, a handful of Skills won't hurt you. Cap it at thirty at most unless you decide to take the route of a Wizard. In general, if you can replicate the effects of a Skill fairly trivially and won't be constantly using it, don't bother taking the actual Skill."

"I need to check, because I'm not sure how Polyglot is working here . . . what do you mean by the 'route of a Wizard'?"

"Building up Skills manually instead of using Paths. Use Firestarting to get Stoke Flames or Summon Spark, leverage that to get Fireball, you know. It's a more tra— I can't say that." She snapped her fingers. "I can't say that."

Huh. So Polyglot could use self-assigned terminology. Unless the System was gauging how English worked based off Edwin's thoughts? Hmm.

A passing thought, a half-remembered question from months previous, bubbled up. "Is there any way to remove Skills? So far as I've heard, there's no accepted way, just contradictory rumors."

"Ooh! Good question! I'm pretty sure that I can . . . yep! Got the all clear. You see . . ." Inion's voice cut out altogether as she tried to say something. Her mouth kept moving, but no sound came out. She realized fairly quickly something was up, though, and it returned a second later, ". . . is still in effect. Huh. So she's still alive then? I wouldn't have ever guessed. Sorry about that. I forgot about that one. I have to keep this one secret as long as the person I Bargained with lives, and I kind of figured she would have passed on centuries ago."

That was what it looked like when a Bargain came into effect? That was interesting, along with the idea that Inion was apparently the weaker party in that Bargain, where she couldn't break the terms. "So where does that leave me?"

She shrugged again. "Can't explain that much. [. . . . .]." Inion threw her head in the air. "That's not even a *secret*! It was *common knowledge*!" she grumbled, then snapped attention back to Edwin. "But

Skills! What are you currently being offered? That'll give a good idea for what you might naturally level!"

Edwin flipped through his still-open prompts, giving Inion a quick rundown of what he had available. The naiad stroked her chin in consideration. "I think Construction, Purify, and Harvesting are probably the most interesting there."

"Construction?" Edwin asked. "Why Construction? Purify makes sense, and maybe Harvesting as well? But I would have thought you'd point me more at . . . well, I don't know. But something other than Construction."

"Construction is a fairly broad Skill." Inion explained, "It's a crafting Skill that covers pretty much anything that involves multiple parts, though doesn't help with any magical aspects of that assembly. You can use magical materials, but it's no Potion-Making or Enchanting. Similar to Assembling, but it also aids in *making* the pieces rather than just combining them. Whatever you need to make should fall *well* within its scope, and you'll have quite a few banked levels from constructing Obairlann. Because it's so broad, you won't get the strongest benefits from it—rather like your Athletics Skill, as it happens—but it will aid you in many endeavors. And! It should level up any time you make essentially *anything*. Possibly even Alchemy, though I don't *really* know about that."

"I guess. Purify I understand as well, heck, I was tempted myself. But why that instead of something like . . ."—Edwin picked another Skill he'd been offered that seemed to fit the "make higher quality" bill—"Precision? That might help with my whole 'wanting better measurements' problem."

"Well, *when* were you offered Precision?"

"Looks like toward the end. Maybe when I was trying to get that last knot whittled out of that log?"

"And Purify?"

"Pretty early on, probably from setting up my distillery one morning . . . Ah. You're saying that Purify is more likely to be used?"

"Ya. Precision might be more broad, but it's *also* kinda similar to high amounts of Dexterity. Purify is something you were complaining you didn't really have the right tools for, right?"

"True." While he had primarily been trying to think of how he could make better tools, it had mostly slipped Edwin's mind that he should try and get *Skills* that would replicate what higher-quality instruments could accomplish. Probably because he wasn't thinking about getting a lot of Skills, and he couldn't afford to replace every tool he might normally need with a Skill.

Purify, though . . . Purifying ingredients was probably the single biggest contributor to experimental replicability. He didn't need a Stirring Skill, but a Distillation or Decontaminating one? Yeah, he could use that.

"Round it off, I suppose. Why Harvesting and not Gathering?"

"That's an easy one. Gathering helps you find places that have stuff you might want, Harvesting helps you to actually get it."

Edwin blinked. "Don't I want both, then?"

Inion motioned uncertainty with her scale-balancing hands. "Maybe. But Gathering is less important if you already know what you're looking for or need to know *exactly* what you want. Gathering, *especially* at normal levels, can only guide you toward things you already know where they are. By the time it would be an actual help, you probably won't need it. Harvesting, though, should help you preserve more magic in whatever you take and will make it last longer! Superuseful."

"Last question, I guess. Shouldn't I try for a Skill like Potion Brewing?"

Inion shook her head. "Nah. Too specific for you. Sure, you'll *use* it when practicing Alchemy, but not even always then. It doesn't seem like you're all that interested in *only*, or even primarily using Potions, but you want to branch out somewhat, right?" Edwin nodded. "There you go. Learn how to replicate what you need here with what you have at hand."

Edwin couldn't say that he was exactly sure about it all, but . . . he did kind of need new Alchemy equipment, and the reasoning made sense. Crucially, it matched up with his own thinking.

You have unlocked the Construction Skill!
Accept Skill? Y/N
You have unlocked the Purify Skill!

Accept Skill? Y/N
You have unlocked the Harvesting Skill!
Accept Skill? Y/N

Yes, yes, and . . . yes.

CHAPTER 18

Assume a Spherical Path in a Vacuum

Construction
We can build it. We have the technology.
Create nonmagical objects.
Proficiency increases with level.
Purify
Not useful in separation of variables.
Remove contaminants.
Purity increases with level.
Harvesting
For getting spoils before they spoil.
Recover resources from natural sources.
Ease of harvesting improves with level.
Level Up!
Skill Points 610→636
Progress to Tier 2: 812/1590
Construction Level 0→15
Harvesting Level 0→6
Purify Level 0→4

"Feel any different?"

"Not . . . really? Am I supposed to?"

"No."

Edwin blinked at Inion. Then why . . . ah, it was either a human thing or a fey thing. Either way, not something worth trying to puzzle out. Honestly, he wasn't sure which would be harder to actually put together, though he almost suspected it might be humans.

"Okay, but Paths now, right?"

"Ya! Tell me what you got."

Edwin pulled up his list. It was getting . . . rather lengthy, but they had time.

Current Plan

Adventurer 0/30, Warrior 0/60, Athlete 0/60, Researcher 0/60, Skilled Arcanist 0/60, Potioneer 0/60, Wanderer 0/60, Stonehide Vanquisher 0/60, Scientist 0/60, Outsider 0/60, Blackstone Conqueror 0/60, Mage 0/60, Novice Pyromancer 0/60, World Traveler 0/60, Physical Arcanist 0/60, Field Medic 0/60, Unkillable 0/90, Path Less Traveled 0/90

Save for Tier 2

Micro-Biomancer 0/90, Realm Traveler 0/120, Alchemical Warrior 0/90, Pioneer 0/60, Alchemical Medic 0/60, Titan Slayer 0/90, Explorer 0/60, Giant Slayer 0/60, Superior Alchemist 0/60, Scientific Revolutionary 0/90

Maybe

Novice 0/12, Trainee 0/60, Trapper 0/60, System Scholar 0/60, Survivor 0/60, Daredevil 0/60, Escapee 0/30, Lecturer 0/30, Steadfast Medic 0/60, Rebel 0/30, Arsonist 0/60

Unsorted

Woodsman 0/30, Hunter 0/30, Novice Ritualist 0/60, Feycaller 0/60, Fey Friend 0/60, Feybound 0/60, Feytouched 0/90, Physical Alchemist 0/90, Makeshift Alchemist 0/60, Practical Alchemist 0/60, Chemist 0/60, Biologist 0/60, Physicist 0/60, Experimenter 0/60, Forerunner 0/60, Purifier 0/30, Master of Obairlann 0/60, Recluse 0/30, Primal Constructor 0/90, Primal Ritualist 0/90, Potter 0/30, Physical Laborer 0/30

Probably Not

Lumberjack 0/60, Way of the Empty Hand 0/60, Pyromaniac 0/30, Exile 0/30, Rebel 0/60, Master of the Ruined Tower 0/60,

Razer of the Ruined Tower 0/60

No

Slave 0/12, Assassin 0/60, Killer 0/30, Traitor 0/60, Burglar 0/60

"Hmmm."

"Any interesting insights? Actually, any thoughts about how to get rid of some of the Paths I don't want?"

"Slave will definitely go away if you take Escapee, but probably if you take Master of Obairlann or any of my Paths."

"*Your* Paths? You mean the fey-related ones?"

Inion nodded. "Feytouched and Fey Friend especially. Killer and Assassin you won't get to go away outside of a Pacifist Path, which you *don't* want; you'd need to get a Loyalty Path or something to be rid of Traitor; and Burglar . . . if you got a Reformed Criminal Path, maybe? It'd probably cover for Assassin, too."

She shrugged. "Not that any of those other than Slave is actually *bad*; you might even benefit from them—Killer would advance one of your Skills to be offensive in nature. Harvesting, maybe, now that you have it. Or perhaps even First Aid. Assassin would do something *similar*, but more subtle in nature. If it could affect Alchemy, you'd end up with *something* poison-related almost certainly.

"Traitor . . . perhaps some sort of concealment Skill, advancing Identify, that would hide aspects of your information *from* Identify and its ilk."

"Wait, from Identify?"

"Ya. It and Status are the main Skills that interact with the System, and while they're both kind of ehhh . . ."—she teeter-tottered her hands. "*Generally*, Status Skills help you connect with the System, whereas Identify helps you connect the System to what's around you. There's probably as many exceptions to that as there are examples, but it helps convey the general trends. What returns when someone Identifies you can be influenced through *lots* of different routes. Status, Identify, even Stealth if he wasn't lying . . ."

"Who?"

She waved her hand dismissively. "Doesn't matter. Somebody I knew back when.

"But ya! Burglar would probably give you a Stealth Skill from Flexibility if you wanted it."

Edwin weighed that possibility. Tempting, but he suspected he didn't want to have Burglar as a part of his Class, at least not this early on. It being one of his first ten Paths completed was bound to have a bigger effect than one of his first hundred, right? "I'll pass, I think, though I suppose I'll keep that in mind." He considered something and asked, "How do you know all this stuff? I thought it was insanely complicated?"

"Experience, mostly. Paths have certain . . . tendencies, shall we say? Learning how to read them takes time, but once you get used to it, it's relatively intuitive. It's . . . okay. This is a drastically imperfect metaphor, but it'll work.

"Think of each Path as a Class of its own. Then imagine what single Skill that Class would most want. For an Assassin, that's probably gonna be a Skill that lets you kill quietly and completely undetected. A Burglar would want a Skill that turned them invisible, intangible, and completely silent. A Mage wants one that allows them to use every kind of magic ever, a Merchant would want something that enables them to have an infinite well of stock and a perfect knowledge of what their customer wants and how much they're willing to pay. You following so far?"

"I think so . . . So, each Class has an 'ideal Skill,' which is based around what their overall concept is based around?"

"Exactly! I knew you were smart. When you take that Path, it tries to make that ideal Skill, and to do so, it takes whatever Skill it has available to it—those which have advanced the fewest times—that's already the closest to its ideal and tries to make a new Skill out of it, using the old Skill as a foundation that more closely matches what it wants."

"Okay, that makes sense. But what about for something simple? Like I can't imagine that a Linguist would want anything more than just Polyglot."

"In the case of a *really* close match, you'll usually find that the new Skill is just a more focused or generalized version of the old Skill, though sometimes it's almost identical to the old one and just provides an even *greater* benefit than before. That usually only happens if you use the same Path a *ton* of times, though."

"What about the Skill Point requirements?"

"You can think of those as the fuel for the change. The more points used, the more drastic a change can be wrought. Though what's considered a drastic change isn't always obvious, it's based on what the System sees, not what you do."

"That . . . makes sense, I suppose. Then what about more abstract Paths, like my . . . 'Feybound' one?"

"Those are a bit more complicated, but you can still think of them as having a certain ideal Skill that they're trying to get to."

"Trophy Paths?"

"The item-granting ones? Same sort of thing. If you fought wolves endlessly, what would you end up with? A lot of wolf pelts and teeth, and so Skills will give you something to approach your end."

"I'm not sure if that entirely follows?"

Inion waved her hand. "It's *all* an abstraction. Sometimes a 'trophy Path,' as you call it, will grant some hidden technique that your foe used. I heard a story about one druid who, upon slaying a menacing panther, received a Skill that allowed her to summon a spirit panther to fight alongside her."

That sounded cool. "You can get Skills for summons? What about like . . . bonding with an animal or something? Getting a companion?"

Inion nodded. "Yep! Though you actually *need* a companion first, then you'll be offered a Path relating to it, and completing it will help you bond in some way. It's a connection Path, a bit like your Slave Path, but more . . . equal? If it takes to Status, you might be able to see and influence or even choose Paths for your companion, if it takes to a Magic Skill, you might get a shapechanging ability, or perhaps a summon-teleport, any number of possibilities."

"So then where does the influence of your current Class come into play? Or you mentioned accomplishments with a Skill changing what you get?"

"Well, it's not a perfect analogy," Inion agreed with a grimace. "Not that one really exists. It's all really complicated, and I *seriously* respect the people who made it." As soon as she finished her statement, she flinched *hard*. "I should *not* have said . . . oh hey, no smiting. I guess I'm okay to talk about the creators, then? Ah. Just what you've already put together. So, what do you think, so I know what I can say?"

That caught Edwin seriously off guard. "What I think? Uhhhh . . . Well, I did put together that the System probably isn't *natural*, but was made by someone, who I did presume was either the moderators or someone connected with them. I *also* think that it doesn't apply to anything outside of Joriah, and though there are other worlds—maybe even another Joriah—*none* of them have the System. Instead, this was made for . . . some reason. Entertainment, perhaps? By beings of other realms, like Arcadia.

"I don't know *how* the System works, but I suspect it overlays some kind of magic over everyone and everything in a way that isn't detectable by normal magical means, either inherently or just by intentionally crafting an exclusion for everything that is System related. There's probably more I could put together with a bit of time, but that's all for now."

Inion's expression was unreadable, but Edwin liked to think that she was in shock. "How'd I do?"

She nodded. "You got a *lot* right, though not *everything*. Of course, I can't tell you *what* you got wrong, or anything like that. But it's nice to know what I don't have to be *as* careful speaking around you."

"Happy to help?"

"I'm sure you are."

"Yea— Hey, wait a minute—"

"You wanted my advice on your Paths?"

" . . .Yes. Can we get to that?"

Inion smiled. "Of course, now that you're no longer pulling us off topic."

"*I* was the one pulling us off topic? You were—"

"Would you *like* my help or not?"

Edwin bit back his retort. "Continue."

"So! You've got yourself a bit of a problem, don't you? Some three hundred points below where you should be, given the Skills of yours that have advanced? You need some careful planning, don't you?"

" . . . Yeah. I'm really not sure what to do in that regard."

"Well, you have a few advanced Skills with loads of levels."

"Shouldn't I wait to use those Skill Points for when I'm evolving them, though?"

"What was I saying about interruptions?"

". . . Sorry."

"*As* I was saying, you have a few high-level advanced Skills, and they'll only be higher level by the time you'd advance *them*. So, I'd say you should use those for any Paths that give you an Attribute."

Edwin frowned.

"You may speak."

He glared at the smug fey. "I was collecting my thoughts. How do Attributes fit into the whole 'ideal Skill' metaphor? Also, how would I know which will? Oh, or do you mean like after they reveal themselves to be Attribute-granting, then I mentally pretend those Skill Points came from Almanac or whatever?"

"Yeah, exactly like that. Attributes . . . they come about when . . . oh man, this is going to be tricky to explain without tripping into stuff I can't say . . . let's say the Class needs some aspect to properly function.

"A Mage needs mana to do anything, a Warrior needs to be able to survive hits they take, a Scout needs to be able to understand whatever they get, a Diplomat needs to influence those they meet, that sort of thing. It'll also happen when the System notices there's an easy Attribute to give, or something *you* really need. Again, it's all quite complicated, I'm just giving a *very* general guide."

"Fair enough. So then what does that mean?"

"Well, it means you only need to worry about your current Skills paying off your point lack, and not about any extra you'll need for Attributes. *That* means you'll want all your Skills to be . . . what is that?"

"Seventeen points above their Path cost." Edwin rolled his eyes at Inion's glare. "You asked!" He sighed dramatically. "Sorry for interrupting."

"I was getting there. But yes, seventeen points. So when all your Skills are at least level seventy-seven, then you should start to advance them. If you're feeling adventurous, get them to a *hundred and seven* and take all ninety point Paths! Now, that'll take a while, but with my help and my Token, we might have you all set in less than a year! Or five years, if you wanna go with pricier Paths."

"So long?"

"Hey, it takes most people some fifteen years to get to level *sixty* in their Skills. Advancing the last one was seen as the mark of an adult back in my day. Getting ten levels past that? Yeah, a year is making good time. Thirty past *that*? You're lucky it isn't a decade."

"What about choosing Paths?"

She shrugged. "We can do that now if you really want, but you might want to just take them later, once you have more to choose between?"

Edwin said, "Whatever you think is best. Though this still feels a bit like 'just do what I've been doing' again."

"Well, what you've been doing has worked well so far."

Well, a year wasn't *that* long, when she put it that way. Still, though. A *year*? That was a long time. But at the same time, that was also a year of being generally alone, with nobody but Inion to talk to save perhaps occasional trips into Vinstead for supplies?

It sounded so very isolated and alone.

"Sounds good to me."

She laughed, "Perfect! Let's get started."

CHAPTER 19

High-pH Training

For the first month, Construction turned out to be essentially trivial to train. It seemed like every time Edwin turned around, he had a new level in the Skill. Granted, that was mostly the result of him officially "moving in" to Obairlann.

While he was forced to use green wood for it all, Edwin managed to make himself a decently sturdy chair out of a few young trees, lashed together with copious amounts of rhoreed and using the same for a woven seat and backing. At Inion's insistence, he made a second chair, which turned out significantly better than the first.

Edwin was able to use much the same method for a "door." It had no hinges and was basically just a frame of wood with rhoreed tightly woven in the center, but it did its purpose serving as a block for wind and insects. He didn't have any sort of latch to it, either, and just had to pressure-fit it all into the doorframe. Not ideal, but sufficient for the time being.

Making a table was somewhat trickier, but after a few failed attempts Edwin was able to cut himself boards and make something that didn't immediately fall apart. Despite his best efforts to try and make glue from the hooves of his hunted deer—though great for training both Harvesting and Purify—it was ultimately fruitless, so he eventually abandoned that approach, and instead tried to make glue from tree sap.

Although the glue that resulted from just melting dried resin and trying to Purify it wasn't *great*, it still worked, and rubbing in sawdust helped take care of the residual stickiness as Edwin used it to keep his table in one piece. It still wasn't anything fancy, just a set of boards glued and lashed together set atop a frame structure similar to his chairs, but it worked well enough to keep his bowls off the floor as he slowly covered it with several layers of rhoreed mats.

His second table he set up in the elevated corner of his house to function as a workbench. While the "basement" might have been a more traditional place for an Alchemy lab, subterranean structures had awful ventilation. Granted, the "upstairs" wasn't *that* much better in the absence of windows or most anything else, but the leaf ceiling allowed fresh air in and contaminants out well enough for the time being.

Speaking of the leaf ceiling, Edwin didn't have the faintest clue how it worked despite many, many experiments. It allowed more nondesirable gases to pass out of it but not into it, which included smoke, but managed to keep heat in quite well. It allowed light through, but was waterproof (Edwin had tested by hauling a giant bowl of water to the top and pouring it out—not a drop made it in). He couldn't fall through it, but when he was inside he could easily move the leaves out of the way to leave. Perhaps most curiously, it shed no leaves on the *inside* of the house, but certainly did on the outside.

Asking Inion was fruitless; she simply said that it was the magic of the place and didn't know how it worked.

Still, a month in, Edwin had a lab bench, a table, chairs, and *loads* of clay bowls and pots. At a certain point, he transitioned from trying to make earthenware to actually making bricks—he still wanted a *proper* kiln, and bricks were the way to do it.

His first batches of brick, being as pure of clay as he could manage—Purify was happy—turned out . . . all right. His test batch was sloppy and irregular, as he wasn't going for consistency until he had a good methodology down. At first, he wasn't firing the bricks long enough, but then found that putting them in for longer just resulted in the outside being . . . singed?

In time, he figured out what was going on and settled on a consistent mixture of clay with sand as a filler, mixed together and dried in a form over the course of several days. Once the bricks were dry, he could stack them inside his kiln—he could only do batches of about ten to twenty bricks at a time at first—and then slowly increase how ferociously the flames burned, providing bursts of Firestarting at times to help up the temperature. Toward the end of the cycle, he had the Skill turned on constantly, producing some insanely hot flames. He never fed Mana Infusion into the mix, though. He'd get around to experimenting with it eventually, but he didn't want to destroy his kiln with a stray explosion.

While the resulting bricks weren't *great,* they were functional. In time, Edwin built up enough of a brick collection to make a more traditional kiln. To aid in insulation, he at first kept using a pit, but dug out his former shelter to the level where the soil turned to clay. From there, he surrounded the kiln with fire on all sides and burned it as long and as hot as he could manage. The bricks helped to diffuse the heat somewhat, and while a couple cracked from the fire, the trial was ultimately a success, as he lost fewer bricks in the firing and the setup wasn't nearly as complex.

A few iterations later had him making a hefty topper to a tower-shaped kiln surrounded on all sides with fire. After a while and a few rebuilds later, that was permanently assembled, mortared together with additional clay, and Edwin kept it burning nearly constantly. Firestarting reaching level 60 meant he could keep it going almost indefinitely if he really tried, though the amount of focus it still required meant he couldn't maintain it while sleeping.

Even between batches, Edwin didn't allow whatever he was making to cool, instead fashioning himself a set of grips that allowed him to pull out the kiln's contents and put in new materials without burning himself. Even then, he needed to use his gloves, which resulted in a few pieces of pottery lost due to fumbled retrievals.

The trade-off was quite worthwhile, though, as his kiln slowly accumulated an outer wall to help contain the fire's heat even better, complete with air intake and chimney.

Now that he'd finally completed it, he decided to try and use his kiln for other purposes, like drying wood for the firepit inside (Obairlann letting smoke freely pass through the ceiling was so convenient) when he didn't feel like keeping Firestarting up.

It was . . . a work in progress. Initial tests had just resulted in the wood he had loaded up catching fire and burning themselves to ashes. Curiously, *Purify* had lent its hand to cleaning all that out, which made Edwin wonder how far its effects spread.

He didn't know for sure what had caused the wood to catch on fire, but he rather suspected that it was the result of the interior of the kiln being within the range of his Firestarting, and in doing so making the drying wood spontaneously combust when the heat was turned up. Unfortunately, turning off Firestarting altogether didn't seem to heat the wood up enough for any significant effects, as the green wood didn't burn hot enough without Skill assistance.

It was a . . . frustrating conundrum. He needed to somehow figure out how to exclude an area from his Firestarting *while* maintaining it for hours on end. Worse still, despite his best efforts, Edwin could barely even shape the area of effect, which seemed to be stuck at an approximately four-meter radius centered on him. Concentrating with all his might allowed him to create a tiny divot in the sphere, changing the border in a small area by a centimeter or two, which at least let him know what he wanted should be *possible*, just really hard.

In the space between Obairlann and Inion's pond, the two of them had started a small garden, primarily using seeds from Edwin's dried foodstuffs. Thanks to Inion's Gardening and related Skills, they had already harvested a bunch of beans and lentils from his first generation, and the second generation was now well underway.

While Inion could speed up maturation of plants and had done so already, letting them harvest their first crop a week after planting, she claimed that doing so repeatedly wasn't good for the soil unless specifically treated, or if she had the right Skill.

Given what Edwin recalled regarding soil fertility, nutritional contents, and crop rotations, that checked out. What surprised him more was that Inion claimed some plants—particularly magical ones— would be utterly ruined trying to speed them up at all. Others could only be sped up with specialist Skills, whereas others required you *didn't* use Skills on them, or perhaps they needed a particular magical fertilizer. . . . It was a whole mess and Edwin was glad Inion could fill in a lot of the *Grimoire*'s gaps of knowledge. Naturally, he dutifully recorded all such tips and techniques via Almanac on the corresponding pages.

Despite the complexity involved, they still had a section of the garden dedicated to said magical plants. Firevine—Inion had managed to locate a sprig of the stuff through some technique she claimed was just raw talent—was growing along the walls of Obairlann, a small shrub of common purple-edged glowleaf stubbornly clung to life near the bond, and Edwin was doing his best to ensure his sunstalk got a proper foothold and survived past sprouting, a task he had thus far been unsuccessful in.

Firevine lived up to its reputation. Its leaves were a deep, dark red, which lightened to white along the edge, and their irregular shapes *did* look reminiscent of tongues of fire. Under careful examination, the sprig felt slightly warm to the touch, and while it hadn't quite spread enough for Edwin to be sure, it looked like it grew in an irregular, firelike pattern.

Glowleaf plants were apparently quite common, but the exact type of bush that he'd found was supposedly less so. With purple edges and greener, more powerfully glowing centers, seeing the bush at night looked mysterious and otherworldly, blue-green and violet hues mixing strangely as he glanced over them.

Sunstalk, or at least what bare scraps of the stuff Edwin had available to him, was the most spectacular-looking plant he had. In direct sunlight, the sprouts seemed to vanish into a mere glitter in the sunbeams, only reappearing when the illumination died down some. When it did so, it would release much of the built-up sunlight, bathing its immediate surroundings in a touch of daylight for about a minute per hour of sunlight exposure.

It probably would have looked significantly cooler if Edwin had more than a half-dozen successfully sprouted grasses, as according to the *Grimoire*, the light-releasing patterns resulted in fields of the grass rippling with sunlight when in darkness, light being transmitted from stalk to stalk and dying out quickly but not without putting on a spectacular light show first. Still, considering what he had, Edwin was content. Heck, he wouldn't have had what he did now if he hadn't noticed some tiny grass seeds mixed in with what he had left of his dried sunstalk.

Well, that was how life went sometimes. He didn't have a strong need for any of the three yet, it was just nice knowing that they were growing. They, particularly Inion, stayed on the lookout for any other plants to add to their collection, especially the healing talsanenris berries, but hadn't had much luck thus far.

Once Edwin had some of those, then he'd be able to make healing potions and have something to sell in Vinstead. He certainly didn't have enough money left over from Lefi to buy everything he'd want. While his hunting had certainly improved with time, and Survival drastically cut back on the amount of food he needed, there was a list of easy-growing plants he wanted to include in his garden.

That wasn't even counting wanting flour, canvas, a whetstone, oil, some more metal bowls to keep him from having to regularly replace his distillery, nails . . . the list went on, but mostly amounted to basic goods that should be relatively cheap to buy yet were impractical to make out in the wilderness. He'd removed soap about a week prior when he'd managed to get a bar of oil and lye mixture to actually turn out properly, but that had only increased his need for oil.

Was it the most comfortable situation he'd been in? No. Was it the most enjoyable time he'd had on Joriah? No.

But it certainly was effective.

Level Up!
Skill Points 635→830
Progress to Tier 2: 989/1770 (Avg level: 45/77)
Alchemy 62→65
Athletics 57→62
Basic Mana Sense 45→51
Breathing 54→57
Construction 15→44
Firestarting 50→62
First Aid 30→34
Flexibility 29→36
Harvesting 6→37
Identify 44→49
Mana Infusion 66→68

CHAPTER 20

Running into Trouble

Edwin jogged alongside Inion, who casually floated through the air at approximately eye level. Well, "jogged" was perhaps something of a misnomer. While prior to Joriah he might have classified his pace as just shy of a sprint, these days the effort didn't even wind him.

". . . and, of course, she decided to finally trust fall *just then* and totally caught me off guard. I technically *caught* her, but that was mainly in the 'my body acted as a shield to make sure she didn't hit the ground' way. She subsequently proceeded to pretend to not trust me for the next six months."

Inion shook her head, chuckling. "That was *entirely* self-inflicted. Did you ever get the chance to redeem yourself?"

Edwin shrugged, a motion lost in the bobbing of his torso as he twisted his way through a tangle of branches. "The . . . last time I saw her, yeah. She was heading out and finally, *finally* let me have another chance to catch her. I succeeded." He smiled sadly.

"That must have been recently, then?"

"No . . . No. It was . . . what, four, five years ago?" *Emotions, get back into your box. Not right now.*

Inion seemed to pick up on how he was feeling, though, and incredibly didn't ask any further questions, the two falling into silence save for Edwin's footfalls across the dry leaves.

Edwin dodged around another tree. While at first his daily runs had been around the clearing, that soon proved to not be enough of a challenge. Jogging through the unexplored parts of the Verdant kept him much more on his toes and helped him also improve some of his other Skills.

Plus, this way he and Inion could cover more ground in search of talsanenris berries and other magical plants. While she'd remained cagey about her limitations, from what Edwin could figure out Inion could leave water more or less freely, but she suffered from a fatigue similar to how Edwin felt when sustaining Firestarting over long periods of time. However, being near him helped alleviate some of that pressure thanks to their Bargain.

On a spur of the moment, Edwin decided to pick up the pace and started to full-on run, pushing himself to a full sprint for short bursts of time. He didn't go at full speed, though. If he exercised too hard, he'd want more food before long, which he tried to generally avoid. Still, he was getting close to the point where he could run at nearly full pace indefinitely. At worst, he had to drop from a sprint into a run to catch his breath. Beyond that, he didn't seem to have any limits beyond purely how much energy he had in his body.

Survival, he found, didn't provide him with extra energy from food—which was what Inion claimed Eating did—so much as it allowed him to go longer without it. It was a subtle difference, and not even one which actually was apparent all that often, but it resulted in Edwin only needing to eat once a day at most, usually once every two to three. After that, he'd start to get hungry . . . and stay hungry, but with no impact to his actual energy levels. It was a similar story with water, though he still got thirsty fairly regularly.

As he waved Inion to slow down, Edwin pulled out his canteen and downed its contents, gratefully chugging the cold water within.

"Water break?"

"Well—" He cut himself off with another swig from the bottle, then, "Yes, but that's not it. I think I felt a twinge from my arcanoception a short way back."

"Your what?"

"My arcanoception. Is there another name for it?"

"Eh, not really. Mana sense sometimes. But you felt something with it?"

"Yeah. Not sure what it was, but . . ."

"You're still hopeful."

He shrugged. "Basically."

"Well, fair enough. How far back was it?"

"Oh, not that far . . ."

Even with both of them keeping their metaphorical mana eyes out, it still took quite a bit of time to actually pin down the location of what Edwin had spotted. Once they did, though, it was quickly apparent why it had been so tricky to find it.

"So . . . does this mean there's a magical oak tree nearby somewhere?" Edwin stared at the tiny object he'd dug up.

"It must. I've never *seen* a magical acorn before, but I don't know what else might have produced it."

"The squirrel that buried it?"

"Couldn't have done it, as I'm sure you've surmised. The mana within it is far more complex than anything even you could do, let alone a Classless critter."

"Any clue how to track it back to where it came from, then?"

Inion just made vaguely noncommittal noises in response.

"Sounds about right." He sighed. "Well, may as well get started?"

It proved to be significantly easier to track down the oak tree than Edwin had anticipated, which was in large part thanks to the sudden appearance of numerous magical plants as he headed toward the northeast. It was turning out to be quite the profitable run today!

With Inion's aid, he was able to dig up a budding hispera bush, prized for its golden berries; a patch of sinbalyne flowers, whose white petals could produce an anesthetic effect; and even a flowering bulb of molai, a neutralizing agent.

Level Up!
Harvesting 37→40

Neither Edwin nor Inion could feel the *cause* of this influx of magical plants, though, which while not inherently strange, did seem slightly odd. Usually, some kind of obvious source of excess mana would encourage the growth of magical flora. That said, with this being the Verdant, such an external source wasn't strictly required, as a powerful nature-attuned ley line ran through the entire forest, prompting rapid growth in mundane plants and encouraging germination of magical plants.

Even then, it was strange to find *so many* magical plants this close to one another, which pointed to there being some replicable cause of higher mana in the area. Edwin had, after all, just doubled the size of his magical plant collection in less than an hour.

After some time walking, the two eventually came across a massive oaklike tree, its trunk stretching far into the canopy above them, casting the entire forest in an emerald glow, the signature indication of a glassleaf tree.

"I think we found it."

"*Really*? What could have *possibly* been your first clue?"

Edwin shot a half-hearted glare at Inion, who merely giggled.

"That." He vaguely indicated the colossal forest titan, towering as it was over even the largest mundane trees around them.

"Hmm. But did you see what's causing *that*?"

"Wait, what are you referring to? Something specific? What?"

Inion nodded toward the trunk of the tree, and while it took a moment, nestled as it was in the shadow of the colossus, Edwin spotted a very particular plant. Black leaves, white berries . . . yep, looked like it.

"Talsanenris?"

"It'd explain the tree," she agreed. "Even without the berries, the bush functions as a . . . node, of sorts, collecting and releasing life-attuned mana. It probably was just a normal oak tree before it picked up that little shrub, and now look at it."

Edwin cast an eye up, and up, and up . . . "All from that tiny little thing? Will it have the same effect growing it at Obairlann?"

If what the *Grimoire*—and Niall, for that matter—said about the berries were even half true, it should be trivial to grow a sustained crop of them. And if it would have this sort of an effect on his garden or possibly even Obairlann itself, then . . . sheesh.

Inion dashed his hopes, though. "No. It's easy enough to cultivate, but unless it's growing in a natural location, it won't have quite the same effect on its environment. Perhaps a slight benefit, but nothing nearly so extreme."

Edwin frowned. "Are we sure that it's actually the bush that's *making* these effects and isn't just a symptom of the sorts of environment that would cause those sorts of things to happen?"

Inion shrugged. He figured. Something to look into if he ever had time.

Still, no sense lollygagging. Edwin didn't know how long his would-be transplanted herbs would survive without being properly planted, so he needed to grab the berries and start heading back. Even approaching the tree, he could feel his Basic Mana Sense lighting up from just *how much* magic was permeating the area. It truly was spectacular.

Edwin knelt down to start picking berries, only for some sixth sense to light up warning him he was In Danger, and as he stood up, his brain starting to process a warning call from Inion—it was already too late, as sharp claws dug deep into his back.

He collapsed to the ground, even as his mind was screaming at him. Well, his mouth was screaming as well, but they were for very different purposes. He felt the piercing pain lessen slightly, and he took the chance to scramble toward the base of the tree and turn around to see what was attacking him.

He couldn't properly see it at first, some Skill getting in the way, but Identify worked well.

Mature Deepwoods Panther

Well, that was just great. What were you supposed to do in a big cat attack again? Edwin didn't have his stick with him—he left it back at camp, but he did have a hunting knife with him. It was easy enough to keep it with him, and with a flourish, he withdrew the shining blade from where he had it holstered.

Just in time, too, as the big cat lunged at him, whatever camouflage it had wearing off just as its claws tore through Edwin's haphazard defense and his shirt, lacerating his shoulders while its jaws opened and tried to go for his throat. Edwin was barely able to fend off getting his throat torn out by tucking his head in and bending forward, Flexibility helping him get his entire head beneath the panther's jaws as they snapped closed on empty air.

He felt the cat's rear claws dig into his legs as it tried to knock him off-balance, but Edwin just laughed. The cat had to weigh some two hundred pounds, which would have absolutely pinned Edwin once upon a time, but now? Compared to the sorts of weights he easily hefted in a single hand these days, two hundred pounds was *nothing*. Sure, it was on giant meathook-like claws instead of carried in his arms, but the weight was the same, allowing him to easily avoid falling.

The jaguar was clearly not anticipating him to resist, and Edwin was able to use the opportunity to twist his arm at what would normally be an unnatural angle and stab at the cat's chest.

The tip of the knife dug in slightly, but nowhere near enough for a finishing blow. The cat yowled in pain and tried to disengage, but Edwin wasn't letting it get away that easily. As its claws were pulled out of his flesh, he grabbed the panther by a limb and threw it into the air. As it slammed into the tree trunk behind him, Edwin took a moment to ensure that he wouldn't be attacked by a second one. Other than Inion warily trying to get close to him, it looked clear.

When he cast his gaze back toward the panther, he did a double take as the beast seemed to have utterly vanished. Could it turn outright invisible? Shoot. He thought its Stealth Skill had worn off. Perhaps it was more effective against the tree bark?

Well, no matter. Edwin had practice dealing with foes he couldn't see. A barrage of Infused Identifies later, he had the blasted cat tagged with a persistent Identify box letting him know where it was.

So far as he could tell, it had grabbed onto the bark of the giant oak tree and was preparing to pounce back onto him. A split second later, the panther was midpounce, trying to take Edwin by surprise once more.

He was actually ready for the attack this time, though, and Edwin was able to twist around; he avoided the cat's teeth but still was struck by one of its paws. Even that, however, didn't go well for the feline, as

Edwin used its own momentum to his advantage, driving his dagger into its paw.

Edwin nearly lashed out with Firestarting as the cat withdrew, trying to burn his assailant to a crisp, but stopped himself. If he accidentally burned the talsanenris bush, then this would be for nothing. Perhaps more crucially, he wouldn't be able to use it to help heal himself afterward . . . which he would definitely need, if he basically unleashed a firebomb centered on himself. He'd keep Firestarting as a backup, but without a way to truly control where the Skill affected, he couldn't use it as a ranged attack.

A melee attack, though. That, he *could* control. Edwin threw his dagger at the circling cat, who tried to dodge. The result was that instead of striking the panther in the throat, the knife just slammed into and destroyed one of its eyes, and it roared in frustration and pain. It wouldn't survive with only a single eye, and Edwin could tell the moment it decided to not flee, but instead try to kill him for the pain he'd inflicted upon it.

It was an oddly cognizant decision for an animal, but he didn't have time to ponder that as he needed to deal with a two-hundred-pound predator lunging at him one last time.

Edwin straightened his back and reached out with his hand. The moment he felt fur touch him, his skin tear under the claws and teeth of the cat, he unleashed everything he had.

Mana Infusion.

Firestarting.

He felt the flames blow back onto him, his magic not protecting him from fire meant to harm, to kill. Edwin screamed in pain as his hand began to burn and fangs closed around his wrist. The teeth pierced effortlessly into skin, tearing through muscle, cracking bones. All the while his hand was literally on fire, and the excruciating pain drove all other thoughts from his mind other than one.

BURN.

BURN WITH ME.

Edwin started to feel faint, and the headache of pushing Firestarting to its limits set in, though it was minor compared to the agony of his arm.

Then, as suddenly as it started, he felt the pressure let up, and the supernatural strength behind the cat's body faded away.

Edwin still took the full weight of an adult mostly-apex predator directly onto his torso, though, and while Packing helped him not be crushed or have any bones break, it didn't keep him from being knocked off-balance before he could avoid it.

He unsteadily stood up, heart pounding as adrenaline flooded his system. A faint grin crossed his face as he looked at the lifeless body of his attacker, smoking as the corpse tried to burn up from the inside out. He canceled his Skill and kicked the corpse. "That's what you get for . . . messing with me."

His thoughts were sluggish, mind clouding over. But at least he had talsanenris berries now! The bush hadn't been crushed. It wasn't a complete loss, and he could use them for healing potions to fix himself right up. Edwin was slick with sweat from exertion, and he wiped his forehead as he retrieved his blade from the panther's skull. He spared a glance at his arm and—

Oh. That wasn't sweat, was it? Was that really all his? Surely at least some of it had to have been the panther's blood, right? Ooh. That didn't look good.

. . . Wait, was it nighttime already? He didn't think he'd been gone *that* long from Obairlann, but why else would it be getting dark?

Inion's voice barely pierced through the murk to reach his mind, but as his consciousness slipped away, he couldn't understand a word she said.

CHAPTER 21

All in the Execution

Edwin's entire world was one of swimming pain when he finally came to, as if his entire body was on fire. His mind was still foggy and slow, trying to piece together what had happened. Slowly, his muddled and distressed mind managed to recall what he'd gone through.

Jogging . . . plants . . . talsanenris . . . panther . . . pain.

The last thing he could really remember was Inion reaching him. She hadn't even been that far away, it had just all happened so *fast*. Perhaps Reflexes might have been a good choice? Or, rather, he needed to prioritize getting Speed . . . however he might manage that.

He tried to open his eyes, but the effort proved to be too much for his exhausted body, bone-deep weariness of the sort he hadn't felt since before he came to Joriah. Still, he didn't need to open his eyes to check his notifications.

Level Up!
Skill Points 833→839
Progress to Tier 2: 998/1770 (Avg level: 45/77)
Firestarting 62→63
Flexibility 36→37
Harvesting 40→41
Packing 43→44

Sleeping 40→41
Walking 49→50

Huh. Nice haul, considering how quick it'd all been. Then Edwin tried moving again and realized it probably hadn't been *that* quick, at least not including recovery. His muscles screamed in protest, lacerations burning like they were on fire, his upper arm especially, as he slowly pulled his eyes open . . .

. . . He was back in Obairlann. Huh. He hadn't really expected that, though he probably would have if he had given thought to the matter. As he cast his gaze around, he realized why his arm burned so much, as Inion gently stroked his forearm, a smile on her face.

"Oh good, you're awake."

"You . . . brought me back?" he asked, his voice cracked and dry, sending him into a coughing fit, which in turn sent renewed waves of agony throughout his battered body.

"Drink this." Inion proffered his canteen, which Edwin struggled to take, but his arms were unresponsively lying dead at his side. He didn't *feel* paralyzed, not that he'd know what that would feel like, but he certainly was without use of his extremities for the time being. Noticing his struggle, Inion carefully helped him prop up his head and trickled the delightfully cool water down his throat.

" . . . How long was I out?"

Inion shook her head, "Not long. Just about a day, *maybe* two?"

"You . . ." He took another sip of water. "You don't know?"

"Time isn't obvious for us. No internal sense of time passing, unlike you messy mortals, and I've been too busy tending to you."

"Tending to me? I can barely move! I feel like half my body is torn to shreds!" Sounding indignant was an art, especially with no voice and an inability to gesture, but Edwin felt like he could manage it.

"Yeah. *That's* the improvement."

"Was it . . . really that bad?"

She started listing things off, counting on her fingers. "Let's see . . . you had Skilled claws tear up your back, followed by you *picking up* a System-empowered cougar *using its claws in your arms and legs as leverage,* your torso got bitten a couple of times that I don't think you even *noticed,* and to end it all, you shoved your hand *down its throat,* getting it almost *completely* bitten off in the process, and burned it to death using your *fingers* as *fuel.* Yes, it *really, really* was that bad."

Edwin tried to wince but found his body wasn't even capable of that much. "Touché," he painfully agreed.

Inion sighed. "I've been doing my best, I even had you in the pond for a few hours at one point, but my healing really only goes so far and so fast. Really, you're lucky the hand was still hanging on by *literal threads*—I didn't think I'd be able to heal it if it was fully severed. Even as it *was,* I was surprised it worked."

"Shrug. Guess it's good it wasn't severed, then."

Inion looked at him strangely. "Did you just *say* the word 'shrug'?"

"What? It's not like I can actually *do* it at the moment. That's the best I can really give at the moment. Can you help me sit up, by any chance? Lying down and drinking water feels like it's about to go badly."

"For the moment, but you do need to generally stay down. Take it easy for a few days, maybe a week or two. I don't trust my work with your hand to hold up to too much."

Edwin sighed. He hated being laid up. He always had been back on his feet way sooner than he really should have been when he got sick or injured, and his inability to do so at the moment was annoying him more than a little.

"Why couldn't you have done anything? Aren't you some great and powerful ancient fey or whatever? Is a single panther really too much for you?" he teased, once he had his water and was lying back on the rhoreed mats he used as a bed.

"Do you *want* my help?" Inion playfully accused before explaining, "I'm waterbound. I can venture away from streams and ponds for some time, absolutely, but I still am giving up a significant amount of my power when doing so. Not only are nearly all my combat-related Skills related to water, I'm just weaker as well being that far from my pond. If I had tried to interfere more than I did, you would have likely had to protect *me.*"

"Oh, really? You're that delicate?"

She made a face at him. "Just you wait, I'll make you take that back when something tries to attack you next to a river or something."

"Sure you will."

"I will! Just you wait."

As Edwin shifted beneath his blanket (really his cloak), a thought occurred to him that he simply hadn't previously noticed on account of his attention being mostly occupied on the burning pain covering his entire body.

". . . Inion, where are my clothes?"

Instead of giving a verbal response, she pointed toward the table. Draped over the back of one of the chairs was Edwin's shirt and pants.

. . . Well, what was left of them, anyway.

"Ah. Yeah, that'd do it, I suppose."

It took another day and a half of resting and being nursed by Inion before Edwin was able to even start to hobble around. Even when he could move his (left) fingers and arm, he spent most of his time Sleeping and tending to his own wounds with First Aid. His right hand was unresponsive for another week, and weak after that. He hadn't properly appreciated the degree to which his Sleeping Skill accelerated his healing, especially as a part of other healing efforts, but given its leveling rate, it had to be doing something impressive.

He even finally managed to attach the two Skills! Running Mana Infusion through First Aid, he then tied them into the nebulous network that was Sleeping; as he activated it, his recovery rate was *drastically* improved. He was even offered a Skill for it! Bed Rest wasn't useful enough to warrant taking it, though. Not when he had his essentially finalized Skill list.

Even with all his and Inion's Skills, it took Edwin almost a week before he was properly back on his feet. He didn't want to waste the time and so spent quite a fair bit of that working on some of his more neglected Skills—namely, Mathematics and Visualization. By linking the two together through Mana Infusion, a long-standing task he *finally* managed after several dedicated days of attempts and for which Inion was of precisely no help, Edwin was able to create almost a three-dimensional graphing calculator. Attaching Status allowed him to adjust Skills flexibly by offloading some of the numbers to the almost computer-like interface, and trying to Almanac his imagination, while unsuccessful, did bring him up to level 90 in the Skill.

**Congratulations! For reaching level 90 in Outsider's Almanac,
you have unlocked the Expert Path!**

Inion confirmed that getting the Expert Path wasn't terribly uncommon, and in the vein of the Novice/Beginner/Trainee Paths. At 60 points, Edwin probably wasn't taking it any time soon, given his wealth of more appealing options, but it was still interesting.

Once he was finally up and moving again, it still took some time before he was at full capacity. He took the time to try and repair his clothing, which even with Construction was no easy task, given he didn't have any sewing materials. In the end, Edwin had to declare his shirt, which was honestly more rags at this point than actual clothing, a lost cause. He managed to patch up his pants with strips of cloth from his former shirt, attached with glue. It . . . wasn't ideal, by any stretch of the imagination. But it worked, and kept Inion from giggling, so he counted it as a win.

Just another thing to get in town, I suppose. It'll have to be my first stop, though.

He still had a couple of marks, picked up from minor wounds here and there, but they were all dwarfed by the massive claw marks he now had covering his arms, legs, and torso. Inion claimed they looked good on him, but Edwin trusted neither the fey nor her fashion sense, so he remained skeptical.

Inion had fortunately kept the magical plants they'd found—even getting a few talsanenris berries, much to Edwin's delight—as well as the body of the panther, though he didn't get much from it beyond some sharp teeth, claws, and a couple levels in Harvesting. Largely, though, he readily accepted "gardening" as his task of choice while his beaten and torn body healed.

Magical healing was *amazing*. If he'd gotten the kinds of wounds he had back on Earth, it would have taken extensive surgery, oh so many stitches, and probably even more for him to fully recover. Here, though? Other than his slowly fading scars, he was up and about, no physical therapy required.

Edwin also ran some experiments with talsanenris. True to their reputation, all it took to grow the white berries once they were picked was to place one of them in the sun, on soil, and pour some water on it. From there, it was possible to watch it grow in real time, a black stem growing while white roots dug into the ground. Within an hour, the resulting bush was the size of his head, and it flowered within two days.

It took about a week for new berries to grow, but that was still an *insane* turnaround. Edwin took several of the fresh berries and planted them around the clearing, growing more and more bushes until he was flush with the magical plants, nearly making himself a hedge out of them. Once he had a larger stock, he could experiment, and he did so with gusto.

Talsanenris placed on stone *would* still germinate when exposed to light and water, but it would swiftly wither if not given soil. He could even hold it in his hand, to much the same result. Dropping it directly into water, strangely, didn't result in growth—until something solid, such as the bank of the stream or the edge of a bowl, came into contact with it, at least. He could trick it with a pebble, though, but the plant withered away just as if it were on rock.

So. It clearly didn't need photosynthesis, or at least needed it much less than normal. However, it was still limited to needing nutrients. He'd need to try and figure out a fertilization method, then he could try hydroponics before to figure it out for sure.

The berries were edible and oddly bland to his tongue, though not to his Basic Mana Sense. However, when he ate them, Edwin could *feel* the magic within them become digested and fill his body with energy, as though he had eaten a pile of sugar. The energy rush took several days to fully dissipate, but Edwin suspected that was due to Survival. The effect didn't seem to lessen any if he picked a berry and then ate it a few days later, though he hadn't tried it on dried berries or any older than a week.

Using talsanenris as a sort of fertilizer had mixed results. The plants he applied the crushed talsanenris to grew incredibly quickly, almost as fast as the bush itself, but also withered if he used too much. Unlike the natural plant, they must not have been used to extracting so many nutrients from the ground in such short order.

Crushing the berries and mixing them with water into a smoothie gave Edwin a *major* boost of energy, like the world's strongest cup of coffee and largest meal all at once. He was hyperactive and didn't sleep for a *day* after drinking it, though admittedly he crashed pretty hard afterward. Not something to be used on a whim, though useful if he wanted to pull an all-nighter.

The berries were already so full of mana he couldn't Infuse them any further, but Infusing the soil where a bush grew seemed to speed up the growing process, allowing it to yield berries in five days rather than seven.

Edwin mixed up another batch of healing salve once his first one was depleted, using them to help himself mend faster, but found he only had enough for two, maybe three more sets. He was fairly certain that some steps and ingredients in the potion were superfluous, but the only question was which.

Well, only one way to find out. It was time to do *science*.

Level Up!
Skill Points 839→878
Progress to Tier 2: 1036/1770 (Avg level: 48/77)
First Aid 34→47
Sleeping 41→44
Mathematics 42→51
Visualization 49→56
Outsider's Almanac 89→90
Purify 32→37
Harvesting 40→42

CHAPTER 22

e^x=book

Edwin was *ecstatic*. While it may have objectively been a relatively minor discovery in the grand scheme of things, certainly not something that would help him survive if he encountered another panther, or even get him to Tier 2 any faster, it was still pretty great.

He'd noticed tiny odd discrepancies in his "Almanac everything he could" strategy at times, when something he wasn't anticipating would already have a tag, but even with Memory he wasn't really able to figure out any sort of pattern. Well, until now at least.

He could tag *words*. Also letters and other symbols, but most importantly, *words*.

Honestly, he should have thought to formally try it when he discovered he could make notes on parts of his Status, but the way it worked was distinct from most of the rules Almanac obeyed. After all, he could tag something either generally or specifically, with specific overriding general. While a particular rock could be tagged with Almanac, he couldn't put two rocks next to each other and have that count as its own object.

Letters, on the other hand, *could* be grouped in that way. Why, Edwin wasn't sure. What was fundamentally different between two rocks and "aa" scratched into the dirt? Was it because letters when combined formed new discrete objects, similar to how materials would form a new object when assembled? That seemed the most likely.

A quick test, which could determine if it really was the word holding the tag, was to write the same word in two places and see if they shared tags. They did.

Okay . . . what about tagging a specific word, seeing if it overrode the general appearance of the word? It did.

How about . . . trying to Almanac a word, then including that word in another Almanac, and trying to pull up the first entry in the second? That . . . also worked. Wow. This made Edwin's note-taking *so much easier*. He could make his own wiki if he wanted to! Sure, he didn't *practically* need to get even more space than his current limit of 1,206 characters—no, wait, 1,336 now; he'd gotten two levels—but he certainly wanted to now! It also removed the final weakness of his notebook, by turning it completely "digital."

Inion, sadly, did not share in Edwin's enthusiasm—she seemed slightly put off by it, actually—but that didn't dampen his excitement in the slightest. After redoing his entire file structure, using Memory and Visualization as a sort of copy/paste system over the course of a long, sleepless night, he set in to do much the same with his current object of study.

Talsanenris Bush

Identifying the word *Talsanenris* itself brought up a more detailed notification. This way, he could still make specific notes on specific bushes without having to worry about character limits or lost access. Much more convenient.

Talsanenris is a magical shrub whose berries apparently contain potent biologically attuned mana.
Simultaneous exposure to light and water causes the berries to spontaneously germinate, and they can be used as a high-energy food or as an ingredient in several healing potions.
TalsanenrisEcology
TalsanenrisLogbookIndex
TalsanenrisFormulaIndex

He considered leaving each "hyperlink"—as the notes basically were—as a more general word, like Ecology, Logbook, or Formula, within the entry, but ultimately decided that using unique words was the way to go. This way, if he ever wanted to reference his Talsanenris-Logbook3, he just needed to write as much on pretty much any surface to access it. Much more convenient than the alternative.

Edwin's Logbook: Talsanenris

First hypothesis (revised since pretesting began): The flesh of talsanenris berries are functionally pluripotent stem cells with a rapid transformation upon exposure to a different type of cell.

Current hypothesis: Talsanenris contains a form of mana that accelerates an organism's metabolism while also providing it with the energy to operate at that increased metabolism, though not any additional nutrition.

Test on plant (1 berry, crushed and mixed in with soil): After about a fifteen-minute delay, the plant grew at an accelerated pace for several minutes before growing sickly, yellowed, and even growing already-dead leaves in some instances. Seems to match nutrient deficiency symptoms based on loose memories.

Test on captured Juvenile Verdant Meadowmouse (1 berry, fed to it inside its clay box): The mouse's activity skyrocketed for several hours, after which it seemed to suffer no serious adverse effects, other than some level of lethargy afterward.

Test on self (1 berry, eaten on a mostly empty stomach early in the morning): Instant shot of energy, like an energy drink. Heart rate increased, breathing stayed mostly steady. Heightened levels of energy persisted for several hours of minimal activity. Repeat trials showed that vigorous activity can reduce the time of effect.

Test on self (1 berry taken while sprinting at maximum speed when stamina began to wane, approximately every five to six minutes): Berries staved off the effects of exhaustion mostly indefinitely; limitation proved to be running out of breath. See BreathingLevelingNotes.

Variations of berry delivery method (eaten whole, crushed and mixed with water) appear to have the same net effect, assuming the same quantity of berry.

Result: Hypothesis not disproven.

Attempted various Mana Sense and Mana Infusion-related experiments.

Attempt: Infuse berry.

Result: Unable to Infuse, seemingly due to a higher concentration of mana already present in the berry than Infusion is capable of providing.

Attempt: Infuse ground around bush.

Result: Faster germination of talsanenris bush, producing berries after five instead of seven days.

Attempt: Infuse sprouting bush.

Result: Infusion did not occur as usual. Bush seemed to suck in mana forcefully, resulting in a relatively unique sensation. First time this occurred, cut off Skill. Resulted in slightly faster germination. Second time this occurred, allowed to happen. Other than being mildly uncomfortable, no adverse effects were noted. Managed to germinate an entire bush, bringing it to flowering within two days of constant supplying of mana (other than sleeping) and berry growth within a third.

Attempt: Infuse ground around bush daily.

Result: Faster germination of talsanenris bush, producing berries after four days instead of seven days.

Hypothesis: Talsanenris utilizes a mana-based variation of photosynthesis, using atmospheric mana in place of sunlight and creating berries with energy supplied via magic instead of sugars.

Test 1: Attempting to grow bush in complete darkness. Planted berries in a set of pots filled with dirt in the basement, each covered by a large bowl.

Result: Berries initially refused to germinate in darkness, regardless of mana Infused into its surroundings. Tried exposing to torchlight to see if it was the result of requiring both light and water. Torchlight did not begin germination. The berry required exposure to direct sunlight to begin germination. Afterward, mana from Mana Infusion did cause some growth to occur, though much slower as compared to the outside trial. Bush did not grow as large as others, and never began to flower. Slight discoloration in leaves. Possible nutrient deficiency?

Test 2: Planted berries outside, covered by a bowl. Exposed to sunlight for initial germination, minimal exposure thereafter. Mana was provided by slipping arm underneath to minimize direct exposure to sunlight. Watered in a similar manner.

Result: Berries germinated as normal, grew as normal, producing berries after an average seven days. Outgrew the bowls they were initially placed under on day 4 to day 6, though.

Test 3: Planted berries outside, covered by a bowl. Exposed to sunlight for initial germination, minimal exposure thereafter. Watered daily by lifting up the edge of the bowl.

Result: Berry germinated as normal, grew as normal though produced berries after nine days. Outgrew its initial bowl after six days.

Edwin pulled at his hair in frustration. What the *heck* was up with these results? Even discounting the occasional bush that just refused to grow—not that there were many of those—nothing made sense!

He'd spent the last two weeks running overlapping growth trials, only to end up with almost contradictory results. It clearly didn't need light to grow, except when it apparently did—or was that just nutrient deficiency? It benefited from mana to grow, but didn't need it . . . where was the energy coming from?

"Okay, what am I doing wrong?" he eventually asked Inion, whose smug countenance was mocking him with silent knowledge.

"Oh, I haven't the faintest clue. I *told* you, I'm no magi."

"Yeah, but you ought to have at least some idea as to what's going on. Like, you have to have a more accurate Mana Sense than I do, if nothing else. Mine's almost useless save as a yes or no detector. It's like my Geiger counter from RadLab but magical!" he ranted.

"Should I understand what that's supposed to mean?"

"No, no. You're fine. Just annoyingly imprecise equipment from back home."

"I see? Well, nope. I don't know. Just know that there is magic in *everything*, but that doesn't mean it can't be stopped."

Edwin blankly stared at her. "Was that supposed to tell me something new? Or are you just trying to confuse me?"

She shrugged, and Edwin rubbed his forehead. "Or are you also clueless and just saying something you hope will sound intelligent?" He sighed at Inion's beaming smile. "I should have known."

Hmmm. Was his bowl adequately blocking mana? Probably not, actually. He had picked it because he knew it would block *light*, but then he'd repurposed it for his nonmana test without thinking twice about it. Actually, he *knew* clay wasn't exactly opaque to mana, given the fact he could Infuse things they were holding.

A bit of testing with his Basic Mana Sense, trying to Infuse objects through the clay, confirmed his suspicions—mana could penetrate through the earthenware bowls with relative ease. In contrast, mana could *not* penetrate into Obairlann, though; perhaps Mana Infusion didn't work because of how thick the walls were? While the inside was perhaps even more magical than the exterior, it was so far the only place a talsanenris plant had not fully sprouted and grown, so it had to be doing something different?

Edwin's Logbook: Talsanenris

Test 4: Planted berries in the soil inside of Obairlann, breaking up a small corner of packed dirt. Some were regularly Infused, some were not.

Results: All plants germinated normally. Infused versions grew more than non-Infused, but neither grew to full maturity. Some stunting of growth and leaf discoloration present. No flowering occurred.

Test 5: Planted berries in pots outside of Obairlann, some covered, some uncovered. Of each, some were regularly Infused, some were not.

Results: All plants germinated normally. Infused and uncovered versions grew somewhat more quickly than non-Infused, but all grew to full maturity. Non-Infused and covered plants grew most slowly, though still eventually bore fruit. All bushes were smaller and more stunted than nonpotted variants, though.

Test 6: Potted berries primarily kept in Obairlann, removed at least daily for exposure to sunlight.

Results: All plants germinated normally and grew to full maturity. Smaller and slower to mature than potted exterior plants, though not by a significant degree.

Conclusion: Mana is needed for berry growth, particularly specific kinds not found inside Obairlann, but while bush growth is significantly less impacted, it is still affected by a lack of mana. Light is not required. Soil nutrients are needed for bush growth but not berry maturation. So long as it has at least some level of sunlight exposure each day, it is capable of reaching full maturity and producing berries essentially normally, though perhaps somewhat slower than normal.

Current hypothesis: Talsanenris is a bush that utilizes mana for growth in place of light, though it does benefit from light in addition to mana. It requires nutrients for the normal parts of the bush and grows at a vastly accelerated rate.

"Inion."

"Yes?"

"There are different types of magic, right?"

"Naturally."

"Okay, great. Can you tell the difference between types of magic?"

"To an extent, yeah," the fey agreed.

"Is there a difference between inside and outside Obairlann?"

"Yeah. Out here is flush with loads of nature magic, like most of the Verdant, plus all the standard types of magic that everything emits. Inside, it's more just normal nature magic for the most part, though a bit of . . . I guess you might call it 'hearth' mana? Protectiveness, comfort, and shelter mana."

"Hearth mana? No, no. Not going down that route right now. Focus." Edwin collected himself. "Everything emits mana?"

"Oh, yeah. Fire mana comes from anything burning, water mana from water, air mana from wind, you name it, it's got magic."

That was strange. "So wait, everything is magical? Why can't I feel it with my Skill?"

"Who's to say you don't? It's also really weak, just barely there. It wouldn't surprise me if you can't. Unless you're in the middle of a massive storm or at a volcano, or in the largest patches of untamed wilderness on Joriah, you won't feel very much of it."

"*Is* the Verdant the largest untamed wilderness on Joriah?" Edwin frowned.

"Blight if I know. *Still* haven't been able to leave, remember? It was one of the largest back in my day, though."

"Right, right. So wait, it's magical because it's so massive? I thought it was so massive because it's magical."

"Eh. Turtle, turtle."

". . . What?"

"Oh, right. That wouldn't translate, would it? Basically, that means it's hard to say which was *first*, but they both play a role now."

Ooookay then. Well. He'd come back to that later.

"So . . . do you know how these berries work, magically speaking?" Sure, he could have asked beforehand, but he wanted to run his experiments with minimal external influence.

"Mm. I'm pretty sure they're just really rich with life mana."

"Life mana?"

"Life mana, nature mana." Inion shrugged. "It's all pretty similar. You can use it in all sorts of different things."

"So . . . how do different types of mana interact, then?"

Inion smiled. "Isn't that your job?"

Level Up!
Skill Points 878→898
Progress to Tier 2: 1053/1770 (Avg level: 48/77)
Basic Mana Sense 51→53
First Aid 47→50
Sleeping 44→46
Outsider's Almanac 90→93
Harvesting 42→47
Memory 40→43
Nutrition 36→41

CHAPTER 23

Nice and Slow

Edwin may have been lacking in magical expertise, so his current testing methodologies, limited as they were to exposing objects to Mana Infusion and Firestarting/Infused Firestarting, were rather inadequate.

The *Grimoire* claimed that loads of materials utilized various kinds of mana. Seagrass was strongly water aligned, firevine was, naturally, fire aspected. A footnote in a mostly unrelated section mentioned that talsanenris was extremely life attuned, far more than the minuscule amount most plants were. He'd have to try to collect some of the more exotic plants at some point.

Magical creatures also had some very magical and very interesting mana affinities that could be Harvested from their bodies. Death-type mana could be found in the marrow of shade vultures, while their wings were more air aligned. Pele wolves had blood that was *literally* magma; storm cicadas didn't have blood or even the normal bug equivalent and were instead filled with lightning-charged air.

The coat of a winter fox acted as a filter, turning ice mana into fire and life. The venom of a death's head wasp (and wasn't that a terrifying name) transformed life mana to death mana.

Hydras naturally produced massive amounts of either poison-infused life mana or life-infused poison mana, meaning their blood could be used for either deadly venoms or potent healing potions. The blood of dragons was so bursting with life mana it spontaneously transformed into other types and infused their bones, scales, and wings, making them utterly obscene powerhouses.

. . . Honestly, there seemed to be a lot of life-rich magical creatures. It made sense to a certain extent—unlike some of the more unusual mana types, everything living had life mana running through its veins. Literally, as it so happened. Blood was the most potent source of mana in any given creature.

He'd have to look into all that later. No matter how much he wanted orchicalcum and its insane magical conductivity, anmanium or phytium to drain mana away from magical sources . . .

Nope! Edwin was going to be focused on what he had here and now. And that was Firestarting and Mana Infusion.

Attempting to use Firestarting on the berries didn't have much of an obvious effect, not that Edwin expected one. It was when he tried to experiment with an Infusion that things got interesting. Though he didn't know what kind of mana he was Infusing with—according to Inion, everyone's was personal, and she didn't know how it was tested beyond it involving a potion. Perhaps he could see about finding out when he was back in Vinstead. Maybe it was like a blood-type test or something? He might be able to swing something with Tara if he asked.

Infusing Firestarting on the berries resulted in burning berries, which went up almost as fast as flash paper, just a small burst of flames and it was gone. Setting Firestarting on a *bush*, however, allowed Edwin to pull a pretty decent Moses impression, as ethereal blue flames danced along the trunk and leaves of the shrub, burning but not consuming it.

As he sustained Firestarting for as long as he could, Edwin noticed the leaves of the bush slowly discoloring, turning from their normal black to become ever so slightly . . . blue? A very, very dark blue but blue nonetheless. Inion had no clue what was happening, but Edwin couldn't help but wonder if it was slowly trying to use the fire mana from Firestarting in place of whatever light mana or whatever it typically utilized.

But why would that make it *blue?*

No matter how long he spent using Infused Firestarting, Edwin could never get the leaves to be anything but a deep shade of midnight blue, and he didn't feel up to keeping his experiment running for a week at the moment.

After he made his trek into Vinstead, perhaps. But not right now. He seriously wanted a new shirt and pants in addition to all his other desires, none of which had lessened. Really, given how his distillery had broken his last spare bowl for it a few days past—the lower bowl cracking under the heat—he seriously wanted to get stronger materials for . . . everything, really.

What did he have to offer, though? He'd need something to trade that either helped despite the existence of Skills or helped Skills themselves. The obvious answer there was talsanenris, but could it really be that rare, given how easy they were to grow? Edwin hadn't seen many on sale when he'd been in town before, but there could be any number of reasons for that.

Well, whatever. That just meant he'd need loads of them to make any appreciable amount of money, and to make up some alchemical potions with them as well. He wished he had more time to experiment and create a reliable healing potion without the need for ingredients he didn't have in overabundance, but he really, really wanted that shirt. He still had time. He had all the time in the world.

Four thousand, two hundred seventy-eight.

That was the number of talsanenris berries he had to trade. He'd used a few dozen making up two final batches of healing salve, which he was prepared to sell, and harvested every ripe berry every bush had.

It might as well have been weightless. Ten pounds was *laughable* to Edwin these days, and he stuffed all of them inside a few clay pots resting inside his backpack. He had his cloak, his stick, all three knives, a dozen dried pitch-soaked pinecones, his filled canteen, a single long-neglected heating stone—he should try to integrate some in place of one of his fires—in case all his healing potions weren't worth much, and his coin pouch.

He was fully rested after a good night's sleep, his shoulder was only a little bit stiff from the panther attack, and he'd just eaten a single tal-sanenris berry for energy.

It was time to head out.

It *had* been time to head out ten minutes prior.

"Inion, if you aren't done in the next two minutes, I *am* leaving without you."

"I'm not ready yet!"

"What do you even need to *get* ready? I have never once seen you take anything anywhere we go, do literally anything with your appearance, and I've only ever seen you sleep a *single* time."

"I'm almost done!"

Edwin buried his face in his hands. "You know, this might count as you interfering with my work. Get moving!"

"Okay, okay! I'm ready."

"Finally. What the heck were you doing?" Edwin was half expecting Inion to look completely different to how she normally did, and so had mentally braced himself for something unusual. What he hadn't expected, though, was there to be absolutely *no* apparent change to her appearance in the slightest.

"Oh . . . this and that."

". . . You know what? I think I decided I don't care enough. Let's just . . . get going."

They traveled alongside Inion's stream, both because it made it easier to avoid getting lost, and because the naiad had an easier time moving when connected to her water. All Edwin's practice moving through the undergrowth seemed to be paying off, as he was able to almost effortlessly navigate the tricky riverbank. Even with Packing offloading the weight of his pack, he still sunk deeply into the soft soil right next to the water, so he was forced to contend more with the tangle of plants where the earth firmed up.

Even with that limitation, they reached a larger stream by noon, which in turn fed into a fairly sizable river (not the Rhothos, though) by early afternoon, and they reached the edge of the forest by midafternoon.

It was, ironically if predictably, there that they encountered their first roadblock. Edwin had wondered what it looked like when Inion had issues leaving the woods, but now he knew.

"It's like . . . trying to go straight from water . . . to a desert!" Inion struggled, pushing against some unseen barrier as though struggling against an impossibly strong wind. Her hair was blown back, her outfit was ruffled, and her hands struggled and failed to find purchase in thin air. "Oh come on, help me!"

"Oh . . . I don't know. I think I'm enjoying the show," he ribbed back. "Bit of a turnabout from all the times you've basked in *my* misery. Just be glad that you still have a *shirt*." It said something about how hard Inion was struggling that she didn't have a comeback to that remark, and Edwin sighed.

"Okay, fine. Let me give you a hand." Edwin set his backpack and cloak off to the side and extended his arm toward Inion, who latched onto it like her life depended on it. Strangely, Packing didn't seem to help him pull the naiad forward, but Edwin still managed, his feet digging into the ground to give him enough traction.

Then, the pressure released, all at once, and the two of them collapsed into a tangled heap, nearly falling into the river before Edwin stabilized and lifted Inion off him with a single hand, setting her down next to him, picking himself up and dusting off his torso and pants before pulling on his bag and cloak once more.

"It feels strange . . . Kind of painful, like I'm *miles* away from my water . . ." Inion frowned. "What sort of spell could have managed that sort of effect?" She prodded at the invisible wall, apparently feeling no resistance. "No, wait. I can still feel it on the other side. What in all the Seasons?"

"What is it that connects you to your pond?" Edwin asked, curious.

"I'm not actually *sure*. I've never needed to know." She scrunched her face together. "*Blight*, this itches. I probably wouldn't be able to come out here at *all* if not for the Bargain's support. Even still, *not* sure how long I can stand it."

"What would happen if you don't get back?"

"Eh, well if not for the Bargain, I'd start dying pretty quickly. I'm not supposed to be apart from my water, like how you need to breathe.

With it, it'll just become more and more uncomfortable, and I *might* still get to the point of dying? It'll take *significantly* longer, though."

"Are you . . . going to be okay?"

"I'll be *fine*. At least for now. Just don't take *too* long, like you did this morning, eh?"

Well, at least Inion was still able to laugh at Edwin's vaguely offended, inarticulate response. She couldn't be *that* bad off.

It ended up not being terribly difficult to find a road, contrary to Edwin's expectations. Simply walking out of the forest into the no-man's-land between the Empire and the Verdant instantly showed them where civilization began. The road, running parallel to the imposing woods, stretched on as far as the normal eye could see, but Edwin was still able to make out where it turned far down the line, heading toward the city.

Interestingly, despite the road only being hard-packed dirt, the river literally running through it didn't soften the soil in the slightest. No mud, no sand, no rocks. There wasn't even a bridge! The water just struck one side of the road and seemed to magically permeate the dirt to emerge unslowed upon the other side. It was as though the river had decided to somehow just *ignore* the presence of a massive dam. As far as magic went, it was pretty interesting, and Edwin mildly started brainstorming the possibility of copying the effect somehow. Maybe he could use it as a filter of sorts?

Inion similarly seemed intrigued, though she refused to elaborate on why beyond voicing unspecified disgust at the "unnatural" Skill. Edwin had to bite his tongue *exceptionally* strongly at that declaration, before he started ranting.

According to Almanac, they were either walking down the same road Edwin had taken to get to the Verdant in the first place or someone had moved every pebble at the side of the road from somewhere he had walked. He figured the former was more likely, though the sights were very different.

Given the way the Rhothos now covered the road on both sides, as opposed to just where it had been on his left, flooding season was still going and possibly still picking up. Like the river, water just seemed to seep through the ground beneath the road, leaving the cobblestones completely dry.

"I'll admit to being impressed. This sort of large-scale project would have *never* been possible back in my day. Too many conflicting Skills. What sort of ability might have even *led* to this sort of effect?"

Edwin chuckled. "If you think this is impressive, just you wait."

They didn't manage to quite make it to Vinstead that day, despite their best efforts. Instead, they found themselves spending the night in one of the Curicn shrines that Lefi was so fond of and had passed appreciation of onto Edwin.

Edwin luxuriated in the sensation of a genuine mattress, infinitely more comfortable than the pile of mats he'd grown used to, as he watched Inion float cross-legged in front of the "shrine" part of the building.

"It's nice to see that some things haven't changed."

"These were around back then?"

Inion nodded. "Car'rakian. God of the hunt, the horizon, and hospitality. He or his messengers would wander the lands and they'd bless those who gave them shelter. In time, a tradition sprang up that every village would have a dedicated shrine to him, which everyone helped to build and would oftentimes be the nicest building in the village. It would be offered to travelers who ventured through, that no individual might claim Car'rakian's blessing solely for themselves, but it might instead be spread throughout the community. I suppose the tradition morphed at some point in the last few centuries to this"—she waved her hand at their surroundings. "But *this* part is exactly the same as it always was. The same symbol, the same layout for prayer . . . it all feels *wonderfully* familiar.

She turned to him. "Sleep now, Edwin. I just need to speak with my god."

"You're religious?"

She didn't answer, but Edwin felt exhaustion press in upon him as her voice began to pick up. She was singing a song, and this one he was not meant to hear.

"O'er the western mounts, to the shining sea beyond.
From the depths below to the skies above.
I see . . ."

Level Up!
Firestarting 63→64

CHAPTER 24

City Troubles

"It's grown so much!"

"Wait, you've been here before?" Edwin furrowed his brow in thought. "I thought you hadn't?"

"What would make you think that?"

"Just . . . actually, huh. I'm not sure. I guess I didn't think it was old enough?"

"Your mistake!"

"So, ah . . . What was it like before?"

"Well . . ."

The two of them were closing in on Vinstead, with some of the outlying homesteads and traffic picking up slowly in density. The city itself had just appeared over the horizon, with its clouds of avior circling and rising and falling.

"It was a lot smaller, right on the border of the Verdant, and there weren't so many birds."

"Those are avior, not . . . wait, on the border of the Verdant?" Edwin asked incredulously.

"Ya!"

"Holy . . ." Edwin tried to imagine how big the forest must have been. "Why is it so much smaller now?" he wondered aloud.

"Less mana in the air."

"Huh?"

"Weren't you asking?" she asked with a knowing grin. "But ya. There's a pretty strong drop of magic between here and in the Verdant proper. The plants won't grow nearly as fast as back there, or for some of the more magical ones, not at all."

That was . . . interesting. "So avior aren't native to the area?"

She shook her head. "Nah. Well. We had a *few*. But humans were dominant up here. That of course meant halflings, and the Verdant was popular among elves and creal."

"The—" Edwin paused as a courier blazed past them, whipping up the air in the wake of their passage and leaving a roar of wind. "The what?"

"Creal? Big, woodlike, fans of nature?"

"Distinct from fey, I take it?"

"Oh yeah. They're more like . . . sentient plants? You might know them as . . .. Talor? Leshys? Treants?"

"Wait, you *have* those?"

"I'll take that as a *no*, then."

"I haven't even heard of them. Well, not in the context of being real, anyway. Elves I've heard rumors of living nearby, but treants? Like, living trees and stuff? Nope."

"Strange. They weren't rare back when. I wonder what happened to them? But anyway! Vinstead is *old*. It's been here longer than I have and gone by lots of names. Vinstead. Vinstead. Vinstead. They all basically mean the same thing, though."

"Let me guess, 'the wine place'?"

"More or less, ya. How did—ah, Polyglot? It translated?"

"More or less, yeah," he tossed back.

The hustle and bustle of their surroundings only increased as the density of homes slowly increased. While the aesthetic was distinctly medieval, the overall layout of the city's sprawl seemed more distinctly modern. Then again, Edwin didn't really know what city layouts back in the early-mid thousands were really like. Maybe it was true to that as well.

In some regards, Edwin could understand why technologically, Joriah might have been somewhat behind Earth. When Skill-powered humanoids and animals were more than capable of outputting more energy than a basic steam engine, why would one ever be developed beyond the state of being a novelty?

Naturally, from Edwin's perspective, that was utter nonsense. Industrialization offered opportunities and capabilities to the masses rather than just specialists, and it opened avenues unimaginable to preindustrial civilizations. But that was the crux of the matter, wasn't it? It was unimaginable, so they didn't push through the initial high-difficulty, low-reward problems of early steam engines.

Inion stopped floating at some point, walking or at least pretending to walk, and her hair also began to follow the normal laws of physics.

"So you *can* control it." Edwin muttered, only to be ignored by Inion. He took it as a victory.

Although Edwin had initially been hesitant to venture into the city itself and possibly leave a trail to where he was for whoever Clan Blackstone might have sent after him . . . after two months in the wilderness, he felt safer. He doubted whoever might be tracking him—if indeed there was anyone, he was starting to suspect that he might just not have been important enough after all—would still be looking around Vinstead, where he officially hadn't been in nearly *three* months.

Risky? Yes. But he wanted to check in, not have to deal with the vendors on the outside of the wall, and report his progress to Rizzali. Edwin had made an agreement, after all, and he intended to follow through on it. He had many, many faults. But being a deal-breaker was *not* one of them. Also, he generally appreciated dealing with the government directly. They'd been the nicest of any organization he'd met so far, after all.

The southern gate of Vinstead wasn't terribly busy when they arrived, and the two of them only waited in line for a few minutes to be allowed in, Inion successfully restraining her tendency to stare at anything and everything. The guards—one a human City Guard, the other an avior Aerial Watchman. The avior took point in questioning them.

"Purpose for visit?" he screeched, *loudly*.

Edwin flinched. "I'm, uh, doing my Adventurer check-in. Also . . . I need to get new shirts."

The guard scoffed. "*Yes*, so you *do*. Show me your license."

Edwin fished it out of one of his pouches and showed it to the Watchman, who looked at it, almost disappointed, then nodded for him to put it away. Edwin obliged and prepared to walk through when the human blocked his way with his spear.

"And your companion?"

"What about her?"

"I need her license as well."

"Uhh . . . she doesn't have one? That's some—"

"Then no entry."

Edwin frowned. "That's something that I'm trying to help with while I'm visiting." It *wasn't*, but that didn't matter. He knew there was no chance Inion would give full details on her Class, but a bit of a white lie seemed like it would help here.

"She may enter when she has a license."

"But you can only get a license inside?"

Edwin wasn't sure how he was able to tell the avior was sneering at him, but he definitely got the impression that he was. "Not my problem."

"So . . . what's she supposed to do?"

The bird shrugged. "Get a license."

"For which, she needs a license?"

Nod.

"Do you not see the problem here?"

"T's not my problem. Your girl wants a license, that's your issue."

Edwin tried to formulate a response, but Inion sauntered over first. "Is there a problem?"

"No admittance for Outlaws."

"I am *no* Outlaw!"

"With a Class like that? Ha! My feathers aren't that blue! Listen, missy, I don't care how big of a shot you may be wherever you are, when you're here, you—"

"Oh, come on now." Inion became undeniably magnetic, attention immediately pulled to her from everyone in the surroundings as her voice became sultry. "Surely there's no reason to be like this?"

Edwin felt a stirring in the back of his mind, pulling him to want to do whatever she asked, but he found it was easy to quash. It wasn't directed at him, and he'd grown used to her presence. If he were to guess, maybe their Bargain also shielded him from the effects. It clearly wasn't weak, though, as there was a bit of muttering from a few random passersby about letting her in, what harm was there?

A glare from the Watchman silenced those murmurs, though, and even Edwin felt it reverberate through his heart, a sudden sense that "something" would Not Be Tolerated.

"Outlaw," the Watchman started, leveling his spear at Inion. "You have committed crimes against the Empire, including but not limited to unlawful use of a Mentalism Skill, use of a Mentalism Skill against an Officer, assault of an Officer, and rejection of Citizen Status. Have you anything to say in your defense?"

"I don't know what you could be talking about!" Inion seemed surprised, though about what specifically Edwin wasn't sure. "I'm innocent."

"Overruled." The avior nodded at his partner, and the second guard moved in a blur, impaling Inion with his spear.

"No!" Edwin started, but stopped when he realized she looked wholly unfazed. On a second look, he noticed that where she was stabbed had turned to water. The avior realized this as well, though, and with a sweep of his wing, she was sent flying into the distance. He turned to Edwin, as well, who held up his hands and took off running after his companion.

He eventually found where Inion had splatted into the ground, hundreds of feet back. She had weakly pulled herself together and was panting on the side of the road, attracting a few odd glances before people hastily pulled their attention back and hustled along.

"Are you okay?"

"Ya . . . Ya. I just wasn't expecting that. He must have a Resistance Skill or something . . . ugh." She winced and held a hand against her stomach.

"Are you *sure*?"

"I'll be fine eventually. Being cut off from my water means it's harder for me to recover. Normally, a mere guard couldn't do anything to me if they tried, but without access . . ."

Edwin raised an eyebrow. "You must have flown three hundred feet there. You could normally just shrug that off?"

"I'm powerful!"

"Sure you are. Hence the panther and now this."

"It's just been bad circumstances!"

"Anyway, what's your plan now? I don't think they're going to let you in, especially now."

"Sneak in?"

"How? I'm *not* going to climb those walls, not when I can literally just walk in so long as you aren't tagging along."

Inion closed her mouth. "How'd you know what I was thinking?"

Edwin glared at her.

"Fine, fine. I'll . . . figure something out. You head on in, and I'll catch up again."

He frowned. "How will you find me?"

"Ancient and mysterious fairy powers, obviously."

"Just try to be somewhat inconspicuous, okay?"

"When am I not?" Edwin glowered at her, which just provoked a pained smile in turn. "Just go on, I'll be fine."

"You sure?"

"Ya. Totally. You couldn't do anything anyway."

"Well . . . fine. If you're sure."

Getting through the gate was much easier without Inion messing things up. Other than another awkward exchange with the guards, there weren't any obstacles for his entry, and Edwin was able to make it into the inner city no problem.

He kept a close eye out for any pickpockets or thieves who would try to pilfer something from his bag and decided he wanted to visit the garrison first. Who knows, they might have somewhere he could sell his talsanenris berries, or at least know where he might.

Now, the trick was just *finding* it. He knew that so long as the buildings kept looking nicer, he was heading in the right direction. While he was stopped a few times by City Guard patrols, presenting his Adventurer's License was enough to get them to move on, and he was able to use their help to point him more directly to where he was trying to go.

* * *

The garrison was just as impressive as Edwin remembered it. A smooth, almost seamless square made entirely of white marble, inset with a black eagle, lay before him, and imposing marble walls loomed on the far side of the plaza, their copper lines tracing geometric patterns and shimmering in the sunlight. Edwin took a deep breath as he stepped on and through the open space, sure he was about to get attacked or called out or . . . something.

When nothing did confront him, Edwin let his shoulders sag in relief as he passed under the arch opening into the complex's courtyard. Then, he picked himself up as he entered the massive, cathedral-like structure once again. The enormous statue of Xares was still in place, and Edwin was able to remember where to go for once, climbing up the cramped stairs to the registrar's office.

"Certainly! It's a pleasure to see you, as always, young miss. I know you'll go on to do great things!" Rizzali's scratchy voice echoed down the stairs, followed by a voice Edwin didn't recognize.

"Thanks so much, Mister Rizzali!" She sounded young, and almost as enthusiastic as the gnome himself. "I can't wait to show Kara!"

He chuckled. "You were the one to do the hard work. We always want to see more young folks taking such an interest in their future. You'll make a wonderful healer one day, Lys."

"Thanks!"

A tiny brown-haired figure in a green-trimmed child's tunic nearly ran headfirst into Edwin as he exited the stairwell. "Whoops! Sorry!"

Edwin turned and watched as the Novice Healer—wow, she seemed young to have a Class. The merchant Aerfa's younger child, whatever her name had been, didn't have one. Was it different in some way for avior? Edwin watched as Lys darted down the stairs, the pitter-patter of her feet swiftly retreating.

"Ah, children. They bring an old gnome so much joy." Edwin turned back toward Rizzali to see the gnome wipe an imaginary tear from his cheek, "And Edwin! Truly, this is a good day for me! Back for a check-in? New Class I see! Do tell."

Edwin cast his gaze back to where the girl had run. "What was up with that?"

"Oh, Lys? Truly a remarkable girl. She's got it in her mind she's going to be a healer one day, and by Hitar, she'll be a force to be reckoned with. She managed to get Status up to level *sixty* by the time she turned eight and had already gotten the Anatomist Path! Ah, it warms a Registrar's heart to see."

"She's already Tier two? Wow, she's beating me."

"What? Oh, no no no no. You see, Anatomist, so long as you don't already have First Aid, will upgrade Status into Diagnosis. So, as long as you have an adequate level of Status, you can freely accept the Path! And Diagnosis is *quite* useful. It allows you to see health problems directly on your Status, and if you upgrade Common Knowledge into Healer's Insight, the two are synergistic enough that you can see a patient's entire list of health concerns all at once. So, I gave her the upgrade and First Aid alike today! Truly, a wonderful day."

Edwin frowned. "How does that all work, anyway? Like, I know that the Empire manages to keep people from just accepting Skills, but I never really thought about what that entails in a practical sense."

"It's quite simple. The Good Emperor Xares has his Management Skill, which sets Registrars such as I as the only ones permitted to confirm Status prompts for all Lirasian citizens. So, when one wishes to complete a Path or accept a Skill, they come visit me or one of my colleagues, and we check to ensure that it is the best choice for them to make given their occupation, then grant it if it is."

"Why not let the individuals make that choice?"

"Well, because they do not know all that we do. If not for us, we would have poor fools taking Knifework instead of Small Blades or Cutting, or Assembly instead of Construction. And we can make sure that they don't take a Path that would mess up all their Skill upgrades.

"It's a full-time job, the average citizen simply doesn't have the time to assess every possible Skill and Path combination for their Class, and even if we tell them, they *still* don't think! They just take every Skill that they unlock with no thoughts for strategy or planning! It's disgraceful, I tell you." He shook his head. "But that's not why you're here, I'm sure. So, tell me of your magnificent adventures, o Adventurer! Hedge Alchemist is fascinating, do tell me!"

* * *

It only took what felt like about an hour to catch Rizzali up with Edwin's new Skills and Paths and explain what happened with the Beginner Path. It seemed to give the gnome a pleasant puzzle, though, as he stroked his colorful chin. "Interesting . . . I've never heard of such a thing happening before. Beginner simply always upgrades Identify. In the rare case where Identify is not available, it tends to help out a Skill to help learn about the world. I suppose I could see how Memory *could* fit into that, but it is still quite a puzzle. Quite a puzzle indeed."

Edwin sat in silence as he waited for the man to finish thinking. "And those Paths! Oh, truly marvelous! I have never heard of many of those Paths before. The academic potential here is *boundless*! Alas, I wish I could encounter the fey you woke up, but the Verdant is far too dangerous for me to venture within; I salute you for making the attempt."

Edwin frowned. "Hold on, I never told you where I went, how did you . . ."

"My dear boy, I'm not an idiot. There's only one place you could have gone to cut down trees and make yourself a house, let alone make friends with a fey! Truly, a stunning achievement, though I wish you could tell me more about it . . ." He must have seen Edwin's expression, because he calmed him with a reassuring gesture. "Don't worry, it won't go on any of my paperwork. I understand the concern, but rest assured I fully support your efforts."

Rizzali paused, and Edwin fell silent in thought.

He was cut off by a familiar voice calling out, causing him to jump, "Edwin? You really are alive?"

CHAPTER 25

Social Niceties

"Lady Tara! Welcome! What brings you to my office today?"

"Rizzali. Good to see you." The Enforcer greeted the gnome and turned back to Edwin. "I thought you'd be dead for sure."

Edwin shrugged awkwardly. "Ummm . . . surprise, I guess? Why would I be dead?"

"You dropped off the map for some three months after leaving Lefi without a trace. The only explanation for *that* incredibly stupid move would be that you got yourself killed somewhere. Which would be an absolute waste, but . . ."—she sighed—"I am pleased to see that you survived. Come, tell me of your endeavors."

"Umm . . . I'm in the middle of my debrief with Rizzali? And I kind of wanted to ask a few questions?" Edwin hazarded.

"Not a worry! The lady's time is far more valuable than mine. If you desire my advice, I shall be here when you return!"

"Come along now. We must speak in an area more private, regarding your more sensitive matters." Tara motioned for Edwin to come along as she entered the stairwell and started climbing.

"Wait, actually? Why?" Edwin hastened to catch up with Tara. "What does it matter to you?"

"Because my . . . superiors"—she hesitated on the last word, seemingly conflicted about something—"have deemed that I be assigned to you as a liaison. You have been deemed interesting enough to be kept up with, and I, with my preexisting relationship with you and geographical proximity, was assigned to the task."

Edwin frowned. "Why am I so interesting? I thought you weren't going to tell them I'm a—" He cut himself off as they passed an open archway, then finished, "My condition."

"I did not. However, it *is* my duty to report low-threat persons of interest to my superior, and you most *certainly* qualify. That I was unable to explain to them *why* I considered you such a person of interest merely heightened their certainty." She sighed. "It is objectively good for you. You have been officially designated as an Ally of the Empire—which I assure you is *not* a simple matter, nor so easy for most individuals—and are granted access to additional services in exchange for task-based taxes."

Edwin frowned. "Don't I get a say in this?"

Tara didn't answer as they reached the floor she was leading him to. They ventured down a short hallway lined with doors far too close together for most purposes until Tara picked one seemingly at random. It opened up to a comfortable, if sparse, room with a few chairs and a table in the center. It was, naturally, far larger than it should have been due to the distance to the doors on either side of it, but that was hardly a surprise by now. They ventured inside, and Tara closed and locked the door behind them.

"There. This is as much privacy as it is possible to find within the garrison."

"Nobody's listening in?" Edwin was hesitant, and Tara picked up on it.

She sighed. "To the best of my knowledge, there are no spies, eavesdroppers, or other parties capable of listening in on the discussion we are to have, save the Emperor himself. Nor am I aware of any efforts to circumvent the Privacy Skill upon this room. This I swear on the Honor of the Empire."

A notification popped up.

Silver Blade Tara Lisana has sworn an Oath of Privacy and Secrecy

Silver Blade Tara Lisana has broken: 0 Oaths

Edwin waved it away. "You didn't say there's nobody listening in. Just that only the Emperor could manage it."

Tara nodded. "Yes, well. This being very decidedly *his* land, he hears all he cares to. I don't think he's trying to do so today, but rest assured that he almost certainly is already aware of your Status. He is quite able to listen to all within his domain if he desires."

Edwin raised an eyebrow, then sighed. The Empire had . . . honestly been pretty good to him thus far. From the sounds of it, they wanted to use him, but he'd take being useful over nothing, he supposed.

"All right, fine. I guess." Edwin sank back into his chair. It felt *so nice*. "What's the 'service tax' thing, though? I'm not going to be enslaved again, you can count on that."

Tara shook her head. "No, nothing of the sort. It just means that if I'm in the area on a mission and deem it useful, I can recruit you to aid me." Edwin eyed her warily, and she clarified, "I am already within my rights to recruit . . . *Adventurers* freely for short-term tasks, and Citizens with appropriate compensation. The service tax merely requires you to do so willingly and not attempt to flee your duties if given the chance. Worry not, I rarely exercise this right with your kind. Adventurers are so unreliable it's usually better to do it all myself."

"I guess that's not too bad," Edwin conceded. "It would have been nice to be consulted first, though."

Tara looked confused. "Why? It was objectively the correct decision, why would you care if you had the opportunity to refuse prior?"

"Just . . . I value having a choice, I guess? Like, even if I already know what I'd pick, the option to do otherwise is valuable."

Tara waved him off. "Nonsense. To do so is to merely grant the chance to worsen your life. You are free to make many choices, but we will not allow persons to waste their life. That is the core belief of the Empire, that all are valuable and may be useful."

"But like . . . you can't know everything about me. What if there was some reason you thought incorrectly about what I would want?"

"Such is impossible. We have teams of individuals working to determine what is best for every Citizen and where they would be the most content and useful. Maximizing productivity and satisfaction is our primary directive."

It still didn't sit right with Edwin, but he let the matter drop for the time being. It wasn't worth pushing, not at the moment. He had an inkling that was probably the philosophy behind their Skill control, which he did have mixed feelings about. It seemed effective, if nothing else. They also had the benefit of being able to regularly evolve their Skills, which he was jealous of.

But still, people ought to have a choice! It only made sense. Actually, no, he wasn't about to let this drop. He would fight Tara over this if he had to.

"Edwin? You went quite quiet there. Are you thinking about something?"

". . . No."

"You're lying, but no matter. Tell me of what you've done."

"Well, Lefi was getting sick of me—"

Tara scoffed. "I have never seen that man act even remotely annoyed with a single person. Ever."

"Yeah, I know the type. It just means they're better at hiding it from what I've found. Nobody likes *everyone*."

"Hmmm. Well, very well. Carry on."

"Lefi was getting sick of me, and I dislike . . . causing a problem for people? Being a bother? Regardless, I don't like being around people who don't want me around. So I left him a note and snuck off one night to keep him from having to put up with me."

"He was mandated to aid you for quite some time. Regardless of his personal thoughts on you, he was still to treat you with respect and patience, and aid you while you found your feet. What does it matter his personal thoughts? He was a valuable asset."

Edwin shrugged. "I guess that's where we disagree. I figured I could make it fine on my own, so I made that choice."

"This is why individual choices don't *work*," Tara muttered. "People like you make utterly absurd mistakes due to the flimsiest of reasons."

"Yeah, but the important thing is that it was *my* mistake to make, so . . ."

Tara made some vaguely exasperated noise, and Edwin pushed on.

"Anyway, after leaving Lefi, I found myself attacked by some bandits,"—he ignored Tara's pointed muttering and pressed onward—"who

I successfully *fought off*. I then decided to follow the one that ran off to see if I could track them down to their base, possibly eliminating them as a threat for further travelers."

Tara nodded approvingly. "I take it that went well?"

"Ehhh . . . Well enough? I found the place, a big abandoned tower in the middle of nowhere. Broke in, ended up *befriending* the Alchemist inside—I guess he saw my Class and figured I'd be interested in learning from him. I *was*, admittedly, at least until I found out he was regularly kidnapping and murdering random passersby for alchemical ingredients."

Tara frowned. "Why did I not hear of this?" she muttered. "I should have heard of this if it were regular."

Edwin replied, "Maybe they were smart about who they grabbed? In any case, I managed to take them out and tied up the survivors, delivered them to the closest town for judgment, and ducked out." He paused. "I did snag a few alchemical ingredients—nothing from humans, just herbs!—and a book on Alchemy, so I count it as a win. I burned the tower down after I was done with it, trying to get rid of any hauntings that might be around." He paused again. "Are ghosts a thing here?"

"Ghosts?" Tara nodded. "Obscenely difficult to be rid of without a priest, they certainly exist, yes. Impossible to predict when they might manifest, though. Good job dealing with the bandits, though next time, just execute them yourself and be done with it. Delivering them for execution is adequate, but runs the risk of them escaping and causing further mayhem."

Edwin frowned. "I dislike the idea of deciding life and death, though. It shouldn't be my call."

"They wasted their life, they had no value, and were harming others. The decision is barely one."

"Maybe," Edwin said hesitantly, "but it's still not my preference."

Tara clearly disapproved, but didn't try to persuade him otherwise, which was nice. She indicated for Edwin to carry on, which he obliged.

"Anyway, I came back this way to try and shake off anyone who might be on my trail."

"You certainly managed that. Even Lefi hadn't the faintest clue where you might have gone." Tara tapped her chin. "Though he may have been lying. He sent a letter, I haven't seen the man since he left with you. It's been . . . blessedly quiet, though that just means it will be even worse when he finally *does* show up again."

"I picked up a few supplies in the outer-city markets."

"Outside the walls?" He nodded, and Tara shook her head. "You were most certainly severely overcharged. There's less oversight out there."

Edwin shrugged. "I wanted to be seen by as few people as possible. You would have sensed me entering the city, wouldn't've you?"

"What makes you say that?"

"You sensed me this time, didn't you? You showed up exactly where I was less than an hour after I crossed the gates. And Rizzali's reaction tells me you don't *usually* go to his office. So you had to have gone there for me."

". . . Very astute. Yes, I suppose there's no harm in saying that much. I do indeed have a Skill—an upgrade of Watchman's Intuition, as it so happens—that broadens the scope of what I am capable of sensing. Persons of interest entering the city is one of them, and I came as soon as I felt you settle in place. So, yes. I suppose if that was your goal, you were right to not venture in, previously." She thought for a moment, and Edwin waited for her to continue. When she didn't, he carried on.

"Anyway, from there I went to the Verdant"—that got an eyebrow raised—"and found a place to settle down." The eyebrow kept climbing. "I ended up building a home out there, working on growing some crops, training up my Skills to help."

"You're *living* in the Verdant?" Tara asked incredulously. "And here I thought I already had examples from you as to why people shouldn't be allowed to make such egregious mistakes."

"Hey! It's not that bad. It's pretty simple, I don't have to worry about other people if I accidentally blow something up. I even met a friendly face. I think that it's not a mistake for me, at least. Lots of magic in there, lots of magical plants, lots of ways for me to level up my Alchemy."

"You met another person living in the Verdant?"

"Basically, I guess? I ran into Inion, who helped me get my home established and nursed me back to health after a run-in with a panther."

"I see. And where is she now?"

"Outside the city. I was going to bring her in, but the guard at the gate refused her entry on the grounds of her not being a Citizen. Then he stabbed her. She's fine, for what it's worth. But yeah. Granted, she *did* somewhat bring it on herself, but the guy didn't need to be so rude about it."

Tara sighed. "It *is* the prerogative of the guards to deny entrance to any non-Citizens they deem worthy of such, but they *should* allow an accompanied Outlaw admittance under the escort of a Citizen—or an Adventurer. I endeavor to encourage them to be polite, yet it is not their responsibility nor mine to do so."

Edwin had been marginally hoping the avior might have gotten a talking-to from Tara, and he was correspondingly disappointed to find out they wouldn't . . . but that was a minor matter. "Well . . . yeah. I came back because I want to get stuff like flour or oil. Also a new shirt, because . . ." He glanced down. Cloak or not, it wasn't hard to tell he didn't have a shirt on. "My old one didn't survive the panther attack I mentioned. Plus"—he patted his backpack on the floor next to his chair—"I have a bunch of talsanenris berries that I was interested in selling. My home is a great climate for them, and I have literally thousands of them."

"Talsanenris berries?"

"Don't you know them?" Edwin asked, mildly confused. "They're superuseful."

He flipped open his backpack and withdrew a handful of the white berries. "I've used them in healing potions, they're a great energy booster, and they seem like they could make supernaturally good fertilizer if processed and used properly."

Tara assessed his handful. "Curious, but it seems like they are a known quantity. Common in some higher-quality rations. You have thousands, you said?" Edwin nodded. "Good. I think we can come to some sort of arrangement, then. Once we're done here, I will introduce you to Fanir. He's the Goldclaw—ah, treasurer? Treasurer. He'll be able to connect you to our cooks and medics, who might know more how to deal with your berries and their value. In the meantime . . ." Tara stretched out a hand and grabbed the air, pinching it between her fingers. A moment later, a shimmering silver shirt wove itself into being, and she tossed it to Edwin.

He caught it and assessed the garment. It didn't light up to his Basic Mana Sense, not that he anticipated that it would. Surprisingly, Identify worked on it.

Armor conjured by a Skill of some sort; it can be used for magical wall formation, too.

"This was made by that Skill you use for your armor?"

"Indeed." Tara frowned. "How could you tell?"

"My Almanac Skill—the Status evolution—lets me leave notes on Skills. It recognizes this as the same as your armor."

"Curious. Regardless, it should last until nightfall at minimum. Was there anything else you require my assistance with?"

"Well, I suppose I do have a few questions about what this 'Ally' thing entails. . . ."

CHAPTER 26

Back to the Grind

Edwin didn't end up leaving Tara for a little while longer. A couple of questions expanded beyond their initial scope, which led into a few additional questions, and . . . well, being an "Ally" involved a fair number of benefits he hadn't anticipated. He was given access to various Citizen services, such as access to the Grand Library in the capital city of Xarenia (one of three, apparently) should he ever manage the lengthy, lengthy trip to a city almost a continent and a half away; consultation with Rizzali for Skill advice—not that he'd likely change his current setup, and even Tara admitted that the gnome would so readily discuss System subjects with anyone who showed even a modicum of interest that it didn't make any practical difference so long as he stayed local to Vinstead; he was allowed to use the postal system if he so desired, and could be a recipient of mail as well, though he'd need to get a tracking token if he wanted to ensure his mail showed up in the right city. Even then, Edwin would have to check in at the postal office to actually *get* said mail unless he wanted to declare a permanent office and pay a recurring fee for delivered packages and letters.

Tara also warned Edwin that his status as an Ally meant that Shash'falara, the local governor, was more likely to take note of him as compared to when he was just another anonymous Adventurer. So he ought to expect receiving a summons to appear before her if he stayed in town more than a day or two. Given he had *no* desire to get caught up with courtly politics, Edwin made a mental note to get out ASAP. He wouldn't be able to dodge it forever, naturally, but it was still something he was *more* than happy to foist off onto future-Edwin.

That conversation had led naturally into Edwin asking about what the Empire was actually structured like, which Tara seemed unusually willing to explain in detail. When he had asked if it was all right he was taking up so much of her time, Tara admitted that she had paperwork that she was trying to avoid doing. Which . . . fair enough. Edwin could sympathize.

In any case, the Empire officially had sixty provinces, though at any given time there were in practice usually only forty-five to fifty due to overlapping governorship, catastrophe, rebellion, or a host of other complicated legal stuff that Edwin found himself completely lost in and even Tara admitted she didn't know all that well.

Each province had three individuals more or less in charge; the governor, who was almost autonomous in their authority; the general, in charge of the military; and the administrator, who handled all the massive amounts of paperwork that kept everything running.

The governor was broadly in charge of everything, akin to a local king or lord. The general was both approximately equal to and yet subordinate to the governor, running the local military recruitment and defense organizations. While they were to report to the governor and were supposed to follow their orders, the general was still paid by and ultimately loyal to the Emperor.

The administrator was in a similar position and was tasked with paying taxes to the Empire, organizing the local registrars, keeping the local postal service running smoothly, and maintaining local information networks with the goal of keeping both the governor and Emperor informed of all the goings-on in the region.

Enforcers like Tara were also apparently on this same level of governors, generals, and administrators in that they reported almost directly to Xares himself, but they were expected to cooperate with their governmental peers, even if they had no administrative power themselves. They were dispatched anywhere it would be either impractical or impossible for normal guards and soldiers to deal with a situation, be it a rampaging monster, a particularly strong bandit group, or other "unusual situations." Most Enforcers knew each other and tended to be on good terms with one another, meaning their effective range of action and authority extended well beyond the single province they were tasked to maintain, though it was usually considered good courtesy to stay within one's home province. Edwin was fairly certain there were *countries* smaller than Rhothos, so even that "limited" area was still massive.

What struck Edwin as remarkably . . . forward thinking of the Empire was the amount of autonomy the governors had. Essentially, so long as neither the province nor its inhabitants started openly rebelling, they kept paying their taxes, and they upheld a few imperial laws, the governor could act as they saw fit. The Skill control was Empire-wide, as were property laws and other forms of protection for Citizens, but other than that, there wasn't much. As a result, a tremendous amount of diversity existed in the governmental structuring.

Some provinces, like Rhothos, had a strictly hierarchical and pseudofeudal structure, with the governor appointing magistrates who ran shires, and some of them appointing mayors who managed townships . . . Meanwhile, the Susa Province near the capital was practically a constitutional monarchy, with democratic elections and everything.

Some provinces had governors who acted like petty tyrants, but those rarely lasted long. Some strictly limited who could become Citizens rather than subjects, while others had the default as Citizenship. Every once in a while, there would be a province that tried something novel, and those . . .

Edwin found it incredibly fascinating until his eyes glazed over, and his brain refused to listen to any more of the Empire's politics. Tara was at least easy enough to talk to, but that still didn't make the specific legal differences between a natural Citizen and a developed Citizen any more interesting. Tara herself admitted that she wasn't entirely certain of the difference herself and was mainly just trying to talk herself through it all in the hopes it would jog her memory.

Even though she didn't talk much about herself, Edwin was still able to pick up a few tidbits about her past. Tara had only been an Enforcer for a few years, was originally from Ecbatana, one of the capital cities, and she'd had a very busy few years since moving out to Rhothos and

Vinstead, putting down several bandit groups that had sprung up in the time preceding her predecessor's retirement.

She'd also managed to pry out a fair bit of information about *Edwin's* past as well, and he managed to stay on topic, explaining parts about Earth when asked for clarifications. Tara had been quite adamant that any political system with no absolute authority figure presiding over it would mean politicians would never do anything even *halfway useful* instead of arguing for argument's sake and purposefully just getting in one another's way, which . . . yeah, he couldn't really argue with that. They had mutually agreed to not get mired in a debate about individualism and set the topic aside for the time being. It wasn't a productive use of their time, not when he had so much to take care of still.

Tara had seemed oddly accepting of the fact that magic didn't exist back on Earth, which Edwin didn't know how to process. But then again, Inion hadn't seemed surprised by it, either, so . . . well, he didn't really know what that meant. He told himself it wasn't important to try and feel better, though it was undoubtedly going to come back to haunt him somehow.

All in all, Edwin found it quite informative and useful. The *rest* of his day couldn't be described nearly so positively, though. He really, *really* didn't care about the logistics of ration-making, which would apparently be the primary use for his talsanenris berries. He had brought *so* many, as it turned out, that they weren't even sure that they'd be able to use them all. They eventually worked out a deal where he'd get paid approximately half their weight in silver this time, and between selling most of his berries and his spare healing salves he was paid a small fortune for his relatively minor crop.

In the end, he got twelve grai (gold), which was more than enough to buy a horse and build a good-size house/workshop. Or buy a really fancy suit. That wasn't even an exaggeration; the clerk at the store he went to, to get a replacement shirt and a few spare changes of clothing, casually said that if he wanted to be fashionable they had high-class outfits starting at merely ten grai. Clothes were *insanely* expensive, apparently.

In the end, Edwin settled for something much, *much* cheaper, and though he was still splurging he found himself in possession of three insanely comfortable tunic-shirts, one in a deep forest green, the other in similar shades of blue. They were also quite durable, even withstanding him directly stabbing the cloth with his knife, and were apparently waterproof. Plus, they would stay clean and resist "a lot of" hazardous materials as part of the Waterproofing Skill. Overall, a fantastic investment. They weren't self-repairing, that was far too expensive sadly, but you couldn't have *everything*.

Edwin also got one outfit in a lighter green for Inion, so her leaf outfit would stop "accidentally" slipping at times. He very nearly didn't get it, but figured that a silver was well worth winning that exchange in their "spars."

Sure, he might be getting a little careless with his money, but he had also found out that what was barely a week of work for him paid him what most laborers would take some six years to earn on their own, so he wasn't too concerned about being stingy. Apparently talsanenris just didn't grow very well outside of the Verdant or something, and nobody had *actually* managed to get a crop of them to fruit before. Edwin wasn't sure why it had been so easy for him, but he also wasn't complaining.

By the end of the day, he'd gotten almost everything he had wanted and had a jug of what was essentially olive oil in an improbably heavy flask on his hip. Apparently the bigger-on-the-inside trend could also apply to containers as well, though it allegedly was a Skill on the oil, rather than the flask. He'd test it anyway at some point. Flour, dried fruits, vegetable seeds, salt . . . he hadn't been sure whether he'd be able to afford much of his list, but the answer was apparently yes.

Though Edwin didn't commission himself any glassware for his Alchemy, he was sorely tempted to. The cost of such things helped dissuade him, though, as he could easily blow through his large-yet-small earnings all at once if he wasn't careful. No, he'd keep things simple for now.

He stopped by Rizzali's office before he left at the end of the day, asking for a bit of advice on how to speed up some of his slower-leveling Skills, mainly Seeing and Flexibility in the hopes the gnome might have some trick to their leveling-up speed. Sadly, he didn't. Edwin did find out that Seeing was generally accepted to just be a slow Skill to level, but it didn't matter much because most people had it their entire lives.

Leaving the city was also fairly uneventful, though Edwin was now laden much more with gear and supplies than when he first entered; he wasn't stopped by any guards or, incredibly, even any pickpockets. He was gone before sunset.

There was still more to do in the city, naturally. He wanted to try to get a healing license, which apparently involved a weeklong course and a test, see if he could get some blacksmithing and glassblowing instruction, and look into what it took to buy an incredibly elusive, true magical item (not counting the minor household magic items made from Skills that everyone used). Not to mention he should probably get some armor and actual weapons, though that would probably fall into the same trap as getting glassware. . . .

Edwin could have probably spent months doing all sorts of things, but he didn't want to stay too long. Both because Inion still hadn't found him and he wanted to make sure she hadn't gotten into too much trouble and also because he wanted to get out of Vinstead before the governor was able to try and meet with him.

Fortunately, he didn't need to look for Inion. As he left the city by the gate he entered through, she slunk up to him from the long shadows cast by the setting sun.

"No luck?" he prodded.

". . . No." She admitted, "There seems to be the same sort of effect that kept me in the Verdant around the city itself. The *gates* don't have it, but . . ."

"You got stabbed again?"

"They're *fast*, okay? I *could* probably get by them, but it would still be so annoying and I'd have to deal with swarms of them and . . . Yeah. It'd be annoying on the best of days."

"And this isn't the best of days."

Inion nodded her head in agreement.

Edwin chuckled darkly. "Well, how much do you have in you tonight? It's been a long day, but I can still push on for a while longer. I wouldn't mind trying to get to the waypoint we were at last night, but it'll be dark by the time we get there."

"I don't need sleep."

"But you do need rest."

She shrugged. "Not unless I do a ritual, usually."

"Fair, I suppose," Edwin conceded. "Guess we keep going."

As promised, Edwin's shirt did indeed fade away around sunset, shortly after they had left Vinstead, the threads unraveling and dissolving into silver motes like so many stars shortly after darkness set in across the landscape. He ignored Inion's playful whistle as he donned one of his new shirts. As light as it was, it still felt oddly heavy in comparison to the essentially weightless Skill construct that he had been wearing.

It was about midnight by the time they reached their destination. Edwin gratefully flopped down on a mattress, his pack carefully placed next to him. He wondered for a few minutes how the shelters were always empty when he came around, but before he could really ponder it too much, Inion started singing and it knocked him out like a magical lullaby.

The next day as they traveled, Edwin found himself marveling at the flooded farmlands, and he thought the sights of barges poking along doing *something* was oddly amusing, even though he didn't have a clue as to what it was.

It was later in the year now, and the sun beat down on Edwin with the intensity of early summer. He'd asked Inion, and it was the equivalent of May or June at this point, which meant Edwin had originally showed up in the middle of winter. It had seemed strange, but the way Inion had put it, they didn't really *get* winter in the Verdant, whatever magic kept it running also blunting the hostility to life the season usually displayed.

When they finally reached the trees, Inion nearly jumped for joy as life flooded back into her, and Edwin watched as color literally returned to her skin and hair. It hadn't been obvious as it happened, but Memory informed him that the naiad had nearly ended up grayscale toward the end of their trip. She claimed she was fine now, but he still kept an eye on her just in case.

Edwin waited until they got back to the clearing to really unpack and give Inion her new tunic and was kind of glad he did. She had accepted it with a grin at his explanation, then promptly stripped before he could successfully look away. Something Edwin hadn't really thought through was the fact Inion's leaf clothes were kind of part of her, while her new outfit *wasn't*, resulting in her losing it any time she discorporated.

Considering Edwin only really objected to the show on principle, and as a steadfast reminder to himself that he should *not* get romantically involved with a fey, he couldn't say he minded *that* much. In time, Inion incorporated changing—always with a smile on her face that let Edwin know that she knew *exactly* what she was doing—in front of him into their standard back-and-forth exchanges.

Overall, Inion and Edwin's daily routine didn't shift all that much in the aftermath of the trip to Vinstead. The new gardening tools made some things significantly easier, his new food options made his meals . . . well, at least they had more variation. He hadn't thought to get yeast so he couldn't make bread properly, but he could still make a sort of flatbread that didn't taste too bad. It's not like he needed to eat that much, anyway.

His new hammock was *amazing* and endlessly more comfortable than his previous sleeping arrangement. No pillow, but that was a minor matter when his rolled-up cloak worked nearly just as well.

Edwin experimented more with his talsanenris bushes, stripping seeds from their berries and trying to grow them—they never sprouted in the two weeks he gave them. Unsurprisingly, the reverse—planting a berry with no seeds (once he made sure there *actually* weren't seeds inside) likewise produced no sprouting. It did make pretty great fertilizer, though. Like his attempts to use the berries to speed up the growths of other plants, anything he planted inside a berry quickly withered as it couldn't keep up with its nutritional requirements.

His soap-making efforts went quite well; his attempts to Purify lye worked surprisingly well, and a few tries (and Alchemy levels) later, he had very soft, very revitalizing soap made from his ever-present talsanenris berries.

Edwin's bricks slowly improved as well, and he gradually made himself an oven built into the ground, a massive pit dug out in front of it for easy access, which was useful for all sorts of stuff, from drying to baking.

His other alchemical ingredients steadily grew as well, under his and Inion's tender care, slowly maturing and spreading as spring rolled over to summer. While the temperature kept slowly rising, the tree cover and mountain spring meant that Edwin never felt like he got too hot.

One *immensely* annoying discovery Edwin had made was that his talsanenris berries suddenly stopped producing one day, once his entire clearing was surrounded by hedges. He still had a sizable stock of the fruit, so it wasn't a crippling blow, but a week of testing made Edwin realize he'd just overused the soil. The only place that could still grow *anything* was the garden, and he wasn't going to risk everything else to try and grow more of the magical berries he had in abundance already.

It was annoying, but manageable. As it turned out, the ash from talsanenris bushes was *ridiculously* nutrient-rich. A 50/50 mixture of ash and dirt let him grow a bean plant in hours when adequately supplied with water and mulched talsanenris fertilizer without the plant instantly withering like it had previously.

Inion still advised that he not try it with their magical plants, but that didn't stop Edwin from trying to grow additional sprouts, separate from their "actual" attempt. Perhaps predictably, the plants didn't turn out, though the way they didn't turn out was what was most interesting. Instead of withering, they turned out oddly stunted and almost . . . grayscale. It was as though someone had leached all color from the plants, turning them various shades of light and dark gray instead, vaguely reminiscent of Inion's state after their trip to Vinstead.

The plants were decidedly not magicless, but they did feel distinctly different from the properly grown plants in his main garden under his Basic Mana Sense.

Edwin found that he could grow new talsanenris bushes in the ash-soil of their predecessors, but he decided to not push things quite so far as before, instead keeping a few bushes tended to and harvesting their berries regularly, keeping himself well stocked though without the obscene levels of surplus he'd had initially.

Really, Edwin had done so many gardening and biology-related tasks, he was expecting to see an absolutely massive number of related Paths and Skills next time he checked those notifications instead of just his Skill levels.

Notifications were a funny thing. He could manipulate them relatively freely, hiding and calling up the pop-ups, but he couldn't minimize anything after it had already appeared, just dismiss it. The ability to block out entire classes of prompts had been a nice discovery when he stumbled upon it, and he used it to avoid being constantly spammed with Skill unlocks. He'd look at them eventually, to see if he had gotten anything truly spectacular, but it was so nice to not be told for the *four hundredth time* that he could take the Clay Sculpting Skill.

Anyway.

His levels were steadily increasing across the board as the average crept into the 50s, and Edwin expressed some amount of skepticism that it would really take him a year to bring them all almost to level 80. Inion had smartly informed him that once they were all at level 60, that just meant they were nearly halfway there.

Ugh.

The days ticked by, one by one.

Edwin built out an irrigation system and even a rudimentary waterwheel, taking water from atop Inion's waterfall, diverting it down a hollowed-out log and delivering it to his garden, keeping it eternally watered. His waterwheel didn't do much at the moment, honestly, but its existence was still cool and something Edwin was very happy with. If he had any further repetitive tasks such as sawing, grinding wheat, or possibly cracking nuts, he could hook something up to the driveshaft to accomplish it.

He was also really happy with the way he'd set up the trickle of water entering the distillery. As the water evaporated from the bottom bowl, a floating bob would sink ever so slightly, lowering a stopper between the heating bowl and the waiting water. As it lowered, the stopper would come out and let in a few drops of fresh water until the bowl refilled and the stopper was replaced. It was awesome and janky and Edwin always felt like just looking at it made his Construction Skill happy.

The rest of Edwin's new distillery setup utilized a cooling stone he'd bought in Vinstead in place of cold water, providing a constant supply of fresh, clean water as he used his heating stones in place of a fire he'd have to tend to. It was slower, yes, but that didn't matter when it ran constantly, eternally dripping out water for him to use in his experiments. He was even able to measure an increase in its speed as his Purify and Alchemy leveled up. Though it was drinkable, he usually got Inion to refill his canteen when he needed it, as the water processed by her Skill tasted fantastic.

Not much of an increase, admittedly, but an increase nonetheless. Sadly, he lacked the precision instruments needed to determine exactly *how* much faster distillation each level-up brought with it. Sure, Outsider's Almanac may have an exponential increase in character limit—each level brought with it a 5 percent increase to how many it could store—but Survival seemed to linearly decrease how much food and water he needed to survive, so it wasn't necessarily consistent between Skills.

The fact that he had once accidentally gone a week without eating or drinking was quite interesting, though. It hadn't been comfortable and Edwin swore that he'd pay more attention to his bodily needs in the future. As it turned out, a tendency to go an entire day without eating or drinking didn't leave when food and water became even less important. He maintained it was important, though.

Edwin had managed to copy all the text from the *Grimoire* into his filing system as a result of the one-week grinding session, and he'd figured out an even *bigger* use of his Almanac as part of it.

As most grand discoveries did, it started off mundane. He had made it through the introduction and first chapter of the *Grimoire*, tucking hundreds of words into every Almanac entry before he'd need to start the next one.

(Prev—Zosiman102)

3. In this production whilst the Soul fashions unto itself a body, there is thus a third thing by which the Soul is now inwardly joined to the body and unto the Spirit of the World, and by which the operation of all natural things are dispensed, and this is called the Vital Spirit.

4. The operations of natural things are dispensed from this Spirit by the organs according to the attunement of the organ and its manifestation within the Spirit of the World.

5. The organ of Intellect, set within the crown, produces Mana. Secondly upon the organ of Life itself according to the reasons of things produces

Health from its place within the chest. Thirdly, unto the organs that motivates things in such a disposition as is within the limbs and thusly produces Stamina.

6. It is thus truly the production of blood from within the heart which is the origin of Health. As seen by the creation of the bile humor in all its endless colors in accordance with the infinity of Mana, which demonstrates their production within the brain. When exposed unto the muscle and skin, the Vital produces Stamina in its immediate form, namely the phlegm, as evidenced by the manifestation of it upon the skin when Stamina is utilized.

7. No bodily thing hath any energy or operation in itself saving so far for as it is an instrument of the same Spirit, or informed by its creations, for that which is merely corporeal is merely passive. It is exclusively Health, Mana, and Stamina that does inform the Spirit of the World to connect with an individual.

8. He that will work great things must (as much as possible) take away corporeity from things, or else he must endeavor to awaken the sleeping Attributes within himself, connecting wholly unto the Spirit of the World, now laboring and undertaking an exchange, he will never do any great works.

9. It is impossible to take all this Spirit from anything whatsoever for by this bond a thing is held from falling back into its first matter and kept in place by the Spirit of the World itself.

(Next—Zosiman104)

(Prev—Zosiman103)

10. This Spirit is somewhere or rather everywhere found as it were free from the body, and he that knows how to join it with a body agreeably possesses a treasure better than all the riches of the world and even the grandest Skill of the Spirit of the World . . .

Edwin stifled a yawn, then mentally cursed as it broke his concentration. Well, at least he had just started a new page, so it wouldn't be too awful to restart and try again. Still annoying. He'd take a quick break first, and he rose from where he was sitting, stretching to get the crick in his neck out. Supernatural flexibility may let him bend so far back around he could nearly touch his nose against his heel, but it didn't keep his muscles from locking up if he stayed too long in the wrong position.

Inion noticed his shift. "Another break?"

He wordlessly nodded, unable to talk past a giant yawn, and the two of them went for another quick run. It was getting harder and harder for Edwin to properly push himself in relative safety, making levels scarcer and scarcer as time went on. It didn't keep him from trying to get levels in Walking or Athletics by going for regular runs, though.

He always brought Inion with him in case he ran into another panther or other dangerous situation. He was still skeptical of her alleged fantastic combat prowess, but she was, if nothing else, strong enough to carry him back to Obairlann if needed.

"How *does* Almanac even work, anyway?" Edwin asked as they ran.

"Was that toward me?"

"Eh. Kind of. You'd know more than I would. Like, where is the information stored? Is it the System itself? Is it with me? How can other people access the information? *Can* they?"

"You're *just now* wondering all that?"

"No." Edwin paused in thought. "I've always wondered about it, it's just becoming more and more prevalent as I translate page upon page of dry Alchemy text into a seemingly limitless database."

"Aren't you even now *still* dropping random phrases onto any odd leaf or pebble that catches your eye?"

"Sure . . . but those feel different because they're a word or sentence at most, then it goes to the next object. Now that I'm uploading an entire *book* into seminonsense words? It's really sinking in."

"I can't *really* answer that, you know."

"Yeah, yeah." They ran in silence for a few moments before Edwin had a thought cross his mind. "So how does the System handle different languages anyway?"

"What?"

"Well, I know for a fact that not all languages use the same alphabet, let alone the Latin alphabet from Earth. But whenever I see a System prompt, even in a different language, it seems like it gets converted to English characters. Is that by phonetics? If so, what happens when there's a phenotype that doesn't appear in English, that it just can't replicate?"

"You're not *actually* asking this, right?"

"You have to ask?"

"Fair."

"But why then is the character limit also in English? What about something like kanji instead? Would they be able to store more information in the same space, like with a tweet?"

"I'm not supposed to even be able to *follow* this, right?"

"I know I can input all letters in both uppercase and lowercase, as well as punctuation, numbers, and even some symbols. I don't think I ever really thought about that last fact much, though it's pretty significant. It makes *no* sense for Joriah's System to run on unicode, so then is it just running based on what I think of as a letter or character?"

"I'm going to assume you don't *actually* care about my understanding."

"Huh? Oh, sorry, Inion. Do you need me to explain more?"

"Nah. I'll be *fine.*"

"Okay, if you insist. Turn around here, say? There's something I want to test when we get back."

So. If Almanac was limited based on characters, then what counted *as* a character? As Edwin experimented, he never quite hit the limit. Even as he pushed it more and more, starting off with just the more unusual characters he knew of that were still essentially part of the English alphabet.

Then, he found that capital and lowercase delta showed up alongside the other Greek letters. Then, letters with accents and modifications. A 7 with a cross along the middle. 0 with a line through the center. Delta but with an equilateral triangle. The single kanji he knew and remembered—火—also worked and only took up a single character slot. It was getting extremely tedious to actually count out his character limits, but he didn't really see any alternative.

From there, Edwin just kept pushing things further and further. So long as he was able to conceptualize something as a single "character" he could insert it. That quickly included countless symbols of various kinds, random squiggles, and letters written in cursive. Thanks to Visualization, he could imagine *very detailed* single characters, and by the end of the day he had managed to upload a semisketched representation of a firevine ivy leaf. Only a single color, and mostly a single line, but it was still an absolutely massive proof of concept.

Further experimentation with Almanac's formatting let him figure out how to change the display of what he wrote. Large letters, small letters, letters in different colors . . . once he figured out how to overlap "characters" everything really went great.

He could do vector art! Triangles, squares, pentagons, circles, and more. Basic geometric shapes were really easy to maintain. Another day of work and Edwin had figured out gradients and distortions. Two days after *that*, he had started figuring out more general pictures. It was absolutely *murder* on his Almanac space, meaning he could only have relatively low-resolution pictures stored, though he jumped up a few levels in the Skill just from this discovery, so said quality kept marginally increasing.

Well, so far, anyway. He could take pictures! This was so cool!

It didn't help all *that* much with his text-copying endeavors, but it did mean he could sort of embed images once he got to the herbology sections. He was only limited by his imagination!

. . . Literally. It worked based off Visualization.

Level Up!
Skill Points 899→1065
Progress to Tier 2: 1191/1770 (Avg level: 56/77)
Alchemy 65→69
Athletics 62→64
Basic Mana Sense 53→57
Bomb Throwing 14→17
Breathing 57→61
Construction 44→61
Firestarting 64→68
First Aid 50→52
Flexibility 37→47
Harvesting 47→59
Identify 49→53
Mana Infusion 68→71

CHAPTER 27

Training Will

Revelations about how Almanac worked and what it could accomplish aside, as summer carried on, it was Edwin's other projects that began to bear fruit. Literally, in some cases. Sadly, he most likely would never get berries from his hispera bush, simply due to its slow life cycle, and it wasn't old enough to flower or bear fruit yet. However, that didn't apply to the rest of his plants, even the other ones he'd gotten on the same day as his talsanenris berries.

Sunstalk, after his initial problems getting it to grow, was one of the few magical plants that actually responded positively to using talsanenris as a fertilizer. The large patch of strange golden grass sparkled and glowed in the shade but turned almost invisible in sunlight. Edwin used it to make a window for Obairlann. A waste of the substance? Perhaps, but Edwin mainly wanted to see how long it would retain its magic. He was still waiting.

According to Inion, Harvesting helped, and he didn't have a reason to disagree. If he could figure out how to somehow magically grab the property he needed, then Edwin might have an ingredient for an invisibility potion. Actually making one was still *well* beyond his grasp, though not for lack of trying. He just didn't even know where to begin, and the *Grimoire* offered no help in that regard—not even a list of ingredients. So his trying basically amounted to trying to grind up the grass and put it in a potion with other ingredients. He found some interesting reactions in his experimentation, but nothing usable yet.

Firevines grew at a pretty decent rate, especially with the rising temperatures that accompanied the warmer seasons. The *Grimoire* was more helpful in figuring out what he could *do* with them as compared to sunstalk, though that wasn't terribly useful. Matches and what more or less amounted to magical, essentially nontoxic (from what he could tell anyway) kerosene—highly flammable amber-colored oil that instantly combusted when exposed to heat, mana, particularly strong light . . . it was basically liquid Firestarting, and thus mostly superfluous to Edwin.

That said, combining the Skill and the oil netted Edwin a few levels in Bomb Throwing, which was appreciated. Putting it on food made it act a bit like liquid fire, scorching what he put it on if he wasn't careful or cooking it if he was, and even the freshly picked leaves of the ivy burned quite well.

His sinbalyne flowers were among his most promising experiments in terms of usefulness, though also his most challenging by *far*. Eating the flowers themselves very, very slightly—to the point where he was pretty sure it was just his imagination—made his tongue and lips feel numb. Mashing the petals into a paste, straining out the liquid, and distilling it in a smaller, more precise still than the one he used for his water gave a slightly lavender liquid that definitely made him feel faintly drowsy when he tasted it.

Inion found his resulting slurred speech *hilarious*, which . . . fair enough. He tested the distilled sinbalyne by smearing a drop of the liquid onto a thoroughly cleaned and sterilized knife, then pricked his finger to try and "inject" it into his finger. It had no effect. In fact, it wasn't until he accidentally sniffed a still-cooling vial of the drug did he realize that it was an *inhaled* anesthetic, which he . . . probably should have realized. Most likely, it was usually burned and that helped reduce sensation.

His stoppered vial of distilled sinbalyne, one of the few he had from Niall's laboratory, was one of his most potent tools and constantly kept on his person for a while. Just a whiff was enough to make him decidedly woozy for a good five minutes, and if he heated it slightly, that time could go up to half an hour.

It didn't affect Inion, not that he really expected it to, but it was still very useful for disorienting pretty much any mammals, something he confirmed in his hunts. It worked all right on birds, though not quite as well.

Molai was kind of boring. It did its job, sure—applying juices from its stalk quickly neutralized the knockout effect of the stronger knockout potion, though not that of the weaker one for some reason. So far as Edwin could tell, it negated or weakened the magical aspects of potions, whereas mundane portions were left unhindered. Was it absorbing the mana? Was it destroying it? If it was the latter, did that mean mana didn't follow the laws of thermodynamics? Further testing was required.

Glowleaf continued glowing even after it was picked, for a day without Harvesting or about a week with it. Well, other than lighting. Mixing the ground plants into distilled water resulted in glowing liquid that seemed to keep glowing at the same intensity more or less indefinitely. Thus, the glowing potion bottles on his shelves just ended up providing some *really* cool ambience. Depending on what else was included in the mixture, he could get the normally purple or green elixirs to take on gold, red, or white tints by utilizing sunstalk, firevine, or sunstalk and talsanenris.

All in all, Edwin had magical kerosene, windows, nitrous oxide, and glowsticks. Truly, he was a force to be reckoned with. May all tremble before him as he *glowed* at them, then tried to pour lighter fluid over them. Was he regressing? Throwing rocks at people had worked just fine for him until now.

What he really needed was to integrate his Skills into his combat style. He needed more Alchemy stuff. He needed to really double down on his training . . . which mostly amounted to the same thing he'd already been doing. Inion claimed she had "ideas" for once he stalled out, which filled him with dread, though he wasn't sure why.

As time progressed, marching on in its inexorable advance, Edwin found his patience slowly being eroded by the *Zosiman Grimoire*. There were only so many times he could read about how the Three Attributes could be seen in all creation, describing certain experiments that had been *demonstrably wrong* on Earth as self-evident.

Some things never changed, it seemed, and Alchemy on Joriah was just as flawed as alchemy had been on Earth. Oh sure, a core of truly fascinating magic was in there, but it wasn't actual *science.*

Edwin hadn't given too much thought to his long-term goals. He wanted to find a place to permanently settle down that wasn't in the middle of nowhere, he wanted to find friends—Inion didn't really count; she was contractually obligated to be his friend no matter how much fun she might be to be around and how well they got along—and he wanted to be strong enough to feel in control of his own life.

The question of what he wanted to do with his life had always been a bit of an annoying question for Edwin. All he really wanted was to be comfortable, to not be stressed, and to have friends. The quickest route to that had been to get a well-paying job, and engineering paid very well. He'd taken quite some time determining which route exactly he wanted to take, before settling on physics because of its increased emphasis on peeling back the mysteries of the universe in comparison to engineering.

He'd essentially settled for mediocrity because there weren't any other options, and he had been genuinely content with that. But some dreams never really died, and the desire to make some game-changing discovery in science was one that any scientist ought to have had at some point. There was just no way on Earth it would ever happen.

Fortunately for Edwin, though, he was no longer on Earth, and he *could* make a difference. Just like Newton had his *Principia,* nothing was stopping Edwin from making his own series of books to revolutionize science and Alchemy as a whole!

Was that what he wanted, then? Maybe. It sounded cool and grand, at least.

Edwin made himself a deal. He wanted to travel to see the world anyway. He could help out people, he could try to make his own Alchemy guide! Starting from base principles. He didn't have that much paper, but that was fine. He'd just write the first draft in his Almanac . . .

Edwin stopped. Outsider's Almanac. How had he never connected the dots before now? Probably because the Almanac had been his first-ever Skill evolution, so it had never been something he had thought about. He'd never *needed* to think about it, never needed to really push the limits for what the Skill was capable of because of how fast it leveled up, but this was what it was meant for, wasn't it? It was right in the name.

The System was *trying* to get him to come in and revolutionize things, wasn't it? The Outsiders of the past had come in and done *things* of all sorts. One had built a flying city. Another was the pioneer of Alchemy. There was apparently a race of machines running around that an Outsider had made . . .

The sudden realization in turn of the absolute crushing expectations he'd stumbled into slammed into Edwin. That . . . that was why Tara had been assigned to him, why the Empire was trying to be nice to him. They thought Edwin would—no, they *expected* him to—change the world. To them, he'd stumbled out of myth and legend, with thousands of years of aggrandization on the side of the bar he would need to clear.

He closed his eyes and breathed slowly. Here he thought that he might be able to escape some of the high hopes people had for him back on Earth, only to stumble into something ten times worse. Before, when people joked about him curing cancer, it was indeed just a joke. Here, though? How could he possibly live up to those standards?

No. No, Edwin. No sliding into depression. There's only one thing you can control. Just like before, people will always have high hopes and expectations for you. There's no point in stressing over it, you can't help that. All you can do is your best, right? Not that that's much better, *at least for stress management.*

It took a few minutes, but Edwin eventually got his emotions back under control. So what, if people literally expected the world from him? He'd just . . . well, not be *himself*. Nobody wanted that. But he could still be the Alchemist. He was going to wander, he knew that much. If nobody knew what to expect, he couldn't disappoint them.

But the System? The System clearly wanted something from him as well, namely his thoughts and observations. Well, he could at least do that. He Identified the plants he was tending to, and a word abstraction later, he was writing again. A bit of finagling got a sketch-picture of the plant's leaves inserted inside the entry, just like any good almanac should have.

Firevine.

Hedera Inflammare

This ivylike vine is, true to its name, usable in alchemical formulae that can utilize fire-based effects. See FirevineUses, FirevineFormula.

On their own, the leaves function as excellent tinder, and if the leaves are crushed and the juices extracted and distilled, the resulting liquid combusts when exposed to a number of different stimuli. See FirevineUses, FirevineStimulants, and FirevineHarvesting.

Native to the Rhothos and Verdant regions.

Related entries: FirevineUses, FirevineFormula, FirevineStimulants, FirevineEcology, FirevineFamily, FirevineHistory, Firevine-Gardening, FirevineHarvesting

It wasn't perfect, but it was a start, and that was what mattered. *Hedera* was the classification for ivies, and while the tree of life was no doubt radically different on Joriah, Edwin imagined it was similar enough for cross-pollination of ideas. Half of the "related entries" didn't even have an Almanac post when he started off, but subdividing everything made it easier to update when he found something new and kept him from having to redraw the picture every time. Hmm. There was probably an edit function, wasn't there? It would only make sense. He made a quick Almanac note to look into it.

"That's what you want me to do, isn't it anyway?" Edwin asked the air. He'd never gotten any indication that the System moderators and admins could hear him, but it didn't hurt, "Fill in information about everything ever?"

"Did you ask me something?" Inion perked up from where she lounged on a rock.

Edwin waved her off and continued with his work.

Sunstalk
Poaceae Solaris . . ..

So, Edwin thought to himself that evening while working on his latest batch of brick, Almanac on his mind. *If I were an immortal System with an interesting individual whose thoughts I want to record via a Skill, what features would I put in that Skill?*

"What'cha thinking about?" Inion dropped down next to him.

"Almanac. I finally got to thinking about it, and now I'm wondering if I can figure out what its other functions might be based on what the admins and mods might have tried to give me. I figure its fast leveling-up speed is part of that, and they clearly want my thoughts on some matters . . . but am I supposed to be able to share it? There's got to be an editing rather than rewrite option. I store data, what are the limits? Can I store audio? Videos? Can I just straight up take pictures of things? Is there a search function I can access somehow?"

He thought for a moment. "Have you gotten any Paths pertaining to me explaining science stuff to you, by any chance?"

"Uhhh . . . lemme check. I don't look that often." Her eyes focused on thin air. "Uhhh . . . Nope. Doesn't look like it."

Edwin hummed to himself softly. "Interesting. I would have suspected something like that. I wonder if there's some clever thing I need to tell you about to get it to unlock?"

He tapped his chin. "Or maybe . . .. Inion, I give you permission to access my Almanac."

She blinked. "Huh. That actually *worked*. 'New Path! By receiving appropriate permission, you have gained the Outsider's Student Path!'"

Edwin blinked. "That was easy. Also nice to know that I don't need to worry about someone getting access to it by accident, if you need permission. How many points is it?"

"Sixty. I'll have to take it, see what it does." She stuck her tongue out at him. "Maybe I'll *finally* get to see all your random thoughts you leave everywhere."

"Oh, shoot. You know what? You don't have to take it. In fact, you should forget you ever unlocked it."

Inion just laughed, and Edwin smiled.

* * *

Almanac wasn't the only Skill that Edwin was working on improving. Firestarting had been a consistent problem for him since he first realized the Skill's limitations. It affected something like a thirty-foot radius around him whenever it was enabled, which was great for keeping all his fires going at full blaze, less so when he wanted to make something specific burn, and nothing else.

Like, for instance, if he was trying to make incendiary grenades.

He'd figured out how to make what mostly amounted to firebombs through use of Firevine extract—two rocks inside a clay ball, along with a small measure of the ivy's oil and a number of the same plant's leaves would break apart into puffs of fire. He didn't have enough extract to make anything like a Molotov cocktail, unfortunately, but if he could find some lamp oil or something he could remedy that.

It didn't hold quite the same punch that he would have wanted, though. Sure, fire was great and all, but he was skeptical that setting someone on fire would really cause lasting harm. Actually, he had evidence that it would, given how often he did set people ablaze as a finishing move with Firestarting, but he still wanted something with more force.

So he turned to pinecones. If he soaked them in a mixture of sap and firevine extract, covered up the stickiness with firevine leaves—leaving a stem poking out to function as a fuse—then covered *that* with a thin layer of clay, he could set the "fuse" on fire with normal Firestarting, and it would reach the main body quickly enough that the entire pinecone would be on fire midflight. Testing in nonflammable areas showed that if he managed to apply Infused Firestarting to it, the grenade would detonate violently, resulting in an explosion of burning smoke and shrapnel.

Edwin had two major obstacles to that goal. First, trying it anywhere other than on barren ground would probably set everything on fire. Second, he could only apply Mana Infusion to things he was touching, or nearly touching.

The former he was slowly making progress on. He'd managed to bring the area of effect for Firestarting down from a sphere to a hemisphere through a colossal effort of will and Visualization, and he was confident he might be able to shrink that into a narrow cone in time. It was just a matter of accomplishing it. In the meantime, Edwin could offset the problem by just pulsing Firestarting, kind of like how it was originally *intended* to be used, but it wasn't perfect as he still ran the risk of starting unrelated fires. At least he was able to shrink the radius it applied in, so he didn't have to worry about a stray ember sending his garden up in flames.

The second was a much bigger problem. Infusing the grenade beforehand actually proved *detrimental,* the mana from his Infusion presumably washing out some of the natural fire mana in the Firevine. Infusing the sap just made it stickier, and Infusing the pinecone had no apparent effect. No, he needed to Infuse it *through* Firestarting, the Skill apparently making his mana fire-attuned.

Eventually, Edwin came across a . . . mostly workable solution.

As it turned out, he could Infuse Bomb Throwing. It had been an utter *nightmare* to figure out, and was the result of many, *many* days of doing nothing but trying to make the two Skills work together, but the results were mostly worth the effort and complexity, and when the explosion actually worked, the result was always *super*satisfying.

However, even just doing the Infusion itself was tricky. He needed to Infuse whatever his "bomb" was *first,* then feed it through Bomb Throwing—specifically instead of Throwing Weapons; the two felt very similar—then back into the bomb. In that last bit of feedback, he could slip Firestarting in as an effect. What that meant was that after a partially random amount of time, Firestarting took effect and ignited whatever his bomb was. Even then, it usually wasn't Infused Firestarting, just the basic Skill, meaning that after all that work, a good three-quarters of the time it wasn't a proper explosion so much as it was just a tiny fireball with a bit of clay shrapnel.

Further practice required.

It took even more work to figure out how to sustain two Infusions at the same time, and even once Edwin did, it still took intense concentration to actually pull off—and thus was not terribly useful under pressure—but when he *did* manage it, he was treated to the wonderful sight of his makeshift grenade exploding midair. Or on the ground. Or right after it left his hand.

. . . So he still had some work to do. Well, as the end of summer rolled around and the biting chill of autumn set in, he was happy to be playing with fire.

While Edwin had originally expected that he would need another trip or two into Vinstead to get supplies, he hadn't accounted for two—well, really three—variables.

The first was Survival. He could go a *week* without feeling so much as a pang of hunger so long as he wasn't too active. The second *was* his activity level. Once he finished building up Obairlann, he just wasn't as physically active as before. Sure, he still went for runs—and always took his stick with him, just in case—but those were rapidly becoming almost trivially easy as Athletics and Walking boosted his physical efficiency to incredible levels. The third was how much food he and Inion managed to grow in their tiny little garden.

All in all, it meant that with the addition of a few deer's worth of jerky slow roasted over his fire, Edwin had plenty of food as fall slowly drew to a close. He could benefit from a few minor things, like yeast, but nothing was critical enough for him to take the multiday trip to Vinstead and back. Plus, he didn't want to put Inion through that ordeal again. She'd steadfastly said that it wasn't so bad that she wouldn't go with him again for whatever reason, but Edwin couldn't believe that literally losing color was good for her.

Inion wouldn't tell him what her plan was when he finally left for good, whether she was staying back at Obairlann or tagging along with him somehow, and he didn't press the issue. Odds were decent she hadn't made up her mind yet.

Yeah. On one hand, she stays here and is bored, the other way she has to put up with me.

Another part of Edwin said that it wasn't that bad, and that she did like him well enough that traveling with him wouldn't be "putting up" with him. Edwin hoped it was more the latter. He'd been in this position before, where a "friend" was just trying to humor him because they were nice, and he wasn't sure that Inion wasn't in a similar position. He was willing to try, though.

He had many flaws, but a lack of social persistence wasn't quite one of them. Or so he liked to think, anyway.

Inion would most likely abandon him as soon as she had a viable alternative, but . . . he didn't want to think about that. He was probably just worrying over nothing, anyway.

Where was I? Oh, right. Trips to Vinstead.

There was no real rush to return to civilization, not with all he already had, and enough reasons to avoid it that Edwin figured he could just buckle down and try to survive the winter. It *had* actually rained a few times over the summer and fall, wispy clouds forming and sprinkling water across the land, but he could still count the number of times on one hand.

So probably not going to be a harsh winter. At least, no snow. It might get chilly, but nothing like Edwin hadn't dealt with many times before. Honestly, if he wasn't trying to be productive, he could most likely *legitimately* hibernate, just sleep the winter away with a use of Sleeping, Survival, and Nutrition.

He had something much better to spend his time on, though.

He wanted to *fly*.

Now, while the ideal case would be to unlock a Skill for it once he succeeded, letting him improve magically, he couldn't accept it before he finished his tier-up. So he'd have to figure out how to unlock the Skill now, then dismiss it and reearn it once the year was up, then train it up until it hit level 60 or more, evolve it, and then level up its *evolution* to whatever level the rest of his Skills were at by that point.

. . . Yeah, he wasn't looking forward to that. There was a reason he needed to be so selective about his Skill choices, now more than ever. He wanted higher-tier Skills, darn it, no matter how much every Skill ever might give him something amazing once it evolved. Something that was amazing from the start would just keep getting amazing. That's what everyone told him. Even Lefi, for that matter.

But he was getting ahead of himself. First, he needed to *learn* how to fly. And to do that, he would need to level up Packing.

So far as Edwin was able to tell, Packing currently reduced the weight of whatever he carried by about 95 percent, so he had to actually carry one-twentieth of whatever he lifted. Air was about 1.2 kilos per cubic meter, and humans were slightly more dense than water, putting him at a thousand kilos per cubic meter.

That meant he still had some ways to go before he could properly lift *himself* with Packing and potentially fly (or rather, swim through the air), but if he was able to assemble a backpack that was about 80 cubic meters in volume, so long as the average density of the backpack and him combined was less than 7 kilos per cubic meter, he would be neutrally buoyant in the air.

He'd *tried* assembling a really big "backpack" by making a canvas-covered cube and strapping it to his back, then jumping off the cliff above Obairlann and trying to see if it slowed his fall at all. It wouldn't be enough for buoyancy, sure, but if he could lighten the air he should at least feel the effects as he fell.

It seemed like it couldn't be cheated like that, sadly. He'd plummeted to the ground about as fast as he should normally, once you adjusted for a massive wooden-framed backpack/parachute on his back anyway.

Inion had enjoyed the resulting splash into her pond, and *Edwin* enjoyed the fact he had spare clothes to change into while his other outfit was drying.

Dreams of flight notwithstanding, Inion had managed to come up with a number of creative "training" regimes for Edwin. She could be so nice at times he almost forgot he needed to not trust her, but that was a serious mistake. Now that his Skills had passed level 60, to actually level them at any kind of half-decent rate, it took, according to Inion, serious effort and required him to push the Skills in new directions. Which was how he ended up with some utterly *brutal* weeks.

With no warning, Inion started waking him up partway through the night, held him under her waterfall with a cloth over his face, and made him breathe through her literal waterboarding *and* fall asleep while doing it. She blindfolded him and threw magical ice at him, making him try and puzzle out where it was coming from solely with Basic Mana Sense and dodge it. Once Edwin had that figured out, she stuck his feet in place by burying him up to his shins in mud and freezing it, making him exercise Flexibility to try and keep avoiding being hit.

She once joked that she had a more *"enjoyable"* way to train Flexibility, and though he nearly gave in and accepted, Edwin first joked that she'd need to twist his arm more than that to get him to agree.

Sadly, she took it literally and didn't ask again afterward. It was almost a pity, he could have used some fun after he de-dislocated his shoulder, though he mentally slapped himself for almost giving in.

She trained Identify in a similar manner. Apparently, using it didn't actually require sight so long as Edwin could, well, identify what the target was. So, as part of Inion's "last" level of training, Edwin was forced to yell out to her *which* chunk of ice she threw at him, while he was blindfolded with his feet frozen in mud, then have to dodge the annoyingly accurate projectiles. Visualization helped there, actually, as he was able to slowly build up a mental picture of the space, and helped him process the input from his sixth sense. Supposedly Perception would help with that, but he didn't *have* that Attribute yet, but it was quickly moving up his list for what he wanted.

Edwin was starting to regret not taking Inion up on her offer without sarcasm, but, ah, well. He wasn't about to ask. Much too awkward, no matter the prize, which by itself was still probably not the best idea.

Once he had graduated from that permutation, Inion changed it up so her "final" version of the training started mixing nonmagical projectiles in, which Edwin had to *listen* for and Identify, then use that information to dodge the attack. She tried not giving him any warning at one point, just throwing her "training tools" at him without shouting she had thrown something, but, well . . . he had at least gotten First Aid levels out of that debacle.

It was hard enough figuring out *where* to dodge from, never mind *if.*

Inion's Walking training wasn't as bad, but running across slick rocks up and down the cliff was *not* pleasant. Then Packing training got added in, and he'd have to do it while also carrying a full-size tree.

Edwin dreaded what dedicated First Aid training would look like, but at least he didn't have to worry about that . . . yet. Even his largest bruises faded overnight, and a broken ankle took a day to heal once he whipped up a basic healing potion from talsanenris berries and a minuscule amount of molai mixed with sinbalyne.

The former provided the basis for the magical healing by unleashing a massive wave of energy and speeding up his metabolism, molai absorbed and slowly released magical energy, preventing him from being hit by all the effects of the healing berries, and the last, when properly prepared and applied, helped encourage blood flow to his feet, concentrating the effect there. It had been an experimental potion, but certainly a rousing success.

It *did* leave his foot swollen for three days after the break was healed, purely from the increased activity and blood flow, so it still required some work. Still, he got a whole Alchemy level for that discovery, and those were getting harder and harder to come by.

A large part of Edwin wondered just *how* much his Alchemy Skill was covering for him, if it was filling in for poor technique, imprecise measurements, or even totally missing ingredients. Inion could rarely replicate his results, but she also, ironically, didn't have the same level of patience for brewing that he did. She also claimed that her own personal magic would mess with things, and that just part of magic—including Alchemy—was *literally* finding what did or didn't work for someone.

He put his ~~rant~~ notes on *that* subject in his Almanac. Not that he expected the mods to somehow patch it or anything, but it didn't hurt to give them the *option* to.

It was also about that time that he discovered his Alchemy Skill hadn't been applying to his sinbalyne knockout potion, resulting in the weaker product. That was remedied by adding a tiny drop of talsanenris juice and gently heating the mixture while he stirred for about a minute. Afterward, if Edwin got so much as a drop of the stuff on him, he'd pretty much instantly black out. It didn't last long—a few minutes at most—but firmly knocked him unconscious nonetheless. If he actually swallowed any, he'd be out cold for a day or more.

Edwin wasn't sure why it changed from being an inhaled poison to a contact or ingested one beyond "Alchemy stuff," but he made sure to prepare vials of both versions. Maybe he could turn the normal liquid into a smoke bomb or something.

That discovery only served to further muddle what exactly the Alchemy Skill did. Did it just directly enhance the potency of his creations? It would fit with his observations, if potentially insignificant effects were magnified into appearing.

Inion made him train Survival with a combination of cutting down trees (she tried to get him to rip them out of the ground to help with Packing, but it didn't work, so she just made him carry them one-handed while she rode on the branches instead) and going without food for extended periods of time, then Nutrition by force-feeding him truly *awful* foods, utterly sublime food, literal dirt, and food that just looked like dirt. He wasn't sure what the point of that last one was.

Actually, Edwin wasn't sure what the point of *any* of those had been, but Inion *swore* she was helping him train Nutrition. She refused to clarify when or how that was the case, though, so he was skeptical.

In comparison, Mathematics was a dream to level up. He just kept running more and more complicated numerical functions into his mental calculator, plugging it all into Visualization.

Well, it was a dream to level up at first. Then Inion had caught on and, as her "final" addition to her stone-throwing training, made him plot the trajectories of her projectiles on top of telling her which ones were which and *still* dodging them all. Edwin eventually got very, very good at dodging projectiles, and as an interesting side effect, calculating where a given throw of his attacks would land became almost second nature.

It was because of that that Edwin realized some kind of force was being applied to his throws, which just smoothed out their arcs regard-less of wind or air turbulence, if he slipped while throwing something, or more. He so desperately wished that he could still be leveling up Throwing Weapons, but he also didn't regret his decision to evolve it when he did. Odds were good that whatever bonus it granted explosives was what helped him get out from the Blackstones as well as he did.

To level up Purify, Edwin had to come up with new purification *methods*, whose required equipment conveniently tended to help with Construction. In particular, he vaguely remembered a spinning-wheel toy centrifuge that was being used to test for malaria or something.

He didn't know how to do that, but his version was at least able to reliably separate oil from water without his Skill applying, and separate the different forms of blood *with* his Skills. It was kind of satisfying, explaining the components of blood to Inion who had no clue about any of it. He got a First Aid level for it as well, which was even *nicer*.

The "final" level so far for Inion's ice-throwing training now included Harvesting, and she would include some small trinket in each ice crystal, and he would (still blindfolded) have to Identify which projectile was flying at him, figure out where it was and where it would be, dodge out of the way, and now use his knife to cut out the prize.

Edwin had no chance, at least not until Inion allowed him to catch the crystals and started throwing at a much slower rate than before.

"I take back . . . every nice thing . . . I've ever said about you." Edwin panted out the words after one particularly grueling training session, wincing as he dabbed healing salve on the hole in his hand.

Inion frowned. "*Have* you ever said anything nice about me?"

"It's the thought that counts, so . . . I'm counting nice thoughts I've had about you," he decided.

Inion just laughed. Edwin wasn't sure whether he loved or hated that laugh.

Probably both.

It was, blessedly, a day off for Edwin. Well, as much of a day off as he ever gave himself. He was fully healed from his latest bout of training, Inion was off wandering the woods doing something, and the sun was shining. He sat by his kiln fire, reveling in the sounds of nature as he tended to the flames. Day off or no, he still had work to do. It was just a question of how painful that work was.

He actually had an idea for how he might be able to improve both Construction and Harvesting at the same time. Wood carving, and possibly rock chiseling, seemed like it might be in the conceptual overlap between the two Skills, and he was eager to give it a try.

Edwin reached down and grabbed a log to work on, tugging it free—hang on, it was caught on something. Ah, it was embedded in the ground, and Packing never helped with anything even partially buried for whatever reason. Most likely, trying to lift the entire planet was beyond the scope of its weight-reduction capabilities.

Edwin freed up his other hand and wrapped it around the wood, yanking on it. Oh come on, was it stuck on something as *well* as being buried? He gave it one last giant pull to try and clear it, and as he wasn't expecting it to actually work, he was knocked off-balance as the tree trunk switched from being "not carried" to being firmly affected by Packing, shedding several hundred pounds all at once.

He most *definitely* wasn't expecting the action to save his life, as a crossbow bolt whizzed right toward his throat, only intercepted by the massive chunk of wood, striking and embedding itself up to the fletching in the bark.

Edwin reacted in the blink of an eye, mass-Identifying everything in the direction the bolt had come from, suddenly thankful for Inion's tutelage in that matter. Amid the flood of meaningless Almanac pop-ups, a single notification caught his eye.

Darkshadow Contract Hunter
Level Up!
Skill Points 1065→1279
Progress to Tier 2: 1362/1770 (Avg level: 66/77)
Alchemy 69→78
Athletics 64→69
Basic Mana Sense 57→68
Bomb Throwing 17→31
Breathing 61→66
Construction 61→68
Firestarting 68→77
First Aid 52→71
Flexibility 47→63
Harvesting 59→66
Identify 53→62
Mana Infusion 71→73
Mathematics 53→65
Memory 43→49
Nutrition 49→59
Outsider's Almanac 102→111
Packing 58→73

CHAPTER 28

A Blast from the Past

Edwin mentally cursed as he ducked behind the "wall" surrounding his kiln, trying to get cover from whatever assassin had been sent at him. He *knew* that his constant paranoia about the dwarves had to have been justified. How had he been tracked down *now*, though? It had been months since he'd been anywhere close to people.

His mind raced as it pulled on instincts he hadn't had to use in months, struggling to get ready for fighting. Inion's training didn't *exactly* prepare him for this, but the required Skills when combined with what he knew were similar.

Take in the surroundings, make a plan, take him out.

Edwin knew his clearing like the back of his hand—possibly even better given he'd never tried to memorize the latter—which put him at a serious home field advantage. He closed his eyes to try and think, but another quarrel coming from a totally different direction broke his concentration as it struck his left arm, pinning him by the bicep to the side of the earthenworks. It was immensely painful, but eminently manageable.

A concerted flex of will had the wooden shaft in his arm burst into flames, incinerating it in the blink of an eye and freeing him. He'd need a potion to fix the muscle damage to his bicep, but that was fine. A drop of very, *very* diluted knockout potion killed the pain in his arm, and he downed a tiny vial of experimental healing potion. Hopefully, the combination of his two emergency-healing potions would help keep him alive. He'd taken efforts to ensure he'd always have something on him after the panther attack, and it was finally paying off.

Before Edwin got the chance to also eat a few talsanenris berries for the energy boost, he was forced to take cover *again* as another bolt flew at him from a new angle.

That made three shots coming from three different directions. Where was this guy? Other than the momentary tag with Identify, Edwin hadn't seen so much as a hint of his assailant. The rate of fire suggested a crossbow rather than a bow, and the Class name suggested he might have something to do with darkness. Or it was just a Clan name. Probably the latter. Maybe both.

Straining his ears let Edwin hear a *clunk* coming from the side, near the top of his cliff, and although Edwin wasn't fast enough to completely dodge the attack, his sudden movement meant it took him in his shoulder rather than his heart.

Any hopes he'd had of his left hand being of any use in this fight fled his mind, but at least he still had his right. That was enough to throw his bombs, though without the counterbalance, his accuracy would suffer.

To test his current aim, he grabbed and threw a rock from his surroundings toward where the last bolt had come from. A moment later, Edwin heard it clatter against stone. A miss, then. Whoever he was facing was smart and kept moving. Some kind of ambush specialist, most likely. *Hopefully* that meant the attacker would be weak close-up, but he'd probably at least have Health.

Running across open ground to try and get inside Obairlann was just inviting a quarrel in his back. He'd need a shield of some form, or some sort of obscuration. Smoke bombs sounded really nice about now, and he wished he had something that would help in that regard, but wishes wouldn't help him survive this attack.

Another quarrel shot, and Edwin flinched, letting the quarrel strike his kiln, a good foot from his face and sending a spray of fired clay into his face. Was it just him, or was the hunter getting less accurate with each attack? Some sort of ambush-type Skill, perhaps?

A thought flickered across Edwin's mind, and he grimaced. It wasn't ideal, but he'd take it over dying. What he needed was something big, loud, distracting, and that would produce a lot of smoke . . .

The sequence of events here wasn't great. But it *would* accomplish his goals, and *only* had a moderately high chance of killing him. It beat dodging crossbow bolts while pinned down in a pit, though.

. . . Maybe. He might also just blow himself up if he didn't do this *perfectly*.

No, he'd blow himself up regardless. Edwin didn't have long, didn't have time to consider many alternatives. There was one thing he might be able to do to increase his odds of survival, but that in itself was a risk. But he was close enough to tiering up that even in the worst-case scenario for his first risk he wouldn't be hurting himself that much. And right now? Right now he'd need all the help he could get.

I really hope you guys are right.

Edwin steeled himself and pulled up his Status, eyes skimming down its length. He flinched as another quarrel shot from the direction of the cliff, but it seemed like his current hiding spot would hold for the time being. Gah, this list was a mess. He'd been ignoring it for months, not that he blamed himself for that.

There it was. Just what he'd need to give him every edge in potentially surviving this. Worst-case scenario, it might . . . he didn't even know. Give him a combat Skill that might be useful in this situation? He'd been lax before, putting long-term plans above all else. It wasn't wrong, perhaps, but not the mindset he needed right now. Besides, this was *already* on his must-have list, it was just moving up the schedule a bit, and as it gave an Attribute, it might genuinely be useful, in contrast to a Skill that he'd need to figure out on the fly and wouldn't even be that strong.

Another bolt whizzing overhead broke him out of his musings. No matter the accuracy or lack thereof of his assailant, who was probably just trying to keep him pinned anyway, Edwin didn't have time to waste.

You have completed the Warrior Path!
Relentless training and a will to survive and thrive has gotten
you far. You have and will face many obstacles in your way. As
an Alchemist, you know the value and power of blood both
that of your own and that of your enemies. You tread a Path of
bloodshed, but will it be one of war or of medicine?

Come on, come on, stop waxing poetical at me. Are you going to give me what I need or not?

Class Change!
Hedge Alchemist → Sapper
Calculating Rewards . . .

Could this thing be *any* slower? He was never trying to complete a Path any time it was time critical ever again. Shoot, that bolt seemed like it had a sharper angle than its predecessors. Was his attacker getting closer?

. . .

Done!
You have unlocked a new Attribute!
Health
Health level set to . . . 7

Edwin gasped as the change set into place. It wasn't a major change, nothing like getting magic for the first time, but warmth blossomed across his body, seeming to anchor him to . . . something. The connection to his body became more pronounced, and for a few moments he was acutely aware of his blood spread out throughout his entire body. No *wonder* Zosiman had said Health was a vital (heh) component of becoming "real." Were all Attributes like this? Stamina had just bumped itself up his to-get list regardless.

A stick snapped on the soil nearby. Heh. Some assassin, if he couldn't even avoid stepping on a stick . . . unless it was a decoy? Nope, not going down that rabbit hole. Edwin needed to do something, and fast, to avoid getting skewered . . . again. He'd almost forgotten the crossbow bolt sticking out of his shoulder in the glow of getting Health, but it was still definitely there.

This would take careful timing, and Edwin prepared himself. After each shot, there was about thirty seconds before the next one. That was still true, even as all the quarrels started coming from the same direction, trying to keep him pinned down.

One, two, three . . . Let the hunter shoot his bolt and . . . now.

Edwin had a fairly long stick within reach, and he grabbed it, used it to push himself out of the pit through what he felt was a *stellar* display of Athletics and Flexibility through the excruciating pain in his shoulder, and fed Mana Infusion in through it. It charged up quickly, and Edwin maneuvered the end of it so it was sticking in the kiln's roaring fire.

He jumped, pushing Athletics as far as possible to let him leap across the open ground. He kept his foot barely touching his pole as he arced through the air. While midflight, his eyes were able to catch a glimpse of the next crossbow bolt hurtling straight toward him from an indistinct figure barely fifteen feet away from him. In the instant before he lost contact with his stick and the moment escaped him, he pulled his trigger.

Mana Infusion. Firestarting.

Edwin pushed as much mana as possible through the stick into the fire. The Skill did what it always did, and his connecting pole burst into flames. The fire beneath the kiln, though . . .

BOOM!

Explosions were not what Hollywood liked to portray them as. Everyone knew that. There was much less fire and much more concussive force. However, even then, there was this idea that the force of an explosion could push you away from the explosion, like a massive fireball-powered leap.

That was wrong. While some might argue it was mere semantics, the shock wave did nothing to push away a person, not when it was traveling so fast through a person that it could rupture any part of them with gas in it. Instead, it was the air *it* pushed that might throw a person, and paradoxically, it was just as possible to be flung toward the epicenter of the explosion as away from it.

However, this close to a roaring kiln simultaneously catching on fire, every piece of charcoal igniting with a speed that would leave any pyrotechnic from Earth jealous, Edwin wasn't worried about where the wind would blow him, midair or not. If it came to that, he was dead, anyway, the blast wave tearing open his lungs, his digestive system, and his ears. He'd hoped there wouldn't be much of a shock wave, but he'd been proven very definitely wrong.

All that to say, Edwin was *very* surprised to be alive.

The resulting explosion that had ripped through the clearing was massive. A fireball had risen into the air alongside shattered pieces of kiln and displaced dirt, pelting Edwin with debris. A crater had replaced much of the ground on that side of Obairlann, and the blast of wind originating from a rippling shock wave had snatched Edwin from the air, tossing him away like a floating leaf, and knocked the bolt aimed at him to places unknown.

When he'd come around to his senses, Edwin gulped, then winced at the pain accompanying the action. He wasn't sure how he was still alive. Well, that wasn't entirely true. Being that close to such a large explosion, even larger than he had anticipated, would have killed him if he were still a normal human, and not magically augmented with his Athletics and Flexibility Skills, and now Health. His ears rang, his ruptured eardrums bleeding slightly, and as his gulp turned into a cough, he felt wetness. The pressure wave had to have ruptured blood vessels in his lungs. Without magical healing, he was a dead man walking.

No.

No.

The Alchemist pulled himself to his feet, his sense of balance wholly shot. He'd make it through long enough to get potions, to get Inion, to get First Aid going. He was a bloody mess, the crossbow bolt in his shoulder shattered and wedging the tip even deeper inside his body, but that explosion would have been undoubtedly heard across the Verdant. Inion would be back soon. Once she came back, they'd have numbers on their side and then he'd be safe.

A figure stirred at the base of the cliff, similarly thrown by the explosion against the rocks. If not for the motion, the hunter would have been indistinguishable from the stone around him.

Edwin narrowed his eyes.

Inion would be on her way. All he needed to do was survive until she arrived. Once she showed up, then he could reassess and figure out what his options were. He could probably manage that.

If she wasn't on her way . . .

Well, "stay alive" was still a priority.

Dust and smoke were sweeping across the area, obscuring everything and giving Edwin the cover he needed to make a break around Obairlann. He dashed around the edge, crossing the distance in an adrenaline-powered flash, half slamming into the outer wall of his house before he was able to reorient himself and barrel his "door" down. Behind him, he slammed it as best as he could and barricaded it with his table and chairs, now smeared with his blood. He couldn't hear anything from outside, which meant . . .

Oh yeah. It meant he should probably heal his eardrums.

Now that he was inside, Edwin had way more than just the random first aid potions he kept on him at all times, and he took full advantage of that. He gently pulled the crossbow bolt from his shoulder—did his left side have a magnet on it for arrows or something? Or did crossbows just lean toward the right when they were shot?

He'd been through this song and dance before, so he wasn't too worried. A few giant dollops of proper healing salve, some of his last, set his skin itching as it and muscle knit themselves back together. First Aid and Alchemy both cooperated when he used healing potions, and alongside the specialized human-only salve, he'd be up to about 70 percent capacity within a few minutes. Already, his hearing was just barely starting to return.

There was a knock at the door. Edwin grabbed his stick and his knockout potion as the knock rapidly turned into pounding, and then with a *crack*, the door broke in half, both halves flying across the room.

The dust cleared, and Edwin finally got a good look at his attacker. Well, not quite a clear look. Shadows wrapped around him, obscuring most of his features, but Edwin could still tell that he was dealing with something tall, large, and gangly.

Not a dwarf, then? Edwin ducked behind where his table had been knocked to with his assailant barging through the door.

The hunter advanced inside Obairlann, hefting a wicked-looking harpoon-spear. He paused, and Edwin tried to tell what was happening. Was he sniffing the air? Could he not see Edwin?

Edwin dashed out from his cover and up the stairs, snatching a row of glowing potions from their shelf. Sure, they didn't actually have any alchemical effect, but he could still throw them and maybe use them for cover?

As soon as the first potion started passing through the strange dark mist surrounding his attacker, he jerked out of the way, and the bottle crashed against the floor, spilling its contents everywhere.

Edwin winced. Intentional or not, it was still painful to see some of his few glass containers shatter in front of him. He'd take it over dying, though. He didn't have any time to really think it through though, as the hunter seemed to use Edwin's attack to find him, and the spear flashed out toward him, fortunately falling short.

Edwin followed up the first throw with several more harmless vials, each of which was effortlessly dodged. He quickly started throwing just his earthenware containers instead of the glass, but even empty ones were all swiftly avoided.

Soon, the hunter's slow advance brought him to the top of the stairs, and Edwin promptly fled through the roof, climbing over the edge of the wall and slipping out of the leaves that made his roof. Once he was on the outside, the magic of Obairlann supported him and he ascended to the top of the roof. There, he had a chance to breathe and let his wounds recover somewhat.

His hearing returned enough to hear a commotion inside, specifically the commotion of pottery and glass breaking, and Edwin winced. He didn't want to know what some of his creations would do when mixed, but it sounded like he was about to find out. He'd also probably have to remake most of his Alchemy equipment as well.

The branches near the edge of the roof rustled and parted as his assailant figured out where he'd gone, and the shadowy figure pulled himself onto the roof, only to be met with Edwin's entire bottle of concentrated knockout potion straight to the skull.

Edwin looked on in dismay as his efforts to make a tough container for what was by far his most impactful potion *succeeded*, and the ceramic vial failed to shatter on contact. Instead, it bounced off the hunter's head and rolled off the edge of the roof, leaving Edwin in the awkward position of having just thrown away his best weapon with nothing to show for it.

By the time he'd prepped a firebomb, the hunter had already closed much of the distance between the two of them, and Edwin frantically slid down the far side of the roof. He managed to stop himself before he fell off the edge, transferred his firebomb from his left hand to his right hand, and lobbed the grenade just in time before he fell.

Edwin took the landing relatively hard, which just meant that he went almost entirely limp to absorb the shock of hitting the ground before springing back up—Flexibility was great—and dashed to the talsanenris hedge. Behind him, he heard the figure curse as the grenade detonated, hopefully as it came into contact with him, but Edwin didn't look back right away.

In the bushes, he finally turned around to see what he needed to prepare for. Edwin's eyes widened in shock as the assassin took a leap from the top of the roof, diving gracefully to the ground. Wait, no. *Through* the ground. He had vanished into the soil without so much as a trace.

Edwin stood back warily, not sure where the assassin might reappear next, and a flash of motion from near the cliff drew Edwin's eye just in time to see him emerge from the rock, face and body tense. The shadows reappeared, enshrouding his body from the head down, but before they did, Edwin managed to make out a powerfully built, furred body with a wide, monstrous head and fanged mouth. As the shadows returned, the hunter looked more relaxed. The light hurt him, then? Or was just uncomfortable? Hmmm. Edwin needed to try and figure out flashbangs.

Edwin's eyes grew wide as the assassin produced a crossbow from . . . somewhere . . . and began the process of loading it. Within ten seconds, it was already cocked and ready to fire. That was *way* faster than the pattern he'd counted out earlier! Was the hunter trying to bait him out before? Probably, come to think of it.

He dashed through the bushes, intentionally rattling some that he wasn't near to try and confuse his assailant as crossbow bolts peppered his surroundings. He managed to remain mostly unharmed, save for some cuts that came from the bushes tearing at him. The bushes seemed to do a good job of foiling accurate shots.

If Edwin were to guess, maybe the assassin was used to underground fighting, and so wasn't used to undergrowth? It would explain stuff like the stone and earth travel and the discomfort with light. That confirmed that he likely was sent by the dwarves, even if he wasn't one himself. Edwin shuddered at the thought of having to deal with this assassin in enclosed spaces.

He really hoped Inion made it back soon. Edwin could only stall so long, especially against someone actually good at his job, no matter how out of his element he was. The assassin seemed mostly unfazed by the explosion, barring some likely disorientation, and Edwin certainly didn't have anything that could hit harder in his arsenal. His next option would be his knockout potion, but that had been knocked off the roof and lost to him for the time being.

So . . . time to just run around and hope that the assassin's accuracy didn't improve? There had to be a better idea than that, and Edwin had a sudden realization about something that might help. He broke from the bushes near the garden and, taking a deep breath, dove into Inion's pond.

It was freezing, naturally. It always was unless Inion specifically willed it otherwise, but Edwin couldn't let that hold him up. He swam to near the bottom of the very, very deep pool and looked up. He could see a couple bolts floating at the top, and another slammed into the water as he watched, disturbing the surface and penetrating just a few feet under before its momentum was sapped and it floated to the surface.

Whew. He was safe down here, for a little while at least. He'd never tested *exactly* how long he could stay underwater before he'd drown, but so long as he wasn't superactive and just let Breathing slowly work its magic, he could last about twenty minutes. Hopefully, that would be more than enough for Inion to return. Edwin gently wedged his foot in the crevasse of a rock to help him keep his position and looked up at his shadowy foe, who had arrived at the edge of the pond and was staring down at him through the crystal-clear waters.

Edwin wasn't sure why the small waterfall pouring into Inion's pond didn't disturb the surface, but he suspected fey shenanigans, especially as he didn't remember it happening before she woke up. Still, in this instance, it was very useful as Edwin and his hunter stared at each other in silence. The assassin prodded the pond with his foot, then withdrew.

If Edwin was above water, he would have sighed in relief. He was safe. Inion was bound to make it here before he needed to go up for air.

An enormous splash broke Edwin out from his reverie. He looked up and released most of his breath in surprise. A massive boulder had broken the top of the pond and was now sinking like, well, a rock directly at him.

He hastily extracted his foot from the crevasse it was wedged in—oh come on, it wasn't this hard last time—and darted out of the way just in time, joining the many fish displaced as the gigantic stone dropped through the water. Athletics was working overtime, and Edwin's lungs began to burn in protest at the sudden exertion, and even then he was still caught by the wake left by the stone, pulled in toward where it had just been while it settled to the bottom with a gentle crack.

There was another splash above Edwin. Then, another one. And a third. And a fourth. He looked up in panic and saw four more stones—not as large as the first, thankfully, but still at least as big as he was—sinking toward him. Ah, shoot.

He needed to do something, and fast. His lungs cried in protest, but how was he supposed to get to and be at the surface safely with boulders being chucked at him? More stones kept raining into the pond, and it was only a matter of time until Edwin was hit.

Hmm . . . He hadn't tried it, but couldn't Packing be of use here? Rock was something like one and a half times denser than water, so if he activated Packing on one of the stones falling toward him, given his current Packing level, it should then be . . . what, one-twentieth of the weight of the water? It would practically function as a flotation device! He could ride it up to the surface, using it as a shield, and then hide under it while taking the occasional breath.

Plan in mind, Edwin pushed himself just a bit farther to grab a slightly concave stone. He grabbed it, the rough surface of the rock hard on his hand, and . . . nothing. Edwin frowned, intentionally trying to get Packing to work. Nothing happened. What was going on?

The rock dragged Edwin down, and another stone crashed into his foot, making Edwin recoil. Why wasn't Packing working? Wait, no. It was, it just . . . wasn't doing anything?

He released the boulder before it could pull him farther underwater, and another rock struck him in the back, driving out the last bit of breath from his lungs and threatening to crush him under it. He rolled out from under it before it could sink so deeply, and he frantically swam toward the surface. He'd take his chance with the boulders, he just needed *air*.

Edwin broke the surface of the pond with a gasp, and immediately dove back underwater, grabbing on to a rock for weight, to avoid the rain of stone projectiles. Yeah, his attacker was *absolutely* geared for underground attacks if he could do this much with stone. There weren't many rocks that big in the surrounding area; he must have been pulling them from the cliff face itself.

Edwin continued the cycle for a little while longer, ducking up to the surface to get air, hitching a ride on a rock down. Then, his hunter caught on and started mixing in crossbow bolts every once in a while, catching Edwin in the side before he started becoming more cautious. Where *was* his attacker, anyway? He wasn't sure how long he could keep this up, not with a crossbow bolt sticking out of his gut and slowly bleeding him out.

The pond was flooding with every boulder thrown in, great splashes drenching the surrounding area and filling the stream to near bursting. Was he just trying to fill up the entire pool? That . . . Honestly, Edwin didn't know if that would work. Inion would be *peeved*, though. Not that she wouldn't be anyway.

The boulders had piled up significantly in the pool, and Edwin was almost considering trying to hide between them for shelter, but immediately dismissed that idea for being utterly idiotic. He'd never have time to make anything stable, and if it wasn't perfect, the shifting rocks as more struck them would make the whole thing collapse.

Come on, where was Inion? She had to know to come when she heard the explosion. How long had it been, anyway? It had felt like hours, but "minutes" was probably the better measure here. Each time he went up for air, Edwin lasted less and less time. While twenty minutes might normally be his limit, this was far from normal. Panicked gulps with highly injured lungs interspersed with playing dodgerock and avoiding being shot at barely got him a minute at a time, if that, and when a rock actually did connect, it tended to knock any remaining air from his lungs.

After what felt like an eternity, salvation arrived.

"Hey!" a voice boomed from the top of the cliff, melodic and terrifying. "Stop throwing rocks at my human!"

The sound echoed through the water, and Edwin looked on with hope, hesitantly climbing onto the shore in utter, pained exhaustion.

"Break it up! *Now!*" She sounded like she was scolding a kid, or maybe a dog. Honestly, that might not be the worst comparison.

The waterfall cut off suddenly, and a low rumble filled the area. A second later, Edwin's attacker was blown *out* of the cliffside, a pressurized blast of water carving a hole in the solid rock and breaking against Obairlann. The hunter, devoid of his shadowy occultations, slumped to the ground.

Then Inion crested the cliff, appearing to ride a wave of water to her pond. She floated over to where Edwin lay, a broken and bloody mess. "Are you okay? I'm sorry I took so long." Her voice was . . . unusually caring. She seemed like she might almost actually care about him personally, rather than just contractually.

Edwin managed a weak smile. "I've . . ."—he coughed, blood and water coming up from his lungs, and his side and entire body a mess of cuts, scrapes, bruises, and crossbow bolt—"I've been better."

"It's all gonna be okay, m'kay, Edwin? I'm here now." She cupped her hand around Edwin's head and gave him a smile, then turned back to a somewhat-recovered assassin who was trying to stand up and flee.

"And just where do you think *you're* going, you little *insect*? Uh-uh. You stay *here*." Inion snapped, and vines burst from the ground, ensnaring the hunter until Inion was able to reach him. Then, the vines retreated.

Before Edwin's former attacker could make a break for it, though, Inion reached out and grabbed him by the heel, her grip supported by a tendril of water, lifting him into the air and assessing him like a particularly interesting piece of meat.

"Eck. Honestly, people like you are why there's such a stereotype about bugbears. Like seriously, *Terror of the Depths? Haunting Nightmare? Abyssal Predator?* What sort of person takes Paths like that? What do you have to do to *get* Paths like that? Someone seriously messed you up at some point."

The hunter—bugbear, apparently—growled something that Polyglot began to translate, but Inion interrupted, returning the speech to snarling. "None of *that*, thank you very much. The children are listening."

Edwin . . . felt like he should be offended by that description, but he was in too much pain to really care.

"Now, what to do with *you*, though? Hmm . . ." Inion paused for dramatic effect. "Ah yes, *I* know."

A tendril of water snaked around her arm and the hulking figure, hefting him like he weighed nothing, and slammed him into the side of Obairlann. Edwin could hear something *crack* from where he was, and the yowl of pain that accompanied it almost hurt his ears. Or maybe that was just his head in general, and sympathetic wince.

Inion wasn't satisfied, though, and brutally slammed the bugbear into the ground a couple more times, each time sending a small spray of blood into the air and leaving a few tufts of fur drifting, then threw him bodily against the cliff. The hunter jumped at his chance and tried to dive into the stone. He was halfway into the rock when Inion suddenly *arrived* next to him, and the tendril of water wrapped itself around his ankle and yanked him out of the stone. "I *told you*. I will have *none* of that."

The assassin didn't come alone, and rocks ripped from the cliff seemed half merged with the bugbear, now a bloody mess even beyond Edwin's current state. One ear was mostly torn off, hanging by a thread. Bone was visibly poking through the fur on his chest, his right arm was at a bad angle, visibly broken yet somehow better off than his left arm, which was half missing. All that was left of his forearm was a splintered fragment of bone, the stump bleeding profusely.

Edwin couldn't help but wince as Inion refused to let up on her savage beating, and the intermittent screams were the only thing that let Edwin know that the bugbear was still, somehow, alive. The air around them, and Inion's water, was starting to turn red from the bloody mist his would-be assassin was slowly becoming.

"This isn't what you wanted? *THIS IS WHAT YOU EARNED*," Inion screamed at the hunter, her appearance shifting somewhat, becoming lankier, more distended, and hands slowly elongating into claws. "THIS IS WHAT YOU GET."

With every blow, she became more and more inhuman, and his attacker looked less and less like a creature. His pitiful cries wormed their way into Edwin's mind even after he looked away and closed his eyes, until he couldn't take it anymore.

"Inion!" Edwin called out, and she dropped the broken attacker in a heap, immediately reappearing next to Edwin.

"Yes, Edwin?" The tonal shift was . . . immense, and sudden. Same with her appearance. She looked no different from how she normally did.

"Just . . . stop." Edwin slumped in his plea. "I can't watch this. Just . . . put him out of his misery, or let him go, or . . . something. But I can't see you doing that to someone anymore."

"He would have killed you. Brutally. Painfully, if possible. Dragging your final moments out into hours, ensuring you were a broken, nervous wreck begging for death."

"I . . . I know. But please. I . . . don't want to return the favor. Give him a clean death at least, I can't stand to watch or hear anymore." She looked unconvinced, so Edwin pulled out what he hoped would work. "And I need your help besides. I can't move . . . hardly anything."

She seemed torn between her conflicting urges, before settling on one and giving a curt nod and a sigh. "Fine. For *you*."

The bugbear hadn't moved from where Inion had dropped him as she reappeared, picking him back up, this time by his splintered arm, "You hear that? You get off easily. *This* time."

With that, she wound back, enshrouded the hunter with water, and *threw* the assassin as hard as she could. The bugbear seemed to rouse slightly at the water's touch, and as he arced through the air, a trick of the light almost made it look like the creature's shadow cloak was remanifesting.

Edwin took a deep, rattling breath and leaned into Inion's embrace as she picked him up and carried him inside Obairlann.

"I really need to stop getting myself injured so much," he muttered as Inion gently laid him down on his "recovery" mat. "Maybe we scale down training a bit?" he tried to joke, but his heart wasn't into it.

"Ya," Inion carefully caressed his face. "Maybe a bit. Now sleep, Edwin. I have a lot of work ahead of me."

"Good luck," he mumbled, and his friend smiled.

"Sleep, Edwin. You need your rest."

Edwin sighed, and with a tug of his Skills, let darkness envelop him.

CHAPTER 29

The Wheel Turns Ever Onward

Edwin slept fitfully, dreaming of fire and water, of shadows and blood. He woke up several times to find Inion next to him, tending to his wounds.

When finally he awoke fully, it was nighttime, and Inion was cradling his head in her lap. While Edwin felt mostly light and sturdy, he was still sore in many places, leading to him trying to pull himself into a sitting position, only for Inion to gently keep him down. Not wanting to really cross her after what he had just seen, he obliged.

"Not yet," she reassured him. "You may *feel* better, but you still need your rest."

"How long?"

"Were you out? Only about a day this time. You still have a few bones that are cracked, and it took a while to get all the poison out, but you're recovering nicely. Health suits you well."

"You can tell? Wait, of course you can. My Class changed besides, and you can apparently see my Status?" He finished processing the rest of what she had said. "Poison?"

Inion nodded. "It was a slow poison, but a poison nonetheless. Quite tricky to purge, but I got it all in the end."

". . . Thanks." Edwin said, "This is what, the second time you've directly saved my life? Have I thanked you properly before?"

"Not *quite*." She replied, and Edwin winced.

"Sorry. I'm not very good at it."

"It's okay. You don't need to say it, I can feel it."

"You can?" Edwin frowned, to which Inion only replied with a smile. Did that mean she was joking or agreeing with him? "But it doesn't matter. I want to get better at it. I *need* to get better at it. You're my friend, and while that can be a thankless job, I don't want it to be."

"I finally managed to be your friend? I feel *honored*," Inion teased him, and he half-heartedly swatted at her leg.

"Best in the whole world."

"You don't . . . *have* any other friends on Joriah."

"Well, how else would you ever come out on top?"

She laughed and shoved him playfully. It hurt, but Edwin was still able to smile through the pain.

"So . . . bugbears?"

Another good night's sleep with First Aid and Sleeping active had Edwin to "mostly functional, though don't push it" Status. That meant his break from training was blessedly extended and left them chatting about the attack. Edwin had a lot of questions.

"Ya." Inion nodded. "Big and strong yet sneaky, *usually* live in the Beneath. Cousin to goblins and orcs with a decided aversion to strong light. They *love* taunting their prey, terrifying them and playing with them until they collapse from fear. They basically never go for the kill at their first opportunity, which probably kept you alive."

Edwin frowned. "I'm pretty sure this one *did* go for the kill right away, but I got lucky."

"Oh? Do tell, do tell."

"I was looking to carve a log," Edwin explained, "and it popped out of the ground just in time to intercept a bolt to my throat. Kind of unnerving, and that was the first glimpse I got of the . . . bugbear."

"Interesting. That's unusual behavior for them. Though you're somewhat wrong about *one* thing."

"Oh?"

"*Probably* not luck that kept you alive."

"What else could it have been?" Edwin cut in. "Were you messing with me?" he accused.

"If you'd let me *finish*."

"Sorry," Edwin mumbled in apology.

"*Anyway*. You mentioned you thought he might have been from the dwarves, ya?" Edwin nodded. "Ya. Their violation of hospitality rights would mean you'll find these little *coincidences* happening a lot more than usual. You've *probably* exhausted it now? What with it saving your life and all, but its effects are a *bit* more pronounced when living with me."

"Why's that—" Edwin cut himself off as he realized, "Fey thing?"

Inion nodded. "You've bound yourself to me, which means that I get some humanlike abilities from you, but that also means that you get some feylike abilities from me. But perhaps most importantly"—she gestured around—"this is your home. A place to be safe, to defend you from attack. Obairlann *itself* will come to your aid in ways much like what you saw. The walls are nigh unbreakable in the face of all but the most *overwhelming* of power, and things will fall in your favor more than with any who try to attack you here."

Huh. That was really interesting. "Does that affect you, too?"

Inion nodded. "I'm far stronger here than I would be anywhere else, because not only is *my* home here, but *your* home is here as well, and I'd *usually* be acting in service to try and protect you, which also lends some aid to my power."

Edwin mentally revised his assessment of Inion's strength from "utterly and obscenely terrifying" to "really darn intimidating, do not annoy." He said, "I'm not sure if that's reassuring or not. If you attack me, who gets the advantage?

"Also . . . I don't think I ever got an answer. Can you see my Status?"

Inion weighed her hands. "I can after a fashion. I can see your Skills to a certain extent, and I could pry further if I tried, but you'd feel it if I did."

"You were able to tell what the bugbear had for his Paths, though?"

"Only vaguely. He had a lot of them aimed in a very particular direction, and that's noticeable."

"I don't suppose you could teach me how to do that?"

"We'll see what Skills you get. Take some of your fey Paths, it might help. You're getting closer, ya?"

"Tell me about it," Edwin agreed, looking at his gains from the past few days.

Level Up!
Skill Points 1219→1235
Progress to Tier 2: 1370/1770 (Avg level: 66/77)
First Aid 71→73
Athletics 69→70
Breathing 66→68
Bomb Throwing 31→39
Sleeping 61→62
Firestarting 77→79

No major jumps, perhaps, but compared to the gains he usually got for a single day, which may have been a single level at *best*, he'd take it. Plus, he got days off! Win-win, if he didn't count the bruise that was his entire body as a negative.

"Just an average of eleven levels, or . . . four hundred total? Wait, no, that's not right."

A couple seconds of math had Edwin realize his mistake. "Ah, that's right. I still have all my Attribute Paths mixed in with my progress section."

"I'm going to *assume* that makes sense in your head, with whatever Status setup you have."

"Yeah, it does. Ah, it's not something I need to worry about at the moment."

They sat in silence for a few moments, broken only by Edwin wincing in pain and stretching his shoulder to try and work out a sore spot.

"So, now that I think about it, what are you going to do with all those rocks in your pond?" Edwin asked after a bit of time.

"Those? Ah, I tossed them out while you were asleep."

Edwin raised an eyebrow at that, but given what he'd seen, it also sounded about right. He wondered idly how long it had taken the pond to refill, but it also reminded him of the *last* thing he'd wanted to confront his friend about.

"What was up with all that with the bugbear, anyway? Was all that . . . brutality . . . really necessary?"

Inion looked at him like he'd said something absurd. "He hurt you," she replied, as though that was all the justification needed.

"I mean, I get that for just killing him, or throwing him away, but like . . . that was beyond any of that."

She shrugged. "Got off *easy*, if you ask me. He *hurt* you."

"Easy? He was beaten half to death, you ripped his arm into pieces, and threw him ten miles!"

"Eh, more like five. And you gotta be sure to be thorough when killing them. Buggers can be *tough*. Like cockroaches, but the size of a bear. Maybe where they got the name, actually."

"Really?"

"Eh, *probably* not, but I dunno how they did. So maybe."

"I'm getting distracted. But, like, why were you so cruel to him?"

"Cruel? Boy, you haven't *seen* what fey cruelty is like." It may have been Edwin's imagination, but Inion seemed to be . . . deeper in some way as she addressed him, something about her shifting to remind Edwin sharply that his friend was *not* human in the slightest. No matter how she looked.

"That someone else does it worse doesn't make what you do any better," he countered.

Inion thought for a moment. "Perhaps. It doesn't make it worse, though."

"Could you . . . try to scale it back a bit, though? I just . . . I dislike seeing that much pain."

"You're fine with *killing*, though?"

"Kind of? That's more a self-defense thing. Torture, on the other hand . . ."

"I don't *torture*," she spat, "I administer payback."

"Seems a bit . . . excessive, perhaps? You scare me like that."

"Oh, Edwin." She wrapped him in a hug. "You don't have anything to fear from me. Not now, not ever."

"I . . . that's not . . ." Edwin sighed. He was too tired for this, and the hug was . . . very nice. He was still holding firm on his "no dating the unknowable nature spirit" stance, particularly after the showing from the other day, but hugs? Hugs he could appreciate.

Something was strange with his Packing Skill. Edwin knew that much: it played around with momentum and weight in strange ways. He let his eyes skim over his Almanac entry for the Skill, reading through it and ensuring his recent reorganization of his old experiments fit properly. If he was going to turn Almanac into the ultimate guide to everything, that included Skills.

Almanac Entry: The Packing Skill
    Description:
    Useful when trying to bear the whole weight of the world on your shoulders
    Carry heavy loads easier
    Strength when carrying objects increased per level
    PackingUnlocks
    [Attempting to put explosives in a bag in such a way that wouldn't result in their detonation]
    PackingLeveling
    [Carrying heavy objects, packing objects in a careful manner]
    PackingEvolutions
    []

Packing is unusual in that the description provided, "Strength when carrying objects increased per level," is demonstrably wrong. The Skill does nothing for brute strength (see PackingTestA1), but instead affects the objects carried in some fashion. Testing (PackingTestB1) indicates that gravity is reduced on the objects affected by Packing.

PackingExploits
    [Objects carried with Packing are less likely to break, and picking up something with Packing will result in lessened internal stress—something flexible will bend less than usual, currently

investigating the possibility of utilizing Packing for flight or levitation (see PackingTestC)]

PackingNotes

[]

PackingCombinations

[When used with Mana Infusion, a carried object will become more durable. This can unlock the Mana Reinforcement Skill.]

PackingTestIndex

[PackingTestA1

PackingTestBConclusions: The B series is pertaining to the investigation of Packing reducing the weight of affected objects.

PackingTestB1

PackingTestB2

. . ..]

Nothing new there . . . Edwin frowned at the reminder of his A series test, and that he needed to relabel A and B into a single series, changing his flight experiments to series B. Series A's tests of whether Packing truly increased his raw strength had just been an attempt to lift tough objects and then see if he could break them, which, if his strength was truly increased, should have been trivial. It hadn't worked out, and he'd abandoned the series after only a single test, as reducing weight seemed to be a better explanation. It had held up to testing, too! He'd done five different tests, and number five had seemed to seal the hypothesis in.

Hypothesis: Packing decreases the weight of objects it is used upon.

Test 5: If weight is decreased, the weight of myself holding heavy objects should be significantly less than the weight of myself and the heavy objects individually. Set heavy object onto a sinking plate, then stepped onto sinking plate, then stepped onto sinking plate holding said heavy object, with depth sank in each step compared.

Results: Set heavy rocks on a flat stone resting on mud. Sank approximately 8 inches.

Reset standing stone and stepped onto. Sank approximately 10 inches.

Reset standing stone and stepped onto. Sank approximately 14 inches.

Conclusion: Hypothesis confirmed. Packing reduces weight of carried objects.

Now, though? With his failure to lift a boulder during the attack? He needed to revisit his tests. First up, seeing if the difficulty of lifting things underwater was replicable.

Hypothesis: Packing decreases the weight of objects it is used upon.

Testing: If weight is decreased, the density of lifted objects ought to be decreased, resulting in the capability of flying akin to a hot-air balloon, or utilizing even very dense objects as flotation devices within water. This test was performed with a Packing level of approximately 70, which from PackingTestA6 should grant a weight reduction of approximately 1/30.

Test 9: Rocks (density of 1.5 g/cm^3) dropped into water (density of 1 g/cm^3) and attempted to lift while underwater. With the current level of Packing, the resulting density of stone should have been approximately .04 g/cm^3 and be highly buoyant in water.

Results: Stone refused to float. Lifting the rocks was just as hard as normal while swimming, though lifting the rocks when bracing against the bottom was quite easy. Similarly, lifting a rock submerged in water from the shore was not significantly easier or harder than lifting the same rock from dry land.

Conclusion: Packing does not reduce the weight of objects. As this contradicts PackingTest5, reattempting Test 5 with more rigorous measurement technique. See PackingTest10.

Edwin was coming to realize he'd likely made some incorrect conclusions regarding the nature of Packing. He'd previously thought it directly lightened whatever he carried, and he wasn't quite convinced that *wasn't* what happened, but his experiments underwater showed a distinct lack of buoyancy from pretty much anything he tested that didn't *already* float, so that meant he would at the very least need to revisit his plans for flight.

Hmm.

Maybe it was a limitation of the water in some form? Skills could seem to be somewhat arbitrary at times, maybe Packing just needed his feet planted. Perhaps that was just the fundamental problem?

Hypothesis: Packing does not decrease the weight of objects it is used upon when in water, but said property is unique to water. Outside of water, weight is reduced by Packing as normal.

Testing: Setting up a makeshift scale, and stepping onto it while holding heavy objects. Once the scale has settled, the heavy objects will be set directly onto the scale and will then be stood upon. If weight is decreased by Packing, the scale should shift significantly once the objects are no longer held and thus having their weight reduced via Packing. If it is not decreased but rather redirected somehow, the scale should shift only a small amount if at all.

This test was performed with a Packing level of approximately 70, which from PackingTestA6 should grant a weight reduction of approximately 1/30.

Test 10: Set a log up as a lever and stood on one end while holding a heavy rock while stones were added to the other side, until the two sides reached parity. Then set down rock and stood upon it.

Results: The scale did not noticeably shift toward the experiment's side, meaning there was no difference in weight measured between holding and standing upon weights.

Conclusion: Results are more in line with PackingTest9, and overturn PackingTest5. Notes have been made. New methodology is required.

So if it didn't help by reducing weight, what *did* it do, then? Did the weight somehow "skip" him?

Hypothesis: Packing "offloads" weight of carried objects, making much of the weight of affected things not apply force to hands, arms, or legs, but are directly supported by the ground beneath the carrier. The percentage of this is determined by Packing's Skill level.

Testing: Attempting to see if this force reduction affects stacked objects when carried via Packing. Placing a heavy object on top of a fragile object while held in hand, then setting down the stack onto another surface.

Test 12: Held a pottery bowl upside down, then placed a large rock on top of the bowl. The bowl did not break. Carefully set the bowl onto the table.

Results: Initial versions of this test had the bowl not break at all, as the rock used was insufficiently large. However, once the stone was large enough, holding the rock and bowl enabled the bowl to support the rock, but the pottery was crushed immediately upon setting it on the table.

Conclusion: Force between carried objects is lessened. Hypothesis tentatively confirmed.

So, Packing offloaded force between objects. Was it a form of tactile tele-kinesis, perhaps? If so, that was even *better* than the gravity-manipulation idea. His dreams of flight weren't yet grounded!

However, that would depend on if he was able to convince the Skill to accept shoes or something he was standing on as part of "him" to exclude from the force distribution. If he did it properly, he might man-age to airwalk!

Hypothesis: Packing shunts force off to the exterior of the individual's frame of reference. Namely, anything that travels alongside the indi-vidual with Packing is excluded from excessive forces, whereas what is stepped on gets the full force of all carried weight.

Testing: Creating relatively fragile platform "shoes" that support full body weight and a matching platform with similar structural stability. Will stand upon platform wearing the shoes, gradually holding more and more weight and see whether the shoes break before the platform. If the platform breaks significantly prior to the shoes, hypothesis is confirmed.

Test 15: Created clay clogs with three half-inch-diameter, two-inch-tall pillars as support, and platforms with matching pillars. Gradually held more and more stones until one broke.

Results: Platforms broke well before the shoes did. Shoes never broke; ran out of ability to hold rocks before they did.

Conclusion: Hypothesis confirmed. The limits of how the System determines what counts as shoes or not needs further testing.

It took more work to properly determine what Edwin could get to count as part of "him" for Packing to work on. The general guideline did end up being what he suspected, however; namely, that if an object moved along with him as he walked, it was freed from internal forces.

He ended up being able to push his Skill pretty far, as well. He made shoes supported by stalks of grass, tiny twigs, even wet clay. It all worked out just fine, breaking only under fairly extreme circumstances . . . most of the time. Every once in a while, it just didn't work, and Edwin couldn't figure out why.

The "attached to him" restriction seemed quite arbitrary. Edwin understood it from a magical perspective, perhaps, where objects could be discrete and laws of nature were more . . . guidelines, than actual rules. But from a physical perspective? He was attached to literally everything in the universe via gravity and electromagnetic forces, no matter how weakly, and gravity and electromagnetism were the *only* forces that kept macroscopic objects together. There was bound to be some kind of trick he could exploit, it was just a question of what. . . .

Edwin kept working at it, though. He still had plenty of time.

That time slowly vanished as Inion ramped her training back up, but it was still, as fall slowly fell past, one of the few things that Edwin had in abundance.

"Huh."

"What's up?"

"I passed a year on Joriah at some point recently."

"You can tell?"

"The age on my Status by default thinks I was born when I fell to Joriah. I was getting suspicious and wanted to check it. Turns out, my meddling didn't do what I thought it would, it just kept me frozen at twenty-two. I took down my programming, which was also really wrong, wow. Maybe that was why it didn't work? Anyway, I took it down and Status now says I'm one year old."

Name
Edwin Maxlin
Age
1
Race
Extraplanar Human
Class
Sapper
Attributes
Mana 5
Health 7
Skills
Magical
Basic Mana Sense: 71, Mana Infusion: 74 (Basic Mana
Manipulation: 9)
Physical
Athletics: 70, Breathing: 68, Flexibility: 65, Nutrition: 59,
Packing: 76, Seeing: 59, Sleeping: 64, Survival: 66, Walking: 62
Mental
Polyglot: 56 (Language: 36), Mathematics: 65, Memory: 49
(Research: 50), Visualization: 69
Combat
Bomb Throwing: 39 (Throwing Weapons: 48)
Utility
Firestarting: 79, Alchemy: 79 (Improvisation: 14), Outsider's
Almanac: 111 (Status: 22), Identify: 63, First Aid: 75

"Happy anniversary?" Inion probed.

"Thanks, I guess. Not sure what the right terminology for the day commemorating being dropped into a new world would be."

She shrugged. "Whatever you wanna call it. I don't *think* there'd be a name for it, and none that'd be in all languages."

"Hmm. Well, I'll think about it."

"Now, you didn't think that would get you out of *training* today, did you?"

"... I mean, I was kind of *hoping* that ..."

"Ha! Get moving!"

Edwin sighed. No rest for the weary, it seemed.

Edwin groaned as he lifted a full-grown tree overhead. It had to have weighed something close to two tons, but Packing made it possible for him to support the whole thing. He winced as an ice crystal tore into the skin on his leg because he didn't move it quickly enough. He wasn't blindfolded in this variation of Inion's training, but that didn't make it any *easier*. Really, he wasn't sure how he wasn't sinking into the ground with the sheer amount of weight that had to be concentrated into the space right below his feet.

. . . Why *wasn't* he sinking into the ground?

Hypothesis: All weight carried by a Packer is concentrated in the space below their feet.

Testing: If all weight is so concentrated, spikes mounted at the bottom of feet ought to sink deep into soil once a moderate amount of weight is applied. The ground itself ought to give way under the pressure of a pinpoint application of massive force.

Test 35: Strapped knives to feet and stood on the soil. They did not immediately sink into the ground. However, it proved possible to "disable" this and sink into the soil. Which happened seems to depend on what is . . . expected to happen.

Conclusion: There is some additional support provided that prevents a Packer from sinking into the ground, but only when they think they ought not to. Possible use in water or airwalking.

Despite Edwin's best efforts, he wasn't able to walk on water by "expecting" not to, though that may well have been a limitation of imagination. He honestly couldn't be sure. However, further testing showed that he *could* walk on mud with more ease if he expected he shouldn't sink in. He would still sink in *somewhat*, but just not as much as he should—determined by a facsimile of him that he'd cobbled together out of branches and rocks.

It was . . . frustrating, and the first true evidence Edwin had that his thoughts could genuinely influence the way his Skills impacted the world around him.

Stupid magic, not following the proper laws of the universe. How *dare* it open an entirely new branch for comprehending and exploiting everything!

It *did* mean that he needed to redo a lot of his old experiments that had confirmed his hypotheses, on the off chance that they had been influenced into performing as they were "supposed" to. Fortunately, there weren't any major discrepancies with the later check. Or was that just because his expectations hadn't changed? Gah!

Despite himself, Edwin was still having a *blast*. He was doing actual, really cool research into his own little slice of the universe! He was slowly learning how to fly! He had *magic!* He had glowing potions in bowls and bottle (only a single surviving glass vial, sadly) on his shelf!

It had taken Edwin some time to rebuild his Alchemy supplies after the bugbear's attack, especially as his magical plants stopped bearing so much fruit, but he'd managed it in the end. (Edwin had been quite relieved to find that his knockout potion hadn't broken after it fell off the roof, and that he was able to safely retrieve it.) Inion's training was painful as always, but it still proved to be a fruitful way to pass the time as winter rolled in.

Then, it was an exhausting way to pass the time as winter rolled out.

Edwin was determined to crack open his Skills, and while Packing may have remained stubbornly out of reach, that didn't mean he let his other abilities fall by the wayside. Well, Inion's training ensured he wasn't able to let their *levels* fall by the wayside, but he still had *science* to perform on them!

While he had varying degrees of confidence with his assessments, Edwin felt that he had a decent handle on how a fair number of his Skills worked "under the hood," so to speak.

Athletics increased the density of his cells: giving him more blood, more bone cells, more and tougher skin cells. He'd need a microscope to confirm it, but he felt certain in his conclusion.

Bomb Throwing magnified the speed of combustion reactions, sometimes of his choosing, other times randomly. Breathing had initially helped him absorb more oxygen with every breath and now aided him in using said oxygen more effectively.

Alchemy gave a combination of instincts for how various procedures worked and magnified the results. Construction functioned similarly in that Edwin got hunches as to how something might be best created, but the Skill likewise aided him in said creation. Glues stuck slightly better, saws cut more easily and left smoother surfaces. Firestarting acted as a catalyst, allowing oxidation reactions to happen a lot easier, other than rust (it made him wonder if thermite would be aided by the Skill).

First Aid worked in a similar manner to talsanenris berries, speeding up metabolism in treated areas and magnifying the body's recovery capabilities. Flexibility made Edwin . . . bendier. His very bones could deform slightly without pain or harm, or not so slightly in other cases, and his joints were slowly becoming almost omnidirectional.

Mathematics felt like a sort of basic calculator stapled to his mind, which could store numbers he put into it and recall them later, like the System had directly connected a computer cable to his brain. Nutrition, Edwin suspected, aided his body in dismantling whatever he ate on a submolecular level and reconstructing it in a more helpful form. He'd managed to stave off hunger at one point by eating a literal stick, despite it normally being indigestible to humans. That meant he should probably still try to get his minerals, but any organic chemicals he would get just from normal life.

Purify made dissimilar molecules repel one another. He'd separated a small pile of sand and dust just by blowing on it, could wash out even bloodstains with trace amounts of water, and he could clean his hands by Infusing Purify, making all dust, dirt, and stains simply flake off and fall to the ground. He still needed some methodology to purify things, but no matter what it was, it worked great.

Edwin suspected that Seeing worked by messing with the Rayleigh resolution formula. *How* a Skill managed to mess with a fundamental property of optics was something Edwin deeply wished he had a full lab and research group to investigate, but considering he could distinguish two points less than a millimeter apart from the far side of the clearing, which a bit of math told him should be physically impossible given the size of his eyes, he didn't see any other possibilities.

For the rest of his Skills, Edwin just didn't have anywhere to start. Be it Basic Mana Sense or Mana Infusion, he simply didn't know enough about mana to make any educated guesses. Its effects clearly depended on what he used it *on*, but beyond vague common-sense intuitions as to what *should* happen with magical rocks or water, there weren't any apparent physical patterns. He could feel Memory working, sharpening recollections—particularly those from Earth—as he actively tried to remember something, but he didn't know enough neuroscience to begin to guess how that might work. He ran into similar problems with Harvesting, Visualization, Survival, Sleeping . . .

Packing still worked when Edwin walked on his hands, interestingly. It didn't help him support his weight on thin branches, but did when he was in a cluster of vines. It didn't help him keep his footing on slippery surfaces, but if his feet were coated with something slippery, like soap, then Packing would help him.

He'd finally figured out what it was that Packing did to help him avoid sinking into the ground, as well! It sort of . . . spread out his weight, under his entire body, but only so long as the ground was at the same level as his feet. Walking with knives for shoes meant the point of the knife was the bottom of his "foot" and the weight was distributed across its normal area. But if he was *standing* on a knife, then it would be driven into the ground until it was flush with its surroundings or it was somehow able to hold Edwin up.

He was still working on translating that to letting him walk on air, but he felt that he was getting close. And after all—

Level Up!
Skill Points 1235→1473
Progress to Tier 2: 1559/1770 (Avg level: 76/77)
Alchemy 78→83
Athletics 70→81
Basic Mana Sense 68→77
Bomb Throwing 39→49
Breathing 68→75
Construction 68→77
Firestarting 79→90
First Aid 73→82

Flexibility 63→74
Harvesting 66→76
Identify 62→71
Mana Infusion 73→83
Mathematics 65→74
Memory 49→56
Nutrition 59→69
Outsider's Almanac 111→124
Packing 73→83
Polyglot 55→59
Purify 63→75
Seeing 58 →70
Sleeping 62→73
Survival 65→76
Visualization 67→78
Walking 62→74

—everything else was coming together *nicely*.

CHAPTER 30

Two Paths Diverged in the Verdant

At long last, it was time for Edwin to make his last few preparations before finally tiering up. Sure, it had taken him some four or five months (he'd stopped keeping track at this point) to get these last ten levels in each of his Skills, but now he was just a handful away before his break-even point was reached at long last!

It hadn't been easy getting this far. He'd managed to get Firestarting to only affect a small area centered around his hand, and his break-through on constraining the Skill's shape had allowed him to finally use his firebombs with a modicum of control, and though he still struggled getting the Infusion to connect properly, he no longer ran quite as much of a risk setting his surroundings on fire.

That breakthrough had managed to get Edwin over the level 90 spike in difficulty, and his current task was trying to turn areas "on" or "off," enabling him to burn patterns into wood. So far, he had managed "square" and "circle," but he was hoping to get a few more levels from it before it evolved.

On the other end of the level spectrum, Seeing and Nutrition were lagging behind. The latter he kind of blamed on his tendency to go weeks without eating, which from what he could tell was the only way Nutrition leveled up with any regularity. That said, he hadn't tried setting up an IV drip to see if he *could* help Nutrition that way. When it came to Seeing, Edwin just didn't get much practice with it, especially given Inion's tendency to blindfold him during their training.

As a result, she'd shifted tack lately, giving him tasks that were more reminiscent of an optometrist's test. It was, if nothing else, a nice relief from the more physically perilous tasks he usually had to deal with. Edwin also spent a fair bit of time trying to combine Seeing with Basic Mana Sense, giving him an improved range where he could "see" mana, but in exchange it only functioned in the direction where he was looking; his omnidirectional sense didn't work when so focused. His attempts at constraining the area of effect like how Firestarting worked were thus far unsuccessful, but it at least wasn't terribly strenuous.

Of course, it was offset by all the time Inion was now having Edwin spend waterboarding himself. It apparently helped both Breathing level as well as Purify, but after each session he couldn't help but wonder if that specific method was really worth it.

Packing, of course, he kept pushing by trying to use it to fly. He was close, he knew it, not that he could vocalize exactly why he felt that way. It was just some combination of his growing proficiency of its use and its own increasing level that pushed him further and further, allowing him to support himself on more and more tenuous supports. The way the Skill worked vaguely hurt his brain at times, as it didn't fit quite with how forces *worked*. He still always felt his own weight, but the weight of things he carried just . . . slid off. But he could still *feel* their weight pressing down on him, and they didn't feel any lighter, just easier to manage.

Edwin rubbed his temples before he could pull himself off topic again, refocusing on what he should be thinking about.

Ideally, he'd unlock the Flight Skill now to maximize the effect of his efforts to level up Packing, then decline it and re-unlock it after he tiered up once he knew the trick. He had time, after all. For the first time since . . . Well, for the first time since he started high school a nigh decade ago, the only pressure on him was his own restlessness. It was . . . freeing. He could really do only so much while he was still at Obairlann, which was why his plan similarly included *not* sticking around once he tiered up.

Yes, it would be smarter to stay and get a solid grasp on his Skills and a good bank of levels under his belt, but he couldn't stand to go through *another* year out here. He kind of missed human interaction, unbelievably. Who would have thought that after months of only interacting with Inion he might want something more? It was shocking, truly shocking. Plus, it was boring here. The only entertainment Edwin really had—training did *not* count, it was a wonder he'd stayed focused on it for as long as he had—were his plants, and he'd *long* since finished cataloging his alchemical ingredients (other than hispera, which didn't grow fast enough) to nearly the full extent of his abilities.

Firevine was the simplest of his plants; every part of it was related to fire in some way. The leaves made good tinder, its sap was highly flammable, and its sticks burned hot and evenly, making them useful for controlled-temperature fires.

Talsanenris acted as magical sugar, giving cells all the energy they could ever need and speeding up their metabolism dramatically. Its leaves and branches were exceptionally nutritious, and when combined, a tiny pellet of the leaves and berries could make highly effective energy tablets—essentially stamina potions, Edwin realized.

Sunstalk had *something* to do with light, and while he was befuddled as to *how* it worked, Edwin had managed to determine that its invisibility in sunlight wasn't actually invisibility. Instead, it absorbed and reemitted any and all light it was exposed to, like some kind of sci-fi cloaking device. This process was much faster in direct sunlight, but still functioned in the shade or in darkness, just with colors far less distinct and with a very delayed reemission.

Sinbalyne functioned as a combination of nerve blocker and vasodilator. When inhaled, it produced light-headedness and slowed reactions, and when applied topically, it encouraged blood flow to an area. Concentrating it made it lose some of its vasodilation properties, which meant its effects stayed quite local. When it was ingested, the concentrate rapidly induced unconsciousness; applying it topically rapidly caused all sensation to fall away from the affected area; and when *injected*, it temporarily paralyzed the limb. Edwin was still figuring out the dosages (for obvious reasons he was hesitant to test it on himself), but it was extremely promising.

Molai acted as a magical resistor of sorts. When it was mixed with another alchemical ingredient, especially a fresh one, it slowed the discharge of said magic, meaning that instead of a powerful effect all at once, the potion would slowly have a lesser effect. Sunstalk glowed more softly but for longer, firevine burned slowly, more like a candle than a blowtorch, talsanenris didn't deliver all its energy at once, transforming the nutrition pellets from a shot of magical caffeine to rations, allowing the life mana to seep into the body over time. Of limited *personal* use to Edwin, molai and sinbalyne worked to make a sleeping potion. Its offensive applications were obvious, but delivery methods were still spotty at best.

By contrast, the seemingly boring glowleaf was ironically the *most* interesting of Edwin's plants. He had noticed some of the originally purple leaves changing color to varying shades of blue or red and had set out to investigate. Over extensive experimentation, he'd found that contrary to what Zosiman had said, glowleaf *did* seem to all be one species, but its color was determined by external factors. Specifically, environmental mana.

Because he didn't know any methods to remove magic from something (his attempts to do so with molai were what led him to realize what the plant truly did), he couldn't use it to make a magic-detection potion, but Edwin was confident that if he found some way to strip all external mana from the glowleaf, then mix it with molai to help dampen environmental "noise," he would create a clear potion that would change color depending on the kind of magic it was exposed to.

Overall, Edwin had found his toolkit included magical fire, light, life, and paralysis. Combined with an indicator and a time-delay, he felt decently confident in his initial alchemical repertoire. He'd made a fair number of potions with different uses, most abundant being firevine bombs, which closely resembled Molotov cocktails in function, striking something and setting it on fire.

He'd confirmed that Bomb Throwing did work on the firebombs, and it made the flames burn hotter, as well as affect a larger area.

Everything had, naturally, been fastidiously recorded in the Almanac. All his findings, all his formulae, all his musings on the plants and potential uses. He would leave a legacy, and if someone got ahold of it and tried to use it against him? Well . . . if it came to that, he'd figure something out. Edwin couldn't help but feel that they deserved it if they managed to pull it off, though he probably wouldn't feel that way then.

Okay, enough stalling. He needed to actually look at and organize his Paths. He'd been putting off the notifications for so long . . . this wouldn't be fun. Or maybe it would be! He needed to look on the bright side as he queried the System.

Instantly, his vision was filled with long-suppressed text.

Congratulations! For developing six unique potion effects, you have unlocked the Alchemist Path!

Congratulations! For granting access to your Almanac unto another, you have unlocked the Almanac Administrator Path!

Congratulations! For going two weeks without eating or drinking, you have unlocked the Ascetic Path!

Congratulations! For setting yourself on fire, you have unlocked the Autopyromaniac Path!

Congratulations! For developing a number of explosives, you have unlocked the Bomber Path!

Congratulations! For developing a system to create bricks, you have unlocked the Brickmaker Path!

Congratulations! For turning one year old, you have unlocked the Child Path!

Congratulations! For spending a year improving yourself and learning about the nature of the world, you have unlocked the Dedicated Student Path!

Congratulations! For slaying a Mature Deepwoods Panther, you have unlocked the Deepwoods Panther-Hunter Path!

Congratulations! For detonating a powerful bomb and destroying a permanent construction in the explosion, you have unlocked the Demolitionist Path!

Congratulations! By spending more than twelve minutes underwater, you have unlocked the Diver Path!

Congratulations! For successfully making a basic waterwheel, you have unlocked the Engineer Path!

Congratulations! For obtaining extensive training from an elder fey, you have unlocked the Fey Scion Path!
Congratulations! For successfully bringing a crop of food to maturity, you have unlocked the Gardener Path!
Congratulations! For killing a foe through self-mutilation, you have unlocked the Heedless Hunter Path!
Congratulations! For being recognized by the Liras Empire as an Ally, you have unlocked the Imperial Ally Path!
Congratulations! For growing and harvesting a crop of magical plants, you have unlocked the Magical Gardener Path!
Congratulations! For healing yourself from the brink of death with the aid of another, you have unlocked the Medic Path!
Congratulations! For arranging the mass sale of products you created, you have unlocked the Merchant Path!
Congratulations! For surpassing level 120 in the Outsider's Almanac Skill, you have unlocked the Outsider's Almanac Specialist Path!
Congratulations! For transcribing an entire book into another form, you have unlocked the Scribe Path!
Congratulations! For your efforts to uncover the fundamental nature by which Skills act upon the world, you have unlocked the Skill Researcher Path!
Congratulations! For having traveled 1,200 miles while away from your home and settling to another permanent residence, you have unlocked the Traveler Path!
Congratulations! For surviving a life-or-death battle and successfully attacking a powerful foe during its course, you have unlocked the Warrior Path!

Huh. That was a lot, and yet it still ended up being . . . quite a bit smaller than Edwin had anticipated. Then again, it wasn't like he'd actually *done* anything all that noteworthy over the past year, not in comparison to his first five or six months on Joriah at least. He'd just been focusing on improving his Skills, which ended up being reflected in the relatively anemic Path selection before him.

"Hey, Inion, is it normal to get a Path for reaching level one hundred twenty in a Skill?" he asked his friend, who wandered over to where he was reclining.

"I can't say I actually *know* the answer to that. Why, didja get something?"

"Outsider's Almanac Specialist, yeah. Ninety points. Any guesses what it might do?"

Inion barely even needed to think. "Either take and enhance the Skill it's based on, giving it a straight upgrade to efficacy, or give another Skill a lot of synergy with it. For you, it might take . . . Visualization, and allow you to include more detailed images in your entries. You can include images already, right?" She frowned.

"Yeah, I can. It's a bit tricky to do so, but probably not worth another Skill. Anyway, you want to help me figure out my Path ordering?" he asked, looking at his massive pile of Paths to choose from.

Adventurer 0/30, Alchemical Medic 0/60, Alchemical Warrior 0/90, Alchemist 0/60, Almanac Administrator 0/60, Arsonist 0/60, Ascetic 0/60, Assassin 0/60, Athlete 0/60, Autopyromaniac 0/60, Biologist 0/60, Blackstone Conqueror 0/60, Bomber 0/60, Brickmaker 0/30, Burglar 0/60, Butcher 0/30, Chemist 0/60, Child 0/12, Daredevil 0/60, Dedicated Student 0/60, Deepwoods Panther-Hunter 0/60, Demolitionist 0/60, Diver 0/30, Engineer 0/60, Escapee 0/30, Exile 0/30, Expert 0/60, Explorer 0/60, Fey Friend 0/60, Feybound 0/60, Feycaller 0/60, Fey Scion 0/60, Feytouched 0/90, Field Medic 0/60, Forerunner 0/60, Gardener 0/30, Giant Slayer 0/60, Heedless Hunter 0/60, Hunter 0/30, Imperial Ally 0/60, Killer 0/30, Lecturer 0/30, Lumberjack 0/60, Mage 0/60, Magical Gardener 0/60, Makeshift Alchemist 0/60, Master of Obairlann 0/60, Master of the Ruined Tower 0/60, Medic 0/30, Merchant 0/30, Micro-Biomancer 0/90, Novice 0/12, Novice Pyromancer 0/60, Novice Ritualist 0/60, Outsider 0/60, Outsider's Almanac Specialist 0/90, Path Less Traveled 0/90, Physical Alchemist 0/90, Physical Arcanist 0/60, Physical Laborer 0/30, Physicist 0/60, Experimenter 0/60, Pioneer 0/60, Potioneer 0/60, Potter 0/30, Practical Alchemist 0/60, Primal Constructor 0/90, Primal Ritualist 0/90, Purifier 0/30, Pyromaniac 0/30, Razer

of the Ruined Tower 0/60, Realm Traveler 0/120, Rebel 0/30,
Recluse 0/30, Researcher 0/60, Scientific Revolutionary 0/90,
Scientist 0/60, Scout 0/60, Scribe 0/30, Skill Researcher 0/60,
Skilled Arcanist 0/60, Slave 0/12, Steadfast Medic 0/60, Stonehide
Vanquisher 0/60, Superior Alchemist 0/60, Survivor 0/60, System
Scholar 0/60, Titan Slayer 0/90, Trainee 0/60, Traitor 0/60,
Trapper 0/60, Traveler 0/30, Unkillable 0/90, Wanderer 0/60,
Warrior 0/60, Way of the Empty Hand 0/60, Woodsman 0/30,
World Traveler 0/60

He'd pulled out all his previous organization details, as he wanted
to reassess them with fresh eyes and with advice from someone he
trusted more than Lefi. Still, Edwin and Inion quickly eliminated some
Paths like Slave, Child, and Novice—Paths with little to no or harmful impact. That was followed by the mundane profession Paths, like
Brickmaker, Gardener, and Physical Laborer. Sure, they might give him
something good, but he also couldn't confess to being terribly interested
in them over their more interesting counterparts. He similarly couldn't
claim to find appeal in his Ascetic, Exile, Rebel, Recluse, Traveler, Revolutionary, and Imperial Ally Paths nor their ilk, so those got cut next.

From there, Inion helped him pick out the Paths that were likely to
give him an Attribute; namely Path Less Traveled, Scout, and Athlete.
He asked about getting Intelligence or some other related Attribute,
hopeful that he might be able to get it through Scientist or Researcher,
but Inion told him that given he already had mind-related Skills pertaining to research, it was unlikely that he would get the Attribute from
anything he had unlocked. In fact, shy of something along the lines of
a Genius Path, he was probably out of luck for Willpower and Intelligence. Edwin didn't really understand it, but Inion seemed certain, so

. . .

Edwin mentally shrugged. It didn't matter *that* much, he supposed.
He liked to think he was already smart enough to survive, but he was
realistic enough to recognize that was an idle hope at best.

Inion also thought there was a good chance that Unkillable would
give him Constitution, which he was initially in favor of, but she also
said that cheaper Paths were liable to give the Attribute. Edwin wasn't

sure if it was worth waiting on something that stood such a good chance of keeping him alive, but the 90-point Path *was* a pretty big commitment.

He'd reassess it once he had everything figured out, but for now he reluctantly set it to the side. He'd probably still take it in the end anyway. Not dying was high on his priority list, after all. Apparently Path Less Traveled was a Big Deal, because Inion said that it was still a priority even with the cost.

That was when it started getting hard. Virtually any of the remaining Skills he would most likely be content with. Assassin would help him survive by staying unseen, Escapee would help him avoid mental ensnarement, Titan Slayer would give some really great combat Skill that would aid him in taking down strong foes . . .

Okay, think. If two Paths had the same point cost, the more general one was probably superior for someone like him, who needed broadly applicable Skills rather than a few specialized tools. Unless, of course, he really liked the sounds of the Path. That was also a factor to consider. However, more expensive Paths would give him Skills that were more distinct from what he currently had, and that was generally a good thing, so . . ..

Edwin still set aside Realm Traveler on account of being just *too* expensive for the time being, World Traveler and Way of the Empty Hand for more or less being more specific variations of Wanderer and Warrior, Almanac Administrator for not being what he could most benefit from. . . . It was a painful process, but he slowly narrowed it down.

Hunter and Killer would be cheap ways to get attack Skills, was that worthwhile?

He only really needed one Medic Skill, what did he want to focus on?

How many fey-related Paths should he go for?

Blackstone Conqueror, Stonehide Vanquisher, Deepwoods Panther-Hunter, Superior Alchemist were all likely trophy Paths. How many did he want? Which did he want? Did he want any?

He only needed one fire-related Skill if he was being honest, but Firestarting had been so useful he should probably take a flame-focused Path to give it a potentially even better use, though he only needed one, and it probably wasn't going to be Autopyromaniac.

Did he want Skill Researcher or System Scholar? Did he want either? Both? Hmm . . .

Master of Obairlann would probably tie him to its eponymous location in some way, and considering he was about to leave, it wouldn't be the most useful. Unless it would be? Ah, maybe if he already had a teleportation Skill. But probably not yet.

He . . . probably didn't need more explosion-related Skills. At least not yet, right? He was cautious about blowing himself up following the assassin's attack.

Primal Ritualist and Primal Constructor were both rather expensive, and Edwin wasn't sure if he wanted the nature overtones they brought with them. The natural world was *fine*, but he was no Biologist.

On something of a whim, he decided to sort his Paths based on what their categories seemed to be. Maybe that would help him figure things out, based on how he wanted his Skill distribution?

Attributes Likely

Path Less Traveled 0/90, Scout 0/60, Athlete 0/60, (Unkillable 0/90)

Trophy: Blackstone Conqueror 0/60, Deepwoods Panther-Hunter 0/60, Stonehide Vanquisher 0/60, Superior Alchemist 0/60

Combat: Alchemical Warrior 0/90, Assassin 0/60, Giant Slayer 0/60, Heedless Hunter 0/60, Hunter 0/30, Killer 0/30, Titan Slayer 0/90, Trapper 0/60, Warrior 0/60

Magic: Mage 0/60, Magical Gardener 0/60, Micro-Biomancer 0/90, Novice Pyromancer 0/60, Novice Ritualist 0/60, Skilled Arcanist 0/60

Science: Alchemist 0/60, Chemist 0/60, Biologist 0/60, Physicist 0/60, Engineer 0/60, Experimenter 0/60, Purifier 0/30, Researcher 0/60, Scientific Revolutionary 0/90, Scientist 0/60

Physical: Physical Alchemist 0/90, Physical Arcanist 0/60

Medical: Alchemical Medic 0/60, Field Medic 0/60, Steadfast Medic 0/60

Alchemical: Makeshift Alchemist 0/60, Potioneer 0/60, Practical Alchemist 0/60

Fey: Fey Friend 0/60, Feybound 0/60, Feycaller 0/60, Fey Scion
0/60, Feytouched 0/90
Other: Adventurer 0/30, Daredevil 0/60, Dedicated Student
0/60, Escapee 0/30, Explorer 0/60, Forerunner 0/60, Outsider
0/60, Pioneer 0/60, Skill Researcher 0/60, System Scholar 0/60,
Wanderer 0/60

Hmm. It didn't make things any *easier*, but it did help Edwin visualize everything better. He had 50 Paths to choose among, and 18 Skills to go with them. This . . . was going to be tricky.

He didn't need that many combat Skills, and so he could eliminate the ones like Hunter, Killer, and Assassin, which . . . well, no, Assassin might be useful given how it stood a chance of giving him some sort of stealth Skill. Well, Trapper, then. Or no. Traps *would* work well with his theoretically perfect fighting style, wouldn't they? Setting up hazards and letting people blunder into them? Well, he could take out the 30- and 90-point Paths if nothing else. He wanted to try and use Alchemical Warrior on Bomb Throwing when the time came. But he could probably reearn it if he tried? He'd gotten it escaping the dwarves, hadn't he?

Darn it, this was supposed to simplify things!

Fine. He'd take out the 30-point ones—with none of his current Skills really all that combat focused, he'd need something with a bigger impact. He'd also take out Heedless Hunter and Warrior, the former because he felt like whatever Skill it provided would involve hurting himself, which he wasn't terribly fond of, and the latter because . . . well, no. He'd leave Warrior in for now, as a nice generic combat Path.

Magical Gardener . . . nah. He wasn't likely to keep growing stuff while on the road. It might be useful if he ever settled down again, but not for the time being. Micro-Biomancer would probably be very cool, but more effective if he already had something . . . Nutrition would probably pair well with it, wouldn't it? Hadn't he gotten the two at the same time? It was still expensive, though. Off to the side for now.

Well, with Science, at least the choice was easy! He was a physicist and alchemist, not a biologist. That said, he certainly was more of a biologist than a doctor, so . . . he moved the Skill over to his "medic" category. Purifier might be nice . . . he'd see if he needed a cheaper Path. Experimenter, Researcher, and Chemist were all great . . . but inferior to the others.

Did he want his physical Skill to involve magic or Alchemy? Hmm . . .

Choosing a medical Skill should have been easy, but did he really want to hyperfocus on Alchemy? It might leave him vulnerable if he was ever caught unawares. So should he take Field Medic? It was between Alchemical and Field for the time being at least. But maybe he should go with Biologist? It would be somewhat out of left field, but he trusted his science background far more than he did his half-remembered first aid skills from his days as a Boy Scout, so it might work in his favor. Between Alchemical Medic, Field Medic, and Biologist, then.

Potioneer . . . Edwin wasn't really sure what that would do. Well, it would help him make potions, that much was obvious, but that was only one part of Alchemy, and one he was already decent at for that matter. Shouldn't he try to expand his capabilities? Makeshift Alchemist would probably help him with difficulties he might encounter from not having adequate supplies, but Practical just sounded . . . well, practical.

His fey Paths . . . well, Feybound and Feycaller both seemed sub-optimal. He wasn't really inclined to try waking up or dealing with any more, making Feycaller superfluous, and Feybound made Edwin think it might make him more susceptible to fey influence. It would no doubt come with some really impressive benefits, but he wasn't sure the added benefits outweighed what he'd get from Fey Scion or Feytouched. Fey Friend seemed fine, but the name just didn't seem quite as impressive to him as Scion or -touched. Petty, perhaps, but he needed *some* way to narrow down what Paths he was taking, and if it came down to personal preference in the end, may as well get a bit ahead of the curve there.

Adventurer . . . well, Edwin wasn't sure what that might provide him. It might give him some sort of general-purpose Skill that aided him as he wandered about, or it might do something tying him to the Empire in some way. Given the Path wasn't *Lirasian* Adventurer, he doubted it, but it was still something to keep in mind.

Daredevil would . . . hmm. He needed to think about that.

A bit of conversing with Inion and general musing later, Edwin felt like it would probably give him some sort of crash-resistance Skill, possibly evolving Flexibility to improve his capabilities of absorbing falls and blunt attacks. The question was, did he really *need* that? Between Health and whatever he ended up choosing to enhance his combat and physical prowess, not to mention his current non-Skill proficiency with ducking and rolling, he could deal with most situations well enough. Did he need more? Eh, probably not. It would be more of a niche Skill if his predictions were right. He'd keep it in mind in case he needed an extra Path for some reason, but he'd take it off for the time being.

Escapee was a cheap path with some utility. Keep for now.

Explorer and Forerunner were similar, but Edwin couldn't say he was terribly inclined to go exploring trackless wildernesses . . . no, that was flatly untrue. He was still in the mindset of Earth, where there wasn't anywhere left to explore. He absolutely needed one of them, but which? And was Adventurer close enough to count? Argh! He wanted everything!

Outsider he absolutely wanted. It was the main Path (alongside Path Less Traveled and the Almanac Skills) that would let him leverage his supposedly mythical status as an Outsider. Well, Realm Traveler also fit into that mold, but he was *not* spending that many points on a Path this tier. The unique aspects of it would probably be largely wasted, but if he *waited* for a tier or two, well, he might well get some kind of teleportation ability.

Inion had told him flat out that nothing he had was close enough to teleportation for even the 120-point Path to get him there, but depending on his advancements, he might get there next tier. Longstrider, which was what Lefi had predicted he'd get by taking Wanderer to evolve Walking, might make it possible—Edwin dropped it on his list of strong contenders. In addition, Wanderer just spoke to him on some level. It encapsulated what he *wanted* to be in this next phase of his life. It was simple, yet profound.

In any case, Outsider was on the shortlist. Pioneer was more debatable, though. It was halfway between his System Paths and Explorer. . . . Would it be better to have more Skills like that, or fewer? Why did this have to be so hard?

Dedicated Student . . . maybe it would help him learn faster? He already had Memory for that sort of thing, though. Maybe a focus Skill? That would be appealing, but given it required a year of work to unlock the Path, it was more likely to give some sort of willpower improvement. That was honestly kind of appealing . . . Hmm. He'd put it to the side for now. While appealing, it didn't seem like the kind of Path or Skill that would help him with his attention span, which was all he really needed assistance with in that regard.

Edwin had *no* clue what Skill Researcher or System Scholar might get him. Maybe some sort of Skill-identifying upgrade to Identify? But he could already sort of mimic that with Almanac. Should he wait for the next tier and see if they would evolve Almanac? Outsider's Almanac was already a fantastic Skill; he couldn't imagine how good it would get if he managed to get it integrated into the System further. System Scholar would be put off to the side for now, then. Skill Researcher, though? He needed to understand the System, and Skill Researcher seemed to fit that bill perfectly.

Tallying them, that left . . . 36 Paths. Still twice as many as he really needed.

Okay, time to get picky. Titan Slayer was cool, but if he was to take a 90-point Path, it wasn't going to be that one. He wanted to invest more points where he actually wanted to *focus*. He wasn't going to be a Forerunner, leading people to new frontiers; Explorer fit him much better. Pioneer met a similar fate. He'd look at them both again when he was ready to teach people.

Escapee and Purifier were both nice, cheap Skills, but he didn't want *cheap*. Ironically, he couldn't *afford* cheap. He could spend a few more months getting the points needed for his more expensive Paths if need be; he could push through a bit more training if needed.

Deepwoods Panther-Hunter and Stonehide Vanquisher . . . they were cool, and trophy Paths were very cool, but he didn't know if they quite stacked up to their competition. Did he really need four trophy Skills, anyway? He'd rather take the ones based on his alchemical prowess rather than his ability to swing on a vine or burn himself half to death.

Okay. He could work with this.

Two trophy Paths, one or maybe two combat-oriented Paths, two or three magic Paths, two or three science Paths, one physical Path, one medical Path, one or two alchemical Paths, one or two fey Paths, and up to five "other" Paths. That was a total of 16 to 21 Paths, which was right in the ballpark of what he needed.

That just left the question of *which*.

Attributes

Path Less Traveled 0/90, Scout 0/60, Athlete 0/60, (Unkillable 0/90)

Skill Improvements

Blackstone Conqueror, Superior Alchemist, Adventurer, Explorer, Outsider, Skill Researcher, Wanderer, (One or two of Alchemical Warrior, Assassin, Giant Slayer, Trapper, Warrior), (two or three of Mage, Novice Pyromancer, Novice Ritualist, Skilled Arcanist), (two or three of Alchemist, Physicist, Engineer, Scientific Revolutionary, Scientist), (one of Physical Alchemist, Physical Arcanist), (one of Alchemical Medic, Field Medic, Biologist), (one or two of Makeshift Alchemist, Practical Alchemist), (one or two of Fey Scion, Feytouched)

He stared at the list for a fair while longer, going back and forth on what he wanted, debating the merits of what each might provide. Alchemical Warrior would lean into what he wanted his strengths to be, Assassin and Trapper would help keep him safe, and who knew what Giant Slayer or Warrior might give him.

Mage was a nice, broad Path that would give him more magic; Novice Pyromancer would give him Basic Pyromancy in conjunction with Firestarting; Novice Ritualist may be exactly what he needed to become a true mage-scientist, if he got a Skill that aided him with rituals in general; and Skilled Arcanist had already given him one of his most powerful Skills with Mana Infusion, who knew what else it might provide?

Alchemist again played to his strengths, Engineer might give him some sort of artificing ability to help with mechanical creations, Physicist played to his experience, Scientific Revolutionary was just *awesome*, Scientist was nice and broad. Physical Alchemist sounded to him like steroids and potions of strength, whereas Physical Arcanist was more of a "punch wizard," if that memeworthy concept translated to Joriah.

Alchemical Medic was more potent, Field Medic less likely to be interfered with. Makeshift Alchemist helped his resiliency, Practical Alchemist was exactly the sort of thing he needed to push ahead with his bombs and potions. Fey Scion and Feytouched . . . he didn't know enough about either (and Inion was no help), but he suspected that Fey Scion would give him fey abilities of some form, whereas Feytouched would change him to *become* more feylike. What that entailed, he wasn't sure.

Edwin just kept going back and forth on what he wanted, what his plans were, and he eventually had to admit he just didn't know. He could play it by ear, he could push it off just a *bit* more. After all, he still had some Skills to level and explore fully.

Edwin worked to eke out a few more levels with Identify, trying something relatively novel and pairing it directly with Basic Mana Sense—something he hadn't really thought to do until recently. By the end, he had pushed his range up to a good fifty meters—quite respectable and absolutely sufficient for his purposes.

He gorged himself on pretty much anything edible he could find, and with Nutrition, that was a lot. Seeing he pushed by trying to mess up his vision, with sheets of ice and glowing potions, mist and smoke, and pushing through even that.

Most of his attention, though . . . mostly, it was focused on Packing and Firestarting, his two all-star Skills.

With Firestarting, his primary focus continued to be on finessing it, trying to manipulate its area of effect. He managed to constrain it to just his fingertip, and then push it out to the end of a stick. That allowed him to burn single dots onto wood held over his fire, but that wasn't enough.

It took Edwin a week, but he managed to get the area burned changed from a dot to a line. Then, a line to a curve. A curve into multiple curves. Curves into simple shapes. Simple shapes to detailed shapes. It took intense focus and significant amounts of time, but he could manage it, in large part thanks to Visualization actually giving him the capability to, well, visualize where the area was affecting.

He tried to get the Skill to help his breathing, and while he got a few levels in the latter, Firestarting didn't seem to do much. It was probably for much the same reason he didn't make iron rust, some intentional safeguard crafted by the System to avoid such a major and obvious side effect. Or maybe he was totally wrong about how the Skill worked. It certainly wouldn't have been the first time.

Edwin didn't stay idle on Packing, either, though he made much less headway. Progress in the manner he was already trying felt akin to hitting his head against a brick wall. He needed some sort of fundamental shift to his approach, but what?

Edwin's balance wasn't improved by Packing, he had found. However, between Flexibility and Athletics, his "natural" balance was nearing the peak of human capability. Thus, he was able to sit not exactly *comfortably*, but at least competently, while balancing on the top of his stick.

However, while using Packing, he should have theoretically been able to lean to the side and not overbalance; it didn't work so well in practice. While the stick didn't just push into the ground thanks to Packing spreading the weight out across the ground, it didn't provide any support to the rest of his body. It all just came from the stick.

It didn't stop him from trying to lean out as far as possible, though. Edwin felt like if he could master this, he might be able to master flight. Unfortunately, it hadn't borne fruit yet.

This time, he was attempting something different. Mana Infusion through Packing helped strengthen objects, but what about if he tried to use it on two different things simultaneously? He threaded a trickle of mana out of his foot and into the wooden rod supporting him, and without letting it finish, he also connected it to his shoe, trying to reinforce them as a single object. It wasn't the first time he'd done this experiment, naturally, but it had never worked before.

It didn't work this time, either. The stick filled up with mana and refused to smoothly bridge the gap to his boot, which frustrated him to no end. It shouldn't make that much of a difference, should it? He could Infuse and reinforce objects made from different materials no problem, so why was this different?

He kept working at it for a while longer, but as night began to set in, he nearly gave up. What even *was* the issue? It wasn't like there was any fundamental difference between the leather of his boots and the wood of his stick. It was all just carbon, hydrogen, and oxygen once you got down there, just arranged in different ways. They may not have been held together by molecular bonds, but then again, neither was a lot of the wood! They were all just different cells, vaguely kept together by electromagnetic forces in the form of friction or bonds. That wasn't different from his boots and his stick! He'd cleaned off the bottom, it wasn't dust getting in the way.

What could be the difference? Edwin cast his mind back to Earth, trying to figure out what kinds of bonds Infusion used to determine what was a single "object," though he could still Infuse an object made of multiple materials.

Hmm . . . hydrogen bonds? Van der Waals? No, that applied to everything. Gah, OChem was so *long* ago. Was there some kind of structure involved in holding cells together or something? A framework of some variation? Though that wasn't true for metals—but metals were essentially just one giant molecule, so maybe they got a pass—and it wouldn't be true for water. Literally just *gluing* the two together should do the trick, and *why was glue special?* A lot of the time, glue was just vaguely hydrogen bonds, but hydrogen bonds existed between *everything*. The only thing that made glue special was that it seeped into microscopic pores and just stayed there, displacing the air!

And then it clicked.

The first thing Edwin noticed was that he no longer needed to work on balancing to stay perched on his stick. Instead, his entire body felt remarkably sturdy, as though he were wrapped in form-fitting foam or buried in sand, though without the pressure associated with the latter.

"Huh. Hey, Inion! I think I got it!" he called out.

"Did you? Good job! Let's see!" Inion was over in a flash and snatched his stick out from under him. Edwin half expected to find himself dragged along with the pole, having used it as an anchor. Instead, he found that his support immediately vanished and he crashed to the ground.

"Uhhh . . . Guess not." He groaned. "I could have *sworn* that I had it that time. It felt so different."

"Well, whaddidya do?"

"I was thinking about what utter nonsense it is for magic to treat 'objects' as distinct in any real meaningful way, especially those made of varying types of materials. Hmm . . ."

Edwin experimentally tried Infusing the rock he was on, and some minutes later when it was complete, he tried imagining much the same thing as before—that the two objects were held together by the exact same forces as the forces within the same object, albeit in a much weaker manner.

That didn't work.

Okay, what was it then? The glue?

A lot of the time, just utilized hydrogen bonds, but hydrogen bonds existed between practically *everything*. What made glue special? It just seeped into microscopic pores and just stayed there. It was as though air was a liquid that could harden into a solid.

If glue made two things the same, then so should air!

Click.

Ah. There we go.

So had Edwin been unintentionally hindering himself by trying to ease himself into supporting himself through air alone? The secret was just to persuade the magic that air was part of "him" and so Packing should apply to it? That was . . . well, it made sense. It wasn't overly simple, it wasn't incredibly obvious, it wasn't some basic trick that he should have gotten ages ago. Rather, it was hard work, practice, and a good understanding of the fundamentals of the universe.

The feeling of support he got from Packing like this was unusual, but not uncomfortable. All the weight of supporting himself, no matter how minuscule, was gone, though he was still able to move more or less freely.

"Yeah, I got it." He settled, drawing Inion's attention back to him. "I just had to apply science to everything I've mastered so far. Not easy, but I might be able to coach someone through the process."

"Can you teach *me*?"

"No, someone with *Packing*, obviously." He sighed. "Besides, you can already fly . . . aaand you're just messing with me. Anyway."

"What's keeping you up? Mana or stamina?"

"Mana, I think. I don't have Stamina, though?"

"Ah, *everyone* has Attributes. When you unlock one, you just get a number for it and have it strengthened. I *think* six or seven is what you might normally start with?"

"Huh. You couldn't have told me this before because . . .?"

"You didn't *ask*," she teased.

"I could have sworn that I did, but you know what? It doesn't matter. Nope."

"How long can you keep it up, do you think?"

"Uhhh . . ."

There *was* a slight ongoing drain on his mana, but it didn't seem like it would run dry any time soon.

"Indefinitely, maybe? There's just a trickle of my mana going into it."

"Really? Can you do anything beyond just sort of floating an inch above the ground?"

"I don't want to try and accept any Skills, though?"

Inion reached out and whacked his head, breaking his concentration and dropping him to the ground. "Ow! What was that for?"

"You *know* that you don't need Skills to do something. It just makes it easier. Now, start floating again and push more mana into it."

Edwin grumbled but complied. Now that he knew the trick, it only took him about a minute to get into the proper mindset needed for him to levitate, but it didn't make it any easier to maintain. Sensing his own mana was easier than sensing any outside of him, but pushing at the mana didn't seem to really do all that much. Or rather, he was already pushing as much as he could at the Skill, and that was what was just barely allowing him to hover.

"I don't think I *can*. My mana manipulation Skill is stuck at level nine."

Inion looked at him, disappointed.

"Hey! I didn't know any better! It was like my fifth day here," he defended himself.

She sighed. "Well, you can always try to improve without the System, or hope that your Skill helps with the cost in some way once you take it."

Edwin could only shrug helplessly. "I guess?"

He checked his notifications. Sure enough, the message he was hoping for was present.

You have unlocked the Flight Skill!
Accept Skill? Y/N

He declined it for the moment—accepting it now would throw off *everything* he'd been working toward—content in the knowledge he could re-unlock it shortly, once he had all his Paths completed. In the meantime, he decided to peek in and see how his Skills were going.

Level Up!
Skill Points 1473→1508
Progress to Tier 2: 1590/1770 (Avg level: 78/77)
Basic Mana Sense 77→82
Breathing 75→76
Firestarting 90→94
Flexibility 74→76
Identify 71→80
Mana Infusion 83→85
Memory 56→57
Nutrition 69→73
Outsider's Almanac 124→125
Packing 83→92
Seeing 70→72
Visualization 78→80

Well then, Edwin thought with a smirk, *Time to get started.*

Name
Edwin Maxlin
Age
1 year
Race
Extraplanar Human

Class

Sapper

Attributes

Mana 5

Health 7

Skills

Magical

Basic Mana Sense: 82, Mana Infusion: 85 (Basic Mana
Manipulation: 9)

Physical

Athletics: 81, Breathing: 76, Flexibility: 74, Nutrition: 73,
Packing: 92, Seeing: 72, Sleeping: 73, Survival: 76, Walking: 74

Mental

Polyglot: 59 (Language: 36), Mathematics: 74, Memory: 57
(Research: 50), Visualization: 80

Combat

Bomb Throwing: 49 (Throwing Weapons: 48)

Utility

Firestarting: 94, Alchemy: 83 (Improvisation: 14), Outsider's
Almanac: 125 (Status: 22), Identify: 80, First Aid: 82, Purify: 75,
Harvesting: 76, Construction: 77

CHAPTER 31

A Classy Ascension

Even with his Paths selected, Edwin still needed to figure out what *order* he wanted to take them. Fortunately, this wasn't nearly as tricky. All that mattered was he took them in approximate order of how cool he thought they were, with perhaps a slight eye toward estimating which Skill each Path might evolve.

His Attribute Paths absolutely would have to be first, as Attributes wouldn't increase until he'd unlocked them. He couldn't imagine *their* order mattered all that much, so he'd just go with what he already had—Path Less Traveled, Scout, Athlete, and finally Unkillable. Then after that . . .

Completed Paths

CharLimitCanttalkmuchNocluewhathappened Didmybesttohelpyouli, Mage, Skilled Arcanist, Physical Alchemist, Bomber, Linguist, Beginner, Warrior

Prospective Paths

Blackstone Conqueror, Superior Alchemist, Adventurer, Explorer, Outsider, Skill Researcher, Wanderer, (one or two of Alchemical Warrior, Assassin, Giant Slayer, Trapper, Warrior), (two or three of Mage, Novice Pyromancer, Novice Ritualist, Skilled Arcanist), (two or three of Alchemist, Physicist, Engineer, Scientific

Revolutionary, Scientist), (one of Physical Alchemist, Physical Arcanist), (one of Alchemical Medic, Field Medic, Biologist), (one or two of Makeshift Alchemist, Practical Alchemist), (one or two of Fey Scion, Feytouched)

Edwin tapped his leg in thought. Did he *really* need even two trophy Paths? Superior Alchemist was a *must*, as it fed too well into his overall hopes for this tier. Blackstone Conqueror, though . . . What might that give him? There wasn't even the slimmest of chances that it would give him some way to summon Blackstone, not that he needed another reason for the dwarves to come after him. In a few tiers it might, though. Should he save it for that possibility, then? A single trophy Path was probably enough. He could reassess later on if he felt like he might benefit from a second, but for now his inclination was *no.*

He struck Blackstone Conqueror from the list. He felt like he could get a better Skill from it in a few years, and he was unlikely to reearn it.

Hmmmmm . . .

Okay, put off the decision for combat choices at the moment. He did want both Makeshift Alchemist and Practical Alchemist, and combine that with his science choices . . . Alchemist, Physicist, and Engineer. Not that he didn't want the others, but the three former Paths seemed decidedly more practical for the time being. He'd take Physical *Arcanist* to avoid overspecializing, and then . . . Novice Pyromancer and Ritualist. Maybe he was breaking his rule to take generalities instead of specific Paths, but it was in an effort to branch out his available Skills, to break into new fields—Rituals—and leverage his existing strength—fire.

After all, the story of human advancement is just the story of mastering fire.

By that token, he'd go with the more unconventional option of Biologist over his actual medic Paths, as it was once again leveraging what made him different to great use. He'd also go with Alchemical Warrior as well. It didn't make sense for him to not leverage that particular strength as much as possible, and it wouldn't require as much setup at the time as traps or the subtlety of assassinations. Warrior and Giant Slayer were in turn perhaps *too* broad for his purposes at the moment.

That meant he could go with both Fey Scion *and* Feytouched. Excellent. He didn't want to have to choose between them; they both seemed good in their own way.

He took a deep breath and began.

You have completed the Path Less Traveled Path!
Your exploits have garnered even the attention of the System.
Going forward, keep in mind all that you have accomplished
and all you shall accomplish, for your every action will have far-
reaching effects. You have already impacted the world, and you
are liable to shake its very foundations going forward.
Class Change!
Sapper → Unconventional Sapper
Calculating Rewards . . .

. . .
Done!
You have unlocked a new Attribute!
Impact
Impact level set to . . . 5

"Impact? What does that do?" he asked, to which Inion just shrugged and smiled mysteriously. Edwin sighed. He didn't *feel* any different. Going by the Path completion description . . . Did it act like karma or something? Did it make his actions more likely to have a broader impact? Or did it enhance the power of his Skills, making them more impactful? It was sure to be impressive if nothing else, whatever it may do.

Well, he was sure to find out eventually, he supposed, and he didn't really know how to test it out, so that put it as a puzzle for future-Edwin.

You have completed the Scout Path!
Your keen eyes have seen much, and your ability to perceive the
world in your unique manner has not gone unnoticed. Keep a
keen eye at all you create, all you encounter, for it shall return
the favor.
Class Change!

Unconventional Sapper → Sapper-Forerunner
Calculating Rewards . . .

. . .

Done!
You have unlocked a new Attribute!
Perception
Perception level set to . . . 8

Edwin half expected that he would be overwhelmed with new sensations, but much the opposite, he found that the flood of sensory input he'd been slowly adjusting to over the last year, leaving his Basic Mana Sense active at all times, became *more* comprehensible, the multiple senses helping instead to build a cohesive picture of his surroundings.

A bit of experimentation showed that he could move his Perception around, in a way. He couldn't reduce his sight below its baseline Seeing-enhanced level, but he could direct his Perception away from feeding a consistent picture of his surroundings into instead focusing on a single sense, giving him far more clarity than he might normally have access to. Pushing it to touch meant he could feel the almost nonexistent breeze tickle his skin, to his smell allowed him to pick out individual scents with ease, his sight allowed him to see massive swathes of his field of view as though he was focusing on it all . . . it was really impressive.

He could put it toward his Skills, too! Basic Mana Sense enabled him to more easily pick out individual sources of magic (though it all still felt the same), and Identify allowed him to target even a single grain of sand from a distance.

Overall, it was very cool, and he needed to figure out how to best use it.

You have completed the Athlete Path!
You have traveled long, and you have traveled far. While you may not yet be road-weary, you still have far, far more travel ahead of you. Obstacles of all manner stand in your Path, yet you will surmount, or blow up, any who dare to oppose you.
Class Change!
Sapper-Forerunner → Tireless Sapper

Calculating Rewards . . .

. . .

Done!

You have unlocked a new Attribute!

Stamina

Stamina level set to . . . 8

Whoa . . . now *that* was a rush. More than any talsanenris snack he'd had, that was for sure. Edwin felt like he could climb a mountain without ever getting tired. That glow faded after just a couple of minutes, but he still felt *great*. More . . . real. His heart beat in his chest, blood rushed through his veins, and he could feel the air entering his lungs. If not for Perception, he might have felt overwhelmed. But as it was? It just felt *right*.

Edwin was still full of energy even after Perception faded. It seemed like he could run a marathon without so much as getting winded. Well, okay, he could have probably already done as much, but with Stamina he actually *felt* like it. Even better, he didn't feel restless or jittery, or like he needed to move to burn off extra energy. He could still sit contentedly, but ready to spring up at a moment's notice.

It was quite nice that everything— *Nope*. Not even thinking that. It was the most surefire way to ensure things *would* get messed up.

Health 7→15

You have completed the Unkillable Path!

Though many have tried, and though many will try to end your journey before it can fully begin, you have emerged victorious against all odds. You are tenacious and persistent, and your way ahead is long and treacherous. Perhaps you'll even survive it.

Class Change!

Tireless Sapper → Indefatigable Sapper

Calculating Rewards . . .

. . .

Done!

You may evolve your Survival Skill into the Adaptive Defense Skill!

Accept Evolution? Y/N
Adaptive Defense
Yes, well, if you had *prep* time, then . . .
Resist harm after initial exposure.
Maximum reduction increases per level.

Right on queue. Why did he have to tempt fate? Ah, well, he'd just . . . ah, screw it. What *would* he drop? Fey Scion? Explorer? Uhhhhh . . .

"I thought you said this would give me Constitution!" he side-eyed Inion.

"I thought it *would!* This isn't an exact science, I'll have you know."

"Fine . . . fine. Whatever. Lemme give this a quick test?"

"Do you *feel* anything?"

"Uh . . . not really?"

"So then . . ."

"Give me a minute, okay?"

Okay, so Adaptive Defense. Finally, a self-explanatory Skill. Because it was only level 1, it wouldn't have that great of an effect, but between his healing potions and Health, he felt a lot more confident sticking his hand in a fire than he did a year ago.

As he approached the roaring fire he always kept active in his kiln, Edwin felt his skin begin to heat up to the point of slight pain, but then it began to fade. He frowned and pushed his hand closer to the fire, letting it heat up again . . .

Level Up!
Adaptive Defense Level 1→2

Ah, the joys of low-level Skills.

After some more experimentation, Edwin found that the longer and more intense his exposure to the fire was, the more he would resist heat, and the more the Skill leveled. He didn't work on it for too long, just enough to get a good idea of its limitations. It wasn't a permanent resistance, but faded over time. He couldn't quite tell how the Skill determined what was or wasn't "harm," but it seemed to try and keep him generally comfortable.

That probably meant he would just never be bothered by extreme temperatures ever again, didn't it? Score!

Overall, the Skill promised to be incredibly useful and, depending on what its limitations were exactly, possibly his strongest Skill yet. Not a bad start, he had to admit. It certainly seemed to live up to its "Unkillable" promise.

Further testing was, naturally, required.

Impact 5→6

Health 15→17

You have completed the Superior Alchemist Path!

You have been challenged as an Alchemist, pitting your Skills and knowledge against one another. While you may have been outnumbered and faced with overwhelming numbers, through quick thinking, superior strategy, luck, and a deeper comprehension, you reigned supreme.

Class Change!

Indefatigable Sapper → Veteran Sapper

Calculating Rewards . . .

. . .

Done!

You may evolve your Construction Skill into the Sapper's Apparatus Skill!

Accept Evolution? Y/N

Sapper's Apparatus

Don't get sappy with it. It'll just blow up in your face if you do.

Conjure basic objects within certain limits.

Limits loosen per level.

Okay, all the surrounding stuff was getting old really fast. He decided to hide the reminder of what his Class *used* to be and the "calculating rewards" bit. They were just getting on his nerves.

That was only a minor quibble, and Edwin quickly found himself enamored with his newest Skill. Thanks to some minor feedback it gave him, it only took a few minutes to figure out how to use it. By focusing on a simple object and activating Sapper's Apparatus, a blue light would coalesce at his fingertips, slowly forming into shape and condensing over the course of about a minute until it created a blue crystal-like substance in his desired shape.

It almost made him think his Makeshift Alchemist Path was suddenly made obsolete, before he caught himself. Redundancy was always a good plan for something this important, after all. What would he do if he didn't have alchemical ingredients?

Besides, the tools were . . . well, rather limited. He could make bottles, much to his delight, as well as stirring sticks, beakers, and other basic lab equipment that fit in his hand, even a sharp scalpel. Unfortunately, none of it was very strong, perhaps less so than even the glass it was modeled after. He tried making tweezers, but they shattered in his grasp, vanishing back into motes of blue light, instead of bending. Overall, they seemed comparable to glass in durability, but with none of the complications of actually *breaking* glass.

They didn't seem to need any concentration on his part after he created them, but he'd need to see how long they lasted before he entrusted any of his creations to them. Perhaps he could use Packing to reinforce them? He tried setting one in his kiln, only to find it shattered into motes of light if it heated up too quickly. He could boil water in them, which was nice, and if he created a hollow object submerged in water, it would manifest filled *with* water, even if his creation didn't have any openings.

There was lots of potential here, he was certain. He'd need to wait and see how long his conjurations lasted before he could tell how much, but it was still quite exciting.

Impact 6→7
You have completed the Outsider Path!
You have come from places unknown, with knowledge strange
and unique and wholly unfamiliar with what you found yourself
confronted with. Yet you did not allow this to hinder you. Those
who would oppose you will find that you approach from a
wholly unique angle.
Sapper-Marauder
You may evolve your Packing Skill into the Improbable Arsenal
Skill!

Accept Evolution? Y/N
Improbable Arsenal
You*can*touchthis,thoughitmaylooklikeit'smissing.
Infused containers are larger on the inside.
Mana efficiency and maximum size increases with level.

Man, these Skills were sounding *fun*. He could make *literal* pocket dimensions! It probably didn't make his backpack redundant, but it did mean he could carry around an arsenal of . . . oh. Improbable size. That was probably the reason for the name, wasn't it?

Edwin pointedly avoided looking at Inion as she mockingly nodded.

There was . . . loads of stuff to unpack in it, but at the moment, it looked to be exactly what it said on the tin, so to speak. When he Infused Improbable Arsenal, he could push through the Skill and into bowls, jars, and boxes. They didn't *look* any different on the outside, but even the small effect his basic Skill provided allowed him to pour more water into a bowl than should have otherwise been possible. Not much, but enough to make him excited.

The Skill didn't work on his shirt or pants, though it *did* on his socks. Taking a random initial guess based on his observations and the "intuitive" limitations of the Skill, it probably only worked on direct containers, possibly only those with a single opening. So no expanding the size of a building or hallway, but something that was just a glorified bag for his feet was fair game.

He could combine his Apparatus with the Skill, and when he used it on one of his sealed water orbs, a tiny gap opened at the top, prompting the inside water to boil for a minute before it settled back to normal.

Edwin's eyes widened. He could use this to create a vacuum, couldn't he? That itself was a phenomenal use of this Skill, even discounting its obvious utility as a bag of holding.

When he tried to use it on his backpack, it didn't have quite so dramatic an effect as it did on his personally created contain-ers. There were two possibilities: either his Skills worked better on his own creations, or the backpack already had some space-warping properties that were minor enough to go unnoticed but that his own

Skill didn't stack with. Probably the latter, but the former wasn't impossible either. He'd need to take some careful measurements to determine it for sure.

He was at three for three of Skills he was exceptionally happy with. Would that continue?

You have completed the Skill Researcher Path!
To you, the System is not some strange and arcane phenomena the likes of which Man Was Not Meant to Understand. It is a machine, like the rest of creation, and it has laws that can be understood and dissected. All that you see falls under your scrutiny, and nothing escapes your inquisitive gaze.
Alchemical Marauder
You may evolve your Seeing Skill into the Skillful Assessment Skill!
Accept Evolution? Y/N
Skillful Assessment
You've got an eye out for those with the right Skills.
See Skills.
Detail improves with level.

"Whoa . . .." Edwin *felt* as the Skill kicked in, and Inion became wreathed in a strange, nonchromatic light. He looked around Obairlann, but other than some colorless illumination around the garden, there wasn't anything else that stood out. To test, Edwin tried using Firestarting at his fingertips, and just as the Skill activated, the same gray light flashed into existence. When he tried again, sustaining the Skill, the light accompanying it stayed active as well. Huh. That was cool. Even if he didn't get *much* information at the moment, being able to see when a Skill was being used could be very useful, especially given his ability to—he checked; yes, he could—pair it with Almanac. He could build up quite a respectable knowledge of Skills being used!

"Hey, Inion, what Skill are you using right now?"

"Wait!" She jerked upright from her floating position. "Does that mean you got a Skill-reading Skill?"

"Uhhh . . . yes? Skillful Assessment. Why?"

"I mean, I was *hoping* you would, but I thought you'd get it from Fey Scion or something! What Path?"

"Skill Researcher. Wait, why would Skills be associated with Fey Scion?"

"Well, that's . . . a secret, actually. I could have told you if you'd gotten it, but because you didn't, ah . . ." She thought for a moment. "Your exposure to fey probably helped."

"I thought the System didn't work like that."

Inion shrugged hopelessly. "I don't know! *You're* the System expert here."

That seemed decidedly untrue, but Edwin wasn't really interested in getting into a fight over it at the moment.

"So . . . Skill?"

"Airborne Wellspring! It lets me treat the air like it's water, but none of my other water-related Skills work alongside it, sadly," she pouted.

Edwin just shook his head, made a note on the Skill that it could be used by fey—any more detail and the Skill would just fail as Inion's Bargain forced him to keep her secrets—and carried on.

You have completed the Physicist Path!
While many say that numbers are an arcane art, you disagree.
Numbers are perfectly comprehensible and endlessly useful. You
boast a mastery of this otherworldly art and can use it with a
great deal of proficiency, a Skill that will aid you greatly in your
future endeavors.
Studied Marauder
You may evolve your Mathematics Skill into the Numeracy Skill!
Accept Evolution? Y/N

"Wait, what's the difference?" Edwin wondered aloud as he accepted the Skill, but as it appeared and shoved its way into his head his question was answered. Hundreds of numbers shoved their way into his brain, overloading even Perception with the sheer quantity of information he was dealing with. He screwed his eyes shut to help deal with it, but it still took a minute of adjustment before he even realized what he could do to *really* help, namely disable the Skill.

Now, what did it say?

Numeracy
Let's assume the elephant is a sphere . . .
See the numbers of the universe.
Precision increases with level.

So it . . . let him measure stuff instinctively? He tentatively tried enabling the Skill just a touch, focusing on Inion as she drifted by. Fortunately, the headache didn't return, and by combining the Skill with Visualization, he wrestled the input into something more comprehensible. According to the Skill, she was floating through the air at a rate of 1 mile per hour, which offended his Physicist sensibilities. A twist of Numeracy fixed that, though, and properly showed that she moved at 0.5 m/s.

Edwin sat on the ground, playing around with his new ability. This was *awesome*. While he couldn't do too much at once without overwhelming even his Perception, he found that he could assess the speed of various objects, determine distance with a great deal of precision, and even overlay free-body diagrams over objects, letting him actually *see* air resistance, friction, and gravity.

It was, in short, the greatest Skill *ever* for a Physicist. Edwin could only imagine how much more accurate he might be able to get with his bombs with all this information; literally more than he could even handle. Hopefully he'd get better with it over time, but for now he set up the Skill to display the world overlayed by a three-dimensional grid of cubes. By default, they showed distance in increments of 2 meters, but he could scale that up if he wished. He couldn't make it any smaller *yet*, but he felt confident that he could make it smaller as the Skill level grew. The minimum size had *already* decreased as the Skill leveled in his experimentation.

Some more testing revealed its limitations. He could only sense everything within about 50 meters, but he could focus to push it beyond that in a specific direction, such as if he was trying to measure how far away something was. Even then, it became less accurate the farther out he tried to reach. Without so much as even clouds to measure on, all he knew was that the sun was out of range. That was probably for the best, as there was no *way* he'd be able to take in all that information at once.

Mana 5→10

You have completed the Novice Pyromancer Path!

Fire is the spark behind all technological innovation since the dawn of time. From the first embers roasting meat to baking clay, melting and forging metals, and pushing fire further and further into the future, powering all life on the planet. You have begun to harness this power, twisting it to your will. Your experiments have never been simpler.

Incendiary Scholar

You may evolve your Firestarting Skill into the Basic Thermokinesis Skill!

Accept Evolution? Y/N

Basic Thermokinesis

Turn up the heat!

Increase the temperature of an object.

Maximum temperature increases with level.

Huh. It wasn't Basic Pyrokinesis like he had expected, but this seemed . . . better? It was no doubt influenced by his Alchemy background even if his Class didn't explicitly show it at the moment. It was less magiclike and more practical, in some ways. Direct manipulation of temperature, even if it were only in one direction, was so utterly *fantastic* it surpassed a lot of Earth tech.

Playing around with the Skill for a little while revealed that it was indeed a magical Skill, not that he expected anything else. He could pour mana into it while touching an object, and it would slowly heat up. It didn't have a terribly high maximum at the moment, but it was already slowly increasing. It was another Skill that was limited by his Basic Mana Manipulation, but he could deal with that.

Edwin couldn't get it to work on Inion or anything alive, much to his relief. No, wait. He could use it to wither some small grasses and cook insects he touched, but that was about it. Still, it was somewhat relieving to know he wouldn't cook someone alive by accident, or even on purpose. It was just an awful way to go, even if it was objectively bad for him from a survival perspective. Ah well, give and take. Maybe one day he'd be strong enough, but for now, he was content *not* being able to magically microwave someone.

Numeracy didn't provide much feedback regarding temperature, but the small amount he was able to prod it into granting *did* indicate that it would probably expand into becoming a thermometer as well as everything else. That would be oh so very nice, and Edwin was seeing in his mind's eye how his toolkit as a proper Alchemist was already expanding. Pity about the Class name, but . . . there was an easy fix for that. He just needed to move his next Path up the schedule a bit.

You have completed the Alchemist Path!
Magic and science. You come from a place where all the former
has been incorporated into the latter. It is the job of the
Alchemist to transmute the impossible into the understood,
and there is much that is impossible before you. Your task is a
daunting one, some might even say impossible, but what is such
a duty to one such as yourself?
Incendiary Alchemist
You may evolve your Identify Skill into the Alchemist's Analysis
Skill!
Accept Evolution? Y/N
Alchemist's Analysis
Knowing what you have to work with is the first step.
Identify parts.
Sensitivity improves with level.

It took a few minutes to figure out what it did, but Edwin eventually figured it out when he used his new Skill on one of his glowleaf potions.

Water
I swear, if I have to explain what this is, I quit.

While he'd need to run more tests to be sure, and level it up more, it looked like the Skill allowed him to see the primary component of something he was dealing with. Granted, that would usually be water, but he figured the Skill might let him pick out more trace ingredients as it leveled.

It was really interesting, seeing his higher-tier Skills have such synergy. He was able to brute-force it with his Skills before, combining Visualization and Mathematics to let him visualize mathematical graphs, but Numeracy started serving as an . . . interpreter, of sorts.

While he couldn't yet determine with any level of precision just how much water was in the potion beyond it being "mostly" water, it felt as though as Numeracy leveled, he would get actual numbers associated with the purity of what he looked at. Meanwhile, as his Analysis leveled, he got the sense he'd get more feedback for what was in mixtures. While right now Analyzing mud only showed that it was "mostly" dirt and wet clay as being "mostly" clay, as it leveled it should also pick out the water involved in each.

Man, Numeracy was awesome. It obviated the need for *so many* measurement tools that would normally be required for pretty much any proper science.

Well, Alchemist's Analysis was cool, too—Edwin didn't know why he felt like he needed to reassure his newest Skill that it was also useful, but he did—and as it leveled up he already saw himself using it to pilfer ingredients from potions he encountered. Could it eventually get to the point where it could measure atomic composition? That would be *very* cool.

Stamina 8→13
You have completed the Wanderer Path!
Your Path has taken you far, far from your home, and while you
have perhaps settled for the moment, that is but a temporary
arrangement. Soon, you will leave even that, your heart and soul
not content to settle down, every footfall blurring into the next.
Wandering Alchemist
Paths Unchosen: Master of Obairlann, Master of the Ruined
Tower, Recluse
You may evolve your Walking Skill into the Longstrider Skill!
Accept Evolution? Y/N

Longstrider
One giant leap for a man, a small step for mankind.
Take longer strides.
Distance increases with level.

So he wasn't *completely* special, it would seem. Lefi had been right about this, if nothing else. Walking did indeed become Longstrider, and it was kind of disorienting to use at first. When it was in use, his every step took him ever so slightly farther than he was used to, and for someone who already had issues with spatial awareness at times, he had needed to lean *hard* on Perception, even wholly disabling Numeracy, to help keep him from repeatedly walking into the cliff or into Obairlann's outer wall.

Hmm. Should he take a couple of Paths that were likely to increase Perception? It might almost be worthwhile just so he would be able to use all his new Skills more effectively. Adventurer and Explorer were likely to help on that front, he'd just have to make *sure* he took them, which meant he'd need to figure out a different Path to skip.

It was also interesting to see himself actually *lose* Paths. Sure, he'd intellectually known it was possible, and Recluse was no great loss. Neither was Master of the Ruined Tower, honestly, but Master of Obairlann might have been nice to take at some point.

Ah well. There was nothing to be done about that now, and only one way to go—forward!

Health 17→20
Stamina 13→16
You have completed the Alchemical Warrior Path!
Your Path has not been a peaceful one. You have had to fight for your freedom, multiple times. Your future is likely to be as conflict-heavy as your past, and you will need to fight for your freedom, safety, and future ingredients every step of the way.
Alchemical Squire
You may evolve your Harvesting Skill into the Alchemical Dismantling Skill!
Accept Evolution? Y/N

Alchemical Dismantling
Oh, sorry, were you using that?
Break down alchemical components.
Power increases with level.

What the heck did "break down components" mean? It would presumably aid him in recovering parts from magical creatures—he really wanted to try and get his hands on pele wolf blood, see if it really was *actually* magma or if that was just creative license—but would it help him if he were to, oh, get hydrogen and oxygen via hydrolysis? That could be quite useful, if it genuinely worked that way. Given it came from a combat Path, perhaps that meant it would also help him cut into particularly tough hides?

He didn't have anything particularly worthy of trying to use it on hand, unfortunately. Even his trick of trying to "harvest" dirt while digging didn't seem to engage it when he tried that—it probably wasn't alchemical enough. He tried boiling water to see if that would have any effect, but couldn't claim to tell if it made an impact. Numeracy wasn't that precise yet, it seemed.

Edwin wanted to try breaking his Blackstone pebble to see if that counted, but he couldn't find it. Maybe it fell out of his backpack somewhere? Normally, he'd be able to find it with his Basic Mana Sense, but with the general background mana within Obairlann, it was like trying to find a specific blade of hay in a haystack. Ah, he'd keep an eye out for it. It might show up eventually.

He might have felt the Skill contribute when he was crushing talsanenris berries—his bushes had finally borne some fruit again, though not many—to see if that would do it, but between the preexisting ease of crushing berries and the Skill's low level, he wasn't sure if . . .

Ah wait, it leveled up. Okay, so it *did* help with that. Good to know. Further testing was required, but it seemed like he had a partial handle on its function at least.

Onward!

Mana 10→15
You have completed the Novice Ritualist Path!

As a man of science, you have had very little experience with the supernatural, with the impossible. Yet you have brushed against it, felt the power of magic, of rituals, and that power calls to you and intrigues you. To you, it is another branch of science to dissect and understand. Such is a Path some have attempted to tread before you; will you succeed in this regard where they once failed? Regardless, your experiences have prepared you for your magical explorations in the future.

Alchemical Initiate

You may evolve your Basic Mana Sense Skill into the Ritual Intuition Skill!

Accept Evolution? Y/N

Ritual Intuition

No, not that kind of ritual. Honestly, this should be intuitive for you.

Sense magical ambiance.

Detail increases with level.

Running contrary to Edwin's expectations, his newfound sense didn't automatically plug into Numeracy to give him a numerical breakdown of . . . whatever it was telling him. Instead, he was able to feel some kind of presence around him, like he was previously able to sense what temperature things were.

Was it just that different, that his scientific analysis wasn't able to properly quantify what was around him? Eh, probably not. He could figure out some kind of numerical system for it in time. Odds were better that whatever feedback he was getting was too intricate for Numeracy to deal with. Or maybe because it was "intuition," it bypassed the Skill altogether. Regardless of *why*, Edwin's sudden onset of a new sense wasn't quantized.

There was a deep, *deep* sense of nature and tranquility all around him, that much was certain. There were also feelings of protectiveness and flourishing emanating from Obairlann, and a cool, watery impression being radiated by Inion, who looked on with curiosity.

"Hang on, just a minute. I think I got a Skill that lets me sense types of mana, and it's a weird sensation."

"Ooh! You're just getting all the goodies, aren't you?"

Edwin shrugged absently. "I guess so." He played with his vial of concentrated firevine sap. Sure enough, he felt a hint of roaring fire trickling from it. He tucked the magical liquid away before anything might happen and nodded. "Yep, looks like it lets me sense mana. Strange that it's not giving me numbers, but this is still really useful."

"Keep an eye on it, ya? Probably has a bit more going on."

Edwin nodded absently, assessing his next choice.

You have completed the Engineer Path!
Coming from a world of machines into one of magic and hard work, you see nothing but inefficiency and impracticality. And like any engineer, you're looking to see how to fix it. Perhaps you'll manage to, perhaps you won't. Regardless, it is a valuable skill set to add to your ever-growing arsenal.
Dabbling Alchemist
You may evolve your Visualization Skill into the Prototyping Skill!
Accept Evolution? Y/N
Prototyping
To predict catastrophic failures and ensure they happen.
Simulate natural phenomena.
Maximum complexity increases with level.

"Oy! Machines *are* hard work!" he half-offendedly exclaimed at the System. "It's just all done up front!"

"What is it this time?" Inion inquired, and Edwin waved her off.

"Doesn't matter."

Edwin had no *clue* where to start figuring out what Prototyping did. The description was *no* help—seriously, that was so vague! Couldn't the System have come up with anything better? The Skill likewise didn't provide him with any immediate feedback, didn't give any clues how it was supposed to be activated. Well, that wasn't entirely true—he *was* able to activate it, but doing so had no apparent effect on anything around him. What was the secret?

It took him about an hour of messing around before Edwin finally got his answer as he Visualized a cube floating a few feet off the ground in front of him before activating Prototyping. As soon as had done so, gravity took ahold of the box and it fell to the ground, thudding into the ground and bouncing slightly.

"Huh." Inion perked up as Edwin broke out of his concentration, but she resumed her seemingly bored float around the area when he waved her off. He'd fill her in later, once he had a good idea as to what this Skill did exactly.

Some more experimentation showed that it, for lack of a better term, did indeed "simulate natural phenomena," much to his annoyance. *Now* how was he supposed to complain about the System when it actually provided a decent Skill description? Ugh.

Anyway, he could imagine a situation by utilizing Visualization, and then by activating the Skill, it would take his Numeracy measurements and apply them to whatever he had imagined. However, the complexity of his Visualizations was starkly limited—at the moment, he could only simulate basic geometric solids, with no variation for material.

As Edwin toyed with it more, he managed to start simulating two basic objects, which could interact with each other as well as their surroundings. This would be eminently useful as it leveled up, he could tell, *especially* if he could figure out how to apply material strength to the Skill. Already, his mind was racing with all manner of possibilities, but he was getting ahead of himself.

Mana 15→21

Stamina 16→20

Health 20→24

Perception 8→10

You have completed the Physical Arcanist Path!

Though many seek to strengthen themselves through physical means, others attempt to surpass the limits of the world through use of magic, you tread the narrow Path between them. It is a hazardous Path for many, and one not taken often, but when threaded appropriately its results are undeniable. Weaving magic into your body directly, without aid of potions or artifacts brings

you ever closer to disaster, but binds you to the world all the
more.
Metabolic Alchemist
You may evolve your Athletics Skill into the Overcharge Skill!
Accept Evolution? Y/N
Overcharge
There is always another horizon to surmount.
Infuse magic into yourself to push past your normal limits, at
great potential cost.
Maximum duration increases with level.

"Great potential cost'" sounded . . . ominous.

"Inion, Skills won't kill you, will they?"

"Oh, they *absolutely* can. I remember one *particularly* bold fellow from back when who got a Water Breathing Skill. He dove down *deep*, only to have the Skill give out on him and he drowned."

"Okay, but that just sounds like Skill misuse, like if I . . . blew myself up in an explosion, or poisoned myself with a failed potion. What about the act of using a Skill being deadly to the user?"

Inion frowned. "I don't *think* that should be possible. Well," she amended, "it's *possible*, but I don't think the System would give out something like that—no, wait. Blood Sacrifice could *absolutely* kill you if you aren't careful."

"What about if you are being careful?"

"Then you *should* be fine. Why, what'd you get?"

Edwin read out his new Skill, to her nodding. "Mixing raw mana with your own body outside of the framework of a Skill or magical organ, like *you* do with your eyes and Seeing, can be harmful without proper training or bodily adaptation. Even at the *best* of times, it creates this vile black goop that can build up in mundane tissues and in extreme cases has to be cleansed. If you're careful, though, and don't overuse it, you *probably* won't have any problems."

The Alchemist frowned. "Cleansing in what way?"

She shrugged. "Eh, some just sort of push it out like sweat, others manage to excrete it into the stomach and vomit it, but there's also some magical and herbal treatments for it."

"And this happens a lot?"

"Oh, it's really minuscule and only really happens with wholly unprocessed magic." Inion saw the frown growing on Edwin's face and clarified, "Your potions should be fine unless you seriously, *seriously* overdo it. Like, drink gallons of concentrated potions in one sitting. Using magical plants already dilutes it because the magic is associated with something physical already and your body is just generally better at *dealing* with that sort of thing, and what tiny amounts you get from that and normal mana exposure is flushed from your body naturally. It's only when you start shoving raw, unstructured mana inside of yourself that issues arise. Even with this Skill, it's probably not something you'd need to worry about so long as you restrain yourself."

Edwin was still somewhat wary. It sounded like it was kind of dangerous to overdose on raw magic, but he would need to use the Skill *sometime* so he could level it, and better that he gave it a try now, right?

Overcharge.

He activated the Skill, Infusing mana into his entire body. Immediately, he felt everything about him become sharper, clearer, and *he* felt stronger and more grounded, as though he had just gotten a new influx of Attributes on *top* of the ones he'd gotten for completing the Path. He abounded with energy, and his muscles flexed with newfound strength. This was amazing!

. . . Then the moment passed, and the feeling suddenly reversed. His muscles cramped, the world grew dim, and exhaustion clamped its jaws over his entire body while a dull ache permeated throughout him, and he slumped to the ground in pain.

Inion stood over him, looking down where he lay. "You okay there?"

"I think so. Ugh. Feels like I got hit by a truck."

"A what?"

"Never mind." He groaned, pulling himself to his feet. "I think that's enough for today. I'm . . . going to sleep now, I think."

Inion gave him a hand, leading him to his bed and gently laying him in it. He nodded in appreciation and let his very, very sore body give way to the peaceful oblivion of sleep.

It had been a very long day, and besides, the sun was beginning to set.

His Paths weren't going anywhere, after all.

CHAPTER 32

Taking Things to the Next Level

It was only when he woke up without so much as a trace of lingering soreness that Edwin finally appreciated just how much work Sleeping must put in to refresh him so completely every night. Still, he couldn't say he wanted to put himself through that ordeal very much. If he were a masochist, he could use Overcharge every night to level it and just sleep off the exhaustion and pain . . . but that sounded like almost-literal torture. Plus, he didn't want to overuse it and maybe poison himself with black sludge? No thanks.

He pulled himself from his hammock, wincing slightly. Okay, so he was still a *bit* sore. Waking up with a tweaked shoulder was something of a novel experience for him these days, after all, and he was so *incredibly* glad that he *did* have Sleeping, or else Overcharge might well have put him in his bed for a *week* rather than a single night.

His personal discomfort notwithstanding, it was a very bright and early morning. The sun was shining, the birds were chirping—wow, were the birds ever chirping. He could identify where dozens of birds were just from listening, and if he changed his Perception's focus to sight, he was able to take in an extraordinarily high-detail view of Obairlann, its walls and roof glistening with morning dew. He allowed his door—a proper door these days, not the contraption he'd initially woven—to swing close, following its trajectory solely through the faint breeze it created as air rushed out of its way.

Perception was *amazing*.

He waved to Inion, only wincing slightly as his arm tweaked a sore muscle, who floated over to him on a cloud of colorless light—one of her Skills, whatever it was. He'd ask about it at some point.

After exchanging standard morning greetings, and Edwin had a small bite to eat, Edwin dropped down to get started on the rest of his Paths. He had another long day ahead of him, that was for certain!

You have completed the Biologist Path!

"The magic of life" is such a ubiquitous phrase that it is common knowledge to almost all that life must be intrinsically linked to magic. But not for you. Life is a natural phenomenon, and that means it follows rules, guidelines, and patterns. It can be studied, it can be predicted, it can be understood. While this is perhaps not what is typically meant by the idea that one ought to "know themselves," it seems to be adequate for your Path.

Metabolic Alchemist

You may evolve your First Aid Skill into the Anatomy Skill!

Accept Evolution? Y/N

Anatomy

Neither cruel nor cowardly. Never give up. Never give in.

Understand the body of yourself and others.

Insight improves with level.

Huh. It didn't change his Class name? Well . . . it made sense after a fashion. Metabolic Alchemist made enough sense for a biologist/alchemist. It did imply that his Class name would stop changing more or less altogether at a certain point, though Inion's Class indicated it would get more complex instead, or perhaps as well?

Edwin asked as much, getting a nodded agreement from his friend. "Ya. Your Class is a cumulation of all the Paths you've taken, each Path you complete does less and less to actually change it. At some point, you'd need a bunch of Paths to budge the Name. Though as you get more completed, the more . . . grandiose it tends to get. Or more definitive. Be *very* wary of *anyone* who has 'The' as part of their Class."

Yeah, Edwin probably didn't need the warning, but it was still nice to have confirmation. He nodded absently while he turned his attention instead to his newest Skill.

The first thing it did was improve his proprioception . . . no wait, that was just his Perception as he turned it toward himself. What it *did* do was help him figure out exactly which muscle in his shoulder was tweaked and that it should work its way back into place if he kept it relaxed today, caused by overstressing it last night. A flex of Numeracy informed him of his precise heart rate—38 beats per minute—and while he couldn't quite feel his exact blood pressure, it felt healthy.

He looked at Inion . . . and frowned. He couldn't put his finger on what it was exactly, but something about her anatomy just seemed . . . wrong. Her proportions, or maybe the way her muscles moved. It was another reminder that she wasn't human, no matter how superficially she may have resembled one, given the way her wet tunic form-fit itself to her . . .

Focus, Edwin, he admonished himself.

Hmm. So, Perception gave him extra feedback on the state of his own body, and let him get further intuition on the bodies of others? Not too shabby. Pity about it being another thing for him to split his Perception between, though. It was funny how he became supernaturally aware of his surroundings, only for him to immediately find his attention split between far more stimuli than before.

He needed to find some Paths that would give him more Perception, and the sooner the better. Then again, he'd probably slowly acclimate to all the information his Skills were feeding him anyway. The human brain was *amazing* at that sort of thing, after all.

Next up was Makeshift Alchemist, and Edwin . . . just wasn't feeling it. He had Purify, Breathing, Flexibility, Nutrition, and Sleeping to go. Makeshift Alchemist would, he was almost certain, give him some kind of ability to turn normal materials into alchemical ingredients by evolving Purify. It was undeniably useful . . . so why was he hesitating?

Well. I do already have Mana Infusion, he mused. *That kind of fills that same role. And Practical Alchemist is also a good Path, which could also evolve Purify into something that might be useful in my research and alchemical experiments.*

On the other hand, he *did* really need some kind of backup in case he found himself without his potions on hand . . . but didn't Overcharge kind of fill that role? He'd gotten a Skill that could be quite a fight finisher if he pulled it off properly, and he'd gotten another Skill that meant he'd always have *something* on hand. If he took too many Skills that were backups, then that weakened his primary strategy, so wasn't it better that he ensure that most of his Skills were ones he'd use all the time? It wasn't like he'd ever be *completely* unarmed these days, right?

To confirm his suspicion, he summoned a knife with his Sapper's Apparatus. The blue light slowly coalesced into the appropriate shape, a blade of crystal, sharp and pointy. He pricked himself with the end—a marginally harder task than anticipated with his newly increased Health—and watched the blood bead at the tip of his finger.

Anatomy helpfully informed him he was bleeding and that it was already clotting. Huh, that was fast. Still, it confirmed that he *could* make weapons with Apparatus, though . . .

Edwin tossed his knife at a nearby rock. It cut through the air with perfect accuracy and shattered as it struck the stone tip-first, vanishing into faint motes of blue light. It wasn't superstrong, admittedly, and took a while to form, but it was the principle that mattered.

Hmm. He would . . . take Practical Alchemist first and see if it evolved Purify. If it did, great. He'd put Makeshift Alchemist off to the side as his one Path he didn't take this time around thanks to Unkillable's unpredictability. If it didn't, he'd take Makeshift Alchemist to evolve it instead. Better that *an* Alchemist Path evolved it than Adventurer or one of his fey Paths, after all.

You have completed the Practical Alchemist Path!
Some Alchemists get so lost in their own experiments, in their
own philosophizing and experiments, that their minds and
tests become wholly divorced from reality even as they seek to
comprehend it. Others run experiment after experiment, seeking
knowledge for the simple fact that it is knowledge, and they

must know it. You may be vulnerable to both of these failings,
but you recognize that the true value of Alchemy is in the
application of the theoretical to reality. You have found how to
use your alchemical knowledge in defense, in aid, and to attack.
You would be well-served to remember this lesson as you venture
forth on your Path.
Alchemist
You may evolve your Purify Skill into the Refining Skill!
Accept Evolution? Y/N
Refining
Better. Faster. Stronger.
Isolate and improve desirable qualities.
Strength of refinement improves with level.

Edwin . . . wasn't sure how that differed from Purify. Not totally, at least. With chemistry, metallurgy, and pretty much all material science, refining something *was* purifying it, removing impurities and concentrating what you wanted. How was this different?

He asked Inion as much, only to get a skeptically raised eyebrow. "Your Class may say you're just an Alchemist, but you don't *think* much like one, do you?"

"What's that supposed to mean? And no, I *don't*. I was a scientist first, and in many ways I still am. I'm an Alchemist because I'm in a land of magic, of course I'm going to be one! Like, do you realize how cool of a job description 'alchemist' is, when it isn't just prechemist? Trying to develop immortality, turning lead to gold, making a universal solvent! Like, those are the things which every chemist *dreams* of. Making the impossible, doing things that flatly break the laws of physics. Of course I'll jump at the chance!"

"Okay, well *that's* your problem."

"I . . . don't follow."

"You said it yourself. 'Making the impossible,' you don't accept that Alchemy and the things you do are possible because Joriah follows different rules from your Earth. To you, you have the laws of your universe, and then there's magic. Magic is impossible, and it doesn't fit with what you know. It is not an intrinsic part of reality."

"That's just an expression, though! I do and see impossible things all the *time*." He gestured around. "Look at me! I'm sitting here talking to a floating nature spirit. And of course magic is in addition! Everything behaves almost exactly the same as on Earth, just with the addition of magic. I can use magic perfectly well, and I can be a scientist-mage, no problem. But refining is literally just the exact same as purification."

"Think, Edwin." Inion floated over him. "What does refining something mean to an *Alchemist*. Not to a scientist, but to someone who views your 'laws of the universe' as interesting guidelines."

Edwin shrugged helplessly, then caught himself. Hmmm.

"Uhh. Huh. Actually . . ." He reread the Skill description, "Isolate and improve . . ." He blinked. "Can I *alter physical parameters* with this? Like, I don't know . . . make something stronger than it should be? Alchemy Essentia, I guess?"

"It's *your* Skill," Inion countered. "Why should I know?"

Edwin sighed. "Yeah, yeah."

Refining ended up being even harder to use than Alchemical Dismantling, and Edwin figured he had to be doing *something* wrong, but he put it off to the side for the time being after an hour of experimentation yielded no results. Four Paths to go, four Skills left. What did it still have in store for him?

Mana 21→28

Stamina 20→23

Perception 10→13

You have completed the Feytouched Path!

Your Path has taken you into the most curious of locales. Among these are the primal corners of Joriah, where powerful spirits slumber, hailing from a world quite unlike the one that currently exists. You bear many resemblances to them and have found yourself in concert with one of these great fey. Inexplicably, you survived this encounter and can now claim a small fraction of their might in your own adventures.

Leighis Alchemist

You may evolve your Flexibility Skill into the Fey's Caress Skill!

Accept Evolution? Y/N

Fey's Caress
Brush against the power of the fey.
Bind yourself to a touched material, gaining some of its
properties.
Depth of binding increases per level.

"Leighis? What's that?"

"Medicine? Where did you hear that— Oh." Inion stopped as she presumably Identified Edwin, and nodded. "Well, it means medicine. Medical, rather."

Edwin wryly nodded. "Got it. Any idea why I have a word in my Class that isn't in a language I understand? And then why Polyglot didn't translate it?"

"You'd know as well as I."

Edwin mumbled a vague half-complaint before he turned his attention more to his newest Skill. For once, the Skill description was actually useful in figuring out what to do, and he laid his fingers on a nearby rock and activated the Skill.

From the point of contact, gray-black stone spread up his arm, bringing a chill and a faint sense of numbness alongside the discoloration. Before it could reach his elbow, he pulled away and the transformation began to reverse, shrinking down the length of his forearm and to his fingers before vanishing altogether.

So it wasn't permanent. That was good. He didn't think it would be—heck, the thought hadn't even occurred to him until after he tried the Skill—but it was still nice to confirm as much.

A bit more poking around, both literal and figurative, alongside some coaching from Inion helped Edwin tease out some of the limits of his new Skill. He could bind to mundane materials around him, like wood, stone, or leather, and take on many of their characteristics. His skin generally became tougher regardless of what he bound to, it would become heavier or lighter, usually lose a bit of flexibility, and get a few other miscellaneous attributes depending on what he absorbed. Metal allowed him to shape-shift his features ever so slightly, deforming his fingers to be pointed; and cloth was actually lighter and more flexible than just using skin, to give the two primary examples he'd found.

Attempting to Caress air . . . hadn't gone well and had resulted in several layers of skin stripped from his hands before he knew what was happening. Inion told him it was because of the Skill's low level, and he might be able to use it to turn wholly into wind at higher levels, once he could transform all of himself at once.

It was apparently similar to the Skill she had gotten as part of binding to her pool—namely Aquatic Presence—except his bindings were strictly temporary, and his nature as a fully corporeal and mortal entity was fighting it. As a result, Inion was able to coach Edwin through how to use his water transformation, especially how to hold the water close to him (preventing a repeat of the air fiasco), and marginally manipulate it. Eventually, he'd be able to turn his entire arm into water, but for now, it didn't even transmute the entirety of his skin.

Flexibility was the only reason that he was even able to move while Caressing stone or metal, and even that was something of a struggle. Edwin also found that how much of himself he could transform was strictly limited to how much stuff he was in contact with. Using one of his few remaining grai only allowed him to turn his fingers into gold, which ended up being surprisingly easy to flex for a metal, though it made sense *why* it was the case.

No matter what, to use his Skill reliably, he'd need a significant amount of materials on hand. Golden fingers would probably be useful in lieu of gloves if not much else, but stone or steel forearms would be useful if Edwin needed to punch someone.

Last, any transformation started with wherever he was touching the material. If he was standing barefoot on stone, it would start with his feet. If he balanced a coin on the back of his hand, it spread from there. Turning his entire body to stone felt *strange*, but not altogether unpleasant. His clothes didn't transform alongside him, but that felt less like a Skill limit and more just not knowing the proper technique (Inion was no help there, to no real surprise).

Overall, a decent Skill. Lots of potential, but it would take time to figure out how to use it optimally and Edwin wasn't sure if it would ever be one of his primary tools in a fight, though he seriously wanted to figure out how that transformation *worked*.

> Mana 28→33
> You have completed the Fey Scion Path!
> You have learned much from your fey mentor, from lessons
> on magic to Paths to how to utilize your Skills. Already, you
> have taken some steps to more fully embody the nature of
> your Arcadian teacher, and with your previous endeavor in
> comprehending the nature of reality from the physical, you have
> taken the first steps needed to comprehend reality from the
> metaphysical.
> Alchemical Scion
> You may evolve your Nutrition Skill into the Arcadian Elixir
> Skill!
> Accept Evolution? Y/N
> Arcadian Elixir
> Once one has sampled perfection, well . . . they can settle for
> you.
> That which you make is like unto ambrosia.
> Potency increases with level.

"Are everyone's Skill notifications as sarcastic as mine?" Edwin asked Inion. She perked up, looking for clarification, and Edwin read the Skill box to her.

"Okay, you can stop laughing now. It wasn't that funny," he finally decreed. "Now are you going to answer my question or not?"

"Fine, fine. It's just funny." Inion wiped away an imaginary tear from her face and composed herself. "To answer your question, no. It's not normally like that, at least for me. I don't know what determines the Skill descriptions, but it's not consistent among everyone who gets the same Skill."

"Great," Edwin grumbled. "I'm so glad I alone have to deal with this sort of thing. Would it kill the System to consistently give me useful Skill descriptions?" Edwin shook his head and started trying to figure out what it did.

. . .

It took a fair bit of trial and error, but Edwin eventually felt like he had the Arcadian Elixir Skill figured out. Anything edible he made now tasted better—particularly noticeable when compared to the same thing he'd made prior to getting the Skill—and was more filling. That seemed . . . rather lacking, so there had to be some kind of further hidden effect he wasn't seeing. It *did* have the side effect of making his previous food taste like cardboard in comparison, but he could live with cardboard so long as it was filling enough. He'd just have to remake a bunch of his supplies, figure out what the bare minimum amount of work needed to get the Skill to activate was, and see if it worked with potions, too.

Oh man, that would be awesome if it worked with healing potions and the like. Better-tasting and possibly more effective potions would be so nice, way better than the vaguely bitter and medicinal taste they usually ended up being.

When she sampled it, Inion agreed that his food tasted better now, as well, and that it reminded her of home. Overall, a win! Perhaps a boring Skill, but one that would at minimum make his trail rations far more tolerable.

Breathing and Sleeping to go, and Explorer and Adventurer to combine with them. He was getting so close he could practically *taste* it. Pity it didn't taste as good as his venison jerky soup.

Stamina 23→29

Perception 13→18

You have completed the Explorer Path!

The Path you have taken is not one many have trod before; going places unseen for generations and finding all the forgotten corners of Joriah. You boldly venture into the unknown, blazing your own trail through calm and storm alike, the only thing murkier than your past being your future.

Alchemist-Errant

You may evolve your Breathing Skill into the Fresh Air Skill!

Accept Evolution? Y/N

Fresh Air

Nothing like the smell of a newly discovered toxic gas in the morning!

Breathe in fresh air.

Purity increases with level.

Edwin felt a dramatic shift in the air the moment he took a breath and collapsed into a coughing fit. He had *not* been expecting such a sudden change from a new Skill, what was causing . . . ah. Purify must have affected it, didn't it? Yeah, that would make sense, if he functionally just had a level 75 Skill suddenly appear out of . . . thin air.

His explanation of the air being *too* pure as to why he suddenly doubled over coughing drew an amused giggle from Inion. Overall, Edwin wasn't sure how the Skill actually functioned, since he could still smell his surroundings. It seemed that pleasant odors were allowed through, whereas anything even marginally unpleasant was filtered away . . . though it was still present if he thought about it, just not obvious.

It was very cool being able to stand in the smoke from a campfire with no issues breathing, but further confusing matters was the fact that his eyes didn't seem to be affected by the smoke *either*. Clearly a lot was packed into the Skill that the description didn't adequately describe, but Edwin had no clue where to start testing its limits. Although maybe he could breathe underwater with it?

. . .

So he, as it turned out, could *not* breathe underwater. At least, not yet. His trial run had still had him inhale water, but far less than a mouthful. Probably, as the Skill leveled up, he would be able to just hang out fully submerged, but that day hadn't come yet.

For now, he'd have to settle for being highly resistant to airborne hazards. It probably worked on diseases and inhaled poisons, though he couldn't exactly *check*—nor had he gotten so much as a sniffle since he'd arrived on Joriah, come to think of it. Weird. He hadn't considered that fact, but if he had, he would have thought that his immune system, being wholly unfamiliar with all the plagues and viruses to be found on Joriah, would fare about as well as that of the Americans when faced with Europeans.

Now, he wasn't complaining that he *hadn't* died of the smallpox-equivalent here, but it was kind of strange. Then again, there was so much overlap in animal life (which was its own kind of weirdness for that matter), maybe there were similar connections in diseases? Asking Inion just confirmed that they did indeed *have* diseases on Joriah, the

System not wholly sufficient to snuff them out, but she wasn't terribly well-informed about what said diseases *were*.

Perhaps his genetics were subtly different enough, being an "extra-planar human," that he got an exemption, as surely as if he were a human among chimpanzees? Well . . . whatever it was, Edwin was just going to be thankful and hope that he never had to deal with it. Something to worry about another day.

Meanwhile, he had one Skill to go, and one Path to complete with it. So, what would Adventurer do to Sleeping? Make him immune to needing such? Let him dream up training situations? Let him adjust a Skill he had overnight?

Health 24→25

Stamina 29→30

Perception 18→19

You have completed the Adventurer Path!

Your Path is your own, and no one else's. From your very first moments upon Joriah, you have broken conventions and defied expectations. Your very existence is unpredictable despite the best efforts of many, and you carry with you many valuable lessons for all who would seek them. You venture forth on your own terms, adventuring for the sake of novelty and excitement—but also to help and learn. Take care you do not lose yourself like so many before you.

Alchemist-Errant

You may evolve your Sleeping Skill into the Watchful Rest Skill!

Accept Evolution? Y/N

Watchful Rest

No more sleepless nights, just sleepless knights.

Retain awareness of your surroundings while asleep.

Awareness increases with level.

. . . Or maybe it would help keep him from being surprised during the night. Well, it may not have been as *glamorous* as some of his other Skills, but perhaps he was getting overly hopeful for a 30-point Path. This would serve him perfectly well going forward, as Inion wouldn't always be able to keep watch for him. Something that reduced his need for sleep would have also been welcome, but this worked perfectly fine as well.

So he was to be an Alchemist-Errant going forward, was he? Well, it at least sounded cool, and did describe him more or less adequately.

It was still earlyish afternoon, his Skill experimentation having only taken a few hours, and that meant Edwin still had one last task to do before he started exploring all his new powers together in earnest.

***

You have unlocked the Flight Skill!
Accept Skill? Y/N
Flight (Magical, Tether)
Raw magic and will: significantly better than wax wings.
Fly.
Efficiency improves with level.
Congratulations! For obtaining a Skill that allows you to fly
unaided while not having wings, you have unlocked the Aerialist
Path!

Using a dedicated Skill was *so* much easier than the way he jury-rigged Packing to lift him off the ground. To start, it was instantaneous. No more carefully getting into the right mindset, convincing the air it ought to support his weight. No, it just took a single flex of Flight to take Edwin off the ground. Mere inches off the ground perhaps, but off the ground nonetheless.

The "tether" referred to in the Skill felt like, well, like a tether connecting Edwin to the ground below him. In attempting to find the limits of his newest ability, he found that it could (after a couple levels) extend about six inches from him and, so long as it connected to something that could support him, allowed him to fly. It didn't matter if it was a ceiling, a wall, or a tree trunk, just that it was solid. Attempting to fly over the pond had resulted in a very wet Edwin, and trying to fly over the edge of his cliff had sent him plummeting to the ground. He'd face-planted firmly into the dirt, not able to reactivate the Skill fast enough to catch himself.

What was really interesting was the way the grass below him bent out of the way, like he was surrounded by a powerful downdraft, but he hadn't figured out how to replicate the phenomena reliably. It couldn't be used as a force push, sadly. If the tether didn't connect to anything strong enough to hold Edwin up, the Skill just failed to engage. Fortunately, Packing didn't seem to count toward that limitation, and Edwin honestly wasn't sure what supported the boulders he lifted to test it. The branches he was using Flight off of certainly didn't look like they had to support several hundred pounds of rock in addition to him, anyway.

The rest of the day passed in more or less a blur. Edwin played around with all his *new Skills*, trying to figure out all their interactions and limitations. He'd done some experimenting as he went along, yes, but now he was actually looking for the synergy.

The first one was pretty easy—Apparatus and Prototyping both worked off Visualization, so it was trivial for Edwin to figure out how to conjure an object he had prototyped. Apparatus still required him to be in contact with his new creation, but he was able to make some pretty interesting "rock" stacks by summoning new levels already balanced.

Basic Thermokinesis *was* usable at range, as it turned out, but required him to have a "focus" point, like his hand were a magnifying glass concentrating heat on a specific object. From there, it was relatively trivial to focus the Skill onto small points, which could either ignite said point if he used Firestarting or just rapidly heat that specific point to the Skill's maximum—something like 15 degrees (Celsius, naturally) above air temperature. Past that, the entire object just started to heat up instead of the point specifically. Once the entire object was at maximum, it radiated heat into its surroundings.

If Edwin was able to channel more mana into the skill, he probably would have been able to then keep heating his target indefinitely, but as it stood, he wasn't able to heat it faster than it lost that energy to its surroundings.

Curiously, until the object reached maximum sustained temperature, it felt as though it stayed at or just *barely* above skin or air temperature. That, and a few other interesting quirks of the Skill led Edwin to deduce that Basic Thermokinesis consisted of two parts: one was directly adding energy to his target, and the other was almost perfectly thermally insulating whatever he used the Skill on until it was overpowered by a significant temperature differential.

For now, the two aspects seemed to be linked—he could only insulate an object he was also heating—but Edwin was hopeful that he might overcome that limitation in time.

The Skill also opened up some interesting revelations about the nature of magic—was it a form of radiation, where it could be focused to a point? It could transfer energy, yes, and seemed to break conservation of energy given mana just appeared from seemingly nowhere, but how did it transfer that energy? Was it radiative? Convective? Conductive? Did the insulation manage to block all three types? Or just conductive (which would also block convective, come to think of it)?

There were so, *so* many questions that Basic Thermokinesis raised, and Edwin had to force himself to step away from it for the time being. He'd give it a thorough, *thorough* investigation at some point in the future, he promised himself. There were thermodynamics shenanigans afoot, and what kind of physicist would he be if he didn't tear into it as much as possible?

Something Edwin found quite interesting was that his Firestarting and Thermokinesis felt *very* different under his Ritual Intuition. The former felt like . . . weakening, and change, for lack of a better term, whereas the latter felt more directly like fire. It reinforced his idea that Firestarting just served as a catalyst rather than an actual fire*starter*, but he still couldn't confirm it.

Curiously, Mana Infusion *also* felt vaguely like fire, Flight felt like a patch of still air deflecting rain, and Fey's Caress reminded Edwin of . . . well, like a mountain spring at night. He wasn't able to get a sense of what his other Skills felt like, as the only mana present that showed up on his arcanoception when he Infused them was from Mana Infusion itself.

Curious. A bit frustrating, perhaps, but still curious. By a similar token, he was also unable to sense anything pertaining to his own mana.

Alchemical Analysis had yet to return anything but whatever an object "mostly" was, but with Numeracy leveling, he was getting a closer idea as to how pure the substances he was Analyzing were exactly.

Numeracy was also growing more precise in other areas, too, and Edwin was approaching one meter being his minimum resolution. Thanks to it, he was able to measure that Improbable Arsenal increased the volume of his unenhanced containers by about a third, and he was nearing a meter and a half per normal Longstrider, in comparison to about one without using the Skill. He'd also gotten . . . somewhat better with the Skill. He didn't trip over his own feet anymore, not that it had happened too often previously, and if he was careful (and double-checked distances with Numeracy) he could walk around without running into anything.

What made the Longstrider Skill so complicated and annoying to use was not only that he didn't have the appropriate muscle memory for how to deal with such large steps, but he couldn't *develop* it either, as every time he adjusted, the Skill leveled up and threw him off once more. He'd get there eventually, but it was going to be something of a process in the meantime.

Skillful Assessment took some getting used to as well. It created or allowed him to see a vague light show around Inion or himself when they used a Skill, roughly corresponding with the utilized ability. All in all, it reminded him of action lines in a comic or cartoon, where it was impossible to tell if a given effect was intended to be visible in-universe or was just there for visual clarity for the watcher or reader.

"As if my life wasn't already enough of a fantasy story," Edwin grumbled. "The question is, am I the main character or supporting cast?"

At least the Skill made the normally mundane-looking aspects of the System more exciting, and it had some potential for him to leverage it to further understand its underlying mechanics. After all, most laws of the universe didn't have literal source code to peel back and stare at.

But the System? Well, that was just *asking* to be hacked.

Level Up!
Skill Points 145→284
Adaptive Defense 1→7
Alchemical Dismantling 1→3
Alchemist's Analysis 1→8
Anatomy 1→6

Arcadian Elixir 1→5

Basic Thermokinesis 1→7

Fey's Caress 1→8

Flight 1→9

Fresh Air 1→3

Improbable Arsenal 1→6

Longstrider 1→7

Mana Infusion 85→86

Numeracy 1→14

Outsider's Almanac 125→127

Overcharge 1→3

Prototyping 1→9

Ritual Intuition 1→8

Sapper's Apparatus 1→13

Skillful Assessment 1→5

Congratulations! For spending 600 Skill Points, you have unlocked the Journeyman Path!

Congratulations! For spending 1,200 Skill Points, you have unlocked the Adept Path!

Name

Edwin Maxlin

Age

1 year

Race

Extraplanar Human

Class

Alchemist-Errant

Attributes

Health 25

Impact 7

Mana 33

Perception 19

Stamina 30

Skills

Alchemical

Alchemy: 83, Alchemical Analysis: 8, Refine: 1, Alchemical Dismantling: 3, Sapper's Apparatus: 13
(Purify: 75)

Magical

Flight: 9, Basic Thermokinesis: 10, Fey's Caress: 8, Ritual Intuition: 8, Mana Infusion: 85
(Basic Mana Sense: 82), (Basic Mana Manipulation: 9)

Physical

Overcharge: 3, Longstrider: 7, Fresh Air: 3
(Athletics: 81), (Breathing: 76), (Flexibility: 74), (Nutrition: 73), (Packing: 92), (Seeing: 72), (Sleeping: 73), (Survival: 76), (Walking: 74)

Mental

Numeracy: 14, Prototyping: 9, Anatomy: 6, Polyglot: 59, Memory: 57
(Language: 36), (Mathematics: 74), (Research: 50), (Visualization: 80)

Combat

Bomb Throwing: 49, Adaptive Defense: 7
(Throwing Weapons: 48)

Utility

Outsider's Almanac: 125, Watchful Rest: 1, Skillful Assessment: 5, Arcadian Elixir: 5, Improbable Arsenal: 6
(Firestarting: 94), (Improvisation: 14), (Status: 22), (Identify: 80), (First Aid: 82), (Harvesting: 76), (Construction: 77)

Paths

Skill Points: 284

Combat

Assassin 0/60, Bomber 0/60, Giant Slayer 0/60, Heedless Hunter 0/60, Hunter 0/30, Killer 0/30, Titan Slayer 0/90, Warrior 0/60, Way of the Empty Hand 0/60, Trapper 0/60,

Alchemy

Alchemical Medic 0/60, Demolitionist 0/60, Makeshift Alchemist 0/60, Potioneer 0/60,

Science

Chemist 0/60, Experimenter 0/60, Researcher 0/60, Purifier 0/30, Scientific Revolutionary 0/90, Scientist 0/60,

Magic

Aerialist 0/60, Fey Friend 0/60, Feybound 0/60, Feycaller 0/60, Mage 0/60, Magical Gardener 0/60, Micro-Biomancer 0/90, Primal Constructor 0/90, Primal Ritualist 0/90, Realm Traveler 0/120, Skilled Arcanist 0/60,

Mental

Dedicated Student 0/60, Lecturer 0/30,

System

Almanac Administrator 0/60, Forerunner 0/60, Outsider's Almanac Specialist 0/90, Pioneer 0/60, System Scholar 0/60,

Trophy

Blackstone Conqueror 0/60, Deepwoods Panther-Hunter 0/60, Stonehide Vanquisher 0/60,

Career

Brickmaker 0/30, Butcher 0/30, Diver 0/30, Gardener 0/30, Lumberjack 0/60, Merchant 0/30, Potter 0/30, Scribe 0/30, Woodsman 0/30,

Physical

Ascetic 0/60, Daredevil 0/60, Physical Alchemist 0/90, Survivor 0/60, Physical Laborer 0/30,

Traveling

Escapee 0/30, Exile 0/30, Traveler 0/30, World Traveler 0/60

Medical

Field Medic 0/60, Medic 0/30, Steadfast Medic 0/60,

Misc

Arsonist 0/60, Autopyromaniac 0/60, Burglar 0/60, Child 0/12, Expert 0/60, Imperial Ally 0/60, Novice 0/12, Pyromaniac 0/30, Razer of the Ruined Tower 0/60, Rebel 0/30, Slave 0/12, Trainee 0/60, Traitor 0/60, Journeyman 0/60, Adept 0/60

Completed Paths

CharLimitCanttalkmuchNocluewhathappened Didmybesttohelpyouli, Mage, Skilled Arcanist, Physical Alchemist, Bomber, Linguist, Beginner, Warrior, Path Less Traveled, Athlete, Scout, Unkillable, Superior Alchemist,

Adventurer, Explorer, Outsider, Skill Researcher, Wanderer, Alchemical Warrior, Novice Pyromancer, Novice Ritualist, Alchemist, Physicist, Engineer, Physical Arcanist, Biologist, Practical Alchemist, Fey Scion, Feytouched

The Silver Legion

Tara breathed out as the Outsider finally left Vinstead. It had been . . . strenuous, to maintain Imposing Presence of the Empire for so long through her Argent Armory alone. It seemed to be worthwhile, as what limited sensory feedback she received from her combination of Mirror's Gaze and Sight of the Silver One indicated that Edwin had managed to leave without incident.

Content, she allowed her active maintenance of the Skill to dissipate, appreciating the levels her task had earned her. Sustained Construction ensured it would not vanish immediately, and with nothing attempting to break it, it should take . . . oh, half an hour to vanish? She'd never investigated.

Meanwhile, she massaged her temples. The strange senses that came from heavy use of Mirror's Gaze always gave her a headache, and she wished that the paperwork required for her to be approved to obtain Perception would finally clear. She'd had Sight of the Silver One for a year now, after all. It hadn't been this hard to get paperwork for "her" Outsider to clear, a thought that prompted her to sigh.

Edwin . . . Edwin was a fascinating case, and such a clear example of why the Empire was so important. He embodied a truly astounding level of wasted potential. If only he had first found his way to Port Torveil or, somehow, Vinstead, in lieu of the bearded barbarians in the mountains.

Tara drummed her fingers on her leg, trying to control her emotions. The dwarves were their *allies*, and it was not her place to allow personal judgment to circumvent what the Empire had decreed.

Trust the system, not the individual.

Edwin's story nearly made her wish to weep. Not only was he an Outsider, but a mage as well! The combination would have been one that echoed throughout history and elevated the entire Empire for the betterment of all, if only they could keep him on their side. And yet, the poor fool had taken Breathing and Sleeping instead of expanding his natural mage talent.

It confused her how he might be a mage if there were none on his "Earth," though perhaps in his travels the spark had been awoken within him? It was the only reasonable conclusion to be made, and she sorely wished that she might be able to ask one of the scholars what their thoughts upon the matter were.

Alas, such was not to be. Her Honor of the Empire would remain untarnished, and there was no direct obligation for her to report on his existence as an Outsider to others. Such an obligation would have to be added in the future, once proposing it would no longer constitute a potential violation of her Oath. Previously, the concept of a Person of Interest being an Outsider was so utterly laughable that no one had even considered coding it into Law. If only ensuring the Law was useful and comprehensive was a direct duty of hers, rather than an implied one . . . perhaps she could propose the matter when she was next prompted, most likely in thirteen months when her six-year review was scheduled.

Then again, perhaps there was a reason that such a duty was not already present, but asking would only bring with it commendation. It was only through such inquiry that progress could be made, by questioning those above your station for the logic behind their actions. Should they have a sufficient reason, you learned. If they did not, they would know of a flaw within their reasoning and could act to correct it.

The Outsider did not seem to share this perspective, beyond as was natural in his station as an Alchemist. Tara supposed that was most likely typical for those who would take the Path of Artifice, that they would be focused upon the material rather than the political. After all, *she* usually cared little for the questions asked by those upon the Path of Administration.

Edwin certainly provoked her to wonder about those questions, and she was uncertain how she ought to feel about that. *Was* it not better for one with a medical Skill to provide lifesaving treatment in the absence of a proper Medic? The answer was apparently no, as doing such would encourage unlicensed medics to first mortally wound patients with otherwise minor injuries such that they could legally heal their clients, resulting in *more* deaths than otherwise.

Regardless of the validity of the answers Tara had received, it still didn't sit right with her, even all these months later. Still, what she technically did not witness and had no technical knowledge of was not under her purview. Even then, was she truly in the right to bend the laws in such a manner?

Trust in the System, not the individual, she reassured herself.

In the future, she might not conduct herself in such a manner, though perhaps she would. Something about the Outsider's position on individual choice struck her as odd. Tara would have to ensure Edwin underwent the proper training for medicine when he next returned to Vinstead. Hopefully she would be around to oversee it. No other Adventurer was liable to cause her to question their qualifications; she knew and had dealt with too many of them. And Citizens were required to take the course when they first received their Skill or were approved to earn it.

A message arrived for her, and Tara sighed. It seemed as though not even a week could pass without some new monster beyond the scope of the local guards showing up and forcing her to personally deal with the situation. Usually it was trivial—some Classed wolf, though it would on occasion be more than seconds of work. What was it this time? She tapped the pebble presented. Tactile use of Identification had always been her preference, despite its shortcomings. Something about feeling the stone under her fingers had always been so reassuring.

Her eyes skimmed across the Identification. Hmm. This might actually be somewhat enjoyable. A small, nameless town near the Frigid Sands was being plagued by a manticore. Winged, no less. With a Class as well. Lord of the Thousand Quills of Death. Lovely. It seemed to have already killed two guards and put their lieutenant in critical condition, and they had sent the message pebble yesterday.

She wasn't as fast as a courier, no. They spent their entire Classes pushing themselves to go as fast as possible. Even avior, winged as they were, couldn't match a true-blood Human for high-speed endurance. All that meant that if it took a full day for one to reach her here, it would take at least three days to make the journey if she pushed herself to her limits.

No time to waste, then. She applied an Imperial Note to her desk regarding her whereabouts and stepped out onto her balcony. A grin flitted across her face as she beheld the clouds of satisfied, safe Citizens going about their daily lives so far below. This was her favorite view in all Vinstead. This was what she *lived* for.

Shining Regalia.

Silver Steps.

Thanks to the high levels she had raised Don Regalia to, Tara's Skill manifested around her in the blink of an eye, silver armor that felt weightless even before Second Skin initiated. As she stepped into thin air, a tiny disc made of silver force materialized beneath her feet, enabling a full sprint across the sky. Sustained Construction meant that she left a set of sparkling footprints in the sky like stars while she set off for the north.

Avior swooped around her, their added maneuverability and lower rank ensuring that they gave way to her instead of the reverse. She sprinted across the evening sky, feeling Endless Endurance engage and grant her already considerable Stamina an even greater boost.

Tara managed to arrive at her destination in just under two days, having stopped only once at a town to sleep before continuing her quest. Upon her arrival at the nameless town, she located the guard encampment with ease—this far out, there were usually a few upon the Artifice Path assigned to local guardsmen. Not a particularly experienced Fortification Builder, from the looks of the building, but the construction was nonetheless fully functional.

A nervous-looking soldier stood outside the temporary barracks. The human looked like he might bar her way, but Tara flashed her badge of office. Insignia might be an ostensibly weak Skill, but its inclusion as the first upgrade to Authority *made* it useful. Supposedly in days past, and even to this day in some of the foreign lands, their methods of identification within their ranks were incredibly prone to forgery. Pathetic.

Inviolable proof of her identity thus presented, Tara was swiftly escorted inside. While the interior was almost uncomfortably cramped, her suspicion of an inexperienced Builder confirmed, there was still enough room for her to address the Senior Lieutenant as she reclined on a medical bed, tended to by one of the natives. A skinwalker of some sort, or at least descended from one, given the medic's eyes and ears.

As she approached, the medic retreated to a respectful distance, eyes downturned. Deferent. Interesting. Not an unpleasant surprise, though rare this far out. Distance seemed to dilute the respect Citizens had for their superiors.

"Enforcer Tara present. Report, Lieutenant."

The lieutenant stirred, an eye meeting Tara's even behind her visor. "You made it," she croaked.

Tara didn't respond, waiting for the continuation. The soldier looked in rough shape, missing several feathers across her head and torso, and her wing looked more dead than alive. If Tara's suspicions were correct, and the lieutenant had been poisoned by the manticore, all she could do was pray for a relatively painless death.

"Blasted thing has a lair out there, an hour north into the Sands. Big rocky outcropping, you can't miss it. It's smart and took down Voral and Aeach faster than you could blink, when we thought we were still at a far enough range. Hit me with a quill, and well, you can see the results."

Indeed. Manticore venom was infamous for rapidly causing the death of whoever it touched. It was said to be more virulent the more Skills one had. Even Poison Resistance purportedly did nothing to halt it, though few were willing to put such claims to the test. It was, after all, utterly incurable and generally excruciatingly painful. The lieutenant seemed to be mostly cogent, which meant her death would not be as harsh as it could be. That she had survived this long was a testament to the tending medic. Few saw the next sunrise when so injured.

A few more probing questions had Tara find the answers she was looking for. The community was an insular one founded by a few families some generations back looking for a quiet place to settle. They'd first caught on to the presence of some predator when their herd animals started going missing, and they had sent a runner to fetch the local patrol. By the time they'd arrived, the predator had begun snatching people who wandered too far afield, though they'd yet to catch so much as a glimpse of it.

When the guards had arrived, they managed to set a trap for it and discover its identity. One of the locals possessed a tracking Skill of some variant and was able to mark the beast to find its lair. They didn't manage to seriously wound the creature, though the small amount of blood they had drawn was sufficient for the monster to retreat back home. From there, it had been merely the story of a failed hunt.

In the past three days, it had been even worse. The manticore had grown bolder and could now be seen flying around the area and picking off sheep with impunity, going so far as to kill and leave, simply to taunt the residents.

Tara thanked the lieutenant for her information and ventured off to sleep. This was a problem best tackled fully rested.

The Frigid Sands lived up to their reputation. The desert almost looked like snow, white sands stretching as far north as anyone had ever ventured. Allegedly, at some point snow and sand mixed until the two were indistinguishable underneath an eternal night or eternal day, depending on who was telling the legend.

The sun shone down on her, the True Light insufficient to fight back against the aura of death the Sands produced. Farther south, such a vast expanse would have been almost deadly for its heat. Here, though, the heat and light were sapped from the air itself, leaving the desolate wasteland inhospitable to all but the hardiest forms of life. Such as, it would seem, a manticore.

With a full night's sleep behind her, it was finally time for Tara to uphold her position, to prove that her existence was not a mistake. Attempting to pioneer a new Class with novel Paths was a stressful matter, and she decidedly wished that the burden had not fallen to her. Still, she could not deny that she enjoyed utilizing what made her special, as scandalous as that may be. Her armor was such a unique and power-ful tool, and she couldn't wait for the time when the Registrars were capable of reliably replicating it, a task thus far unsuccessful. Still, she felt uncomfortable with the idea that she might have been chosen. Was she truly so otherwise worthless as to be considered expendable? Yet she *had* agreed to the gamble. It was . . . confusing.

Trust the System, she reassured herself. *There will always be those needed to lay down their lives and usefulness for all others.*

Silver Steps made the hour-long journey to cross the shifting sands trivial, Tara's every footfall landing upon a manifestation of her Regalia fixed in place. She still maintained her vigilance and kept a keen eye out for any possible signs of her target.

In time, the rocky outcropping began to loom over her like a shat-tered crown of stone, cast down by some ancient giant of unmatched proportions. The sky was an endless expanse of blue, save for a single dot swooping from the tip of the crown, and Tara narrowed her eyes. The manticore, she was certain.

As it drew closer, the Enforcer hardened her resolve. This was what she lived for, both literally and metaphorically. A pull upon Argent Armory manifested a gleaming blade for her to wield against the beast. While the Skill enabled her to fashion all sorts of weapons and simple objects from her Shining Regalia, swords were what she was most famil-iar with and would be sufficient to begin.

Unlike when facing bandits, there were no negotiations, no calls to surrender. Just the Silver Blade standing steadfast against a ravenous beast. It flew toward her like a bolt of lightning, and Tara closed her eyes to concentrate the instant after her Identify landed.

Lord of the Thousand Quills of Death
Manticore
Manticores are ferocious and savage, yet cunning beasts. With a roar that instills terror in all that fear it, this creature jealously guards its territory and prey with an incurably venomous tail.

Around her, she opened her Mirror's Gaze, and the world opened up. The Skill had been one of her more recent upgrades to Seeing and allowed her to sense the world through reflective surfaces such as her armor, with Sight of the Silver One only improving the quality and enabling her to see in truth in place of metaphor. It was eminently useful in combat, though without Perception, her ability to process all she saw was limited.

The manticore opened with a devastating roar, powerful enough to whip up the sands at the Silver Blade's feet into a small sandstorm, but that merely left her standing in midair, her mind shielded from the unnatural terror by Steadfast Ally.

The beast, crimson as the final sunset it represented for so many, swooped at her, unleashing a volley of its quills at the Enforcer. Time seemed to slow as she called upon Lightning Perceptions, giving her plenty of time to call up a Mirror Shield at the tip of her sword, Reflective Mirror causing the quills to rebound back at the beast with twice the power they had at first.

The manticore changed directions in an instant, letting the half-dozen spikes arc through the air, vanishing off into the distance. It attempted a few more attacks, probing at her defense, but a barrage of Mirror Shields easily reflected every last one.

The creature eventually changed tactics when it realized it would have no success as it was, and it instead called upon something within it and launched nigh every quill from its tail. There were far more than there ought to have been, and for a moment the shadow cast by the beast was eclipsed by the sheer mass of deadly quills it had thrown.

The Enforcer remained unworried. Another conjuration of a Mirror Shield intercepted the quills, sending them flying to places unknown.

Then the shield broke, and Tara's eyes shot open in concern. That had never happened before, let alone with an attack that used quantity in place of strength. Now, she was faced with an endless tide of quills, gleaming with black-green venom. So much as a single touch would surely spell her death, and after Mirror Shield had shattered she did not trust her Shining Regalia to adequately protect her.

Slowed time ran slower, and then it utterly froze as Eternal Moment intervened. The Skill had an utterly massive time between uses, but it would still save her here.

Sudden Reposition.

Then, the Silver Blade was *gone*, only a flash of silver light left in her wake as her Skill simply moved her outside the area of the quill attack. Hundreds of needles slammed into the ground, hissing and dissolving the sand where they struck. She frowned. Manticore venom was venom, not acid. Did this one possess some special Skill that allowed it to "kill" inanimate objects?

The manticore was furious at her survival, and with another roar, it swooped down to attempt to claw at her, a single scorpion-like stinger left upon its tail.

Dance of the Silver Blade brought Tara between the beast's attacks, forbidding the creature from rending naught but air. Her blade flashed up and caught it in the stomach, though the simple attack proved insufficient to pierce its hide.

Tara would not allow herself to grow frustrated, and she drew her blade back, using Sudden Reposition to avoid the beast's retaliatory claw. It possessed some rapid movement Skill of its own and reappeared midstrike less than a stride away from her.

Parry.

The Skill was a fraction of an instant too slow, and the attack slammed into her side and sent her flying. The Silver Blade slammed into the ground, skipping across the sands. While her Regalia protected her, Tara could tell that it would not survive a second blow, and she was uncertain whether the claws upon her foe carried the same deadly toxin as its stingers, having no desire to find out herself.

Kip Up.

The Skill jerked her upright, going from horizontal to vertical in the blink of an eye, and not a moment too soon, as the beast was once more upon her. It was all she could manage, to conjure a Mirror Shield and slow the beast before it could reach her. The shield was not tested against the charge, as with a flap of its wings, the manticore merely leapt over the barrier, diving down at her.

Brace.

Silver Steps.

For all that she rarely used it for such, Silver Steps was initially meant for this very purpose—giving Tara a firm footing regardless of the terrain. Brace combined with it well, as it allowed her to give no ground against even the fiercest attacks.

The Enforcer cast aside her sword, using the last moment before her prey slammed into her to conjure a spear from her Armory.

The beast's own momentum carried it onto the silver spearpoint, driving it deep into its own body as the first blood of their fight. Far from being a decisive strike, however, it only served to enrage the creature, and with a roar that would have knocked Tara back if not for her continued Brace.

The manticore attempted to flee, but the Silver Blade effortlessly maintained her Silver Steps in pursuit into the air, where they continued their deadly dance.

The manticore was a formidable opponent, Tara had to admit. It had been quite some time since she had last needed to push herself quite so far in a fight, and she relished the feeling. Regardless, there was never a doubt in her mind that she would prove victorious, it was merely a matter of time. Endless Endurance and Enforcer's Physique meant she simply would not tire, not without significantly more Stamina-intensive Skill usage, but the beast had no such Skill. It was an ambush predator, not a true fighter.

It had tried to flee a few times. However, the Silver Blade had taught the beast why attempting such was a terrible idea. The first time, she had used the opportunity to cut off the tip of its stinger, though the action had forced her to discard and re-create her sword, as the venom corroded and shattered the Skill. The second time, she opened a long slice on its flank, and most recently, she had cut a long slit in its batlike wings, forcing it back to the ground.

It was now fully aware of how little time it had left, and was beginning to panic. Tara's non-Skill-enhanced attacks, or even Sudden Strike, still could not pierce its hide, though its rage and panic were giving her more opportunities to use Power Attack and Piercing Blow, allowing her to slowly whittle away at its health, likely even Health. Attributes were not infinite, after all, and even the strongest Health had its limits.

The manticore had lost a lot of black blood, and given the amount Tara had gotten on herself throughout the fight, she was fortunate it too was not toxic. The spear she had lodged in its chest near the start of the fight had long broken, naturally, as had the second, and as Skill constructs, left nothing in the wound to continue wounding the creature.

It knew it was dying, and now sought only to end Tara's life before its soul left Joriah. She would not leave it to succumb to its wounds, as doing such ran too much of a risk that it might survive against all odds, possibly with the aid of a new Skill or Path, and continue to menace the town. That was unacceptable, and so the Enforcer stayed.

A Mirror shield intercepted a claw, and Flowing Steps took her out of range from the beast's bite. Sudden Strike thrust her sword inside the creature's humanlike mouth, and as it bit down, the blade cut into the manticore's soft skin, prompting it to yowl in pain and rage.

Tara didn't pass up the opportunity it presented, and Sudden Reposition brought her in close, her sword striking at the base of the creature's neck. Sudden Strike reinforced her attack, but it still managed little more than a scratch upon the beast's hide.

That wasn't the point, though, and as the manticore attempted to retreat beyond the reach of the Silver Blade, she had enough of an opportunity to chain together every attacking Skill she had into a single, mighty blow.

Her sword slammed into the creature's hide, piercing its skin and cutting deeply into its muscle, only stopping when her attack hit its bones with such force her sword shattered. Another attack was already on its way, a curved sickle-sword slipping into the same cut she'd just opened and hooking onto the interior of the beast. This time, when it pulled away, Tara kept part of it with her. Brace and Silver Steps kept her and her weapon motionless while the manticore used its movement to flee, and tore open its own guts as it did so.

Blood and bile spilled over Tara, showering her in gore. While disgusting, it was nothing in comparison to the corpse of the beast itself falling upon her a moment later. It was only thanks to Reflexive Shield that she hadn't been squished underneath its body. While it wouldn't have been dangerous, it *would* have been rather embarrassing, never mind that few eyes were upon her.

Tara stepped back, opening her eyes as she dismissed and reconjured her armor piece by piece to avoid getting any blood upon her. She looked upon the body of the marauding manticore with satisfaction. This was her role in the Empire, ensuring the land was safe for the common folk, and she would do her job proudly until her dying day.

Tomorrow, she would begin her long return to the capital, keeping her ears open for other nuisances she could deal with while in the area, such as bandits or a pack of wolves. When she finally did arrive in Vinstead, there would no doubt be some minor incident she needed to give her opinion on, and some days following that, there would be another incident to investigate or intervene upon.

Such was the life of the Silver Blade.

She would have it no other way.

Kaleb England, also known as NorskDaedalus, is an author who loves to integrate magic and science to tell interesting stories. England holds a bachelor's degree in physics.

9 781039 412934